I0658324

MAGIC OF THE NILE

BY VERONICA SCOTT

Bookmark: copyright 2014 by Jean D. Walker

This book is a work of fiction. The names, places, characters and incidents are products of the writer's imagination or have been used fictitiously and are not to be construed as real. Any resemblance to persons, living or dead, actual events, locales or organizations is entirely coincidental.

All rights reserved. No part of this book may be reproduced, scanned or distributed in any manner whatsoever without written permission from the author except in the case of brief quotation embodied in critical articles and reviews.

Cover Art by Frauke of CROCO Designs

To my daughters Valerie and Elizabeth, and to Alison D,
who wanted to know more about Tyema

ACKNOWLEDGMENT

The E-book Formatting Fairies!

CHAPTER ONE

Patience running thin, Tyema tried in vain to focus on the endless details her head crocodile keeper Hotepre was only too eager to share. Proper care for Sobek's animals was her responsibility as high priestess but the god didn't expect her to know about every chipped tooth and broken claw.

"Did you want to inspect the new clutch of eggs?" Hotepre asked as they left the pond where promising juvenile crocodiles were kept.

Glancing at the sun sinking over the Nile, she shook her head. "I'd intended to, but the ceremonies ran long today. We had so many petitioners. Can I see the eggs tomorrow?"

"Of course, my lady." Hotepre's frown deepened the wrinkles on his aged face as they climbed the gravel path from the ponds, winding up the cliff where the temple itself was located. "Are you going to the festival in town tonight?"

Surprised into laughter, Tyema paused for a moment. "When have you ever known me to do such a thing? And especially for a festival honoring Horus, the rival of our god Sobek?"

"You stay cooped up here as if *you* were in an enclosure," he said. "Hiding yourself away isn't good for a young woman like you." He spat.

"Thank you, Hotepre," she said, smiling with clenched teeth, trying to hide her annoyance. He might be one of her most important functionaries at the temple, and older than the Nile, but it still didn't give him the latitude to lecture her about her personal life. *If I wasn't so young to be in charge of a major temple, would people feel as free to gift me with unasked-for advice?*

Dusting her hands on her skirt, Tyema paused at the rear entrance to the temple's extensive grounds. "Don't let me keep you from the festivities."

Broad smile revealing more than one missing tooth, Hotepre chortled. "Indeed, my lady, not even the god could do that! I'll see you tomorrow." Whistling a popular tune from the taverns, he continued along the path, heading toward the staff quarters, moving out of her sight.

Happy to be alone, done with her responsibilities, Tyema sighed. Rubbing her forehead, she enjoyed the soft breeze on the cliff's edge. Changing out of the ornate headdress, the elaborate wig, the jewelry and the elaborate ceremonial garments into a simple sheath before going to meet Hotepre had been a good idea. Now she could relax, with all the day's tasks checked off. Stomach rumbling, Tyema knew her dinner would be set out in the privacy of her apartment, but for now she was content to stand high above the Nile, savoring the beauty of the sunset.

"Hello? Excuse me?"

Hearing a man's voice where no one should be, startled her out of her reverie. She wasn't afraid—no one would ever dare lay a hand on her again, not protected as she was by Sobek—but she was annoyed as she turned on her heel. *Who in the Seven Hells would dare to trespass here?*

"You're too late for the evening ceremonies," she said, barely polite. "The temple is closed."

"I was afraid I'd missed the time." As if his tardiness couldn't possibly be an issue, the newcomer's wide smile lit his cleancut face, accented by high cheekbones and a square jaw. He was a tall, broad-shouldered warrior, wearing a crisp white kilt, with leather straps crisscrossing an impressively muscled chest. The black and gold *nemes* headcloth framing his face denoted a high-ranking officer, as did the golden-handled flail tucked into his waistband. The man covered the last yards of the path in a few steps, joining her at the cliff's edge, taking a quick view over the silvery Nile. "Beautiful. I can see why the crocodile god wanted a temple here."

Hand on the ornate golden falcon hilt of his sword, this unusual supplicant bowed. "I'm Sahure, captain in pharaoh's army, nephew to the nomarch of this province."

Tyema inclined her head with a smile. She was fond of the nomarch who ruled the Ibis Province for Pharaoh. Being his relative was a point in this newcomer's favor. She saw no need to introduce herself, not wanting to listen to any petitions at this late hour, but her curiosity was piqued. "What brings you to the temple? The nome's capital is a day's ride away from here."

"I'm visiting my uncle, combining business with pleasure, inspecting fortifications for Pharaoh and admiring some of the local wonders." His appreciative glance at her was pure flattery.

She pointed at the golden falcon badge on the shoulder of his tunic, so rarely seen in this remote province. "You're one of Pharaoh's Own Guard?"

He laughed. "I have that honor, yes. The Great One sent me to evaluate the Nile in this area, see if there might be potential for a port. Nowadays there's so much river traffic, with the Hyksos menace repelled and the increase in prosperity Nat-re-Akhte has brought to the Black Lands in the last fifteen years, we could use another commerce hub." Studying her with narrowed eyes, he said, "Why am I talking of civil engineering when you shiver in the twilight breeze? Don't let me keep you here on the bluff while night falls."

Rather than entering the grounds, Tyema took a different direction, walking along the path toward the main temple complex, good manners forcing him to accompany her. "Indeed, it's chilly when the sun goes down and the wind rises," she said, rubbing the goose bumps on her arms, most likely brought on by mention of the Hyksos rather than the weather.

But Sahure was already apologizing. "I'm sorry, perhaps I was insensitive to mention the enemy. Your village suffered a Hyksos raid during the worst of the times, didn't it?"

She nodded. "Yes, long ago. What brings you to the temple today?"

"Other than sightseeing?" He laughed. "I wanted to meet the high priestess, tell her my plans, in case the god had any objection, any portion of the river he doesn't want developed. And I might need her help in examining possible sites. This temple is a significant influence in the local area, I have to consider its needs in the new development."

Tyema opened her mouth to speak. "I—"

He was intent on finishing his thought. "But as I've obviously missed my chance tonight, is there an inn in the town you'd recommend?"

"You're not staying with the headman?" She was surprised. A guest of such high rank would normally take over the official's fine house, not rent a room at one of the inns like some poor pilgrim.

"I'd rather not." Taking her elbow as they walked up the slight incline to the gates, he leaned closer. "I've been told he has five hopeful daughters of marrying age."

"Say no more." Thinking about how desirous the headman and his wife were of marrying their daughters well made her chuckle. A nephew of the nomarch would be an enticing target. "You'd be dragged into a round of feasts and celebrations for sure. All five of them would volunteer to help you survey, then distract you from your duty by pulling each other's hair in daily catfights over your wandering attention." The mayor's daughters weren't favorites with Tyema.

"Yes and I have serious work to do while I'm here, no time to referee catfights. Pharaoh gave me a deadline and one doesn't ignore his orders." Sahure grinned and she wondered how anyone could speak so easily and familiarly about the ruler of all Egypt. She might be on speaking terms with the god Sobek, but Pharaoh was so far above her in the human scheme of things, she couldn't imagine even being in his presence.

Realizing Sahure was waiting for her to say something, she rushed into the recommendation he'd requested. "Well, many of the religious pilgrims stay at the Blue Crocodile inn." One of her married sisters ran the place, but Tyema had no qualms in putting it first. Her family did a good job, charged fair prices. "I'm told it's quite satisfactory as to accommodations and food."

He rubbed his jaw. "I think I saw it when I was passing through town to come here. A well kept place by the looks of it."

They'd reached the gate to the new temple enclosure. Tyema paused in the pool of ruddy light from the torches set into the sconces on either side, reluctant to have the encounter end. It was pleasant to chat with a handsome, well spoken man. Sometimes her evenings spent reading or learning new songs were a bit too quiet, maybe even lonely. Hotepre's effort to get her to consider attending the festival in town was the first time in a long time anyone had dared to broach the subject of her self-imposed isolation. *Settling into a peaceful old age before I've actually grown old.* The thought made her uneasy, bitter.

Sahure's next words were almost as if he was reading her mind. "I noticed the town was preparing for a festival of some kind," he said. "You don't attend?"

"It's in honor of Horus, not Sobek." *An easy answer, which should deflect further questions.* Sometimes she wished her defenses weren't so well honed, so automatic. *So imprisoning.* Putting her hand on the gate, she pushed the painted gilt panel ajar.

"Well then, I must certainly put in an appearance, since Horus is my patron god." He peered through the open gate at the deserted temple compound. "Will you come with me?"

"What?" Pausing, Tyema stared over her shoulder at him.

"Well they've obviously all gone off to enjoy the festivities and left you stuck here by yourself, which doesn't seem fair to *me*. " He smiled and she was taken yet again by how handsome he was. "Surely Sobek doesn't begrudge your attendance at someone else's festival? You did say the day's required observances were done."

I prefer my peace and quiet, the temple to myself. Yet why did her thoughts sound wistful? Sometimes it was lonely to be the chosen one of the god.

Sahure held out one hand, palm up. "I'd enjoy your company."

In a moment of wild abandon, heart thumping, Tyema touched his hand with the tip of her fingers and heard herself accepting the invitation, "Let me just run and fetch a shawl first." *What's come over me tonight?*

Leaning against the wall, Sahure nodded. "Take your time, I'll wait."

Tyema hastened to her quarters, the whole time asking herself what she was doing. She rarely set foot in town, with all its sad memories, not even to visit her sisters. Never to attend festivals! *Am I so susceptible to a handsome stranger?* She giggled, thinking of her half-sister Merys and the handsome stranger *she'd* met, who of course was revealed to be the god Sobek himself. "I don't think this Sahure is a god in disguise," she laughed to herself as she returned to the gate, half expecting to find him gone. *But he's a pleasing companion and tonight I'm in the mood to be wild, to do the unexpected.*

"You were quick, my lady," he said, pushing away from the wall and coming to take her hand.

"My name is Ema." The moment she spoke, she wondered why she'd given him the nickname that only her family used. Too late to correct the error without awkward explanation..

"Unusual. Pretty." He conducted her solicitously down the long stairway from the cliff to the plateau, hand on her elbow as they navigated the stone risers, each inscribed with a blessing to Sobek.

"Oh, what a glorious chariot," she said as they approached the waiting vehicle, eyeing the horses with fascination. Her brother-in-law, captain of the town guard, had a team and an old but serviceable chariot. Those were about the extent locally, even now that the town received so many pilgrims and visitors. On the rare visits from the nomarch, she'd seen his chariot, but his was nothing like this. Sahure's was a burnished war chariot, with wide axles, sturdy wooden wheels, gleaming leather side panels and an electrum front plate ornamented with Pharaoh's cartouche, set off by gold-crowned falcons of Horus on either side. The horses wore elaborately striped blankets to cushion the wooden yoke and harness, accented with shining bits of gold-trimmed leather. Saucy white ostrich plums stood tall on their bridles.

But Tyema barely registered any of details of the chariot itself, as she focused on the team of horses. "May I pet them?"

Eyebrow raised, Sahure said, "Of course. This is Nahkti and his partner is Senbi."

"Oh you're so beautiful," she crooned, as the dapple gray sniffed her hand. Stroking his velvety nose while the other horse nudged her shoulder, she said, "I should have brought them a treat, shouldn't I?"

"Next time," he said, untying the reins from a handy post.

"I've never ridden in a chariot," she confided as he handed her up into the vehicle. She clutched the side as he stepped into the driver's position and the chariot rocked a bit on the axle.

"A war chariot is hardly the normal mode of transport for a lady," he agreed. Raising the reins, he set the horses into motion. Wheels rumbling, the chariot rolled faster and faster down the broad dirt road. The horses tossed their heads, making the feathers on their harness dance. At first the team trotted but as they reached the main road to the village, Sahure glanced at her for permission. Seeing her nod, he set the team into a gallop and the chariot shot forward as the powerful animals responded to his command.

Hair flying, Tyema laughed in sheer pleasure. "This is wonderful! Oh to be able to move so fast through the world!" She reveled in the ride, knowing all too soon they'd be at their destination. Deciding this was a night for daring, working up her courage, she said, "May I drive?"

"In the twilight, on an unknown road? Hardly the place for me to teach you to handle a high spirited team," he demurred.

"When will I ever have such a chance again? You must be one of Pharaoh's best charioteers, surely? Who better to learn from?"

Glancing at her face, which must have shown her disappointment despite her wheedling tone, he laughed, drawing the horses to a halt in a cloud of dust. "I can't resist such a charmingly worded request. All right, as a compromise, you can hold the reins with me, if you'd like."

He stood back as she sidled to a position in front of him and he folded the leather reins into her hands, never actually releasing them himself. "You wanted to drive, lift the reins and click your tongue so they know to run."

Tyema was exhilarated as they flew along the road in the moonlight. Fear was the farthest emotion from her heart right now, which was a blessed relief. Keeping her balance with difficulty, she yelled, "We're moving so fast, like gods!" Only the sense of invulnerability that swept over her at the height of conducting a major ceremony for Sobek rivaled this feeling of rushing through the world like a goddess. So much sheer power harnessed to do her bidding! *If I had a chariot and a team, I could experience this joy, this freedom from daily fear and boredom whenever I wished. And I don't need anyone else to participate, only the horses.* Although Sahure standing so warm and close behind her was also a pleasant sensation, her body tingling where they touched as he supervised her driving. She wished the trip could last forever but moments later the captain was extricating the reins from her grasp, pulling the team into a slower gait as they approached the town gates.

Trying to smooth her hair into some semblance of order as the chariot rolled past the guards, Tyema laughed from sheer pleasure. "Thank you, handling the reins was wonderful! I might have to get one of these myself."

He looked at her askance. "A chariot? For a temple?"

"Why not?" She'd tasted the glory of traveling with the speed of the wind and she craved more, enthralled by the idea of escaping the confines of her normal life any time she pleased, going so fast no one in the nome could ever catch her.

"Keep in mind you'll need a groom, a proper stable—horses are expensive to feed." Sahure waved his hand at Nahkti and Senbi, now walking docilely down the crowded road. "They're beautiful but they eat their heads off. Your head priestess might not like the idea much."

Tyema laughed. "Oh there's no problem there, I assure you."

They rode farther into town, through the square and past the temple of Horus, stopping at the inn she'd recommended to him. A small squad of soldiers waited with their gear in the side yard.

"I see my men already found the place on their own," he said.

A grizzled sergeant came to take the horses' heads, eyeing Tyema with open curiosity as he saluted the captain. "Good evening, sir."

"We'll stay here while we're in the area," Sahure declared. "The priestess highly recommends it."

He helped her descend from the chariot. Suddenly feeling shy, Tyema stood to the side as he gave the sergeant more orders. *Does this Sahure collect a new woman in every town they visit?* She hoped none of her family members would come outside the inn and see her standing with a stranger. The questions and sly gossiping would be endless.

Finally Sahure was done with giving orders. Taking her arm, he said, "Are you ready to show me the wonders of your town?"

"If you're accustomed to Thebes, you're not likely to find our hamlet of Ta'sobeksef more than insignificant, although I grant you the temple of Horus has its charms, with the murals and columns."

Tyema was thinking herself an impulsive fool, but as she strolled through the streets with Sahure, she felt less on edge, more relaxed. Her heart beat more slowly and she could breathe without undue effort. Most of the people they encountered were strangers come to town for the religious festivities. She enjoyed the rare entertainment provided by the musicians, acrobats and dancers performing for deben, thinking perhaps she should arrange something similar when the next major festival day for Sobek occurred. With Sahure at her side, no one bothered her, not even the beggars. The few townspeople she met seemed startled to see her but bowed their heads quickly and moved on.

He bought roasted quail for them at one of the stalls and seated her on a nearby bench, going back for a pitcher of beer. "Your town is pleasant, welcoming," he said, setting the container down before accepting the drumstick she handed him.

Sipping at the beer, Tyema smiled. "You're too kind. I'm sure it must seem rural and ordinary to someone who's traveled the length of the Nile or lived in Thebes."

"I've been to the wilds of Kush, seen the mountains where the Nile is born, I've been many places and each has its own form of charm. Right now I can't remember anywhere half so attractive," he said with a wink. "I'm under the spell, of the town and the company."

Feeling her cheeks grow hot with a blush, Tyema took another swallow of the beer, although she rarely drank. "I'm sure the glib words go well with the ladies in Thebes." *Oh dear, he'll take offense at my blunt speech, but he does sound quite practiced at flattery.*

Sahure was unfazed, grinning, little crinkles of amusement around his eyes. "Ah, you see right through me." Breaking apart the quail, he offered her a succulent morsel on the tip of his knife. "Most women smile and don't examine my words like a scribe with a messy slate."

"I—I'm no good at social chatter," she confessed, taking the small bite in her fingertips and carrying it to her mouth. She chewed daintily, savoring the taste before swallowing. "I'm too direct."

"We're conversing, Lady Ema, not chattering. And I enjoy a challenge. Clearly more diligence on my part is required, to offer you only the most exquisitely crafted compliments. Or none at all." He took a long drink of the beer. "Tell me more about the temple of Horus. I've been told the building hasn't been here as long as the original temple of Sobek. From what I could see of the ruins earlier, your temple must have been established hundreds of years ago? Well, the town's name itself says as much."

She nodded. "We believe Sobek's temple has been in this spot on the Nile since the time of the first pharaohs, even before the pyramids were built. The temple of Horus was erected a mere thirty or forty years ago." Tyema felt safer, more at ease, sticking to a factual discussion of landmarks and local history. She was well versed in both. "Our new temple to Sobek was built by your uncle fifteen years ago."

Sahure didn't offer any more outrageous compliments during dinner. She couldn't decide whether to be glad or sorry. Flirting was a dangerous, intoxicating novelty to her, no matter how practiced his tongue might be, so on the whole she was probably better off not trying to match him honeyed word for word.

After they'd finished eating, he escorted her to the square to watch a performance of the old scribes' tale "The Shipwrecked Sailor", put on by a traveling company. Tyema laughed and applauded along with everyone else. She couldn't remember an evening where she'd just had fun, or felt so at ease.

"I've been shipwrecked and let me tell you, it isn't nearly as entertaining as these players make it appear," he said in her ear as they left the play. "Of course the island I washed up on had no fifty foot talking snakes, no enchanted dancing girls, nothing but scrub palms and sand." Reaching out, he snagged a red flower from the stall they were passing, dropping a small coin in the vendor's palm. "Stand still," he ordered. Tucking the flower behind Tyema's ear, he kissed her cheek before taking her hand again. "Now what, my lovely lady? Shall we go inspect the temple of Horus, compare it to yours?"

Flustered, wondering if anyone she knew had seen his bold gesture, she put a hand to the flower, pulling it from her hair. "I think I'd better be going." She sniffed the bruised petals.

"But it's early yet—surely the festivities will go until dawn." He waved his hand at the crowd around them. "I see no signs of flagging energy or loss of enthusiasm. The beer still flows in rivers."

"I have duties, rituals to conduct at midmorning." Truth, as far as it went, she did have to sing while the effigy of Sobek was offered food and drink, before the lesser priestesses draped the statue in fine linen robes and golden jewelry set with turquoise and other gems.

Sahure made an opening through the throng and led her to a less crowded part of the main street. "If you insist on cutting the night short, we'll go to the inn, have my horses put to the chariot and I'll drive you back."

"No need for me to cause you the trouble. I've family in town." Tyema pointed vaguely to the east. "I'll stay with them and walk to the temple at dawn."

"Now that I cannot allow," he said, gazing into her eyes, a frown on his face. "It's quite a distance and you'll doubtless have a full day of work."

Twirling the flower in her fingers, she chuckled at the idea of requiring so much cosseting. "I walk back and forth to town all the time." *Well I would if I ever left the temple grounds.* "I'm not one of your delicate Theban girls. Out here in the country we walk everywhere."

He escorted her to her family's home, where her oldest sister and her husband, the captain of the guard, now dwelt. He didn't try to kiss her again, saying good night before she slipped through the gate. Tyema wasn't sure whether she felt relieved or regretful. She waited in the deserted courtyard for a good ten minutes, before re-entering the street. Glancing over her shoulder at the house, she shuddered and pulled her shawl more closely around her shoulders. *I swore not to ever spend another night under their roof and I'm not starting now.* As always she was secure in the knowledge that no one—not human, animal or demon—would interfere with her, protected as she was by Sobek's amulet around her neck. A deserted road in the moonlight held no terrors for her, unlike the crowded, brightly lit village. Or her late father's old home.

***

As Tyema led the midmorning ceremony, chanting the hymns to Sobek, she was more conscious than usual of the small but attentive crowd of worshippers. Normally she blotted out any thought of the onlookers and lost herself in singing the sacred music. Today she wondered if Sahure was there in the outer sanctuary and whether he'd be upset to learn she hadn't told him her true identity. Her anxiety wasn't relieved any by the fact he'd appeared in at least one of her dreams as well, smiling and holding out another red flower she'd been too frightened to accept. Awakening from the dream with a gasp, she couldn't go back to sleep, disturbed by unfamiliar thoughts and desires. Tossing and turning left her tired. By the time the ceremony was over and she was free to retreat to her office in the temple's new wing, tension was rising in her like a wave. A small headache pounded over her left eye, spreading tentacles of pain through her head.

The temple scribe Jemkhufu was waiting in her private study, arms full of scrolls and tablets. He bowed as she entered, already enumerating the tasks ahead. "We've a busy morning ahead of us, my lady. Reports on the grain harvest, the tally sheets for the papyrus shipment—"

Tyema thanked her maids as they removed the complicated headdress and wig, substituting a simpler style, accented with a small circlet bearing Sobek's cartouche in relief. As the women took the ceremonial items away to be stored for tomorrow's rituals, she rubbed her forehead and sat in her gold—and—ebony chair. Putting her feet on the hippo shaped stool, she forced herself to ask the one thing she cared about right now. "Are there any audiences?"

Surprised, he moved his quill down the list of items on the scroll, ticking each off as he went. "Why, yes, there's a Captain Sahure who requests a meeting." With a satisfied sneer on his thin lips, the scribe raised one eyebrow. "I told him to wait until tomorrow as your schedule was full today."

"I'll see him now." *Might as well get it over with. Last night was a pleasant diversion, but he'll be angry I deceived him and I've no more time to indulge myself in foolishness. Why did I let myself be tempted into spending the entire evening in his company?* She rubbed her forehead where the ceremonial sun-disk had ridden so heavily on her head.

"Are you sure, my lady?" Jemkhufu set down his tablet and quill and came around the table to stand next to her, exaggerated concern in his every move, as if she were a fragile piece of statuary. He patted her shoulder. "You're pale. Another headache?"

Trapped in the chair, Tyema leaned back, shrugging his hand off her body. "I'll be fine. I have herb infused syrup here, made from my late grandmother's recipe." She indicated the duck shaped pitcher on her table. "It's not your job to worry after my health."

He retreated a step or two but stayed in the room. "Your health concerns me because I care, my lady. You're important to the temple—and to me." Tilting his head, he gave her a look of such studied significance, Tyema was tempted to laugh. Unfortunately she knew he was utterly serious.

"The Great One Sobek watches over me at all times." *Probably best to remind this overly familiar scribe of the fact.* "I need no human intervention so turn your attentiveness in other directions." From the downcast expression on his face, now she was sure she'd hurt his feelings. Exasperation made her tone unusually sharp. "Summon the captain so I can hear his business with our temple." She waved one hand at the door.

The scribe bowed low and left the chamber.

He's getting to be a bit much, too solicitous. He needs to find a nice girl in the village and settle down. There's never going to be anything between us. The scribe was short, older than her by several seasons of the Nile, full of his own importance and prone to long speeches. He'd lost a few teeth and he wore too much body perfume. Shaking her head and blowing out a breath in disgust at the mere idea of an affair with the man, Tyema fanned herself and took a sip of water. She probably needed to contact another temple and arrange a transfer of scribes before Jemkhufu crossed the line and said or did something she couldn't ignore. Sobek would kill him and throw his *ka* to Ammit the Destroyer for breakfast if the scribe made advances to Tyema against her will.

Guess this is one letter I'll have to write myself.

Raising a hand to stroke her cheek, she relived Sahure's chaste kiss and the way her body had reacted favorably to *his* proximity. She knew why she'd been tempted to visit the festival with him, aside from his obvious attractiveness and smooth Theban charm. Her life was calm, orderly, peaceful…and lonely. *I run the temple, I lead the observances, I give direction to the staff, and I see my family occasionally.* But she'd deliberately constructed her life to be tranquil, after the turbulent, awful events of her childhood, hadn't she? So how could she complain now, if safe routine had become a cell, one she saw no way of escaping? At least her decision to venture out for one night with a stranger had been fun.

"May I present Captain Sahure, of Pharaoh's Own Guards, nephew of Nomarch Ienhotep," said the scribe as he reentered the room, followed by the warrior. Bowing to Tyema, Jemkhufu added an admonition to the visitor. "Be honored to enter the presence of High Priestess Tyema."

She caught her breath as Sahure sauntered in, resplendent in his full uniform, the golden falcon badge prominent on the leather straps crossing his broad chest, scarlet cloak swirling around his legs. He was even more handsome than she'd remembered. He bowed, "Good morning to you, my lady."

"And to you, captain." With great effort, she kept a smile from forming on her lips. Unfamiliar heat pulsed in her core and she suppressed the urge to shift her hips in response.

"I appreciate your seeing me today instead of tomorrow," he said, staring at her with narrowed eyes.

Oh, I couldn't wait till tomorrow. Tyema remained regally seated in her chair with an effort, curling her fingers tight against the desire to touch him. "I'm sure your business is urgent."

"Indeed, I'm here at the command of Pharaoh, very pressing affairs." He raised his eyebrows and gave a sideways glance at the scribe.

"You may go, Jemkhufu," she said, following Sahure's line of sight.

"But, my lady, what if notes need to be taken?" The scribe was startled, his eyes opening wide and his mouth hanging open. Tyema never met with anyone alone, other than the god Sobek, so she wasn't surprised by Jemkhufu's reaction. Swallowing hard, the scribe glared at Sahure while questioning her order for privacy again. "Are you sure you won't need me?"

She tapped her fingers on the arm of her chair. "I'll call you when we're done."

The scribe gathered up his tablets, rolls of blank papyrus and sharpened quills in an untidy armful and backed from the room, closing the door. She heard him complaining to the guard about the unscheduled audience interfering with the day as the portal closed.

Before she could say anything, Sahure was standing in front of her, his arms caging her in the chair. "And I thought *Theban* ladies played games," he said. "Imagine my surprise this morning to see that the high priestess of Sobek was none other than my little waif from the previous evening. She whom I thought to be Ema was in reality the legendary and rarely seen Tyema herself."

"Waif?" Tyema couldn't decide whether to be amused or insulted. True the plain dress wasn't the best garment in her wardrobe but surely it didn't give such an insignificant impression?

"Were you laughing at me the entire evening?" His tone was cold. "Did you enjoy your masquerade?"

She put one hand on his chest, trying to push him away, but under her fingers his body was solid muscle, an unyielding wall. "I'm sorry, I didn't set out to deceive you."

He stared at her for a long moment before releasing the chair. He backed up a step. Hands on hips, he asked, "Then why the lie?"

Pointing a finger at him, she said, "You just assumed I was a simple priestess. Ema is the pet name my family calls me, if you must know. Please, I had such a lovely, rare time last night, don't ruin it with anger today. I'm sorry."

"You're right, I did assume." Eyes narrowed, he studied her more closely. "The innkeeper was saying this morning you never come to the village, you're never seen away from this temple. Of course he wasn't addressing this remark to me and when he noticed me standing there, he shut up and scurried into the kitchen. His embarrassed departure was my first clue perhaps the girl I'd been enchanted by wasn't what she seemed."

"Oh dear, I was hoping no one in the family had seen me." Tyema knew she'd be dealing with the gossip and fallout of her excursion for a long time. Her aunts, nieces and female cousins would want all the details, none of which she planned to supply, innocuous though the night had been.

"Apparently we're the talk of the entire town today, I assure you. Not that I care," he said.

No, for you'll be departing for Thebes all too soon, while I stay here. Tyema didn't know what to say next. She was unused to dealing with a man on a personal level. All her encounters with people were about the temple, about Sobek's business, and those interactions she could handle. She decided to switch the conversation to his reason for visiting the area. "I'm sure the Great One will be fine with anywhere you decide to build a river port, as long as the site isn't close to this temple complex. The beach below is private for his use."

"Oh no you don't, we aren't done with the subject of last night yet." He picked up a gilded crocodile statue on the desk, examined it briefly before setting it down. "Does the god restrict your comings and goings? Are you going to be in trouble?" He frowned.

"What?" Wrinkling her brow, Tyema tried to follow the train of thought. "No, Sobek is very considerate of me."

The captain from Thebes didn't seem pleased by the answer, clenching his jaw. "Are you sworn to serve him personally, then?"

Now she saw where his thoughts were running. "Of course not! Sobek refers to me as his little sister, when I see him." She bit her lip. It wasn't her place to explain to this relative stranger what the exact relationship between the god and herself was. No one this side of the Afterlife knew the Great One was married to her half-sister Merys, living with her in the home of the gods, by grace of the goddess Isis. "I merely do him honor as a priestess. Many in my family have been priestesses at this temple in past generations. He protects me."

Throwing out his arms, palms up, Sahure had exasperation written on his face. "Then *why* is your attending the festivities in the village with me such wonderment? Even the god Horus is probably speaking of it today."

"I rarely go outside the temple compound, and my reasons are strictly my own," she said, striving for dignity, her heart racing a bit. "I thank you again for the dinner and the evening's entertainment. Now, I'm sure I must have others waiting for a moment of my time on temple business. My scribe said there was a full slate."

He wandered over to admire a fresco on the east wall, of Sobek amid a gathering of his crocodiles, rendered in vivid colors. "Too bad you never leave the grounds. That's going to present a challenge to me teaching you to drive a chariot while I'm here." Glancing at her over his shoulder, Sahure grinned, one eyebrow raised.

Mouth open, she simply stared at him for a long moment.

"Shifting into the frog goddess Heqet now?" he teased. "Careful, you'll be catching flying insects."

Shutting her mouth with an audible snap of her teeth, she started to chuckle, then laughed. "Could we start over?" She held out one hand. "I'm Tyema, high priestess of Sobek in the Ibis Nome, but you may call me Ema."

He walked to her chair. "Much better," he said, taking her hand and bowing respectfully as if she were the queen. "I'm Captain Sahure, sent by Pharaoh to survey the Nile in this area, to further his investigation into the possibility of building a new port."

"And the Great One Sobek does *not* set limits on what I do with my personal time." Tyema smiled, gazing into his dark brown eyes, enjoying the warmth of his reciprocating grin.

He relinquished her hand. "I'm on a tight schedule for accomplishing this task as Pharaoh has other duties for me in the near future. I'd appreciate your help finding suitable inlets to recommend for the new port. In return I'll teach you to drive the chariot," he offered. "Although, gods help me, it's not a skill most women have any interest in. You did well enough last night."

Glancing at the piles of tablets and the rolled papyri on her desk, Tyema said, "I can't abandon my daily duties."

"No, I understand but surely you can delegate some tasks, spend a portion of the days with me while I'm here? The afternoons at least?" Sahure picked up a tablet from Jemkhufu's desk at random, scanning the hieratic writing. "A request for prayers about the birthing of the new calves?" Staring at her, one eyebrow raised, he said, "You don't handle every single aspect of this temple's business and religious activities yourself, do you?"

Actually, I do. She studied him closely. "I can't tell— are you proposing we conduct business or pleasure together?"

Dropping the tablet on top of the others, he nodded. "Oh, I'm all business, I assure you. I have a scroll of authority from Pharaoh attesting to my mission, which I can duly show you if required. I've a feeling your overly protective scribe is going to demand the proof," he said with a deep chuckle. "But I see no reason why a job must be pure drudgery, not when there's such pleasant company available."

Careful, this man is a high born noble, used to verbal foreplay with the women at Court before he beds them, no doubt. You can't take his honeyed words too seriously. Even as she was inwardly chiding herself, Tyema nodded. His friendly, teasing manner put her at ease as no one else other than Merys ever had. What harm could it do to enjoy this rare opportunity, to indulge in seductive flirtation? *Someone who knows nothing of my past? I can keep my head, even if I do find him so attractive. And if we let it drift further, into more intimate territory, what harm after all? I'm a grown woman with no commitments.*

"Well, do we have a bargain? You'd better decide before your officious scribe forces his way back in here to preserve the day's precious schedule." Sahure's bantering words interrupted her musing.

With a little start, Tyema nodded. "I'll help speed your mission, in exchange for the chariot lessons, yes. Although I'd put the resources of the temple at Pharaoh's disposal in any case, up to the limits my Great One imposed."

"I'll take my leave and return tomorrow at the first hour past noon. You should be done with ceremonies by then?"

"Yes, that's fine." Tyema tried to remember what little she knew of boats and harbors. Neither was a subject of which she was fond.

Bowing, Sahure left the office. Tyema sank back into her chair as a flustered Jemkhufu shoved past the captain in the doorway and tried to find his place on the list of priorities for the day, muttering imprecations at the delay in the schedule.

I hope I haven't made a huge mistake. Resisting the urge to go to the window for one last glimpse of the Theban as he left the grounds, Tyema leaned her head against the winged sun depicted on the back of the chair and closed her eyes for a moment, before reaching for the medicinal water, as her headache made a pounding reappearance.

***

Next morning she had butterflies in her stomach which wouldn't subside, no matter what she was doing. The hours crawled by, Tyema felt she was walking through the ceremonies by rote and wondered what occupied Sahure this morning. Finally the noontime devotions were finished and she changed her dress before eating a hasty lunch, in case he arrived early.

Promptly as the shadow of the sundial moved to cover the hour, she heard Sahure's deep voice in the outer chambers and then a frowning Jemkhufu was ushering him into her office. The captain was dressed more plainly today, still in uniform but a serviceable kilt and blue tunic, golden falcon badge pinned to the shoulder. His bare arms revealed the powerful muscles of a charioteer, the tattoo of the Great One Horus's cartouche accenting his left bicep. The belt knife with a golden falcon's head handle and the sword at his hip reinforced his profession as a warrior, if there was any doubt.

Taking a deep breath to steady herself in the presence of so much unaccustomed energy and masculine power, Tyema rose from her chair. "Welcome, captain. I trust your morning was productive?"

He bowed slightly. "Indeed, but I can't make significant progress on my mission for Pharaoh without more knowledge of the aspects of the Nile in this area, especially the flood plain at inundation time. Does your temple library have any maps?"

"We've gathered quite the store of local knowledge over the years," Jemkhufu said before Tyema could get a word in edgewise. Chewing his lip, he added, "Although I'm not sure we have river maps specifically. Inundation records, yes."

Sahure glanced at Tyema, one eyebrow raised, plainly waiting to see what she'd do next, as far as the officious scribe's attempt to insert himself into the discussion.

"The Great One Sobek instructed me to provide Captain Sahure with the knowledge he seeks," she said. "You may spend the afternoon dealing with the issue of the cattle tally from the western farm." Pasting a smile on her face that felt so fake her cheeks ached, Tyema continued addressing Jemkhufu in a determinedly cheerful tone. "I know you were anxious to resolve the issue of how many male calves they were reporting, as opposed to last season's."

Glancing from her to Sahure, the scribe drew himself up taller, still failing miserably to match their visitor's impressive height. "As you wish, my lady, but

I'd be glad to conduct the captain to the library and help him search through the scrolls, so your afternoon remains free for other duties."

A flash of irritation made her voice sharper than usual. Seeing Sahure trying in vain to suppress a smile was also annoying. "Assisting the captain is my primary duty today. Yours is to resolve the cattle tally. I'll expect a tablet with the corrected count on my desk first thing in the morning, so you'd best be off to start the audit."

Face reddening, Jemkhufu said nothing more, merely placed his hand over his heart and bowed, exiting the room with an aggrieved demeanor, chin raised.

"You handled his insubordination well," Sahure said. "Does he take such a tone with you often?"

"Jemkhufu is invaluable in helping me coordinate all the temple's business," she answered, feeling compelled to defend her scribe. "But he does get carried away at times."

"So your library holds nothing that will be of service in my mission? Other than the flood measurements?"

"I have something better." She held out her hand, feeling excitement bubbling in her gut. "I think you'll be surprised."

"Nothing you do will surprise me too much, Lady Ema," he said, taking her hand in his and squeezing her fingers gently. "Where are we going?"

"To the garden beside the old temple." Tyema could barely restrain her grin, anxious to show him what had been prepared at her request.

Forehead wrinkled in a puzzled frown, he allowed her to draw him outside, walking beside her on the crushed stone paths of the formal garden until they moved onto the broken flagstones of the ancient sanctuary. "Your gardeners don't bother to trim the shrubs here, I notice."

"Sobek prefers things to be left untouched in the oldest areas," she said. "I like this part of the garden. The newer complex feels too formal to me sometimes, but it's necessary for pilgrims and temple staff to move freely in the compound so the grounds have to be well kept. No one comes here but me." *And the overgrown foliage ensures my total privacy.*

"I'm honored, but I have to say I don't quite understand how my assignment to identify potential harbor sites brings us on a walk in the garden." Sahure's dark brown eyes held an amused gleam as he cleared encroaching palm fronds from the path for her.

Glancing at him, Tyema felt her cheeks grow hot. *Does he think I'm bringing him here for dalliance?* Fortunately they'd arrived at her destination. "I believe you'll find this immensely helpful." She gestured at what had been a flowerbed in front of them, where now nothing grew.

Sahure drew in a sharp breath of surprise and dropped her hand, striding to the edge of the long planter. "Is this what I think it is?"

"A three dimensional rendering in miniature of the Nile in this area, yes." Pleased at his reaction, Tyema joined him, equally enchanted by the model of the river before them. A small stream representing the Nile flowed through the center of the map, draining into a pool choked with water lilies.

Sahure gazed at their surroundings, overgrown gardens, broken pillars, half-toppled statues. "But you said this is the ancient temple?"

Wondering what his concern could be, she nodded. "Yes."

"Lady Ema, forgive me, this is a fantastic map, but the Nile changes her aspects every year with the floods. I have to work from something current, something accurate in modern times." His tone was gentle, as if he was trying not to hurt her feelings.

She laughed, going to sit on the raised edge of the planter, trailing her fingers in the cool water of the stream. Tiny iridescent fish darted away. "This map is current as of last night, when the Great One Sobek created it for you."

"Are you serious?" Stepping closer to the twelve foot display, he hunkered down and peered closely at the glittering golden sands the god had molded into a map.

"I told him what your mission was for Pharaoh and the Great One was gracious enough to use his power to create this." Tyema smiled, remembering how surprised Sobek had been at the unusual request. "He's the keeper of the Nile after all, so no one is better acquainted with her twists and turns. I think he was pleased to be consulted."

Reaching out, Sahure touched the closest miniature hilltop. The sand stayed firmly in place, not one grain shifting. "This is amazing. I can't believe you asked the god to make me a map." Rising, he paced along the edge, stopping to examine an area a few miles away from Tyema's temple. Voice charged with excitement, he said, "I never expected him to get personally involved. I'm honored beyond words."

"He had a recommendation for you, told me where he felt would be the best spot." Tyema went to stand next to Sahure.

"And?" He raised one brow.

She felt mischievous. "Why don't you tell me first, where you think might be best?"

"I don't presume to put my knowledge against the omniscience of a Great One," he said. "But I think this large inlet with a peninsula seems the most promising. I'll investigate this locale before any other."

Tyema was impressed. "The exact spot Sobek indicated as well."

"I need to copy this onto a papyrus," Sahure said. "May I borrow some sheets from your scribe's supply?"

"Of course, but the Great One promised the map would last for as long as you needed it. He gave me a spell word to dissolve the sands for the wind to scatter later. He'd no wish for it to be permanent."

"I must go see each site in person, make extensive notes while I'm there, take measurements, outline what would be required to make the place a workable port, estimate costs and manpower, advantages, disadvantages. Pharaoh expects a thorough report. I have to be his eyes on this matter," Sahure said. "I can't report back to him without doing the work, not even with a map from a god to help me."

"I see. I'd no idea it was all so complicated." Tyema walked with him as they returned to the newer temple to get the supplies Sahure desired.

Evidently picking up on the disappointment in her voice, Sahure said, "But having the map from the hand of the god himself is a tremendous advantage. I owe you a great debt for obtaining this special favor for me. My work will proceed much faster, and it will do me no harm to mention the god's direct involvement to Pharaoh."

I'm not sure Sahure's early departure was necessarily the result I had in mind. A little ripple of dismay went through her like a chill wind. *I'm not in any rush for him to leave the area. It would take a long time, if ever, for the novelty of Sahure's company to wear off.*

"So this afternoon, I'll be copying the map onto a scroll," Sahure said, oblivious to her thoughts. "But tomorrow we'll drive out there and see for ourselves. At what hour can you be free to leave?"

"You were serious, you want me to inspect the sites?"

"I think it's wise to have the god's representative present, yes." Sahure stopped to let her precede him into the temple office. "And you can get some practice on handling the reins, because an officer of Pharaoh keeps his word and I'll teach you to drive, as promised." He leaned closer. "And perhaps most importantly, it's an excellent excuse for me to spend more time with you, my elusive lady Ema."

She fidgeted with her lotus-shaped earrings before smoothing the neckline of her simple linen dress. *Well, clearly Sobek is favorably disposed to this or he wouldn't have made the map, so it must be appropriate for me to accompany Sahure instead of performing my normal duties.* "I need to conduct the morning observances personally," she said, making a bargain with her conscience. "But by the tenth hour of the day, midmorning, I could leave."

"I'll be here then."

***

Next morning, as Sahure tethered the horses to the stone anchor at the base of the stairs leading to the plateau where Sobek's temple complex was situated, he wondered if Tyema would actually take him up on his offer to teach her to drive. Holding the reins while he stood behind her ready to take control should there be a problem was much different than actually driving. *Today will be interesting in many ways.*

"You're timely," Tyema said from above his head, interrupting his thoughts. "I'd scarcely taken my seat on the bench at the summit, to watch for your arrival, and here you are."

Startled, Sahure realized she was coming down the long stairs to meet him, dressed sensibly in a plain linen sheath, sturdy sandals and a gauzy blue shawl over one arm. Her hair was caught up in a simple twist, her only jewelry the raw emerald pendant of Sobek around her neck. Hastily he went to meet her. "You stand on little ceremony here."

"What would be the point of making you toil up all the stairs, only to engage in another unpleasant exchange with my scribe, no doubt? You and I would still have to make our way back to the chariot and you'd be in a grumpy mood from sparring with Jemkhufu. Or else insufferably amused." Tyema stepped past him, walking to the horses and offering them the carrots she'd been holding in one hand, stroking their noses and murmuring little endearments. Smiling, she looked over her shoulder at him. "I'm saving time."

Practical. He couldn't imagine any priestess in Thebes, or any woman he knew at Court, tossing aside protocol to make life simpler in a case like this.

Apparently struck by misgiving, Tyema regarded him in dismay. "Did you need to see the map of Sobek again, before we leave?"

Genuinely amused, he laughed, tapping a leather case strapped to the side of the chariot. "No, I've all the copied maps and my notes here, along with ink and a stylus. And tools for taking measurements. Shall we set out? I think we're in for a drive of several hours."

She wound her shawl around herself and took his hand to step into the chariot. "And you'll give me a driving lesson?"

"On the return trip," he said, unfastening the reins and joining her, backing the horses up carefully before directing them out onto the road which ran along the Nile. "They'll be less frisky then, easier for a beginner to handle. I intend to let them have their heads and gallop, as soon as we're away from your temple." He gave her a glance and was pleased to see her smile and nod enthusiastically, even as she clutched the top rail of the chariot. "All right then, let's make good time to the spot your god and I believe is the top candidate for Pharaoh's next harbor."

***

She was an excellent companion, choosing to stroll with him on the periodic breaks where he walked the horses. She had many lively questions about a wide range of topics, from what Pharaoh was like to his own adventures in the military. Sahure told her how he'd visited his uncle the nomarch of Ibis Province several times as a boy and fallen in love with the area, which made his present assignment even more agreeable. "But we never came to your village. I would have remembered. My uncle is an excellent administrator and travels throughout the Nome periodically."

"He's been to Ta'sobeksef on occasion," Tyema answered, drawing her shawl closer as if chilled, although the day was hot and the sun beat down on them. "We exchange letters about temple business from time to time, but there's nothing here meriting his personal attention. I like him, but of course I don't know him beyond his official capacity."

Sahure was thankful for the gentle breeze blowing off the river. Wiping his forehead, he checked to see how his companion was faring in the heat. "Do you need another drink of water?"

"I've had plenty for now, thank you." She shook her head. "We must be getting close to the spot?"

"Yes, I think over the next rise." He packed the water skin away and they returned to the chariot, horses picking up their pace to a trot as Sahure directed them over the hard packed earth. Portions of the journey from the site of Tyema's temple had been on what seemed to be the remnants of an ancient thoroughfare, but in other places where no road ran, the ground was firm enough to allow the vehicle an easy passage.

"Oh, so beautiful," Tyema said as the horses reached the top of the small hill and the inlet came into view, a swath of pale blue water, partially enclosed by a slender peninsula on the south. Shielding her eyes with one hand, she gazed at the river.

"And large," Sahure answered, feeling satisfaction sweep over him. *This is the spot, I'm sure. Pharaoh will be pleased. We can build an efficient harbor complex here.* He drove to a small stand of palm trees providing a welcome spot of shade.

"Do you mind if I take some notes before we see what your relative the innkeeper packed for our noonday meal?"

"Go ahead—of course the work must take precedence. Can I help?"

He assisted her from the chariot. "If you aren't too tired you can pace out the area with me."

Tyema laughed. "All I've done is stand in the chariot and walk with you a few times when we rested the horses. My normal day's activities are much more strenuous, inspecting the temple's businesses, our farms, conducting ceremonies—"

Sahure held up one hand. "I'm convinced." As they strolled from one side to the other of the wide basin and he took notes and measurements on his clay tablet, she began asking questions about the need for a new harbor.

"We've done without one in Ibis province since the time of the earliest pharaohs. Even your uncle's capital city is inland, on the caravan route, rather than the river," she said. "What new condition has arisen to require a port here?"

Sahure regarded her with respect, surprised by the incisive question. "It's not to be known generally, you understand, but a new source of copper has been located deep inside Ibis Province. Pharaoh is anxious to establish mining and smelting operations there and have an easy way to ship the ore north."

"Copper is a valuable commodity," Tyema said, fanning herself lazily.

"Pharaoh has been doing much work for the past ten years rebuilding Egypt after driving out the Hyksos, to make us strong enough to withstand any new attempt at invasion. These efforts are a severe draw on his treasury. New mines could help refill the coffers. And in addition, his ambassadors are negotiating treaties with the nations to the east, for spices, principally. The most direct route would be to this general area and then north by boat. The Nile is a much faster way to travel than caravan. Cargo ships can carry greater loads."

Tyema nodded her agreement with his points. "I'll have to make sure a suitable tithe is paid to Sobek then, when the new trade develops."

A bit startled at her matter of fact tone, Sahure stared. "Your temple will negotiate this with my uncle?"

"Of course I'll negotiate it with him," Tyema said, her voice crisp. "The temple treasury always has need of funds. Don't look so horrified, the deben is put to excellent use. We run several schools, maintain a medical clinic where the poor can come for treatment, an orphanage…"

"I see." Sahure had a mental image of his imposing uncle sitting at the negotiating table in full regalia with Tyema in her simple gown on the other side and the picture wasn't as amusing as he might have thought a few hours earlier. This priestess had a level head and seemed able to accomplish what she set out to do. "Your god is well served, Lady Ema."

"I only do what's required for Sobek's honor, to make sure he receives his due and the temple can care for the people. I have my duties." She shrugged. "So explain to me what makes this particular bend in the river a top choice for the harbor. I assume it has to do with the peninsula?"

"Yes, we can enlarge upon what nature has already given us, creating a stable and long quay where numerous ships can load and unload. The terrain here is suitable for launching ships or loading ore directly onto barges. Pharaoh might even build ships here. The water appears quite deep, even close to shore, and of course we can dredge if necessary." Sahure gestured at the group of trees where the chariot waited. "There must be a supply of underground water for so much vegetation to have grown. A port town could be built here fairly easily. And if your inundation records show the area isn't prone to too much flooding, I see no reason why we couldn't establish a bustling trade center in just a few years. And lastly, the contours of the terrain provide some shelter from storms."

"I can see it all clearly when you describe the scene," she said with a smile. "All you need now is a name for your fair city. May I suggest something honoring Sobek?"

"Naming the place will be up to Pharaoh and the gods." He grinned. Talking to Ema about his plans and dreams for the city he knew he could build if given the chance was exhilarating. He couldn't remember any other conversation with a woman that produced such feelings. Court ladies might feign an interest in his civic engineering for a few moments, before they retired to the shade to nap in boredom.

She challenged him as if she were going to be a partner in the construction. "But for now I suggest we have lunch."

"And after lunch?"

Anticipating her question, he felt a smile coming on. "It'll be time to drive back to your temple and yes, I'll give you the first lesson about handling chariot horses."

As they strolled toward the palm trees and the horses, Tyema pursued the subject a bit further. "Are you going to teach me to harness them properly? Not today obviously, but at some point?"

He was surprised. "Do you wish to learn? Surely you'll hire a trained team of stable keepers, since deben must not be an object."

"If I'm going to spend the temple's deben on something, I need to understand all aspects of the investment," she said, her voice brisk. "How else can I be sure things are being done properly in the future?"

"A fair point." *She's as thorough about this as she is about everything, apparently.* "Very well, I'll treat you as we do the cadets at the military academy and drill you thoroughly on all the procedures, not just handling the reins."

***

The week sped by, became two weeks. Tyema conducted her ceremonies and her official duties as efficiently as ever, although she did delegate an unusual number of tasks to her most trusted underpriestess and even a few things to the young priest who'd just transferred in from another nome, which raised Jemkhufu's eyebrows. On the appointed days, Sahure would sweep up to the temple gates in his chariot, the horses full of energy and ready to run, and off they'd go, Tyema dressed in simple clothing, Sahure in his workaday uniform.

Each evening when they ate their picnic dinners, packed by the staff at the Blue Crocodile, he regaled her with stories from his wide ranging travels and what he admitted were heavily edited versions of his times in battle, fighting by Pharaoh's side. Sahure made it clear he admired their ruler's skills as a warrior. "Nat-re-Akhte is a tremendous commander, wily, fearless in battle. When we went against an incursion by Mitanni forces in the north a few years ago, it was our chariots versus theirs. Pharaoh led the way and I was privileged to be assigned to his right flank. In battle, each war chariot has a driver and an archer, you know."

"So you're an expert bowman as well?" Tyema said. "I'd like to see a demonstration some day."

"You may have noticed I keep my war bow and a full quiver of arrows on the chariot at all times." He rose from the blanket where their dinner was spread out and returned a moment later with a gleaming recurved bow and one arrow. Making the movements seem effortless, he strung the bow. "After we eat I'll be glad to do some target shooting for you. But you'll have to help me retrieve the arrows. Can't waste weaponry."

"Gladly, although I have a feeling you're being too modest. You probably don't miss what you're aiming for very often." Tyema held out her hands. "May I see the bow?"

"Can't afford to miss the target in combat." He handed the weapon over and sat down, picking up his mug of beer. "Try to pull the bowstring," he invited.

Struggling against the tension of the bow, Tyema found she could only move the string a few inches. "Clearly I'm not meant to be an archer."

"We train endlessly for a reason," Sahure said. He thumped one bicep with his fist. "It takes awhile to gain the strength to use a bow well and then the power must be maintained through frequent exercise. Speed, strength, stability make for a good bow and an effective fighter."

"And a keen eye, no doubt." She turned the bow over, examining the construction. "What kind of horn is this on the underside?"

"We call that the belly of the bow," he said. "Mine is made with the finest ibyx horn. The rest is willow, the parts bound together with sinew of the gazelle and glue. It's served me well. When I was younger, learning my warcraft, I had smaller bows, with less power, easier to draw. Those are packed away in my family's armory now, for training my sons, if someday I might be so blessed as to have any."

Setting aside the bow, Tyema examined the arrow, running her fingers over the striped feathers at the end and then touching the sharp point with her thumb. "Bronze tipped?"

He nodded. "Pharaoh's armorers turn these out by the thousands."

"But did the Mitanni have archers too?"

"They no doubt thought themselves to be gods of warfare, having placed three men in a chariot. The enemy that day had a driver, a shield bearer and a spearman in each vehicle." Sahure laughed, as if the memory was a pleasing one. "Fools."

Seeing his amusement, Tyema was puzzled. "Extra manpower and weapons must give an advantage, surely?"

"But consider the weight of three men such as myself in a chariot," he said. "Requires the vehicle to be heavier and therefore slower. Ours turn in the wink of an eye, you've experienced that yourself when we've practiced driving."

Tyema nodded agreement, remembering the excitement of the horses galloping full out and then wheeling in a great arc, dust flying, as she redirected them in a maneuver Sahure had assured her was typical on the battlefield. "Without toppling over."

He pointed a cautionary finger at her. "If done right. Their cumbersome vehicles could barely maneuver at all. And I can shoot a volley of arrows from a distance, where their soldiers could only hurl spear after spear from fairly close in. They ran out of spears well before we exhausted our arrows."

"So victory was easily obtained then?" Tyema tried to imagine hundreds of chariots coming together in combat. She shivered at the mental picture.

Face set in grave lines, no trace of his amusement remaining, Sahure reached to take the bow, setting it beside him. "No, victory is never easy. Even with our advantage of speed and maneuverability, many good men fell that day to win the battle for Egypt."

There was a little pause and then Tyema changed the subject, sensing he didn't wish to discuss the details of combat any further. He'd given her a glimpse of another aspect of his life, one she'd never known much about, other than experiencing the shock of the Hyksos attack on her village as a child. *I wish we'd had defenders like Sahure when the enemy swept down upon us that day.*

She'd never met anyone like Sahure before, certainly not in her rural village. He was so far above anyone in the town, in rank, knowledge and accomplishments, even the headman and the captain of the guard. Yet he wasn't boastful or mocking.

At times he spoke of his hopes for the future, for rising in Pharaoh's service, maybe even becoming a provincial governor himself someday. Tyema thought he could probably achieve whatever he set his mind to. In her admiring viewpoint, Sahure was destined for a great future. He was smart, with the all important family connections to leverage at Court.

But try as Sahure might, Tyema would never tell him anything of herself, beyond a bare recitation of how many sisters and nieces and nephews she had, or the latest news about the temple's business. Deflecting questions was second nature to her. A self protective instinct took over her tongue, or so it seemed, and she soon made the other person forget whatever they'd asked her, sidetracked into answering Tyema's artless questions about them. But Sahure was persistent.

"Yes, I can see how highly interesting one might find the fact the grain harvest is twice as big this year as last year's," he said after one such conversation, "But what does it mean for you? Will you buy a new dress? Travel to the nomarch's capital for the winter festival?" He toyed with a loose curl of her hair. "What do you do for you?"

She rubbed her fingers over her emerald crocodile amulet, hanging from a gold chain around her neck. Sobek himself had given it to her when she reached fifteen, creating the charm in the blink of an eye from one of his tears, the god's powers carving the stone with ease. "You don't understand."

"Make me understand then," Sahure said, sitting up and taking her hand. "So far all I see is you working your heart out for the benefit of the crocodile god and while he's been good to your village, how does the extra time and work you put in make you happy?"

"My life is so much better now than when I was a child." She withdrew her hand, got up from the blanket they were sitting on and walked down the shore to the Nile. "Why do you care?" she asked over her shoulder.

"Because I care about you," he said, rising and following her. "When I get you away from the temple and all your duties and burdens, I see this amazing woman blossom forth. She's smart and funny and kind and she can drive a war chariot better than most men. She entrances me."

Tyema smiled. *Who knew I'd enjoy driving a team so much?* She did thrive on the speed and power of strong horses pulling a chariot along at a gallop. The feeling of being in control of all that energy was exhilarating. She never felt in control of anything much in her life, other than matters concerning her temple. Sobek had made her the high priestess and that was that. Carry out the Great One's wishes, ensure things were done properly, follow the rules and everything ran smoothly. If only the rest of life's day to day events could be so well regulated.

Oh yes, buying a chariot and several teams of horses for the temple was definitely on her list of things to do. She almost never spent any of the deben allotted to her from the temple's treasury and while she supposed a high priestess would normally use her portion to buy clothing, jewels or goods for her tomb, Tyema wanted to enjoy driving a chariot in the here and now, to be transported away from her daily cares and duties and set free, even if only for a few hours. Clothing and jewels had never interested her much and as for the tomb, there was plenty of time to furnish it properly. *I wish I could ask Sahure to select horses for me but he won't be here long enough.*

"I have a good teacher when it comes to handling the reins," she said.

"Don't attempt to confuse me with praise." He raised one hand, mock stern. "It's like you deliberately hide inside the robes of the priestess, the same way you shelter within the temple enclosure. When we're out here, alone, you seem freer, happier, yet still there's some kind of a wall."

Closer to the truth than you'll ever know. Why is he so determined to press the issue today? Uneasily, Tyema strolled away from him, proceeding along the river bank.

Walking usually made her feel calmer when her feelings threatened to overwhelm her. To soothe herself as she walked, she hummed one of her favorite songs, one she'd learned as a child from her half-sister Merys.

She heard his footfalls on the sand, following her, and apparently he wasn't going to abandon this topic either. "At first I thought you concealed your inner self merely to be intriguing, but now I've spent more time with you, I'm increasingly puzzled. If I hadn't met you by chance on the first night and persuaded you, gods know how, to come to the festival with me, I never would have gotten the chance to know you, would I?" He skipped a flat stone across the river's surface, startling some birds into taking flight before he caught up to her. "I've inquired in town and what I overheard the first morning *is* true— you never set foot outside the temple grounds."

"I'm not required to," she said, turning to stare at him. Little threads of worry were constricting the beating of her heart, creating pressure in her chest. *I can't have this conversation with him. I won't.* Rubbing her chest to ease the binding sensation, she hummed the opening verse of her song again, then faced the setting sun and sang, full throated, glorious notes. Music always relaxed her, swept her away from whatever tensions she felt, released the bonds of fear.

As the last note died away, echoing over the river, Sahure took her in his arms and kissed her, gently at first, then more insistently as she responded to him, slipping her arms around his neck and pressing herself against his hard body, signs of his arousal unmistakable. Finally he raised his head and hugged her close. "Forgive me, I hope I haven't shocked you, but I've wanted to kiss you properly for days."

"Don't apologize." Tyema blushed but kept her gaze locked on his face. "I've wanted you to touch me as a woman that a man could desire."

"*Could* desire? You have no idea how lovely you are, how much being with you stirs my loins." He stared at the deserted beach. "This isn't the time or place I'd choose to show you how much I long for you, how much you mean to me. I'm not taking you on a blanket in the middle of an open beach where anyone could sail by and ogle us, not like some peasant farmer with his drudge who has nowhere more suitable to couple. You deserve much better." He gazed into her eyes, a frown wrinkling his forehead. "Yet we can't go to my lodging in your family's inn, either. Awkward for you."

"Tomorrow night, I'll make sure the temple staff goes to the village for the end of the month celebrations. We can have privacy in my chambers," she offered. "You can come to me at sunset."

"Are you sure?" He held her close and she could feel his cock straining against his loincloth, beneath the linen kilt.

An ache she'd never felt so strongly before stirred deep within her and Tyema reached a decision she'd been considering for the past week. *Time to take a risk.* "I'll show you the forbidden beach below my temple as the sun sets over the Nile, and then we can have dinner in my private quarters, continue this conversation, see what happens. If you still desire me tomorrow."

"Tomorrow and all the tomorrows, have no doubt." He laughed and kissed her again, one hand holding her close while the other stroked the side of her breast through the thin linen of her dress, thumb gently rubbing her nipple as it pebbled. Tyema pressed her body against his, enjoying the unfamiliar sensations. She shifted her hips to rock against his hard cock, seeking to soothe the ache in her own loins and Sahure ended the kiss with a groan. "Sweetheart, if you keep that up, I'll be tempted to forget my intentions to bed you properly and we *will* tumble here on the sand." He kissed her throat, gently nibbling his way to her collarbone.

Tyema shivered with pleasure, tilting her head to give him better access. She spread her hands on his back, enjoying the feel of the smooth skin and firm muscles under her fingers as she caressed him.

Sahure recaptured her lips for a brief moment, his tongue gently forcing them apart so he could explore the warm recesses of her mouth. Shyly she tangled her tongue with his, caught in the magic of being so desired by this man who tempted her to take unprecedented risks. Eyes closed, lost in sensation, she let one hand drift down his back, over his butt. Feeling surprisingly bold, she slid her fingers across his skin, exploring between their bodies where his aroused manhood tented his kilt.

Sahure permitted her to caress him for only a moment. "Oh, now we *are* done," he said, setting her back a step or two and readjusting himself. "Your touch is hard to resist, but I'm determined our first time together won't be hurried."

She made a small whimper of protest, hand to her lips. "But I want—"

"Tomorrow night, I'll satisfy all your wants, gods willing, I promise." He kissed her on the forehead and took her hand. "The loving will be all the better for having waited, you'll see. Anticipation has its own magic."

"I'm not patient," she said, walking with him toward the chariot. "The hours until tomorrow night seem an eternity. I'm not sure why you object to the beach for our tryst. We've been here quite awhile and have seen no one else."

"Sand isn't the most ideal surface for what we both desire." Sahure laughed as he handed her into the chariot before going to untie the reins from a small palm tree. "I have tasks to accomplish, some land contracts to review in the town library and a report to draft for Pharaoh. It may be an eternity until tomorrow night, but my duty must come first."

***

The next day passed in a blur for Tyema. One minute she was confident of his affection for her, sure it was the right thing to lie with him. The fact he was a high born noble from Thebes, used to having his pick of women but so obviously desiring *her*, was an undeniable part of the appeal. All the many facets of his personality and the exciting life he'd led, so different than hers, or anyone else she knew, captivated her, made her want to know even more. She knew the depth of her feelings for him, and when might she ever have another chance to make love to a man she cared for so desperately?

Just once I want to experience some part of what other, more fortunate women have—to be held and caressed, made love to. I'll gladly pay the price of a broken heart when he leaves the nome and returns to Thebes, but until that day comes, I want the happiness.

I want him.

Distracted by her eagerness to be with Sahure, she made mistakes in the morning ceremony for the first time anyone could remember, which occasioned considerable discussion behind her back, she knew. Tyema held her head high and offered no explanations or apologies. *Sobek will understand my distraction, and he's the only one whose opinion matters.*

After the final devotions for the day were concluded, Tyema firmly reiterated her orders for the staff to demonstrate their support for the new village headman by attending the festival.

Going to her own quarters where her maids had laid everything out before they too departed for Ta'sobeksef, Tyema took her time in preparation for the evening to come. She bathed in lily-scented waters and selected her most becoming linen dress, one with green papyrus leaves embroidered at the hem, from the meager stack in her wardrobe, annoyed with herself for not bothering to have at least one special gown made to keep on hand for a rare occasion like this one. *The robes of a priestess aren't suitable for what I plan tonight.* And all the other garments in the baskets reflected her country life. Certainly nothing to impress a Theban nobleman. *Not that I plan to be in the dress for the better part of the evening.* Smiling as she set a blue cornflower blossom in her hair, the way Sahure had placed the lush red blossom on their first evening together, Tyema admired her reflection in the silver mirror and strolled outside to wait.

Sitting on the bench near the cliff's edge, in her private garden set among the ruins of the first temple, her nerves thrummed with anticipation, mixed with a little fear about the future after this night. But she trusted Sahure. This chance to please and be pleased by a man she cared for might never come her way again, given the restricted life she'd chosen. "Don't look the gifts of the god in the mouth," she said.

"Always sound advice," Sahure agreed, walking up the path. "Are we talking about some particular gift?"

Rising, Tyema ran to meet him. She gave him a big hug and a sweet kiss on the lips. "I'm so glad you're here—I thought the day would never be over. Come, I want to show you the beach before the sun sets completely."

"Let me set this down first." He put a small basket on the bench. "I brought honeyed dates and other delicacies to contribute to our dinner." He pulled a red flower from the basket and placed it in her hair next to the blue one she'd adorned herself with. "Beautiful!"

"Very thoughtful, and I thank you." She tugged at his hand. "Come on, Ra the sun god won't wait, and I want you to see how beautiful Sobek's beach is."

"You certainly aren't a patient woman, are you?" He chuckled before kissing her lips. "All right, I'm ready to see this fabled beach."

They took the path leading from the old temple to the deserted shores of the Nile. Sahure gazed appreciatively to the west as he descended the steep slope behind her. "I feel privileged to be viewing the sunset from the god's private retreat by the river. Are you sure he won't mind?"

"Sobek rarely comes these days and when he does, I always receive a warning from him ahead of time," she answered, walking onto the sandy shore. "There was no indication from him today." Pointing at a group of five crocodiles catching the final rays of the sun on the far bank of the Nile, Tyema said, "We needn't worry about them. As Sobek's high priestess, I was given the power to control his creatures to some extent. They wouldn't harm me in any case, but I'll keep them from bothering you."

"Gracious of you, my lady." Sahure laughed. "I've no desire to tangle with crocodiles tonight. It's entanglement of a different kind I'm anticipating." He caught her for a quick caress. "Will you sing for me? The one about the sailor coming home to his lady love might be appropriate."

"Gladly." She left his embrace and walked to the water's edge. Taking a deep breath, Tyema stood straight and launched into the requested song, tapping time with her toes in the warm, damp sand as she sang. Since she wasn't in the temple, she swayed from side to side a bit, dancing a little from sheer joy. Sahure sat on a fallen log where he could watch her, illuminated in the pink-and-gold of the setting sun, and was generous with his applause as she sang the final notes.

"You have the most enchanting voice," he said.

"I—I write songs myself sometimes," she said shyly, coming to stand between his knees. "They aren't as good as the ancient hymns but they please me."

"I must hear one of your songs, then."

She felt her cheeks growing warm. She never sang her own tunes for anyone but herself. Mentioning them to Sahure had been an impulsive moment, one of the few she'd allowed herself in all her hours with him, but now she was trapped. Refusing Sahure anything wasn't possible. "All right, I call this one 'The Impudent Bird'." Tyema put all her energy into a lilting, fast paced ditty quite unlike the hymns she usually sang, telling the story of a small bird flying over the Nile, teasing the Hippo Goddess Tawaret until the Great One turned him into a fish and devoured him.

He seemed tremendously amused, clapping at the end. "I've never heard the like, but I enjoyed the lyrics and tune. You could have had a career as an entertainer if you'd not been a priestess."

Uncomfortable as always with accepting too much praise, even from Sahure, Tyema glanced away. "Well, hippos don't regularly eat anything but plants, but I thought since the bird was so annoying, the goddess might have made an exception. Shall we go have our dinner now? We'd better climb the cliff stairs before the night grows too dark." Nerves made her light headed, giddy as if she'd been twirled in a dance but her heart beat faster in anticipation of the intimacies to come.

He followed her, stopped once they reached the bench on the heights above to retrieve the basket of food he'd brought from the village. Together they went through the gate to her exclusive area of the grounds and entered her living quarters adjacent to the old temple.

Setting the basket down next to the table where dinner awaited them, Sahure said, "A lovely, inviting setting for the most beautiful priestess in the Black Lands of Egypt."

The flattery sounded a bit too practiced to Tyema. "I suppose you say that to all the priestesses you seduce," she said, fussing with the plates her maid had set on the table.

Putting his hands gently on her shoulders, Sahure drew her into an embrace. "You're not like any other woman I ever met. The words I say in your presence come straight from my heart, flying to your ears alone."

Gazing into her eyes, he slowly lowered his head to kiss her, checking for a moment to scan her face before closing his eyes and kissing her.

Tyema melted into his embrace, her own eyes closed, feeling the warmth of his body igniting a fire in her own.

Breaking off the kiss, he slid her dress from her shoulders, baring her breasts. He gazed at her, heavy-lidded, his expression admiring, satisfied. Cupping her breasts with his hands, he said one word, "Beautiful." He kissed the pillowy top of one and then the other, his thumbs circling the pebbled nipples. Tyema arched her back, pushing into the embrace, a delicious sensation thrumming deep within her. Kissing her the whole time, tongue exploring the intimacies of her mouth while his hand was busy, Sahure undid the knot of the fringed shawl cinching the dress. Tyema held him close, arms clasped around his neck, her lower body undulating against the hard rod of his cock as he undressed her. The dress slid to the floor in a pool of blue-and-green, leaving her naked.

Sahure swept her into his arms and carried her to the adjoining room, standing her on her own two feet beside the bed. "Good, it's big enough for two to share."

"I've never shared it with anyone before," she said, shyly.

"I'm honored." He ran his hands over her back, cupping her butt and squeezing gently as he resumed kissing her.

She tugged at his tunic with both hands, pulling it free of the belted kilt, breaking off the kiss to say, "Fair is fair—you've seen me and now I want to see you."

Obligingly, he helped her work the garment up over his arms, tossing it to the floor himself. Impatient now, Tyema unfastened the leather belt cinching the kilt around his waist. The fabric fell away and Sahure stood in only his loincloth. He unwound the garment in a quick motion and Tyema smiled with pleasure as she saw him naked in her bedroom.

Old scars slashed across his back and abdomen, reminders of the combat he'd faced in Pharaoh's service. The cartouche of Horus was tattooed on his upper arm. Tyema ran her fingers over the ink, but her attention was for his proud cock, jutting from his smooth-shaven loins. She cupped his sac for a moment, enjoying the weight in her hand, before stroking him root to tip. Sinking to her knees, Tyema took as much of him into her mouth as she could, so large was his endowment. Her bolder sisters and cousins talked of doing this for their men, and of the pleasure derived by both partners in the act. The idea had seemed odd to Tyema but now, running her tongue over the smooth head of his cock, enjoying the feel of holding him in her mouth, she could understand. Sahure fisted his hands through her hair, hips rocking back and forth despite his best efforts as she applied her nimble tongue. Licking and suckling with pleasure, Tyema hummed, pleased at his obvious enjoyment of her fledgling attempts to torment him with her tongue.

"Enough for the moment," he gasped out. "Gods, woman, you drive me to the brink."

She gave the head of his cock a last swirl with her tongue and smiled mischievously. "Do I not please you, my lord?"

"Too much, if we're to make it into the bed together. I want to be deep within you when I come, watch you experience the pleasure I hope to give, share the passion, not be selfish. I'll gladly give you more opportunities to work your spell." He picked her up and laid her on the thin mattress atop the strong webbing, moving to join her.

Tyema smiled as he took her nipple into his mouth, tugging and sucking with just enough force to be arousing. His other hand slid down her abdomen, between her legs and stroked the slick, wet entrance to her aching inner core. She grabbed at the headboard of the bed and arched her body to his touch. All that time spent listening to her sisters and nieces talk of pleasing their men and being pleased hadn't been wasted after all. What man anywhere near her renowned temple was going to risk bedding the priestess of Sobek? The men of her village were none too sure she wasn't the consort of the god. But inexperienced didn't have to mean ignorant and she was glad she'd surprised him with her attentions to his cock.

Sahure's focus now was all about her pleasure, what felt good to her, although he was clearly enjoying himself, as his hard cock pressing against her thigh attested.

"Your skin is soft, so warm," he said with pleasure, kissing the sensitive area where her neck met her shoulders.

"I've been thinking of nothing else all day but lying with you," she said, arching as he inserted first one and then two fingers into her, rubbing and teasing.

"Very flattering for a man to hear but we're doing too much talking, don't you think?" He captured her lips, his tongue making its entry into her eager mouth.

He brought her to climax with just his skillful fingers and caresses. Tyema clutched at his shoulders, her body convulsing in waves of unstoppable pleasure as she came, head thrown back. She felt as if she was trying to catch every last particle of the amazing feelings, clenching herself around his questing fingers. Pleasuring herself, even lately as she'd fantasized about him, had never been this intense.

Sahure held her close as the final shivers of pleasure faded, working their way outward from her overheated core, like the ripples on a pond, leaving her langorous. "Beautiful as that was to watch, sweetheart, next time, I plan to be buried deep inside you, with your limbs wrapped around me," he whispered. "If you're ready for such enjoyment? I've no desire to rush you, we have all night."

Moving her hand to caress his heavy cock where it pressed against her upper thigh, Tyema rubbed her thumb across the plum shaped head, smearing the beads of silk moisture and then licking her fingers. "Now who's doing too much talking?"

"Mmmm," he captured her lips and rolled himself on top of her, his weight pressing her into the mattress with just the right amount of pressure. She felt safely caged, protected while they made love. His cock nudged at the slick outer folds of her womanhood and she spread her legs to make entrance easier for him. Using his hand to guide himself, Sahure thrust carefully, kissing her the whole time.

He managed to withhold his own climax until she'd come apart in his arms, clutching him as tightly as she could, trying to take him as deeply into herself as possible, lost in the pleasure of their bodies joined together as one. Sahure came a moment after, while she was still trembling in ecstasy. She felt his seed spurt hot and virile into her womb and she rejoiced in satisfying his needs as well as he'd taken care of hers.

***

Much later, in the last hours of the night, he ran one hand lightly over her breast, leaning in to taste the nipple with his tongue while she shivered, before trailing his hand down to rest on her flat stomach. "Although I hate to cloud a perfect evening with business matters, I should tell you I've been recalled to Thebes. Pharaoh has a new assignment for me, or so the orders indicate."

Tyema sat upright, clutching the sheet. Hearing his news, she felt as if he'd thrown cold water over her. *Why didn't he tell me this before?* "When do you leave?"

"The day after tomorrow." He sat up too, kissing her shoulder. "But my men and I go to the capital tomorrow and depart for Thebes from there. Good thing I can trust my horses, drive even when half asleep. I have to brief my uncle, Nomarch Ienhotep, on my findings, get his seal on the report."

"So soon?" She felt the pain of loss sink its claws into her heart.

"Don't fret." Lazily he reached out to snag some grapes from the bedside table. "I want you to go with me."

Tyema stared at him, not sure she'd heard the words right. "Go with you? Are you mad?"

"You don't think I'm the kind of man who would make love to you for one night and leave, do you? Of course I intend for you to come with me. Or at the outside, if you can't get clear of your duties so rapidly, to join me in Thebes before the next new moon."

She blinked, shaking her head a little, trying to ignore the sinking feeling in the pit of her stomach. "Come with you as what?"

"My wife, Ema, Mistress of my House, what else?" He stared at her, brow furrowed, eyes narrowed. "When I bed a woman purely for mutual pleasure, I make sure she knows my intent before we ever enter the bedroom. With you, it's so much more. My heart is yours. I've never offered marriage to anyone before, never wanted to speak those words. I expected to make a strategic union for political advantage with a daughter of a noble house this year and perhaps affection would come later, if the gods favored the woman and me, but I never dreamt of falling headlong into love as I've now done." He grinned. "Like a schoolboy."

"You—you spoke no words of love to me before this moment, why would I think you wished me for your wife?" Tyema could barely get the words out. He offered her something she'd never dreamt of— love and marriage—much as she might have longed for it deep in her soul, and then in the next breath imposed an impossible condition. "I can't go to Thebes. What a mad idea!" She left the bed, snatching up her robe from the stool and walking to the open door facing the cliff and the Nile below, all the while struggling into the garment. She was dizzy, her heart was breaking, and anger was building a fire in her gut, burning her pleasure into ashes. Knotting the robe's fringed belt with a savage tug, she said, "I can't leave this place."

"I understand you're the high priestess here, but priests and priestesses are allowed to be married. You don't have to work all the time, unceasingly, sweetheart. Let others step in and carry some of the load. I'm sure the Great One Sobek will agree to let you transfer to his temple in Thebes so we can be together, and you can continue to honor him while married to me." Sahure came to stand behind her, the warmth of his body failing to touch the chill in hers. She moved a few steps away, evading the hand he put out to her. Hands fisted on his hips, he tilted his head, a puzzled expression on his face, eyebrows raised. "What did you think would happen when I was done with the survey for the new port?"

Never had she even dared to think theirs would be more than a fleeting relationship—the love of a lifetime for her and a pleasant interlude for him. Yet her traitor heart betrayed her into speaking of the dream she didn't even know she'd cherished. Shaking her head, she said, "You could take a position here." But as the words left her lips, Tyema knew she voiced a forlorn hope. He'd talked often enough of his true dreams and plans in their time together.

"*Here?* Set's teeth, I can't believe you'd suggest such a thing." Taking her by the shoulders, his touch gentle but firm, Sahure swung her around to meet his gaze. "I can't resign from Pharaoh's service. I *won't* resign, to do what? Be a temple guard?" His tone was scathing as he went on. "Stand at the village gates maybe, with a spear, under the command of your brother-in-law? When I'm accustomed to taking my orders directly from Pharaoh's lips? Commanding hundreds of soldiers and charioteers? You can't be serious." His face was incredulous as he tried to find the words to reach her, to explain himself. "I'm a warrior, through and through. I'm an ambitious man, I have goals—I told you about them. I thought you shared my hopes. I'm rising in Pharaoh Nat-re-Akhte's favor with each assignment I complete. My future— our future—can be golden."

"You don't need me, then," Tyema said, allowing some of her anger to color her voice with heat "You need to pursue your original, *sensible* plan, marry a fine lady at Court, with connections and a big dowry. She can help your career. I can't."

"Why are you pushing me away like this? Why are you raising so many objections? I need you." He kissed her but she was unresponsive. "I love you." He laughed a little. "I never thought to say those words to a woman, but then I met you and I was lost."

She framed his beloved face with her hands, the pain from her breaking heart a stabbing wound in her chest. "I cannot be what you want and I certainly can't go to Thebes. You don't understand."

"Make me understand then," he pleaded. "Tell me what's going on in your beautiful, stubborn mind. What is it I don't know?"

Everything. She shook her head, throat choked with emotion. There was no use to try explaining herself. His dreams and hers had nothing in common she could see, except for the love she bore for him in her heart.

Hands on her shoulders, he said, "I'll ask you one more time, please come to Thebes and be my wife. Or tell me once and for all why you can't leave this temple. Why you're refusing all I have to offer."

"I can't. I'm sorry, Sahure, I'd no idea it was going to come to this. It was never my intent to hurt you." Breaking his hold, rejecting his touch as firmly as she was refusing his proposal, she walked away a few steps, toying with the robe's belt.

"Why did you lead me on then? Why sleep with me? Did you just decide it was time to experience a man's embrace, and I was a more exciting partner than the local temple guards? " He injected so much scorn into the words that she winced as if struck. "I thought, I hoped, you loved me, felt what I feel."

She whirled around, her hand going out. "I do, oh, Sahure, I do love you."

He shook his head, going to the bed to gather up his loincloth and kilt. "No. If you truly loved me, we'd be discussing whatever it is binding you to this place. You'd trust me, certainly not leave me to beg for explanations like a supplicant. We'd work through the obstacle together." Belting the pleated linen around his hips, he said, not sparing a glance for her, "I never dreamt I'd be fortunate enough to fall in love, to meet a woman I truly wanted to bind myself to, heart and soul, rather than just a cold political union for ambition's sake. How I envied Pharaoh his long, happy marriage! What a laugh the gods must be having now—I've met the lady and she doesn't want *me*."

Tyema was speechless, emotion clogging her throat. She'd known this affair would end hard for her, but she'd never expected to hurt Sahure. Her heart pounded, sweat dotted her brow despite the night chill and black spots were in her vision. Terrified, because never had the symptoms of her malady assaulted her here, in the safety of the temple, she pressed both hands to her chest and fled out the door into the garden, sobbing. The need for fresh air and open space was driving her. Prayers he wouldn't follow her mixed with wild hopes he would. There was no other answer she could give and the sheer terror assaulting her now was the proof she was right. She of all people could never marry a high born, ambitious man, not even Sahure, wonderful as he was. *I can't even walk in my own village, the place I was born, where everyone knows me, without fear of passing out in the street, disgracing myself with bodily ills, dying in the road like a diseased beggar. How could I keep household for him in Thebes?* "I'm only myself, my real self, in this one tiny spot," she said out loud, gazing around the garden in the moonlight, her voice catching. She knew she'd hurt his pride. But how could she explain to a proud, confident warrior like him, much as she loved him, the way terror caught her by the throat the second she stepped outside the temple grounds, had to deal with people on a personal level? Unreasoning fear never let go until she was safely home again.

"I felt safe with you," she said, leaning on the trunk of a tree and gazing out across the moonlit Nile as she addressed the absent Sahure. "But I couldn't be with you every moment of the day, could I? I'd be an embarrassment, a laughingstock in Thebes. And your career would suffer, your hopes for promotion and honors dashed because of your wife's strange behaviors, until you hated me and regretted we'd ever met. Took other wives and concubines, perhaps. Maybe even divorced me."

She stayed in the garden until dawn, weeping herself hoarse, catching a chill so deep her bones ached. As the sun rose, she crept back to her room, where all trace of his presence was gone, other than the rumpled sheets on her bed. Picking up the now-crushed flower he'd brought for her hair, Tyema collapsed onto the bed, wrapping herself in the linen, breathing in his masculine scent.

Her maids found her there when they brought breakfast.

She told them in a whisper that was all she had left of a voice to get out. She was taking the day off from duty.

And the next day, the day she knew Sahure would be leaving the province—and her—forever, she rose and went silently about her duties, refusing to have the town physician summoned. In the ensuing weeks, she grew even more reclusive, if such a thing were possible, until her staff and her family despaired.

CHAPTER TWO

Sahure had been in a dark mood during the entire journey back to Thebes. As the dusty miles passed under the wheels of his chariot, he kept reliving the last night with Tyema and trying to understand what had gone wrong after such a wonderful start. Angry at her rejection, hoping never to think of her again, his heart hurt and his pride was severely wounded. As the days wore on while he and his men traveled north to the capital, he began to think more clearly and to regret the hasty way he'd left, not even seeking her out in the garden to say farewell and make sure she was all right. He cursed himself for losing his temper.

Arriving in Thebes in the late afternoon, he left his chariot and the horses for the grooms to attend to and headed for his room in the officers' quarters. He needed a bath, fresh clothing and time to unwind enough to get himself into a proper military mindset before reporting to Pharaoh. The Great One wanted to hear a straightforward report about locations for his new harbor, not a sad tale of love gone awry. No sooner had Sahure entered the building, however, than a military scribe sought him out.

"Pharaoh requires you to report immediately, sir," the man said. "The palace sent over a standing order a few days ago to the effect you should waste no time presenting yourself once you arrived in Thebes."

Disbelieving, Sahure gestured at his dusty, travel stained uniform. "I can't go before the Great One like this. Give me at least a few moments to clean up and change."

"All right," the scribe agreed, inspecting him from head to toe and grimacing. "We'll send a messenger to the palace to let them know you're on your way, so don't linger too long."

A short time later, wearing a new uniform, a refreshed Sahure was being ushered into the audience chamber Pharaoh used for discussing military matters.

As he crossed the threshold and his name was announced, Sahure saluted crisply.

Pharaoh put aside the tablet he'd been reading, dismissed the other courtiers and officers and beckoned him closer as the group left the room, greeting him warmly in passing. As the door closed, Nat-re-Akhte said, "I'm glad to see you had a safe journey from the Ibis Nome, Captain Sahure. Is your uncle the Nomarch well?"

Sahure stood at parade rest in front of Pharaoh's desk. "As far as I'm aware, he and his wife are both in good health, sir. I haven't had time to have my preliminary report on the opportunities for a new port transcribed into a proper final draft, but I can recount the high points to you." He had his major recommendations ready to recite. A little flicker of pain struck his heart, remembering all the help and advice he'd had from Tyema in developing those. Clenching his fist, he willed himself to concentrate.

Holding up one hand, Pharaoh shook his head. "I'll see the report in due time, I'm sure. I've called you here on another, far more urgent matter. In the last two weeks, no caravans have arrived out of the south."

"None?" Sahure was surprised, shifting focus to call on his knowledge of the area. "It's not sandstorm weather. What news from the Southern Oasis?"

"Therein lies the crux of the matter." Nat-re-Akhte nodded, forehead wrinkled in a frown, as Sahure pinpointed the key issue. "I've received no word from the commander for the past few weeks either. No couriers, no carrier pigeons. The last report to arrive indicated situation was normal, so obviously something untoward has happened since then. I want you to assume command of the oasis. Take 50 chariots, with drivers and archers and a company of 250 foot soldiers. I'm assigning you three members of my own Guard to be your officers and shield mates." Pharaoh smiled. "I leave the selection of the three men to you—you've served with them, you'll know who best fits the assignment. The Great Overseer of the Army, General Marnamaret, is ready to confer with you about logistical support, but I think you'll find he has all in readiness for your departure. I want you to leave at dawn the day after tomorrow."

Although honored and pleased to be given the challenging assignment, Sahure's head was spinning a bit as he took in the orders. His last military action had been months ago, chasing a small army of bandits in a southern nome. He wondered which of the dire possibilities crowding his thoughts—attack, famine, illness—he was going to find at the Oasis when he got there. *A plan will be required for dealing with each possibility. And which of my brother officers from Pharaoh's Guard do I want to select? Who do I trust the most?*

"The assignment is for at least a year," Pharaoh added. "I need stability there, once you've gotten the place in order. As you're aware, the trade goods brought north by the caravans and the taxes due to the throne are critical to my treasury, necessary for administration of Egypt's affairs, maintaining her defense, feeding my people in time of famine." He pointed his quill at Sahure. "You're one of my best men, I've no desire to immure you in the desert for the rest of your career. I have other plans for your future, but now isn't the time to discuss those." Setting the quill down, Pharaoh leaned closer, staring Sahure in the eyes. "Get my oasis and my caravan route back in order, establish the structure needed to prevent future mishaps, and I'll be *very* impressed. Grateful. Gold of valor shall be the least of your rewards."

"I'm honored, Great One." This was a rare opportunity, the kind of thing he and all his peers craved—a chance to do a true service to Pharaoh and their country. Since the Hyksos invaders had been driven beyond Egypt's borders for a decade, a major operation of this nature had been nearly nonexistent. Sahure was also happy about the length of the posting. Time enough to make his mark on the Southern Oasis, but not so long his hopes for promotion would be sidetracked. He was relieved to hear Pharaoh's praise. It was a pity about the Ibis Nome project, though. He had so much of himself invested in the planning, not to mention the unresolved issues with Tyema.

Pharaoh had already picked up the tablet again, moving on to his next concern, which didn't involve Sahure. "Submit your report on the Ibis Nome matter to my Chief Scribe before you go, although I'm not likely to move forward with it for a while."

"Of course, Great One."

Dismissed, he emerged into the hall, guards closing the door behind him. Knowing he needed to find General Marnamaret, commander of Pharaoh's armies, he set off in the direction of the military annex, only to meet the Great Royal wife, Queen Ashayet, in the central hallway as she approached her husband's study.

He bowed.

"Captain Sahure, well met," she said with a delighted smile. "We've missed you at Court these past few weeks. I'm pleased to see you home from Ibis."

"Then I must disappoint you in the same moment, your majesty. I've just been ordered to the Southern Oasis, leaving the day after tomorrow," he answered.

"I wish you well in the assignment." She smiled. "Unfortunate timing in some ways—I know you were planning to set up your household in Thebes this year, take a wife. My husband does prefer his highest officials to be established, married. I know he has his eye on you for the future."

"Marriage won't be possible right now, I'm afraid. I'd never take a woman to the Southern Oasis, especially when we don't know why it's fallen silent." Sahure found he was actually glad he couldn't pursue a political marriage as soon as he'd originally planned. A vision of Tyema crossed his mind.

"I do see the logic, captain, but there are some ladies in my court who might risk a trip to the Southern Oasis, to be your chosen one." Ashayet's tone was teasing. She pointed her fan at a cluster of younger ladies-in-waiting. "Baufratet perhaps? You were childhood sweethearts, according to her. Or maybe Nidiamhet? You certainly seemed taken by her artistic talents when you were stationed here last." Something must have changed in his demeanor as she listed the names because the queen dropped her bantering tone. She searched his face for a moment, while her fan bearers, guards, and ladies-in-waiting stood discreetly and silently by. Gesturing for her retinue to remain where they were, Ashayet took Sahure by the arm and led him a few steps away, until they were standing partially hidden in the lee of a great granite pillar. "What is it? What's happened?"

He'd always had a good relationship with the queen. Ashayet was genuinely interested in the people who served her husband, so he told her the truth. It eased the pain a bit to be able to speak of Tyema to a sympathetic ear after keeping the emotions bottled up for days. "I met someone in Ibis Nome, someone special."

"This is cause for rejoicing, but I see only stress and concern on your face," the queen said. "Is she coming to Thebes? I'd be happy to take your wife under my wing while you're gone on this task for my husband."

"She refused me, your majesty." Pain burned in his heart again as he uttered the words.

Ashayet seemed amused rather than dismayed on his behalf. "How did you ask her? I know you soldiers sometimes treat women as objectives to be won, not wooed." She chuckled, perhaps over some private memory, Nat-re-Akhte having been a hard driving military man before ascending to the throne.

Swallowing hard, Sahure admitted his mistake. "My proposal was badly done, I freely confess to you. I assumed—"

Holding up a beringed hand to stop him in mid sentence, Ashayet laughed but it was a sympathetic amusement, easy to bear. "I see, my worst fears realized. So in short, you didn't plead your case? You didn't consider the effect on her of moving to Thebes at all, did you? This life we live at Court would be a huge adjustment for a girl from rural Ibis Nome, even if she be high born, not to mention leaving behind her family and everything familiar."

He realized what the queen was saying was true. He'd never thought through what Tyema would have had to do if she'd accepted his proposal, beyond the idea of her transferring to another temple of Sobek. The thought striking him like a blow, now he saw how he'd assumed she'd simply give up being a high priestess, stop running what was by all tokens a successful temple with extensive businesses, to become an ordinary celebrant in Thebes and keep house for him. *And I was so adamant and proud about my station in life and position, never giving hers full credit. I'm an idiot.* "She's the daughter of a village scribe, ma'am, not high born, but she does serve as a high priestess." He knew Ashayet herself would keep his confidence but others were in earshot, however politely they pretended not to be listening, so he didn't tell her any more about Tyema.

Elegant brows drawn together in a frown, Ashayet toyed with the red ribbons on her white ostrich feather fan, which matched the trim of her elegant linen sheath. "I'm afraid I've no advice to offer, not knowing the lady in question."

Rubbing the back of his neck to ease the tension he was feeling, Sahure admitted the queen further into his confidence. "I'd been thinking about taking some leave, going back to talk to her, but now with my urgent new orders, such a trip isn't possible."

Touching his arm lightly, Ashayet said, "Write her a letter before you go. I'll ensure the Chief Scribe finds someone to carry it to the girl for you."

Genuinely grateful for the suggestion and her offer to take on responsibility for getting the message to Tyema, he felt his spirits lighten for the first time since leaving Ibis Nome. "Very kind of you, your majesty. I'd be extremely appreciative."

She nodded, stepping away from the pillar and gestured for her retainers to come forward. "I'd best be on my way," she said to Sahure. "Pharaoh and I have an audience to conduct with newly arrived ambassadors from King Minos of Crete. I'll see about the letter. May the gods go with you to the Southern Oasis and bring you safely back to us when your tasks are done."

***

It was literally the middle of the night. Sahure sat at the desk in his private quarters, one candle burning low. His stool was surrounded by crumpled papyrus, representing his many attempts to find the right way to plead his case with Tyema, to explain, to apologize. "I'm no hand with words," he said out loud, reaching for the wineskin. "I'm no scribe with a smooth tongue. If poetry is what she wants, it's better we parted in anger." Idly, he kicked at one of the balled up papyrus sheets from an early attempt. He'd copied out some lines from a popular love poem but felt ridiculous addressing Tyema in those terms, with fancy words he'd never utter. He'd written facts, he'd written apologies, he'd written—well, attempts to communicate in all possible styles. And not one word of it felt adequate, hence the discarded sheets. "I need to talk to her." *And she needs to talk to me, by the seven hells.* Picking up the wine, he moved to the bed, easing his back against the wall. In awe at the way the room was spinning, he realized he was more than a little drunk. After capping the wine skin, although it took three tries, he closed his eyes, just for a moment.

Only to be shaken awake by his sergeant with the morning light streaming into the room.

"Sir, you're due in General Marnamaret's office right now," the sergeant said.

Hand to his aching forehead, Sahure swore. "Set's teeth, I must have dozed off."

The sergeant eyed the wineskin lying on the bed but said nothing.

Holding his aching head, Sahure got out of bed and made haste to get into appropriate shape to discuss military matters with his commanding officer. He kicked one of the little balls of papyrus with his bare foot and swore again. It had seemed like such a good idea yesterday, when the queen proposed he write to Tyema, but it hadn't worked out. "Throw these in the cooking fire while I shave and get my kilt on," he told the sergeant.

"Waste of good papyrus, sir," the other man said but he gathered up the fragments and dutifully carried them out of the room, to consign to the flames as ordered. By the time the sergeant reentered the bedroom, Sahure was in his uniform after hastily scraping his face with the razor. Adjusting his nemes head cloth, Sahure searched for his sword. The sergeant handed him his weapons and they were on their way to a day of planning for the column to move out of Thebes tomorrow.

Sahure was exhausted by the time he made his way to his quarters, late at night, but confident all the arrangements were in order for a dawn departure. He'd selected three of his most trusted companions in Pharaoh's Guard to be his officers. The men he'd chosen were battle hardened and smart, pleased and grateful to have an opportunity for demonstrating their valor and devotion to Pharaoh, just as he'd been. *I couldn't do better than having Menkheperr and the others at my back, no matter what the situation may be at the oasis.*

Wearily, Sahure tossed his nemes onto the table and unbuckled the sword. Getting a small army ready to march in such a short time was a daunting amount of work, even with Pharaoh's well oiled administrative structure.

A single sheet of papyrus lay on the desk, the only survivor from his tortured attempts to draft a letter to Tyema the night before. "By the seven hells," he swore. Picking up the quill and dipping it into the ink, he wrote the standard greeting followed by a two sentence factual note in hieratic and signed it.

"She'll know where I am, she'll know what I'm doing, she'll know I think of her," he said as he rolled the papyrus up. "She'll know matters between us aren't over." He sealed it, imprinting his cartouche on the congealing red wax with his ring. Resolving to have a courier deliver the scroll to Queen Ashayet in the morning, he went in search of dinner, with one more thing checked off in his mental tablet of tasks to do before the chariots rolled from Thebes at dawn.

***

"Are you unwell again this morning, my lady?" asked her maid, smoothing the coverlet over Tyema and adjusting the wooden headrest ever so slightly to be more comfortable.

"I caught cold last month and never recovered, I think." Tyema couldn't decide which was worse, the constant burning nausea in the pit of her stomach or the crushing weight of tiredness. Nausea won for the moment. Hand at her lips, she asked, "Did you bring me the crusts of dry bread as I requested?"

The maid exchanged glances with the other serving girl. "I did, my lady."

Tyema pointed at the table close to the bed. "Leave the plate and you can go—I won't need you this morning. Please tell the under priestess I asked her to sing the morning devotions again."

Tyema waited until the girls had left, closing the door behind them, before she got out of bed, munching on one of the crusts like a beggar woman. She wandered to the open doors leading to the garden and the ruined temple. Shuffling into a pair of sandals and grabbing an embroidered blue robe to cover her filmy nightgown, she walked outside, hoping the fresh air would calm her stomach enough to keep the bread down.

She strolled over to the ruins of the ancient temple, making her way along the cracked flagstones in the path, then entering the now roofless outer sanctuary. The original statue of the god had been moved with great fanfare and many incantations and blessings, once the new temple had been finished, but she'd had another effigy carved and installed in the old sanctuary, and hung one of Sobek's emerald tears around its neck, to create a private place of worship for herself.

Today she sought out the peace and quiet of that refuge, taking a moment to cleanse her hands and feet in the small pond outside the temple, before opening the door with a spell Sobek had given her. Lighting one of the torches piled outside the inner sanctum and setting it into the bronze holder just across the threshold, Tyema studied the representation of the god she served. Half human, half crocodile, Sobek stood larger than man-sized, leaning on his staff, golden crown and plumes reaching to the ceiling of the tiny enclosure. She'd seen him in this incarnation as a child and never forgotten her awe. The sculptor had done a good job of capturing the grandeur of the god. Going to her knees in front of the statue, she leaned her head on the cold pink-and-gray granite and said, "Why can't I get over this? When will my heart stop aching for the sound of his voice? For the touch of his hand? I never should have gone to the village festival with him on the first evening we met."

She sat back on her heels, hands covering her stomach, feeling a fresh wave of nausea. She couldn't throw up here, in the sanctuary. Swallowing hard to force the bile in her throat to subside, after a moment Tyema said, "I can't regret having taken the risk of getting to know him though. How could I, when now I know what it's like to be truly loved? But what he asked of me on our final night together was impossible." Even now she was tempted to write Sahure a letter, try to explain she hadn't been rejecting him so much as she'd been fleeing the terrible malady she was cursed with, the invisible but real chains of her fearfulness.

"But it's better he just be allowed to forget me, isn't it? Not to be further embarrassed by what we shared? After all, I'll never see him again. And where would I direct such a letter? He could be assigned anywhere in the Black Lands by now."

There was no answer from the god but she hadn't expected one. Her sister Merys had once described Sobek as a force of nature. He wasn't a Great One who dealt much with human emotions, human problems. He tended the Nile itself, ensuring the waters ran properly, thereby benefitting all Egypt. It made sense he had little time for mundane issues, including the broken heart of one of his priestesses. Tyema sighed, rising to her feet. *What I want is to talk to Merys. But she hasn't visited me in years.* Feeling the prickle of tears, she took the torch and left the sanctuary, the door closing behind her. A sudden breeze extinguished the flame. Blinking in surprise, Tyema set the brand aside for her next visit as a shadow fell on the broken pavement in front of her. When she glanced up, heart pounding, her half-sister was standing there, arms out.

"Oh, Merys!" Bursting into tears, Tyema rushed to hug her. "You're really here."

Patting her on the back, Merys made shushing sounds for a few moments, allowing Tyema to weep before coaxing her toward the shade trees. "Come, let's sit on the bench over here and you can tell me what's wrong, little sister."

Tyema felt herself relaxing in her half-sister's warm embrace. Merys had always fixed problems for her when she was a little girl. This current heartbreak was too much for even a beloved sister to mend, but having her to lean on and talk to made the misery recede a little. Hugging her sister close, Tyema said, "How did you know to come? I needed you so badly today."

"Sobek told me. He heard your lamentation as he was going about his duties. You're dear to his heart, sister, so he listens for your voice and his ears are sharp." Arm around Tyema's waist, Merys drew her into the garden and a seat on the bench underneath a towering palm, next to a cracked, dry fountain. As Tyema dried her eyes on the sleeve of her robe, Merys patted her hand. "I can't stay long, you know the rules Isis set forth for my journeys from the Afterlife. Tell me, what besets you so?"

Tyema grimaced, tried to smile, felt her eyes filling with the hot tears again. "It's a short tale—I fell in love." Sniffling, she leaned her head on her sister's shoulder and let the tears fall.

"And he didn't love you?" Merys combed her fingers gently though Tyema's hair, as she'd done many times during their grim childhood when her abusive mother had been alive.

Wiping away tears, Tyema shook her head, a flash of hot annoyance in her heart at the incorrect assumption Merys had made. She sat up and moved away ever so slightly. "On the contrary, he loved me so much he wanted to marry me."

"Oh, I see." Merys frowned. "Difficult but surely not impossible, if he's from anywhere in this nome. Sobek wouldn't put barriers between you and someone you loved. He only wants your happiness."

"Sahure's a noble, a warrior reporting directly to Pharaoh." Tyema couldn't keep herself from singing his praises, proud of the man she loved, sighing as she remembered how handsome he was in uniform. Then her shoulders slumped and she leaned against the filigree of the bench back. "He expected me to go to Thebes with him, to be his wife. You know I can't," she said.

Nodding, her older sister patted her hand. "Did you explain your challenges to him? If he truly loved you—"

Tyema shook her head. "I couldn't tell him. He thinks I'm this strong, confident woman because I run the temple for Sobek and we both know outside these walls, I'm useless."

"Not useless, dear one," Merys protested immediately, rushing to defend her as always. "Shy perhaps, easily startled and upset—"

Tyema sighed, leaving the bench and pacing beside the fountain, unable to sit still with all the emotions pent up inside her. "There's no use in dreaming. I refused him, he was angry and hurt, and he left for Thebes, where he belongs. I have to be able to move on, forget him. I *must*. I'm shirking my duties." She stopped, clutching at her stomach as a fresh wave of nausea swept over her. "Perhaps it's the depth of my grief, but I can't seem to get over this illness."

Merys came to support her as she shuffled to the bench and sat down. "I don't get the sense of a malady of the spirit or the body. Odd." She laid one hand on Tyema's flat stomach. "Let me concentrate for a moment. Living in the Afterlife has given me some abilities I never had here in daily life, maybe I can divine the cause, suggest a remedy." Suddenly she lifted her hand away and stared at Tyema. "Not ill, sister. You're—"

"Pregnant," Tyema whispered, hand to her mouth as the realization flooded over her. "By the tides of the Nile, I'm going to have his baby."

Her sister hugged her hard, rocking her back and forth. "It happens. It happened to me, remember?" Pushing the hair from Tyema's face, Merys stared into her eyes. "Do you want this man's child?"

Laying a hand over her abdomen protectively, Tyema said, "*My* child. And his. Oh, of course I want the baby. I never dreamt I'd have the chance to be a mother."

"People will talk," Merys warned. "They may even assume the child is Sobek's, as you're known to be high in his regard."

"Will such rumors upset you?" Tyema's voice faltered. Determination to have this baby mixed with distress in her heart at the idea of causing Merys any pain, even from gossip.

Merys kissed her on the cheek. "Of course not, silly goose. We know the truth and rumors, if they arise, may make life easier for you and for the child. I wish you well," she said firmly, dispelling any worries Tyema felt on the issue. "I'll be watching, although I must confess time runs differently in the Afterlife and it's hard to remember my connections here." She studied the advancing shadows in the garden as the morning sun rose higher. "I must go. The terms set down by Isis are stringent. She does not like me to come here, but when Sobek said you were in such distress—"

"Thank you." Tyema gave Merys's hand a squeeze and watched as her sister walked away toward the cliff with a wave, growing fainter with each step, like an old fresco bleaching off the wall in the sun, until she was gone. *Merys never changes, never ages. I'm actually older now than she was when she went to the Afterlife.* It was a startling thought, one she'd never had before. *And now I'm to be a mother.* Joy mixed with fear of the unknown swept over her, bringing goosebumps to her flesh and she laid a hand on her abdomen. "I promise you, little one, I'll be a much better mother for you than my mother was for me." Longing for Sahure was a physical pain in her heart, so desperately did she want to share the joyous tidings. *Would he be happy?*

Again, more seriously, she considered sending him a letter, to advise him of the news, but hesitated. I don't know where he's stationed, *I don't know how to address such a missive, other than in care of Pharaoh's palace, which might cause Sahure embarrassment, ridicule even, receiving a letter from a provincial priestess in such a way.* Of course she could write to the local nomarch, his uncle. Nodding at the less audacious thought, she decided that might be a better way to begin. A fresh wave of nausea pushed the vexing subject of communicating with Sahure from the forefront of her mind. Time enough to worry about all of that later, perhaps after the child was safely born.

***

One day, six months along in her pregnancy, no longer troubled by the morning sickness, but able to keep busy and handle her duties, Tyema walked into her office at the temple to find her scribe waiting with a perplexed frown. "What is it?"

He glanced at the object in his hand. "You received a private scroll."

"A what?" Bemused by the baby's sudden, vigorous kicking, she laid a hand on the side of her belly to feel the movement. Smiling, she gave her attention back to the scribe. "I'm sorry, what did you say?"

"A scroll, delivered this morning by military messenger. The man was specific he carried a personal note, not something involving temple business." Jemkhufu's lips were pursed as if he'd bitten into a spoiled fruit. He stood poised to sever the red wax with his short knife. "Shall I open the seal?"

Tyema held out her hand. "I'll read it myself, thank you. Did the messenger wait? Is he here?"

"No, my lady." He hesitated. "I had the feeling they'd gone out of their way to stop here. Both the driver and the officer were impatient to be gone. They certainly weren't the usual mail couriers of the province."

"Was the officer the one who came before, six months ago, on pharaoh's business? You met him, remember?" She was casual but couldn't meet her scribe's gaze, instead fussing with the tablets on her desk.

"No, my lady, I'd never seen this person before." Jemkhufu sounded happy to make this statement.

Tyema took the tiny rolled up papyrus he handed her. Glancing at the cartouche imprinted in the red sealing wax, she saw it was Sahure's. Relieved to a degree the letter was from him and not some message *about* him, she tucked it into a side pocket on her voluminous dress. *I need to be alone when I read this.*

"Aren't you going to open it?" Jemkhufu raised his eyebrows, as if he was expecting her to read it to him.

For the thousandth time she reminded herself of the many things to do after the baby was born and things settled down for her, finding Jemkhufu another temple to serve was imperative. His attitude toward her now varied between unctuous pity and hinting if her child was a boy, he'd need a man's influence as he grew up. *And I'm sure Jemkhufu thinks he's the right person to provide the influence and guidance.* Tyema sighed, not having the energy to rebuke him and then spend the morning dealing with his hurt feelings. She walked around the desk and pulled out the chair. "Not now. I'm sure the message can wait, since it apparently isn't temple-related."

"But what if a response is required?" The scribe wasn't giving up, apparently driven by curiousity.

"You know I was taught to read and write hieratic as part of my training for the duties of high priestess. I'm perfectly capable of writing my own response." Impatience made Tyema's voice sharper than she'd meant the tone to be. She took a deep, calming breath and smiled. "Tell me about the number of new students enrolling in our school next month, hoping to become fine scribes." She sat down, trying to find enough support for her aching back as the chair creaked under her.

"We have fifteen, my lady, from all over the nome. The superiority of our graduates is becoming widely acknowledged." Jemkhufu consulted his notes and launched into a discussion of the incoming students and the arrangements for them.

Tyema forced her lips to curve in apparent good humor and nodded at the appropriate points as best she could, finishing the day's work and finally escaping into the private garden a few hours later. The whole time her fingers itched to pull the private letter out of her pocket and read it. The baby was unusually restless as well, perhaps sensing her own inner turmoil.

She sat on her favorite bench, under a large acacia tree, next to an unruly bed of chrysanthemums. Taking the scroll out of her pocket and balancing it in one hand, she stared at it for a long moment. Resting the other hand on top of her swollen abdomen, she said, "This is from your father, little one. Do you think he'd write me if he bore me ill will?" It warmed her to think she'd been on Sahure's mind, wherever he was. "Well, only one way to find out." She broke the seal with her fingernail, sending little shards of red wax falling to the pavement, and unrolled the scroll. The writing was bold, slashing black hieratic. *From Sahure, Captain in Pharaoh's Own Regiment to Tyema, High Priestess of Sobek in the Ibis Nome, may the gods grant you life, prosperity, health. Now posted by Pharaoh to take command of the Southern Oasis. I think of you often.* His personal cartouche was scrawled at the bottom of the papyrus. A bit disappointed, Tyema flipped the scroll over to be sure she hadn't missed anything. "Not lover-like in the least." She remembered how proud he was of his station as a warrior. "You never claimed to be a poet, did you, my love?" Shaking her head, she levered herself from the bench. It was frustrating to be so big and awkward. "Still, baby, it's a tremendous promotion for him. Huge responsibilities."

And the dangerous, remote Southern Oasis isn't a place he'd take a wife to, so maybe he hasn't gotten married yet. Immediately Tyema took herself to task. It was no business of hers where he went, what he did, who he did it with. She'd refused him for her own compelling reasons and nothing had changed. Glancing at her belly as the baby kicked hard, she laughed. "Well, all right, one thing *has* changed, even if Sahure remains unaware." As she walked into her bedroom, her smile faded. *Now that I know where he is, I'm going to have to tell him about our child. He deserves to know.* Deciding today wasn't the day for composing a demanding letter, she pushed the thought away. Time to change out of her simple dress into a robe suitable for singing the evening devotions. But first she put the scroll inside her ivory-and-turquoise embellished keepsake chest, pushing the papyrus to the back, under her tattered doll from childhood and the dried red petals from the flower Sahure had placed in her hair.

***

Her older sister Paratiti, who'd been chosen by Sobek years ago to be Tyema's guardian until she took over the temple, arrived from her home in the village one day late in the eighth month, by prearrangement bringing her daughters and the wives of her sons, as well as a gaggle of girl children. The group ate lunch with Tyema in the temple's private gardens, laughing and chattering in the shade of towering palms and fragrant acacias. The older ones talked about when their babies had been born, exchanging funny stories and teasing each other. Tyema sat in the midst of her extended family, marveling at what a strange feeling it was to be with them all, but the impending birth of her child gave them common ground. She felt relaxed, unworried, since they were in her home and she was the hostess. *In control.* The baby moved and kicked just enough to remind her the two of them were in this together, and after all the entire gathering was in Tyema's honor, organized by Paratiti. Some of the women had brought embroidered swaddling clothes for the baby and there was one big parcel they refused to let her open. It had taken two of them to carry the basket from the donkey cart at the front gate to the garden where the lunch was being held.

Finally, as the temple servants brought plates of honeyed cakes and figs at the end of the meal, Paratiti gestured at the oversized basket. "Bring the gift now."

Her daughters hauled the sturdy container to Tyema, setting it on the ground next to her. Smiling, she said, "I can't imagine what this might be." Lifting off the lid, she set it aside and removed the top layer of straw packing. Below the straw she found a fine pair of birthing bricks, smooth, freshly painted in white, with stunning portraits of the goddesses Hathor and Tawaret drawn on the sides in turquoise, gold and red. Protective spells were inked in black hieratic. Tyema sat with a brick in either hand, examining the art.

"Do you like them? I made the bricks myself," Paratiti said anxiously. "I said blessings to Hathor as I mixed the mud and straw in the brick-making forms."

"And we had the best artisan in the village do the paintings," Tyema's favorite niece, Renebti, added. "He wouldn't take payment since it was for you."

"I—I don't know what to say," Tyema stammered. "I'm touched."

"I hope your god won't mind, but birthing a child is a female mystery and he isn't known for involvement with such things. His crocodiles come from eggs after all. We were afraid you wouldn't have proper bricks here when the time comes." Paratiti gestured at the temple behind the garden.

"You do know this isn't Sobek's baby?" Tyema asked.

Her sister patted her on the hand. "No matter whose baby this is, you'll need all the magic and charms and assistance you can get when the child arrives." She eyed Tyema's belly. "You're so tiny and the baby is so big!"

The older women laughed conspiratorially. Tears burning in her eyes, Tyema fought not to cry. For the first time ever she felt a part of the family, cherished and cared for. She set the bricks down with care, so as not to risk breaking or chipping them, and turned to Paratiti. Suddenly frightened at what might lie ahead when labor began, Tyema said, "You will come, won't you? To help me?"

"Of course, little sister. You don't even need to ask." She hugged Tyema hard. "But you'll be fine. The women in our family give birth easily."

***

Surveying the neat lines of his temporary camp, humming with activity behind the shield barricade on the seventh night out from Thebes, Sahure was well satisfied with the progress his small army had made since leaving the capital. They'd had few breakdowns of chariots or support wagons, and the logistics staff under the chief military scribe was some of the best in the army. Marnamaret had given him seasoned infantry troops so the pace of the daily march was fast. Sahure sent scouts ranging ahead and always the report was the same— other than local traffic, the great caravan road was empty. *An unprecedented and ominous state of affairs.*

Soon he and his three captains would gather around the fire to eat dinner and discuss strategy as they'd done each of the evenings on the march. He'd unroll the great map of the Southern Oasis issued to him by Pharaoh's archivist and he and his staff would work on designing an approach to counter any eventuality the group could think of. *Including the senior sergeants was a good move. Even if they mostly sit by the fire, listening and occasionally offering a suggestion, better they understand the entire picture so they can convey the strategy to the men. Soldiers fight better when they know the bigger picture. And Menkheperr is doing an excellent job as my second in command. He'll always have my back, has ever since we were cadets together.*

Wheeling on the small hill, he admired the sunset—flaming reds and purples heralding the descent of the god Ra into the underworld, only to rise again in the morning. Not much time for personal reflection when marching to battle. *Yet sunset reminds me of Tyema without fail, especially the haunting songs she sang to the setting sun, there on Sobek's private beach.* Under his breath he hummed a bit of the song she'd written herself. The more he considered the matter, aside from his own arrogance and ham handedness, the more he came to believe something else had been in play, something he'd been too in love to realize.

The truth is she does hide herself away in Sobek's temple complex. I may have teased her about it, but now I know I unwittingly hit on an underlying truth. Her elusive behavior wasn't just village gossip and it wasn't required by Sobek. Priestesses mingled with citizens in Thebes, were married, had families—so why was Tyema so reclusive? He didn't feel she'd been false, or playing a role, but she'd hidden much beneath the serene surface. How often had she told him she was freer to be herself with him than at any other time? The girl learned to drive a chariot, by the gods. He chuckled at the memory.

But when he reflected over their whirlwind two weeks together, he saw how in nearly every conversation she'd deflected the talk to him and he of course had been only too happy to pour his dreams, plans and hopes into her willing ears. *No wonder she was overwhelmed when I casually assumed she'd marry me and move to Thebes.*

She always asked him excellent questions when he talked about his travels or Court life and politics, made good points when they debated some issue or surveyed potential sites for the new port. She had an undeniable grasp of business and administration. Tyema was no figurehead high priestess, propped up by scribes. She was shrewd, with a knack for running the complicated affairs of her temple. So she was beautiful, talented, brave, funny, smart—and somehow he'd lost her.

When this assignment to the Southern Oasis is over, I'll return to Ibis Nome and sort this out with her. I can't imagine what barrier she sees in our way, but my love can withstand anything she might tell me.

As darkness overtook the glorious sunset, he thought briefly of the girls the queen had named that afternoon in Thebes—Baufratet, his childhood playmate, and Nidiamhet the poetess, both the daughters of old noble families in the capital. Either would be a wonderful asset to an ambitious man trying to rise in the politics of Pharaoh's Court. *Neither holds a candle to my paradoxical little priestess.*

His heart was given. *If I can't sort things out with Tyema, maybe I'll go to the Afterlife a bachelor. And my younger brothers will have to ensure the family name carries on.*

"Sir?" Menkheperr stood next to him. "The scout has returned from the Southern Oasis, with news."

"Bring him to me at once. And summon the other officers and the senior sergeants." Pushing aside the personal musings, Sahure descended the hill and went to his small tent. He was unrolling the papyrus map of the Oasis to facilitate a more detailed debriefing from the scout as the men crowded into his tent.

Wine was brought. Worn and shaking from exhaustion, the scout needed only a single gulp to drain the mug of beer handed to him. "The Oasis is besieged," he said, wiping his lips.

A murmur went through the ring of listening warriors.

"Who dares to attack Pharaoh's outpost?" Sahure asked, relieved to hear he faced a problem requiring a military solution.

The scout accepted a second cup of wine from the manservant. "It's a mixed force, sir. Primarily nomads, a few mercenary warriors from the southern tribes, but also a small troop of Hyksos."

Now there was cursing from his audience.

Sahure clenched his fist on the hilt of his sword. "Hyksos! You're sure?"

The scout nodded. "There's no mistake. I was with Pharaoh in the year he took Thebes from the Usurper Queen and in other battles of the campaign as well. I recognize Hyksos. This is a small detachment, maybe fifteen men."

"They've probably recruited this tribe of nomads to be their allies, made them extravagant promises," Sahure told his officers. "It's the Hyksos style nowadays to get others to fight their battles."

"Clever tactic. If the Hyksos can choke off the rich trade from Punt and Kush, Pharaoh's treasury will be impacted. Which can create a ripple effect to harm Egypt." Menkheperr took a deep drink of his wine, quizzing the scout, eyes narrowed. "Besieged, you say, not surrendered?"

The scout shook his head. "The fort is plainly still resisting." Moving to the table where the map had been set up, he traced the topography for them. "The oasis is basically a large bowl in the desert, ringed with limestone cliffs and canyons. The fort lies here, on a slightly upraised ridge at the entrance to the main portion of the oasis." He stabbed a finger at the red dot on the chart. "The town is outside the fort and has a few wells, but the majority of the water is deep inside the oasis. The enemy can't gain access to the water without taking our fort."

"I imagine rations are growing short inside the fort," Sahure said. "Water wouldn't be a problem for them, but if they were attacked several weeks ago, the stores of rations must be growing thin. They can't go out to hunt either."

"What of the villagers?" Menkheperr asked.

The scout shook his head. "I saw a few people moving about in the town without hindrance from the invaders. The locals seem to be staying clear of the fight."

"The townspeople are the *Ta-itjawy*, sent by a great Egyptian pharaoh centuries ago to settle this oasis and hold the caravan route. They believe they're descended from the goddess Sekhmet," Sahure said. "They're Egyptians, but through the long years they've grown independent minded, more allegiant to their goddess and the local chiefs than to Pharaoh." He shared his new concern with the circle of his officers. "A high priority challenge once we've retaken the oasis is building closer ties to the villagers again. Clearly we need them as allies, not neutral parties who wait out any problem, or worse, who might help the enemy."

"Certainly they did nothing to alert Pharaoh," Menkheperr agreed.

Nodding, Sahure gave his renewed attention to the scout. "Did you see any caravans?"

"Massed to the south, sir, in a big camp, loosely guarded by the nomads and mercenaries. The Hyksos didn't appear to be involved in directly managing the caravans. I've never seen so many in one place at one time before. Must be five to ten separate caravans, hundreds of camels and donkeys, all trying to stay as close to the oasis as they can."

"What water are they drinking?" Menkheperr said. "Caravans travel from oasis to oasis. They don't bring their own supply."

"The invaders must be giving them rations from one of the small wells outside the oasis proper." Sahure studied the map for a moment. "Were there any Egyptian-led caravans?"

"I saw the standards for one or two. " The scout ticked off a few names of caravan masters, then said, "Ptahnetamun—"

"Wait," Sahure stopped his recitation with an upraised hand. "You're sure Ptahnetamun is one of the stranded caravan masters?" At the scout's nod, Sahure said, "The gods may have given us an advantage in the game. He and I have mutual friends, so he's unlikely to betray me to the enemy if I can sneak into his camp. By questioning him, I may learn more about the situation and the odds we're facing in retaking the oasis." Sahure nodded to the scout. "You've done a good job. Rest, regain your strength, and then tonight you'll guide me to where the caravans are sequestered. I'll attempt to contact Ptahnetamun."

***

Dressed in a plain tunic designed to blend into the brown of the landscape and label him as a common caravan worker rather than a soldier if caught, Sahure followed the scout as they crept the last few yards to overlook the spot where the invaders had interned the caravans. In the moonlight, Sahure could see how the various caravans had made circles of their animals and cargo, close but not mingling.

"Ptahnetamun's camped over there, sir." The scout pointed to the western edge of the sprawling area.

Assessing the odds for success of his plan, Sahure evaluated the terrain between his location and the caravan he was seeking as best he could in the poor light. "Does the enemy patrol regularly?"

His man shook his head. "I think they rely on the threat of no water to keep the caravans docile until the fort has fallen."

"Which probably works." Sahure checked his belt daggers and issued his final orders. "Wait here. If I don't return by dawn or am taken, report back to Menkheperr."

Barely waiting for the scout's acknowledgment, Sahure crept down the escarpment and closer to the perimeter of the caravan camp. Taking cover in what sparse brush there was, he circled the area to get closer to Ptahnetamun's position, evading one half-awake nomad guard with ease. Sneaking between the restive camels and donkeys belonging to the caravan master he was seeking, Sahure crossed the line into the small, packed camp.

He was immediately accosted by two large caravan workers, blocking his camp with drawn knives and hostile demeanor. "And who might you be?"

"A friend of your master's," Sahure said, not intimidated. "I need to speak with him at once, and quietly."

The man who seemed to be in charge eyed him. "You've the speech and manner of an Egyptian officer in disguise to me. Deserter from the fort?"

"None of your business," Sahure answered, hand on the hilt of one dagger.

"Don't waste time, take him to Ptahnetamun," the other guard urged. "The master'll get to the truth of this in a hurry."

Motioning for Sahure to walk ahead of them, the first man said, "We'll conduct you to the caravan master as you request and if you're a deserter, he'll deal with you quick enough. He hates cowards. Move one hand toward the pretty knife in your belt and you'll die, whoever you are."

"I'm not here to assassinate Ptahnetamun." Sahure set a path to the tent the men indicated. "He'd already be dead and none of you would be the wiser if I had been, although your sentinels are more observant than the enemy's, I'll grant you."

"Big talk." The guard put a beefy hand on Sahure's shoulder, apparently intending to shove him into the tent, but yanked his hand back as Sahure gave him a glare.

Ptahnetamun was heavy-set, bald, showing the effects of his age and many years on the caravan trail, but still a commanding presence. He surveyed Sahure as he spoke to his men. "What have you brought me, then?"

"Says he's a friend. Looks Egyptian to me. Deserter maybe, wanting us to hide him."

"Send them away and we'll talk," Sahure said. "I bring greetings from an old friend of yours."

Ptahnetamun stroked his goatee, leaning back in his chair. "And who might that be?"

Crossing his arms, Sahure leaned against a stout tent pole. "A dancer you once met, Lady Nima."

"You've seen her dance?"

Sahure grinned despite the seriousness of his mission. "Alas, I've never had the honor. Her husband is a most jealous man. But I've lost at senet to her countless times." He leaned closer and lowered his voice. "She cheats so skillfully the gods must assist her."

"Seems you do know her." Apparently satisfied, Ptahnetamun sank back in his chair. "Leave us," he said to his men. He motioned to the other chair. "Sit. I'm afraid I can't offer you anything more than a sip of wine as the thrice damned nomads keep us on short rations. I'm raiding my own cargo to keep my crew alive."

Sahure waited till the two burly caravan workers had left the tent, although he was sure they wouldn't go far. Then he sat and accepted a small amount of wine, nodding his thanks.

"Are you from a relief column?" Ptahnetamun said, wasting no time. "What do you need to know?"

Without confirming or denying his status, Sahure went to the heart of the matter. "What are the conditions at the fort? How big is the enemy force?"

"If you're here to relieve the garrison, you'd better move fast. They're negotiating terms for surrender, or trying to."

Sahure was astonished. "I can't imagine the commander would surrender. He must know Pharaoh will send reinforcements."

"The commander died in the first attack, is how I heard it. The nomads entered the area under the guise of a small caravan, then launched a surprise attack. The

Egyptian troops here were able to keep the invaders from gaining entry into the fort itself but took heavy losses. I think the fort is down to some junior officer in command now, and he's out of food and hope. He's trying to negotiate life for the women and children who took refuge behind the walls." Ptahnetamun cracked his knuckles. "The enemy has falcons which tore apart the carrier pigeons the garrison tried to send off, and I know for a fact they've caught and killed several messengers the fort tried to send under cover of night. Tortured them to death in front of the gates." He spat. "Filthy Hyksos. The nomads at least deal a clean death to a captured enemy, but the Hyksos always want to show off their god's black magic and appetite for human blood."

Sahure was also well acquainted with the methods and beliefs of the barbaric Hyksos, so he kept a tight rein on his hot emotions over the needless deaths of good men. *I'll say prayers for their kas later and see to proper burial. After the battle.* "My scout says the enemy force is primarily nomads, with a small group of Hyksos. Maybe a few mercenaries from the south."

Ptahnetamun nodded. "Aye. It sits wrong with me as a good Egyptian citizen to see the Hyksos making yet another attempt to gain a toehold in our country. I know too much about their evil god and his demands for human sacrifice. But I'm a caravan master, not a soldier." He shrugged, pouring more wine. "I live by the sacred oath of my peers, to protect my people, my cargo, and my passengers. I'll pay my toll and continue north whoever opens the road, you know? I'd let the authorities in the next Egyptian city know what was going on when I arrived, but it's not my job to fight the battle. I only care when the road is opened for traffic. Let Pharaoh regain his own."

"He sent me here to accomplish the task," Sahure answered.

Ptahnetamun raised his mug as if in salute. "And I wish you well with it, but expect no help in battle from me, or the other caravan masters."

"I expect none," Sahure assured him. "But any information will be useful. What of the local villagers?"

"Now there you can help yourself." Ptahnetamun leaned forward. "The nomads took hostages, which I believe is why the villagers have stayed on the sidelines."

Sahure was unsurprised, this being a standard ploy on the part of the enemy. "Where are they holding the hostages? Any idea how many?"

"In their own camp, on the southern rim of this compound. Not too many, I believe, but the most important are relatives of the old woman who's the matriarch of this place. Believe me, if old Iensesu tells you to do something, you don't ask twice. Even an outsider like me knows enough to attend to her wishes." Ptahn-etamun leaned closer. "She's a priestess of Sekhmet in addition to being the village's hereditary chief. The townspeople say she usually protects them with her black magic, although the enemy stymied her this time by seizing her loved ones, lest they die as punishment for rebellion on her part."

Sahure filed the information away, asked a few more questions about the size, discipline and experience of the forces ranked against him and then took his leave of Ptahnetamun. Wrapping his nondescript cloak tightly around himself and slipping into the predawn night, he detoured to spy on the nomad encampment, pinpointing the most likely tent for the hostages. As with the area where the caravans were being detained, the guards were few and far between and not very attentive. The length of the siege and its coming end seemed to have the enemy celebrating their victory prematurely.

Rejoining his waiting scout, Sahure set a fast pace to where he'd left his chariot and a small guard. He raced back to his own camp, where his officers waited eagerly for the results of his reconnaissance.

***

At dawn the next day, Sahure stood beside the driver in his chariot, at the head of the column, watching while his 250 foot soldiers raced in a defiantly screaming wave across the plain to attack the combined nomad and Hyksos forces. As he'd hoped, the nomads lacked the discipline of seasoned troops and poured out of their camp to engage in hand to hand combat with the Egyptians. Sahure gave the command to set his chariots in motion. They swept out of concealment and down upon the enemy, moving as fast as the horses could go, archers in each chariot launching arrows with deadly effect as each wave swept up to the combat zone and wheeled away, executing their standard maneuver. Sahure was in the thick of the battle, leading a wedge of ten chariots, trying to break through to the town and the fort beyond. He heard his trumpets answered by a clarion call from the fort and saw the gates open, a pitifully depleted force of Egyptian soldiers emerging, determined to do their best to assist the relief column by attacking from the rear.

A thin line of Hyksos warriors augmented by mercenaries formed between Sahure and the fort but with his momentum, the deadly aim of his archers, and the pent up ferocity of the defenders, the Egyptians made quick work of the enemy. Sahure jumped from his chariot to engage in hand to hand combat with the last few Hyksos, who gathered in a rough circle, surrounded by Egyptian warriors. Wading into the fray, Sahure slashed the sword arm of a Hyksos about to gut a downed foot soldier and then parried a blow from another with his shield. The newcomer who'd attacked him pressed close, landing powerful blows on Sahure's shield, driving him back. Digging his heels into the loose soil, Sahure took a stand, shoved the attacker off balance with the shield, launching his own series of blows in the next moment. The Hyksos retreated, his defense growing weaker until at last he fell, Sahure's sword drinking deep of his blood. Breathing hard, surveying the field of combat, Sahure was satisfied the oasis and fort would soon be his. The well trained Egyptian infantry were more than a match for the few Hyksos professional soldiers and the mercenary rabble had already broken ranks and fled.

He'd hoped to capture a few Hyksos alive, for questioning so now he had the drums and trumpets sound the all clear but as the smoke and dust settled, it was obvious the remaining Hyksos had to be mercifully dispatched to meet their god, too wounded to be patched up for interrogation and imprisonment. Most were already dead, having a no-surrender code as part of their warrior oath.

Pulling his sword from the corpse of the Hyksos officer he'd just defeated, Sahure made a quick check of the battlefield. His men were in command, the remaining nomads fleeing to the south, pursued by chariots.

Proud his well disciplined standard bearer and shield mates were still with him, Sahure returned to his chariot and drove through the village, through the scarred gates of the battered fort. Cheers went up around him as his driver pulled the horses to a halt in the big courtyard.

A gaunt young officer with one arm wrapped in blood stained bandages and a half-healed cut across the face, marched up to Sahure and saluted. "Lieutenant Kagemni, reporting, sir."

Sahure returned the salute. "Sahure, sent by Pharaoh. Are you the current commander of the fort?"

Standing at attention as best he could, the officer clenched his jaw and nodded, although Sahure saw the man trembling with the effort it was taking him to remain on his feet. "Yes, sir, I am. Although now, I yield command to you."

"You did a valiant job, holding out until we could arrive." Sahure rested one hand on the injured Kagemni's shoulder for a moment. "I'll want a full report later today, after our physician has tended those wounds and you've eaten. For now, point me in the direction of the commandant's office so the scribes can set up my headquarters."

"I'll be glad to escort you myself, sir, before I see the doctor."

But before they could leave the courtyard, a runner darted in through the open gate, heading straight to Sahure. Saluting both officers, the man said, "Captain Menkheperr requests your presence at the enemy camp, sir."

Knowing his second in command wouldn't ask him to attend unless there was something seriously amiss, Sahure beckoned to his driver and was soon on his way across the battlefield, flanked by two chariots full of guards.

The nomad compound was a scene of carefully controlled chaos, as the Egyptian forces checked the tents for any hidden enemy soldiers and gathered weapons, maps and other useful prizes. Sahure's driver pulled the chariot to a halt in front of a medium-sized black tent. Menkheperr exited the tent, apparently having heard the chariot arrive.

"Are all the hostages alive?" Sahure asked, descending from the chariot.

"Yes, we were successful in rescuing them. The special unit you sent in from the west was able to create a defensive perimeter around the hostage tent, kill the guards and hold off the enemy until two squads of my men relieved them. I've sent word to the village and the chief is coming. I thought you'd want to meet her." Menkheperr stepped closer and lowered his voice. "There's another issue as well, sir. Some unexpected hostages."

Sahure followed Menkheperr into the patched and sagging brown tent and found his soldiers busily striking the chains from a small group of the Oasis residents— men, women, and several children. Anger burned in his heart that the Hyksos had told the nomads to take the innocents as prisoners. He thought of Tyema briefly, remembering the stories surrounding the Hyksos's pillaging of her village when she was a child. *I hope she was never their victim. Another topic we never discussed.*

Acknowledging the fervent thanks from the villagers with a nod, he asked Menkheperr, "Where are the unexpected prisoners?"

"Step over here, my lord."

A totally different group of hostages stood in chains against the far wall of the tent, apparently members of some tribe from the far southern reaches. One man stood in front of the others, fists clenched and raised in defiance, as if he was ready to defend his comrades no matter how hopeless his cause. There were two other men and a woman, all haggard and bruised, skin over bones as if they'd been starved.

"They don't speak Egyptian," Menkheperr said as he and Sahure came to a halt in front of the prisoners. "Or any language I know. The villagers said these people were already in chains when they were brought in here. They were trying to shield the children of the village from the enemy when my men arrived."

Sahure stared into the leader's eyes. "You come from beyond the mountains where the sacred Nile begins?" he asked in a pidgin trade dialect he'd picked up during his travels in Kush and Punt.

The prisoner was startled and behind him his companions whispered excitedly. The man answered, "Far to the south, where the elephants and gazelles roam great plains. Till we were brought here we knew nothing of your river."

Sahure was curious, his interest piqued by the mention of the grasslands, which he knew were a tremendous distance away, on the other side of several mountain ranges. "How came you to be the prisoners of these nomads and Hyksos? They don't roam the jungles and plains so far south."

"It was the others, the traitors from our own tribe, the Nkwondola." The man spat. "Old rivalries, revenge for past events. They took my sister and me and these other unfortunates by treachery, when they attacked our home. They hoped to break the heart of my father, the great chief, by stealing his son and daughter, never to be seen in our home again."

So the mercenaries kidnapped them and brought them north. Sahure extended his hand. "I'm Sahure, sent by my chief, the Pharaoh of all Egypt, to recapture this town and defeat his enemies. We've no quarrel with you or your tribe, and are grateful to you for trying to protect our children while your own lives were endangered."

Lowering his fists, the man stared at Sahure, ignoring the outstretched hand. "What do you plan to do with us?"

"Set you free. Have your wounds tended to by my physicians. I'll give you weapons and supplies and then you're on your own. Can you find your way home again? For it must be a far distance to your father's lands."

Eyes narrowed, the man exchanged a quick glance with his companions before addressing Sahure. "We will find our home or die trying. Why do you do this?"

"The enemy of my enemy is my friend," Sahure said. "My Pharaoh would have you and your people as our allies."

Flashing a wide grin, the man nodded and shook Sahure's hand with surprising strength. "I'm N'ruhi, prince of my people." He spoke with his comrades in rapid fire dialect.

Sahure gave crisp orders to Menkheperr. "Release them. I've promised them medical care, food and weapons, and then they're free to go. See if anyone in the ranks speaks trade talk so I don't have to keep translating while they're still here."

"Yes, sir." Menkheperr saluted and gestured for a pair of soldiers to come forward and start working on the chains.

"Magnanimous and well done," said an approving voice behind him.

Sahure wheeled to find himself facing a petite elderly woman, dressed in green robes, with a purple sash elaborately tied, her wrinkled face made up as elegantly as any lady at Pharaoh's Court. Her wig was tightly curled and set with red-and-black striped beads and garnets. She was flanked by four burly men who were unmistakably her sons or grandsons. The family resemblance was strong. Before Sahure could say anything, two of the recently freed children ran past him, throwing themselves into the woman's arms, nearly knocking her over. Two of the men braced them all.

He stepped away, drawing Menkheperr with him. "Give them a moment." The family reunion was noisy and emotional, with much weeping, but eventually the village leader patted her grandchildren on the back as they clung to her and said, "I must speak with the men who rescued you now. Go with your father as quickly as you can and let your mother rejoice." The children kissed her wrinkled cheeks and left the tent holding hands, shepherded by two of the men. The elderly woman adjusted her robes, shifting her focus to Sahure.

"Bring a chair for the headwoman," he said, seeing how she trembled, whether from age or emotion he didn't know, but he was sure maintaining her dignity was important to her.

Inclining her head graciously, Iensesu took a seat in the chair Menkheperr rushed to provide. Her two remaining sons took up a position behind her. Folding her hands in her lap, the elderly woman kept her gaze on Sahure. "As I was saying before my exuberant grandchildren interrupted us, I approve of how you treated the hostages from the south. And I'm grateful to you for rescuing my family and my village."

Hand on the hilt of his sword, Sahure bowed. "It was my honor, Lady Iensesu. Pharaoh sent me to find out what was wrong here and solve the problem."

"You solved it most handily. Clearly he assigned the right man." She laughed, but her face quickly grew serious again and her sparkling black eyes focused on him. "What next? Do you leave us to our own devices and march back to Thebes?"

"No, I'm assigned here, to repair the damage and then to make improvements for the future. I'm anticipating a meeting with you at your convenience, my lady, and to hear your suggestions about how the Southern Oasis caravan station might be managed more efficiently, as well as better protected. I'm sure you must have many valuable ideas for what can be done to avoid any future incursions by the enemy. "

"It will be my pleasure. Bad for trade, bad for the village. Not to mention the bastard who commanded the Hyksos threatened to sacrifice my grandchildren to his hideous god. I offered myself in their place, but he only laughed and said the god preferred children. I begged him to relent but he said they would die if we made any attempt to help the fort or send a warning up the caravan road." She put her hand to her forehead for a moment, partially covering her eyes, which seemed full of tears. "The Hyksos killed people, good people, over such trifles. We were very much afraid."

Sahure exchanged glances with his second in command, wondering if he should send for wine, or perhaps the physician.

Taking her hand away from her eyes and smoothing her wig, Iensesu drew a deep breath. "Tomorrow will be a day of rejoicing and observances at the temple of Sekhmet such as we have never done before, so I can't meet with you." Tilting her head, she stared at him.

Sahure nodded. "I understand. Although I'm sworn to Horus, I'd count it as an honor to contribute something to the celebrations, food and wine perhaps. I'll send my chief scribe to you in the morning for a list of your suggestions and will of course present the offerings myself at the temple of Sekhmet."

"I see Pharaoh has sent me a diplomat in the body of a warrior," she answered, inspecting him up and down with a raised eyebrow. In a younger woman the speculative way she was gazing at him would have signaled a definite invitation. "I approve of your suggestions. You must dine with me in the evening, after the ceremonies."

She was probably a real temptress in her day. Suppressing a grin, Sahure said, "It will be my honor to attend your dinner, my lady. Now if you'll excuse me, I have much to do." He left the tent and directed his driver back to the fort, confident Menkheperr had the situation well in hand out here. He had a great deal to do here at the Southern Oasis on Pharaoh's behalf in the next year, and not a day to waste. *And I should send Tyema a line or two, let her know I'm thinking of her, even in the midst of battle and rebuilding. She and I are not done with the subject of our future, no matter what she may think.*

***

Tyema's labor wasn't going well. Her water had broken at the conclusion of the evening ceremony the night before and her temple guards had carried her to her rooms under Jemkhufu's worried supervision. Paratiti had been summoned from the village, along with the physician.

They arrived by oxcart together an hour later, along with Tyema's niece Renebti, who was to be an attendant for the baby after its birth. A few other family members arrived separately. The women joined the priestesses and maids in Tyema's room, while the doctor drank beer with Jemkhufu and the under priest in the hallway. At first all was well, proceeding normally, or at least that's what her relatives assured Tyema. She was relieved to find her labor pains were widely spaced, not much worse than monthly cramps. Then, as the night progressed, so did her labor. The women made her walk around in between the pains and when it seemed as if she might be close to delivering, in midafternoon the next day, they helped her stand on her birthing bricks, squatting with her sister and her favorite niece on either side, helping her keep her balance and providing resistance to push against, but the baby didn't come.

After an hour of this, Tyema was weeping from pain and fright, trembling and exhausted. Paratiti pushed her wig back on her head, exchanging glances with her daughter Renebti when they thought Tyema wasn't paying attention. "Let's get you back to the bed," her sister said calmly, steadying Tyema as she half fell off the bricks. "And perhaps we ought to have the physician come in and give his opinion, just to be on the safe side."

Renebti ran to fetch the doctor, her haste betraying the amount of worry she and her mother felt about Tyema's condition.

Tyema collapsed into the bed, her entire body enveloped in pain and nausea. Weeping, she curled on her side, cradling her abdomen, praying for the baby to be all right. Physicians were rarely summoned to a childbirth, so the fact her sister was suggesting the man attend her now was not an encouraging sign. "I haven't felt the baby move, no kicking in a while," she said, gritting her teeth as another contraction swept through her. Screaming in frustration and pain, she tried to push with the wave of power but nothing happened and she fell back against the pillows the women had stacked for her. Arriving with the physician in tow, Renebti bent to wipe Tyema's brow with a damp cloth.

I want Merys, I want Sahure. Most of all I want you to be born safely, my baby. Tyema clung to consciousness, rubbing her abdomen with a trembling hand, terrified her child might not make it into the world.

The physician was grave as he examined her in between pains. "The baby is turned the wrong way," he said to the room in general.

"What—what must I do?" Tyema demanded fiercely, raising herself on her elbows. "I won't fail my child."

"Can you shift the infant?" her sister asked the physician.

He shook his head, washing his hands in the basin on a nearby table. "Her channel is narrow and the babe's foot is blocking the entrance."

"Nothing? There's nothing you can do?" Tyema screamed, in the throes of another contraction, her shrill voice echoing off the walls. Panting as the waves of pain faded, she grabbed at the physician's arm. "I don't care about myself, you must save my baby."

"I'm sorry," the doctor said, patting her hand before disengaging himself from her claw-like grip. "You and the child are in the hands of the gods, best pray for mercy from the Great Ones."

"Can you give her something for the pain then, at least?" asked her sister.

"Merys, help me!" Tyema shrieked as the next labor pain took control of her body.

The door leading to the gardens slammed open on a gust of wind and the scent of the Nile lotus filled the room.

Renebti moved to close the exterior door but her mother stopped her with an outflung hand. "Wait!"

A woman wreathed in blue veils stepped into the room from the garden, followed by two more women, also enveloped in filmy layers of cloth. The perfume of the lotus intensified as the trio approached the bed and Tyema took a deep breath, feeling her head clear a bit.

"You may entrust the high priestess to us now," the first newcomer said, her voice low and musical. She raised one hand and made a shooing motion. "Clear the room."

"Who are you?" Seeming determined to defend her helpless sister if necessary, Paratiti took a stand beside the bed, as the doctor scurried out, followed by most of the women.

The second newcomer threw back her veil, smoothing the cloth from her face so the lamplight fell upon her features. "Don't you know me, sister?"

Hand to her mouth, shrinking against the bed frame, Paratiti whispered, "This can't be. *Merys?* But you died—"

Pointing at Paratiti, the first woman said, "Don't seek to keep us from attending your sister. Stay if you wish, but move aside. Or get out, but stop wasting our time."

Paratiti glanced at Tyema, squeezed her hand and then, hugging the wall, made her way out of the chamber, following the other attendants and the physician, all of them staying as far away from the new arrivals as they could. With a crash the door to the corridor shut behind Tyema's sister.

Merys—for the second woman was she—ran to the bed, sinking to her knees and grabbing Tyema's hand. "I'm here, dear one. You're going to be fine."

"The baby," Tyema rasped out, her throat raw, pushing herself up on one elbow with the last of her strength.

The first woman threw off her enveloping cloak and stood forth as the goddess Hathor in all her glory. Her body glowed in the dark room, even without the light cast by the golden sun disk on her headdress. Two curving, gold tipped cow horns grew from her head and her wig was adorned with gold and malachite beads. Dyed a deep red, her gown was the finest pleated linen, and around her neck she wore her *menit* necklace—strands of turquoise beads, from which was suspended the long pendant bearing her cartouche. Gazing at Tyema with large, almond shaped brown eyes, fringed by lush lashes, the goddess said, "It isn't your time or the child's to cross to the Afterlife, but things have progressed needlessly far down a bad path." Running the strand of turquoise beads through her fingers, Hathor glanced around the room, a frown on her flawless face, as if she could see a threat in the very air. "Sobek needs to do a better job of safeguarding his temple and his priestesses from evil influences."

"Black magic?" Merys gasped. "Directed at Tyema? Who would dare, and why?"

"Sort the issue out later," said the third woman, throwing aside her blue veils, revealing herself to be Tawaret, the Hippopotamus, in human guise. Her dress was a one shouldered green sheath, barely containing her pendulous breasts and large belly. Barefoot, she padded awkwardly across the room, her feet the paws of a lioness. Her golden headpiece was cylindrical, offset with black tipped feather plumes, resting atop her long, straight black hair and she carried an inscribed ivory ankh. Walking to the bed with the clumsy gait of one who is far more graceful in the water, she took a stand on the other side from Hathor. Tawaret touched her ankh to the thin turquoise amulet Tyema wore, which bore the cartouche of this very goddess. Paratiti had tied it loosely around her wrist as soon as she'd arrived, saying the charm would assist with an easy labor. Tyema felt a pulse of hot energy flow through her, starting at the place where the amulet touched her skin.

"Thank you for coming," Tyema whispered, licking her dry, cracked lips.

"We watch over all women in childbirth," Tawaret reminded her. "But your case is unusual. Merys persuaded us direct intervention was required, and our friend Sobek also petitioned us for the favor on your behalf. Now rest for a few moments."

Hathor laid one hand on Tyema's forehead and she felt calm, a reviving coolness spreading from the place where the goddess's fingers rested on her skin. The crippling contractions in her lower body receded, then stopped. Merys bathed her arms and face with a damp cloth, murmuring soothing endearments. Tyema straightened out on the bed, breathing more easily as she was free from pain for the first time in hours.

After helping her lie flat on her back, Tawaret rested her hands on Tyema's distended abdomen for a moment. Frowning, the goddess exchanged glances with Hathor. "The doctor was right, the child has turned wrong." The Hippo Goddess brushed Tyema's hair back from her brow and leaned close. Her breath held the clean crisp scent of the Nile at dawn. "What I must do will feel uncomfortable. I'm sorry, but my ministrations are necessary for the child's sake. I'll be quick."

Tyema nodded, clenching her hands in the crumpled sheets under her. "Anything, just save my baby, please."

Tawaret opened her hands as wide as the fingers would spread and rotated them right to left above Tyema's swollen belly without actually touching her. A pale green luminescence glowed in the air between Tyema and the goddess's hands. "Unborn child of Tyema and Sahure, listen to my words and put aside your fear. My sister Hathor and I are here to usher you into the world, but you must do your part." Her voice was breathy, almost wheezing from her lips, but compelling in tone. She put one hand over Tyema's distended belly button. "I command you to rotate in your mother's womb."

Tyema felt the cramping start again, as if spreading from the spot where Tawaret was touching her, but the contractions weren't as painful as they'd become in the long hours before the goddesses and Merys arrived. The baby kicked her in the side, under her ribs, but she didn't mind. The pummeling was proof the child was moving the right way to be born with Tarawet's magical assistance, head down, as the Great One ordered.

Hathor leaned in close, speaking in Tyema's ear. Carrying the refreshing scent of spring flowers, her breath puffed against Tyema's sweaty skin, creating welcome coolness. "We're going to take you to the birthing bricks now."

"I don't know if I can move," Tyema said, panic racing through her tired body at the thought of attempting to reach the bricks, much less squat on them to push the baby out.

"We'll help you, daughter. It's time for the child to be born." Hathor was stern, her voice gentle but firm. "Stay in this bed and you and the child will die."

"You must endure a few moments longer, follow the rituals of birth as all human women do," Tawaret agreed. "Then matters will be well."

With no further discussion, the two goddesses, one on either side, lifted Tyema from the soaked sheets and helped her walk to where the birthing bricks waited. Over her shoulder, Tyema saw Merys working rapidly to change the sheets, substituting the blue veils the goddesses had worn into the room for the earthly linen. Done with remaking the bed, Merys snatched up the waiting swaddling clothes and the knife to cut the cord. She took up a position kneeling in front of Tyema.

Hathor and Tawaret made sure Tyema was squatting firmly on the bricks. "When I tell you to push, I want you to put all your will and love for this child into the effort," Hathor said, staring directly into Tyema's eyes, her own velvet brown eyes wide in concern. "Breathe deep."

Tyema nodded, taking in air. She clenched her teeth and closed her eyes. *Please let this be over soon.* "I'm ready."

"Push then, and let the new *ka* embodied in this child enter the world." Hathor laid one hand on Tyema's swollen belly, massaging the skin ever so slightly. Heat radiated from the goddess's touch.

With no warning, the hard, driving labor pains started again and Tyema tried to ride them, tried not to fight. The sensations were different this time, not only because the goddesses held her in an iron grip, but the baby seemed to be trying to cooperate now. An indescribable urge to push seized Tyema and she bore down with every muscle in her body, holding her breath to give even more power to the effort.

All of a sudden she felt physically lighter as there was a great gush of fluids and a baby emerging from her body, to be caught by Tawaret. The contractions stopped. Leaning on Hathor, the goddess's arm around her waist in support, Tyema watched Merys cut the cord. The strong, outraged cries of a lusty infant sounded in the room. Hathor massaged Tyema's belly until the afterbirth was safely expelled and then the goddesses helped her back to the refreshed bed. The unearthly blue sheets were cool to her overheated skin, smelling faintly of lotus. With tears of joy running down her cheeks, Merys brought Tyema the red, wrinkled, screaming baby, wrapped in one of the embroidered blankets sewn by their family.

"You have a son, a fine boy," she said over the outraged child's squalling as she placed the baby in Tyema's arms.

Trembling, Tyema cradled her son in one arm and pushed back the swaddling clothes with her free hand, looking in wonder at the scrunched up, flushed face, the perfect toes and the tiny fingers. The large baby had amazing muscle tone and coordination already. He turned his head to her, clearly wanting to nurse. Merys helped her arrange herself and the baby more comfortably, and the infant latched on with strong suction and a greedy gurgle. Tyema felt her milk let down with a tingling rush and stared at Merys in awe and surprise, causing her sister to laugh and give her a hug. The child curled one hand around Tyema's finger, staring up at her face.

"How handsome he is, so like his father," Tyema whispered. "All this time I thought I was having a girl. How foolish of me. Of course Sahure would give me a warrior."

"We must leave you now, daughter," Hathor said, bending over to kiss the child. "But first tell us the name which has whispered itself to you."

"Yes, who did we assist into this world?" Tawaret asked with a broad smile. She stroked the baby's hair with one finger.

"Seknehure, his name is Seknehure," Tyema whispered, suddenly sleepy. She leaned back on the pillows rearranged by Merys.

"An excellent name, for a boy with a shining destiny. His future will be full of challenges befitting a warrior, but he will prevail and bring honor to Egypt, and his parents," Hathor pronounced, her voice sonorous, echoing in the bedchamber. She touched the newly named child on the forehead with the tip of her *menit* diadem. "Blessings upon him and those he loves."

"Thank you, for everything," Tyema said, gazing from one goddess to the other. "We would have both died if you hadn't come to help."

"Long life and happiness to him," Tawaret said, laying her ivory ankh on his sturdy body for a heartbeat. The baby blinked but continued nursing, one fist lying on his mother's chest.

"You did well, daughter," Hathor said before she linked arms with Tawaret. The two goddesses strolled out the open door into the garden and were gone in a blaze of green light between one step and the next.

Merys lingered a moment. "I would so love to hold my new nephew again, but after what he's been through, I don't want to disturb him while he nurses. What a gorgeous, big baby."

"How can I ever thank you?" Tyema said. "We both would have died if you hadn't brought the Great Ones."

"No need for thanks." Merys kissed her forehead. She seemed sad, tears glinting in her eyes. "But this is the last time I can help—I can't come again."

Tyema was surprised and dismayed. "Never?"

Merys shook her head. "Isis demanded the condition before she'd allow me to accompany Hathor and Tawaret tonight. One who dwells in the Afterlife as I do isn't supposed to mingle with the living, not even those we love most. My time for being here is done, long past. Isis says it's a loose end in the tapestry and must be cut."

Tyema twined the fingers of her free hand around Merys's and squeezed. "Although more children seem unlikely for me, if I ever have a daughter, I'll name her for you, I promise."

Merys smiled. "We'll meet again, in the Afterlife, for I'm positive your heart will be Judged as true when that day comes." Gently she withdrew her hand from Tyema's. "I wish you well, with the baby and with your man Sahure, if ever the chance arises to make amends with him. I'm not a Great One, I can't prophesy for you how it might turn out, but I hope you find true love, if not with him, then with another."

Awkwardly, trying not to disturb the baby, Tyema hugged her beloved sister, while tears flowed down her cheeks. "I know we've been unusually blessed to be able to continue meeting all these years, but it's hard to say a final goodbye."

"You won't miss me, you'll be busy mothering Seknehure. You don't need me anymore, little sister," Merys said, brave words belied by the sadness in her eyes.

"Perhaps not in the way I did as a child, but I'll always love you," Tyema answered.

"Give the rest of our family more of a chance," Merys said, nodding at the closed door. "They love you too and I know they're proud of you, of what you've done here at the temple, of the woman you grew to be."

"I will, I promise." Tyema stroked her son's downy cheek. Family had a whole new meaning for her today.

"I'm proud of you, as if I'd been your mother in truth, not your half-sister." Merys kissed Tyema on the forehead. "I must go before Isis grows angry. My place in Sobek's home is secure, she gave us her word I'd dwell there in the Afterlife with him for all time, but she's fearsome to deal with when she's upset. Even for a few more moments with you, I can't risk her wrath. She takes her anger out on Sobek, which pains me more than if she punished me and well she knows it. Life, prosperity, health until we meet again."

Walking out of the room into the garden beyond, Merys followed the path the goddesses had taken a moment before.

Tyema saw Sobek stride out of the mists in full human form, taking her sister's hand. He glanced into the room, smiling when he met her gaze, and then they too were gone in a burst of green light.

"Well," she said to the disinterested baby, still suckling contentedly, "Has anyone ever had such a birth night as you managed? Paratiti? Renebti?" she called, "I need some help with the baby!"

The door inched open and after a moment, her older sister peeked around the edge of the panel, white knuckled, eyes wide as saucers. "Are the Great Ones gone?"

"All gone. Come meet your newest nephew," Tyema said proudly. "Come and greet Seknehure."

CHAPTER THREE

The day had been unseasonably hot, even for the desert. The air carried an unusual, oppressive mugginess and the slight breeze gave no relief. Sahure found himself gazing at the skies to the south often as he went about his duties, expecting a sandstorm. None had come. Late in the afternoon thunder rumbled and the skies darkened but there was no rain, either. Although he had no appetite, he forced down his dinner, eating in his quarters rather than with his men tonight, and then tried to concentrate on the reports the scribes had given him, but it was no use. He felt jumpy, restless, as if he was about to go into battle. The hairs on the back of his neck prickled, as if someone or something was sneaking up on him, but he was alone in the room.

Pushing the scrolls and tablets away with a curse, he left his office and walked along the elevated walls of the fort, pausing to speak to each sentry. When he reached the southernmost wall, he stared in awe at the towering gray and green clouds in the distance. Massive bolts of lightning arced from the clouds to the ground. *We've been here for nearly nine months and I've never seen such a display in the sky before.* Pulling his billowing cloak a little more closely around him, Sahure marveled at the unseasonal chill in the air.

"Never seen the sky so angry before, sir," said the corporal next to him, echoing his own thought. "I heard lions roaring earlier." He fingered his sandstone amulet nervously. "What do you think these strange omens mean?"

"Whatever the sky and the lions are foretelling, we'll be fine." Sahure hid his own misgivings and clapped the man on the shoulder. "No wind or storm can breach our stout walls, and the wings of Horus always protect us."

Cowhide shield on his back, a soldier toiled up the ladder to the walkway, saluting as soon as he saw Sahure. "Sir, there's someone here to see you."

Surprised, Sahure checked the sky again, noting the position of the moon as it emerged from a bank of clouds. "At this hour?"

The man caught at his cloak as the winds whipped the folds around his body. "The lady said it was urgent, sir, said she had to talk to you, so the guards at the gate let her in."

As he left the walkway and headed toward the gate, Sahure found himself thinking of Tyema, even though he knew it was impossible she was the guest. When he walked up to the fort's heavily guarded entrance, he saw Menkheperr and Iensesu the town's headwoman, standing together, as his men struggled against the wind to close the pedestrian gate they'd opened to allow the elderly woman entry. Wrapped in a fringed blue shawl, she looked as if the slightest wind could carry her away.

Where are her sons? She never comes here alone. Walking against the winds must have exhausted her. "What brings you to my gate on such a night, my lady?" he asked her. "Is something wrong in the village?"

"The goddess bade me to seek you out," she said, striding away from the gate toward the officers' wing of the fort's central building. Surprised at her vigor when she usually limped and moved with the caution of fragile old age, Sahure hastened to catch up. Gesturing at the ominous skies, Iensesu added, "This turmoil of the heavens is on your account."

Startled, not sure what she meant, he took her elbow to guide her over a rough patch in the parade ground. "Won't you come to my quarters, out of this infernal wind?" Glancing over his shoulder, he said to his second-in-command, who was following them in case any orders were to be forthcoming, "Menkheperr, bring us some wine, please."

Iensesu didn't add anything to her pronouncements until Sahure ushered her into the safety of his office. She allowed him to take her cloak as she said, "The goddess sent me to tell you there's a battle raging, one affecting you and those you love. You should be there, not here." Her voice was also stronger than usual and he felt she was standing taller than normal.

Reacting to the almost accusatory note in her words, he said, "Forgive me, my lady, I don't understand." His thoughts flew to Tyema again and with a curse he took a deep breath and cleared his thoughts. "A battle?" Setting her cloak over the back of a chair, he walked to shut the door.

"Combat of a sort," Iensesu agreed. "But as you lack the power to be in two places, I've been sent to watch over you this night."

Amused at the idea of the elderly priestess attempting to defend a seasoned warrior like him, Sahure grinned and turned to make some properly appreciative remark to humor her. He liked Iensesu. He stopped in his tracks, the breath leaving his body in a whoosh.

The Great One Sekhmet stood in the center of his office, not the stooped little chief of the town. He blinked, astonishment flooding over him, but the goddess herself was definitely in his office, staring at him from her glowing amber cat eyes. Clad in formfitting red robes hugging the curves of her voluptuous human body, curious rosettes of gold at the shoulders, she was barefoot. Her shapely arms ended in the deadly paws of the lioness. On her leonine head, atop an elaborately dressed wig, she was crowned with a golden sun disk, the symbolic uraeus wrapped around the glimmering diadem. Red and gold sparks of light flew from her crown as she regarded him. Leaning on a staff crowned with papyrus buds, her expression was unfathomable. Slowly he went to his knees, arms crossed in respect.

"I'm honored, Great One."

"I would taste the beverage you offered, had I more time to spend with mortal concerns," she said, tilting her head, feline whiskers twitching. Her sinuous tail curled around her ankles.

"I fear until my man gets here with the wine I requested, I've nothing suitable to offer one as lofty as yourself." He hoped she wouldn't take offense. Sekhmet was renowned among all the Great Ones for her sheer unpredictability.

"No matter. I meant to take you by surprise and can't complain at my own success." She waved one paw, claws half extended, and he thought he heard what might have been a cross between a growl and a chuckle, deep in her throat, as if she'd read his thoughts. "To business, mortal. My sisters are taking part in the battle on your behalf tonight, the combat of which I spoke," she said. "I'm here to intervene for you."

Caught in her hypnotic gaze, Sahure felt as if he'd drunk deep from a highly intoxicating vintage, although he'd only had one cup of ordinary, military-issue wine at dinner. The room was spinning around him. Blinking, he drew a deep breath to steady himself. "I don't understand, my lady. Intervene in what? I mean no disrespect, but I'm sworn to Horus the Falcon and he's given me no orders, requested no action on my part tonight." His thoughts flew again to Tyema, never far from his mind, but she certainly had no connection to Sekhmet and would never be anywhere near combat. *Focus, fool, you're dealing with one of the most dangerous of the Great Ones.*

"I don't speak of combat with sword and shield," she said, revealing a glimpse of her impressive fangs, her voice almost a purr. "All things will become known to you in the proper time. Explanation tonight beyond what I've already revealed would be useless. There is no move in the game available to you right now."

Sahure kept a frown off his face with supreme effort. *I'd like to be the judge of that.*

But the goddess was still talking. "I acknowledge you're not one of my children, but you saved my beloved village of Kharga from the nomads and the Hyksos." Her tail lashed angrily at the mention of the enemy, thumping the hard-packed dirt floor and now she did growl, an ominous sound that sent a chill down Sahure's spine. Sighing, she stood taller. "You rescued those who are my children, the people here. You honored my priestess, gave freely to my celebrations, showed proper deference."

Realizing she seemed to expect him to say something, Sahure nodded. "It was my honor to be of service, Great One."

"In return I'll guard you while you're here in this place." She pointed her paw at him, one claw extended. "When you are once again in Thebes, it will be the task of others to watch over you, help you and those you love. Your task to protect Pharaoh."

Why do the Great Ones love to speak in veiled terms? Thoroughly frustrated, Sahure took the risk of standing up. "I'm sorry, Great One, but I don't understand—"

She extended her golden-furred paw to him, palm up. A curious amulet lay in the middle, in the shape of a tiny hand no bigger than his thumbnail and made of crystalline stone, deep blue in color, with a cat's eye depicted in the center delineated in yellow, purple, and black beads. The talisman was woven into a black leather wristband. "This is for you," Sekhmet said. "Give me your wrist."

He extended his arm and the goddess tied the cord around his wrist, skillfully using her claws in place of fingers. Sahure felt a wave of cold run up his arm from where the curious blue hand touched his pulse. The chill ran through his heart and for a moment he couldn't breathe. He felt Sekhmet's tail curling around his ankles.

"I deal in magic of all kinds, mortal." Sekhmet moved closer, putting one paw on his chest. "Therefore I know how to guard against the most evil sorcery, when I choose to intervene."

"I—I don't traffic with magic," he said, searching his mind for any time he'd even remotely been involved with sorcery and spells and coming up empty. The heady smell of her blue lotus perfume was making his vertigo worse, interfering with his concentration on her words. "I'm a simple soldier, loyal to my Pharaoh."

She nodded, patting his cheek with her massive paw, claws sheathed, before stepping away. "I know this. So I've given you a shield."

He touched the amulet with his fingertips. "Why do I need to be shielded?"

"All things will be revealed in due time. You must promise you'll wear my amulet, perhaps even in Thebes." She smiled, the effect strange on the face of a lioness. "Horus won't mind."

"I give you my word." What else could he say, when facing the goddess herself? Sekhmet nodded. "And now we're done."

There was a crash of thunder almost directly overhead and a flash of lightning so bright Sahure was blinded. As he blinked his watering eyes and stared around his office, there was no sign of either Sekhmet or the elderly headwoman. The door was closed tight and he'd not heard it open. Quickly he walked to fling open the portal, practically running into Menkheperr, bearing a wineskin and juggling some mugs.

"Did you see her?" Sahure asked, sticking his head into the hall and checking in both directions. "Did you pass her in the corridor?"

"Pass who?" Menkheperr walked into the room and glanced around curiously. "Your guest left already? Quick visit. What did she want?"

After one more lingering glance down the empty hall, Sahure closed the door. "I'm not sure," he answered. "But I'll definitely have some wine." *And then I'm writing another letter to Tyema, damn it, whether or not she ever deigns to reply.*

***

Tyema always knew when Sobek wanted to speak with her. There would be a faint whispering of her name into her left ear, as if the syllables were carried on the breeze. After awhile her head would start to ache and lightning would flash in her vision, and she knew she must seek the god out. Today was one of those days, so she hurried down the cliff to his private beach below the temple as soon as the headache started, after the noon hour. They rarely met in the sanctuary in the heart of the costly new temple. Sobek preferred the open air, next to the Nile. Sometimes she wondered how it went at other temples dedicated to this god, since he didn't appear to enjoy being cooped up inside.

Or maybe it's just the relationship we have because he's married to my sister, and they met on this very beach.

Arriving on the sandy expanse, Tyema ignored the lingering Nile crocodiles. She took a deep breath, straightened her spine and sang one of the oldest songs she knew, one Merys said their great grandmother had taught her. Sobek always said he especially enjoyed the lilting melody. She loved singing on the shore of the Nile, letting her voice expand and fly over the water. Sure enough, as she finished the last verse, there was a flash of green light and Sobek came striding down the beach toward her, taking his fully human form.

Her headache faded and the lightning flashes in her vision had been consumed by the light of his arrival. Tyema took a deep breath in relief.

He always appeared to her as a man, dressed like a wealthy noble, although she'd also seen him as half shifted, between forms, wearing his crown and plumes on the head of a crocodile. Never as the Crocodile, although she'd seen the damage he could wreak, as well as the aftermath of his anger.

Tyema sank to her knees in the cooling sand, arms crossed over her chest. "I'm honored to be in your presence today, Great One."

He extended one hand, palm up. "This will always be my favorite temple, and you my most beloved priestess, after Merys herself. The song was lovely. No one else knows the oldest verses but you and your sister. The tablets and papyri on which they were written have long crumbled to dust, I fear."

Placing her hand in his, Tyema rose to her feet. "If I have daughters someday I'll teach the song to them, I promise, my lord."

"Walk with me." He tucked her hand into the crook of his elbow.

They strolled along the beach, the huge black and gray crocodiles hissing a greeting as they slid out of the god's path. Sobek nodded and the creatures slid into the Nile, one by one, swimming away in formation.

Wondering what had brought the god to seek her out today, Tyema kept her silence. Sobek would tell her when he was ready. She realized they were walking to the breeding pens on the far side of the temple.

Sure enough, a few minutes later she stood in front of the enclosed pond. All the crocodiles, large and small, came crowding to the fence, crawling over one another to be close to their lord and master. Sobek extended his hand in a silent blessing for a moment, after which the group disbanded, reverting suddenly to normal crocodile behavior, sunbathing in the fading light, drifting in the water, dining on the chickens and other offerings Tyema's staff provided daily.

Only one crocodile remained, the young bull named "Pharaoh" by the keepers. He basked in the sun directly in front of Tyema, as if displaying himself for the god. He had the extremely rare purple belly found occasionally on Nile crocodiles and all the confidence of a ruler.

"You'll have to take him to Thebes," Sobek said.

Sure she hadn't heard him correctly, she did a double take. "I'm sorry, Great One, to Thebes?"

"Yes, I require you to convey this fine fellow to my temple in Thebes in two weeks' time, so he can take charge of the float there. The bull crocodile ensconced in Thebes is dying after many long years of adoration. I've told my High Priest and Pharaoh you'll be sailing shortly, to bring my Chosen One. He'll sire many clutches of eggs over the coming years."

"But why must *I* accompany him? I have an excellent staff of keepers—" Even though she was in the presence of the god, Tyema felt panic clawing at her throat. Her chest grew tight as she tried to think about all the details such a journey would entail. *What if Sahure has been reassigned to Thebes? What if he's taken a wife?* "I—I can't leave my baby—"

Human face set in kindly lines, Sobek's glittering yellow crocodilian eyes were sharp, predatory. "Take the child with you. You forget I have a half-human son; I understand what a child needs and at this age, your baby needs only you." His face crinkled with good humor. "Babies are portable. Even my crocodiles carry their young on their backs."

Her knees were threatening to buckle. Fortunately Sobek took her hand a moment later and they walked to a nearby bench, under a towering palm beside a small ornamental pond filled with fat fish. He made Tyema sit before he waded into the pond, plucking a blue lotus and bringing the entire stalk to the bench. As she watched in fascination, he picked apart the stem and leaves of the plant, industriously braiding the fibers into a bracelet, with the deep blue flower like a gem set into the top. Eyes on his work, the god said, "You don't *have* to go, Tyema. It will be as you choose. Merys has explained to me something of the challenges you face going among the people, leaving this temple. Although I confess I can't understand the problem, knowing you're always under my protection."

Although her throat felt choked, she managed to say, "I desire to do my duty to you, Great One. I owe you so much—"

"We don't have debts and payment between us, little sister." Sobek's voice was kind, warm. "Perhaps you need to hear why I wish you to undertake the journey, before you decide?"

Heart pounding, half terrified at the idea of a Great One explaining his reasons for the unusual request to a mortal, high priestess or not, Tyema nodded.

Sobek admired his half finished handiwork before glancing at her. "The situation is this. Pharaoh Nat-re-Akhte has ruled for nearly twenty years now and has brought peace to Egypt. He threw the Usurper off the throne, drove the Hyksos and their evil god out of Egypt, has kept them at bay ever since. Agreed?"

She nodded, throat too parched to speak. Concentrating on his words helped her alleviate the formless terror assaulting her at the idea of a journey up the Nile. *Maybe if I understand the stakes, the reasons, I can conquer the fear.* She clenched one hand into a fist, nails digging into her palm, the small pain helping her concentrate on the god's words rather than her dizziness.

Tugging at the fibers he was braiding, to make the weave tight, Sobek continued. "The Hyksos haven't given up. They roam just outside Egypt's borders, still make raids from time to time, try to build alliances with other nations jealous of Egypt's wealth and power. The Hyksos god Qemteshub desires to destroy Osiris, my king, in the world inhabited by the gods. The battle rages on."

"But Nat-re-Akhte holds Egypt," Tyema said, not quite voicing a question.

Sobek nodded. "He's been an excellent champion, for the gods and for your people."

Struck by a new thought, Tyema felt a chill sweep over her, despite the hot sun. "Is he— is he voyaging to the Afterlife soon?"

"A shrewd question, my little priestess." Sobek was approving. "Such is not his destiny, not yet. And his son, the crown prince, will be a strong ruler when his time arrives. Egypt should remain secure. You know one of my major duties is to protect Pharaoh from black magic?"

"Yes." The assignment had always seemed odd to her, given his nature, given his primary concern being care of the Nile. But then Pharaoh is the heart and *ka* of Egypt, just as the Nile is the life giver. So who but a fierce, immortal warrior to defend him from sorcerers?

"Ever since Nat-re-Akhte deposed the Usurper, the primary source of black magic in Thebes was removed. There have always been little hints and touches of sorcery. One cannot clean the world of negative magical influence entirely, but nothing threatening Pharaoh himself." Sobek frowned and his golden eyes glowed. "In the past two years, the small trickles of black magic have strengthened, become more cohesive. They swirl around Pharaoh, yet so far don't seem to be directed at him. This is where you come in."

She remembered the night of Seknehure's birth and what had been said to her by the Great Ones, although at the time she'd hardly listened, being in the throes of labor. "Did Hathor tell you there was black magic striving to harm my son and me, the night he was born?"

Sobek frowned. "She did, although I don't understand what reason there could be, any more than I understand the patterns of black magic weaving a tapestry in Thebes at present." He gazed across the crocodile pond. "I tried to get the goddess Nephthys interested in exploring the problem as she's so good at schemes and plots, but she's too grand for my concerns, wouldn't listen, much less get involved. And I *cannot* act unless there's a direct threat to Pharaoh." He clenched one fist, the hand going scaled and clawed for a moment with his sheer frustration. "The other Great Ones tend to think as she does, saying I see a problem where none exists, but I remain worried. Sometimes a pattern only becomes clear in the instant before catastrophe strikes."

Still puzzled as to her role, Tyema asked, "What would my going to Thebes accomplish, Great One?"

The scales and claws of his hand fading back to their human appearance, he tapped one finger on the lotus bracelet sitting on the bench between them. "This will enable you to see the glints and threads of the black magic whenever you encounter them in Thebes. The death of the bull crocodile there is fortuitous, provides an excuse to insert you into the court for a time without arousing the sorcerer's suspicions. I've spoken in private with Pharaoh, after which he insisted publicly the replacement animal must come from this temple and no other. If you can find out who is wielding forbidden magic, then I can get Isis or Nephthys to intervene and crush the sorcerer." He pointed at his massive chest and laughed. "I've no way to fit unobtrusively into the world of Pharaoh's courtiers. No time for it either. The Nile is much troubled this year with sand bars where none should be."

"So I just have to spend some time there after I deliver the crocodile, after the ceremonies are complete? Watch people from the edges of the court and then let you know what I see?" *Maybe I could handle merely observing, if Pharaoh knows what I'm about and smoothes the way for me to stay.* With a shudder and rising nausea, Tyema remembered it would be at least a week's sail up the Nile to Thebes and a week back, depending on the winds. She hadn't been on a boat since the Hyksos incident in her childhood. Hand at her throat, she tried to control her breathing.

Sobek was watching her closely, citrine eyes narrowed. "You can send the crocodile to Thebes with your head keeper and your second priestess if what I ask is too much for you. I've put Pharaoh on the alert, perhaps my warning will suffice."

Marriage to my sister has taught him a lot about the fragility of humans. Tyema left the bench and walked to the fence. The juvenile crocodile shifted lazily, keeping one half-open eye on her. Most of the trip would be in her official role. She never had problems when acting in Sobek's name. *And this task is clearly important. Pharaoh has enough on his shoulders without worrying about some dabbler in black magic.* "All right," she said. "I'll do it."

Sobek came to stand beside her. Taking her by the hand, he slid the fragrant green circle over her outstretched fingers, to rest just above the wrist bones. Green light flared and Tyema watched in amazement as the living plant became shining gold, the flower highlighted with cobalt enamel. "I'm grateful," he said as the green sparks winked out.

"How do I get there? We usually send crocodiles to other temples on cargo vessels, and I can't travel on such a ship." She shivered, visualizing the tiny cabins and close quarters of a typical freighter on the Nile.

Sobek shrugged. "Ask the nomarch to lend you his personal ship."

"And keep it at my command in Thebes for weeks?" *He's a pleasant person, but he isn't going to like that idea.*

"The nomarch wishes a favor from me, albeit one I can't grant. He'll be here in two days to make his request," Sobek said.

"But if you're not granting his petition—"

"I can't. Certain acts are forbidden to me and meddling with the decree of Shai, god of Fate, is one of them. Not on behalf of any human, not even Pharaoh himself. As it is written in the oldest texts, 'there is no one who can ignore Shai, for every man there is his appointed time'. I'm sorry to burden you with providing this answer to the nomarch on my behalf." Sobek looked her full in the face. "Tell Nomarch Ienhotep I'll testify for him at the Judging of his heart. I'll ease his way past Anubis and the other Judges and into the Afterlife. I owe him for his efforts in the past on behalf of my Merys, but I can only exert so much influence. Tell him he doesn't have much time, he needs to get his affairs in order. His tomb must be ready to receive him before the next inundation of the Nile."

Tyema shivered. It seemed the sun went behind a cloud and the day grew gray for a moment as she realized the Great One was tasking her with the delivery of a hard message to a man she respected and liked. Today's visit from Sobek was the most stressful she could ever recall. Tracing the design of the lotus flower on her new bracelet, she sighed. "I'll deliver the message exactly, Great One."

Sobek rose and stretched. "I'll keep an ear open for any summons from you, little sister, while you're in Thebes." He rested one hand on her shoulder for a moment. "I can't lie, this trip will affect your life as well."

"It'll be a temporary challenge, Great One, but then I can bring my son home and resume my normal life," she said, trying to master her runaway pulse and wheezy breathing.

"The Nile doesn't always return to her accustomed river bed after the floods," he answered. "You may find new twists and bends in your own path."

She couldn't stop the gasp of dismay. "Are you warning me?"

"Perhaps a reminder."

With those words, he strolled toward the Nile, disappearing in a flash of blinding green light, sizzling with the power Sobek exerted so easily. Tyema spun on her heel to gaze through the fence at the juvenile crocodile, now destined for a new home in Thebes. The animal stared back at her, opening his jaws and yawning.

"Well, my friend, seems we're going to take a trip together," she said. Rotating the lotus bracelet on her wrist, she began her mental list of all the tasks she must accomplish before she could embark on this distasteful, frightening journey.

***

The trip from her temple to the small port that was Ibis Nome's only formal access to the Nile took three days by donkey cart. Tyema grew increasingly nauseous and short of breath the longer the journey went on, even though she was surrounded by her kinsmen, her temple workers and her niece Renebti and scribe Jemkhufu. All of them did their utmost to make her comfortable, especially Renebti, who was a gentle soul and obviously distressed to see her aunt in such turmoil. Usually Tyema did a good job of hiding her symptoms but in the close quarters of the cart, and the tent the two women shared at night, she feared her problems were all too obvious.

Infant Seknehure was well behaved, watching the world go by from the safety of a sling Tyema wore. He was her solace. Taking care of his simple needs, snuggling him, breathing in his sweet baby scent all calmed her and enabled her to shut out the world. Even when he was fussy and she had to walk beside the cart, trying to soothe him, the activity relieved her symptoms as well.

But her dread of the river voyage ahead came rushing back in a dizzying wave as her small caravan wound its way through the crowded, smelly harbor town. People stared at her since the High Priestess of Sobek was legendary in the province, rarely seen. Tyema held her head high, feeling her blushes staining her cheeks, and tried to smile. It didn't help that she was wearing a simple traveling dress and cloak, not her ceremonial robes and crown. Nothing to hide behind.

The nomarch's private ship, the *Swift*, was much larger than any other vessel in the choked harbor. Comparing the tiny inlet to the sweeping peninsula she and Sahure had surveyed, Tyema could certainly see why Pharaoh had sent him to investigate the possibility of building a new port for the increased trade he was contemplating.

Captain Djedefhor was waiting to greet her on the pier, dressed in a simple white shirt, dyed blue kilt and matching nemes. Around his neck he wore two amulets, one of Sobek and the other of Ra, the sun god who sailed the sky and the Underworld. Djedefhor bowed as she dismounted from the cart and shook out her skirts. "It's my honor and pleasure to convey you to Thebes, Lady Tyema. I hope my poor ship will meet with your approval."

"I'm not used to traveling on ships at all, captain," she answered honestly. "It's very kind of the nomarch to lend me his vessel for the journey."

Djedefhor smiled broadly. "We'll set a high standard for you to compare all other ships to in the future. The nomarch's orders were to ensure your every comfort while conveying you to Thebes as fast as possible." His easy manner toward Tyema bordered on flirtation, his glances at her appreciative. "Are you ready to board?"

"I must see to the comfort of my crocodile before I can worry about myself," Tyema answered. "This is my crocodile keeper, Hotepre."

As the grizzled older man came forward, the ship's captain frowned. "Ah yes, the crocodile. I must confess I prefer taking you on as a passenger over inviting one of the Nile beasts onto my deck," Djedefhor said with disarming honesty. Tyema liked him all the more for his candor. "I don't suppose we can put it in the hold?"

"Not before I've died and gone to the Afterlife," Hotepre said, hands on his hips. His two underkeepers crowded behind him, ready to defend their crocodile.

Djedefhor surveyed the crate on the last donkey cart. It was rocking side to side and much clawing and noise could be heard. The harnessed donkey was wide eyed, sidling nervously while the driver held the bridle tight.

"I can order the animal to walk onto the ship," Tyema said. "Our idea was to chain him by the hind leg to the mast, or perhaps the rail at the stern? One of my men will watch the crocodile at all times. We'll have to catch fish to feed it periodically during the voyage."

Djedefhor had apparently not heard anything she said after the part about walking the crocodile onto his vessel. He swallowed hard. "For the sake of my crew, can you bring it aboard in the crate? I'll agree to let it travel on deck, as long as I'm satisfied with the restraints, but I'd rather not risk having such a dangerous animal walk freely." He glanced at the massive crate again. "I expected to treat the beast as cargo, not a passenger."

"This animal was personally selected by Sobek, to honor Pharaoh. I assure you Sobek has given me the power to command his creatures," Tyema said. Deciding she didn't want to push the point and incur the captain's hostility before the voyage had even begun, she went on in a more positive tone, "But we can certainly load him onto the ship inside the crate and then allow him to have the fresh air. The box is constructed to come apart easily. Hotepre, can you take care of this for me?"

"Well, then it's settled," Seeming pleased, Djedefhor offered her his hand to ascend the wooden gangplank. "It's a bit tricky for nonsailors. And of course you have the baby to balance as well. "

Trying to decide if the captain actually was trying to flirt with her, Tyema allowed him to escort her onto the *Swift*. Renebti and Jemkhufu brought up the rear. The deck was reassuringly wide but flashes of the day she'd been carried aboard a Hyksos vessel as a terrified prisoner came and went in her mind. Tyema froze, clutching the baby so tightly he cried. Her vision was narrowing and she knew she was going to faint. From a distance she heard Renebti's voice asking if she was all right and the captain's deeper tones as he said something, but she couldn't stop the escalation of her terror. Someone tried to take Seknehure away from her and as she was resisting the attempt, backing away, she tripped.

There was a flash of pain in the back of her skull and the world went black.

***

Tyema woke feeling confused, unsure where she was. Lying still for a moment, she remembered the scene she'd made on deck. With a sinking feeling in her gut, she wondered how she was going to face any of her traveling companions again after embarrassing herself in public. She sat up, immediately putting a hand to the back of her head, which hurt a bit. Although the light was dim, she could see she was in a ship's cabin, surprisingly large and well appointed. She was in a bunk, built into the side of the ship, and she could tell they were in motion. "Seknehure!" The baby wasn't in the small basket at the foot of her bed. Feeling panicky, unsure if she'd fallen with him still in her arms, Tyema got out of the bed. Grabbing at the high side to steady herself, she tried to get her balance to match the movement of the deck.

There was a knock on the sliding wooden door. "Aunt Tyema?" Renebti peeked into the cabin, advancing with a smile as she saw her aunt was awake.

Tyema was relieved to see her child in his cousin's arms and held out her own. "Is he all right? I didn't drop him when I fainted, did I?"

"No, no don't worry, I managed to snatch him away as you went down. He's fine, hungry maybe. Why don't you get back into the bunk and I'll hand him to you?"

"Good idea." Tyema still felt traces of the nausea and vertigo. The up and down motion of the ship as it plowed through the Nile's waves wasn't helping. As soon as she was settled, Renebti set the baby in her arms and Tyema checked every inch of his squirmy little body for bruises or bumps. Finding none, she allowed him to nurse and felt herself calming in the process.

Moving the basket, Renebti sat down at the end of the bunk, studying Tyema's face. "You look better now, Aunt. More yourself. Less pale."

"How long was I unconscious?"

"Well, when you woke from your faint, you were disoriented." Renebti looked down at the deck, drawing patterns in the blanket with one finger. "You seemed to think we were Hyksos, trying to kidnap you."

Tyema closed her eyes and slumped against the bulkhead, smelling the pleasant, if faint, tang of cedar. "My worst nightmare." Opening her eyes again, she met her niece's gaze. "You might as well tell me the rest."

"Really, it wasn't much. The captain carried you here, to the cabin, and Jemkhufu suggested we give you some tincture of poppy, the stuff you use for your worst headaches. I fetched the vial from your baggage and we got you to drink a bit. Then you went to sleep. We're underway," Renebti added somewhat unnecessarily.

"Which is a good thing, for that means we're closer to Thebes and the end of this nightmare of a voyage," Tyema said, wondering if maybe Jemkhufu had unwittingly hit on a solution to her bigger problem. Could she stay drugged on the syrup until they reached Thebes? Just sleep the voyage away?

The baby frowned and stopped nursing. She adjusted Seknehure, putting him to her shoulder for a moment, patting his back, getting a good burp before putting him to the other side. Of course she couldn't sleep away the trip, she had a child who needed her. She'd just have to manage. Holding out her free hand to her niece, she said, "Thank you for taking care of us. I'm so glad you agreed to come with me on this trip. Not just because of today's incident, but it'll be comforting for me and the baby to have you as company while dealing with all the strangers in Thebes."

Renebti smiled and came to give her a hug. "I'm the envy of everyone in Ta'sobeksef, going to Thebes. No one ever travels from our village to Pharaoh's court! I'm grateful you asked me to be your companion and his nursemaid."

"I don't know what things will be like in Thebes," Tyema said. "I'll do my best to ensure you have a good time, that it isn't all tending the baby's needs."

Her niece waved a careless hand and made a shushing sound. "Just having been there will surely be the highlight on the walls of my tomb someday. If I see Pharaoh with my own eyes, I'll be satisfied. Blessed! And you know how much I adore your son. I hope my children will be as healthy, if I'm ever married and have a family."

"So how long have we been sailing?" Tyema knew the poppy syrup ordinarily gave her deep, dreamless sleep for several hours. And Seknehure would've been complaining loudly if she'd been unavailable to him longer than that.

Confirming her unspoken estimate, Renebti said, "Three hours. Oh, the crocodile is doing well although the crew is scared to death of him." She laughed. "Captain Djedefhor is still put out that you insisted the animal ride on deck."

Tyema eyed her, a bit concerned by the amusement she was showing over the captain's annoyance. *I hope my niece isn't becoming too fascinated with Djedefhor. He's too old for her and a sailor besides.*

As if her thoughts had summoned him, the captain knocked on the door jamb. "Just came to see how you're doing, Lady Tyema. I'm happy to see you awake and calmer, shall we say?"

"I apologize for my behavior earlier—"

He waved off her earnest words. "Your niece explained you'd not had enough to eat today. I'm sure the movement of the boat was disorienting for someone who's never sailed. And of course everyone knows you were kidnapped by the Hyksos as a child. Quite natural you'd be reminded of that unpleasant episode." He stood taller and grinned. "Although I'm a bit insulted that my beautiful *Swift* reminded you of those clunker boats the enemy sailed."

Relieved to get past the embarrassing incident so easily, Tyema took a deep breath, resolving to exert utmost effort not to suffer another attack for the rest of this nightmare voyage. People could accept excuses for one breakdown, but sympathy would flee in a hurry if she let anyone—even Renebti—see how unsettled she was, being on a boat and totally out of her own sphere of iron control over events.

"I don't know how well acquainted you are with the nomarch's chief wife?" Djedefhor cocked an eyebrow as he asked the question.

"I've only met her once or twice. She's very pleasant." Tyema bounced Seknehure a bit against her shoulder, enjoying his chortles.

"She hates to sail. Absolutely loathes being on the water. That's why this cabin is built bigger than most, so she'd feel more comfortable. For her benefit I usually rig up a pavilion on the bow, so she can have privacy, catch the breezes, watch the scenery—"

"Sounds wonderful," Tyema said, feeling suddenly very cordial toward the nomarch's wife.

"I've been sitting there with the baby," Renebti chimed in. "Jemkhufu and I played a game of senet. If you're feeling better, aunt, please do come join us."

"The fresh river air will do you good," Djedefhor said.

"I need to check on my crocodile too." The plan of going on deck was sounding more and more appealing to Tyema. Handing the baby to Renebti, she accepted a shawl in return, realizing with a warm rush of gratitude her niece had done some unpacking as well. "You take such good care of me," she said, squeezing Renebti's shoulder. "Thank you."

The captain escorted her on deck, his arm solicitously wrapped around her waist "until she got her sea legs". Tyema detached herself from his grasp as soon as possible, discovering it was pleasant to be in the afternoon sunlight and the fresh air.

Djedefhor took her subtle rejection of his tentative advance in good spirits, grinning broadly as he accompanied her first to check on the crocodile and then to sit in the patch of shade in the pavilion. "We'll be pulling into shore before sundown," he said. "We never sail at night, too many sand bars and other obstacles in the Nile. You, your niece and the infant can sleep on the ship or onshore in a tent, whichever seems more appealing to you. I post guards all around of course."

"I challenge you to a game of senet, Aunt," Renebti said, rattling the throwing sticks. "Pass the time until dinner?"

The captain left the ladies to their game, going off to supervise his crew as they adjusted the sails. Tyema set the baby in the center of a soft blanket between herself and Renebti. Putting her hand over her eyes, she watched a flock of colorful kingfishers soar and dive over the Nile, catching their dinner. The ship was gliding past a stand of gray-green tamarack trees on the shore and she caught a whiff of deep evergreen scent. *Maybe this voyage won't be as arduous as I'd feared.*

One of the sailors let out a shout, pointing urgently at the river. Scooping up the baby, Tyema and Renebti joined everyone at the port rail, to see a vee-shaped formation of ten crocodiles swimming alongside, keeping perfect alignment with the ship.

"Seems your god feels we need an escort," the captain said, leaning on the rail next to Tyema. "I'm honored. Never seen that before."

"Oh, Aunt, it must be a sign, an omen that we're protected on this journey," Renebti exclaimed.

Tyema nodded, trying not to let the memories of the past crowd into her mind. Surely Sobek was subtly reassuring her that at least this portion of her trip would be safe. Time enough to think about what lay ahead in Thebes when she arrived there.

CHAPTER FOUR

"Now what?" Tyema asked Captain Djedefhor several weeks later, after he'd displayed amazing seamanship in bringing the *Swift* safely through the crowded Theban harbor, deftly steering her between fat merchantmen and sleek warships, avoiding pesky little fishing boats that swarmed like mosquitoes. The yacht now rested next to the pier designated for visiting dignitaries, securely tied down, and Tyema's voyage was at an end.

"I've sent word of your arrival to Thebes' harbor master. He'll notify Pharaoh's Chief Scribe." The captain's voice was soothing. "Don't worry, I'm sure the palace has all the arrangements made for you and your interesting cargo."

Mind at ease on the issue of telling some authority she'd arrived, Tyema addressed her crocodile keeper. "You might as well go ahead and crate the animal for the next phase of the journey."

"He'll be happy when he reaches the temple breeding ponds and doesn't have to travel any farther," Hotepre said, beckoning to his helpers. The three men walked off toward the stern of the ship, where the purple bellied predator was tethered.

Murmuring her thanks to the captain, Tyema reentered her cabin, taking the fussy baby to nurse. She preferred sitting in their private, screened-off area at the bow, but now the ship was tied to a dock in the busy harbor, other boats moored close by, she felt there were far too many eyes watching. Nursing little Seknehure until he slept, she sat and watched him frown as he snored. *So like his father, with a strong face and stubborn jaw.* Leaning against the bulkhead, she supposed this might be one of her last peaceful moments while in the capital. *I wish I could put the crocodile ashore in his crate, order the anchor raised and sail home now. So many trials ahead and always the task Sobek needs accomplished haunts my dreams. Who am I to go up against black magic?* But she'd told the Great One she'd search out the troublemaker for him and now here she was in Thebes. No use to think of fleeing.

A knock at the door interrupted her peaceful reverie and Jemkhufu poked his head into the cabin, eyes wide with excitement. "You're needed on deck, my lady. Pharaoh has sent an escort to guide us to the palace."

"We're to stay at the palace?" Rearranging her dress, she rose, handing the baby to her niece Renebti, who'd slipped into the tiny cabin around the scribe as soon as he'd opened the door.

"So it seems." Jemkhufu stood aside for her to walk up the stairs to the deck in front of him. "I think you might know the officer in charge."

And that was all the warning Tyema received before she was face to face with Sahure for the first time in over a year. Heart pounding in her chest, breath catching, she stopped in mid step, Jemkhufu bumping into her back.

"My lady." Sahure bowed but his eyes never left her face. His own was set in stern lines, giving nothing away about how he felt at seeing her again.

"You—you're back from the Southern Oasis," she stammered, feeling the warmth rise in her cheeks as she blushed. She was sure he could probably hear her heart beating, the way seeing him again was affecting her. *He seems the same, maybe a bit more careworn in appearance, around the eyes. A difficult year in the desert, surely. What's he going to think about the baby? What will he say to me? What do I say to him?* Her thoughts were all over the place, like the gulls swooping over the harbor. Words suitable to utter refused to come to mind. She had to clench her hand on the railing to keep from touching him. For a moment she simply stared.

"And you've come to Thebes, the place you said you'd never visit," he answered. His eyes flicked to Renebti, standing on the bottom stair behind the scribe and holding the baby. Glancing at Tyema, he raised his eyebrows, lips compressed in a thin line.

Clearing her throat painfully, she rushed into speech. "I can explain—"

"No explanation to me is required. At the moment." His tone left it abundantly clear there would have to be discussion in the near future. "We should make haste to the palace. Pharaoh has decreed the crocodile will be housed in a suitable, fenced pond at his private zoo until the procession and ceremonies occur. A suite of rooms at the palace has been set aside for your party." He stepped aside to allow her to step onto the deck.

"Very kind of him, I'm sure." Tyema gestured at the large cedar crate sitting near the ship's stern, surrounded by Hotepre and his assistants. Thumping noises could be heard as the crocodile took exception to being enclosed after ten days of relative freedom. The crate shifted on the deck as the creature vented his displeasure from inside. "The animal is in there. We boxed him in as soon as we reached our mooring."

Apparently uninterested in the state of the crocodile, Sahure sounded bored. "If the logistics for the animal are organized, we can leave when you're ready."

"Oh, I'm ready now," she assured him.

He stared at her, his gaze traveling from her head to her toes. Brow furrowed, he glanced across the crowded harbor for a moment before taking one step to grab her by the elbow and pull her aside from her retinue. His voice was low and stern. "You can't seriously be planning to proceed through the streets of Thebes like this?"

"Like what?" Tyema was bewildered.

"In your plain travel dress? With your obviously rural companions and servants at your side? Did you bring no other priestesses? No musicians or dancers?"

Growing more bewildered by the moment, Tyema shook her head. "I left my staff to continue the required rituals of worship at our temple. And why should I need the musicians and dancers? You know we have only a small troupe. I assumed the temple here would supply performers for the procession."

He bit his lip, closing his eyes for a brief moment before glaring at her, jaw clenched. "Tell me you at least brought ceremonial robes, wig and crown?"

"Well of course, they'll be needed for the dedication of the new crocodile to his service here." Irritated, she yanked her elbow from his loose clasp. "What *is* the matter?" Djedefhor made as if to come to her assistance but she shook her head slightly, warning him off.

"Tyema, this is *Thebes*." Ignoring the momentary byplay with the ship's captain, Sahure gestured at the bustling city beyond the waterfront. "You can't just walk around in your everyday dress, like an ordinary person. We're not among villagers who've known you your entire life. You're here as a High Priestess of Sobek in the Ibis Nome. All eyes are going to be on you as we proceed from the harbor to the palace. It's common knowledge the high priest of Sobek here has his nose out of joint because Pharaoh insisted *you* had to supply the new bull crocodile for the temple, and lead the ceremonies. You owe it to Pharaoh to present yourself in the best possible light, and believe me when I say wearing a patched dress and a pair of sandals with a mended strap don't make the case."

She was silent for a moment, shocked by his vehemence. It had literally never occurred to her anyone in Thebes would care what she wore or how many retainers she had, much less that anything to do with her could reflect on Pharaoh. Along with her dismay, a flicker of sadness swept through her mind. *I was so right. I could never be the mistress of Sahure's house, having to worry about protocol and appearances.* These things seemed so petty and unimportant. Swallowing hard, pushing away her anger at his lecture because she had to admit he knew more than she did about Thebes, she asked, "What should I do? I don't want to cause Pharaoh any embarrassment."

Face grim, eyes narrowed, he said, "It's all politics in Thebes, which you need to remember while you're here. Don't trust too easily, either. Nat-re-Akhte is more powerful in his own right than most pharaohs have been since the time of the pyramid builders, but still there are endless games around him. I don't understand why my uncle the nomarch didn't warn you, prepare you a bit better, when he lent you his ship." Sahure gestured at the deck on which they stood.

Remembering the sad message from Sobek she'd had to deliver to the nomarch about his rapidly declining health, Tyema sighed. "Your uncle has other things on his mind."

"Yes, I received a private message from him and the knowledge weighs on my heart. My uncle is a good man." The expression on Sahure's face softened for a moment, his brown eyes warming. "Will you take my advice today?"

She nodded. "With gratitude."

Pointing at the stairway she'd emerged from, he said, "Go below, change into the best clothing you have, the ceremonial robes if there's no other choice, and let's get going on this trip to the palace. We can't do anything about your retainers and servants today, but at least *you* can appear as someone to be reckoned with. The first impression is important at court."

"I'll be quick." She hurried across the deck, calling to her niece, who was waiting by the gangplank with the baby, to come help her. She asked Djedefhor to order her trunks, which had already been packed and brought on deck, carried into the cabin again. Going below, followed by her retainers bringing the baskets and crates, she managed to change in record time, donning her finest white linen sheath, with gold embroidery at the hem, and her ceremonial crown—a smaller version of the one Sobek himself wore, a golden sun orb, with fine white ostrich plumes on either side. Around her neck she draped the six large emerald Tears of the god, set into a turquoise-and-gold beaded collar. Her best sandals were still new, smelling of freshly tanned leather, and stiff on her feet, the thong between her toes likely to chafe, but by the time she was ready to return to the deck, Tyema felt confident in her appearance and her dignity. She'd regained some of her composure while dressing.

All right, now I've seen him and yes, he's every bit as handsome as I remembered and there are so many things I long to talk to him about, to ask, but he seems so distant, so formal. I guess our angry parting still burns for him. And for all I know he's married and I'm going to have to meet his wife. Well, I gave him his first child, no other can have the honor. The fierceness of her pride in bearing his son surprised her. Lost in thought, she climbed the short staircase to the deck.

As soon as he saw her, Sahure bowed, a small smile on his lips. "Now you're ready to travel through the city, my lady. Well done." He held out his hand to escort her off the ship and down the gangplank to the dock, where his men had been waiting all this time.

"Oh, Nahkti and Senbi!" Tyema broke free of his clasp, pulled her formal skirts up to her knees with one hand for more freedom of movement and hurried to where the two chariot horses stood, held by a groom. "I missed you, my lovelies." She stroked their glossy necks, murmuring her apology for not having any treats as they nuzzled her. When Sahure came up behind her, she said, "May I go in the chariot with you? I won't ask to drive—"

At his renewed frown, she bit her lip and fell silent. *I've got to be less impulsive in his presence. Here in Thebes he's not the same carefree man I knew in Ibis Nome.* Allowing her dress to fall to its normal appearance, she toyed with the largest emerald in the collar, the cool smoothness of the gem soothing to the touch.

"Pharaoh has sent this fine litter for you," he said, gesturing off to the side where the impressive, gilded conveyance sat, riotous black and white ostrich plumes at each corner, plump red cushions awaiting her pleasure. Two fan bearers prepared to walk on either side. The litter was open, with no curtains. "He does you honor, High Priestess."

"Oh." Tyema knew her smile faltered. She leaned closer to him. "I suppose priestesses don't ride in chariots in Thebes?"

Biting his lip as if to hold back a grin, he shook his head and extended a hand. "Allow me." He led her to the litter and assisted her in gracefully taking her place, with a final instruction. "It'll be best if you endeavor to smile, seem pleased to be here and wave to the crowd as we go."

The burly men who had been waiting picked the litter up with an energy that took her breath away. Startled, she gripped the sides of the conveyance, afraid of being tumbled in the dust. Sahure mounted his chariot and the column set off, with her companions and the boxed up crocodile behind, carried by the men from her temple, using lifting poles inserted through the metal hoops set at the corners of the crate. Tyema checked to make sure her niece and the baby were safely in the middle of the group before giving all her attention to Sahure, handling his high spirited horses. *We're going to have to talk about Seknehure. Why didn't I raise the subject of our child while we had some privacy on the ship? Because Sahure took me by surprise and then he gave me no chance, with all his chiding about my appearance.* And he clearly didn't want to talk about personal matters when she was supposed to be on her way to the palace.

Tyema hoped he was wrong about the crowds, but as the procession marched slowly out of the harbor district, toward the palace, people gathered along the road. Feeling like a fool, Tyema waved, trying to smile, trying to make eye contact with any friendly faces she saw. Her stomach was roiling, sending acid into the back of her throat, and her head swam. The breeze from the fan bearers helped, but not much. Thebes was ten times larger than the nomarch's capital, which was the only city she'd ever been in, for her sister Merys's funeral. The crowds in the street were amazing to her, the many goods for sale enticing, the aroma of food cooking and the other, less savory smells assaulted her. It was all too much, overwhelming. The closer the procession came to the palace, the more she noticed the richness of the clothing, makeup and ornamentation, especially on the women.

By the time Sahure led the group through the huge gates of the palace, flanked by towering pink-and-gray granite statues of impassive pharaohs from an older time, and turned down a wide promenade lined with fierce sphinxes that ran the length of the massive collection of buildings, Tyema was clenching her fist to her chest, fighting to breathe. She prayed not to pass out. There were hardly any people here, mostly servants hurrying on errands, too busy to do more than spare a glance for her, and a few impassive guards. She slumped on the pillows, closed her eyes and counted her breaths in and out, knowing she had to be ready for whatever came next.

At length the litter bearers entered a garden complex of such beauty Tyema's jagged emotions calmed. Studying the mixture of familiar and strange trees, plants and flowers was soothing, as each turn in the path revealed new beauties of nature. An artfully created stream meandered in the midst of the garden and there were lotus ponds and places to sit in the shade. The air was a rich perfume of the mingled flowers, welcome after the odors of the city streets.

She realized they'd come to a halt. The litter was lowered to the ground and Sahure was there to help her rise and step away. He scrutinized her as she made a little business of smoothing her dress and adjusting her crown.

"Are you all right? Is the heat bothering you?" He made an interrupted motion as if to touch her cheek, then stopped himself, clenched hand dropping to his side. "You're alarmingly pale."

"I'm fine. Can we get this over with and be shown to our rooms?" Tyema wasn't sure how much longer she could handle the worry, dizziness and nausea. The fainting spell on the boat at the beginning of her journey had shaken her badly and terror of repeating the episode in a much more public place left her trembling now. *I need to lie down, preferably in a quiet place.*

"We're waiting for Pharaoh," he told her.

"Pharaoh?" *Surely I'm not important enough for the Great One to come to the gardens to greet me, am I?* Her heart sank and the vertigo, which had abated somewhat since entering the beautiful, secluded area, flooded over her in a rush. She swayed, putting her hand on Sahure's arm to steady herself.

Eyes narrowed, he was studying her. "Pharaoh does you great honor, coming to welcome you. I know he also wants to see the new crocodile."

"Sahure—" she turned to him with determination. Part of her trouble today was seeing him, being with him with so much lying unsaid between them, not least of which was the subject of their son. *And my own anxiety over whether Sahure is or isn't married.* Perhaps if they cleared the air, she could relax a bit and do her duties.

"*Not* now." His rebuke was instant, stern.

"But there are things I need to tell you."

A muscle twitched in his clenched jaw. "One of which must concern the baby your woman is swaddling. Is the child mine, Tyema?"

She nodded. "Your son. Our son. I sent word to you as soon as I knew I was with child."

Eyes locked on her face, he gave her a sceptical look. "I never received a single line from you."

Tyema stared. *No wonder he's upset.* "But I wrote three times more as the pregnancy progressed, and once again after the child was born."

Trumpets blared in the distance and Sahure glanced in the direction of the sound. "We can't discuss this here. There'll be time later." He moved away. "Have your men uncrate the beast, ready to allow Pharaoh to inspect it."

As he walked to check on the condition of the crate, Tyema felt as if she'd been doused with cold water from the heart of the Nile. Black and purple flickers surrounded Sahure, shimmering in the sunlight. The bracelet around her wrist tightened for a moment, reinforcing the warning with subtle pressure. Tyema rubbed the braided band, seeking to ease the constriction as well as her own shock. *Black magic? How can he be involved with such things? Not Sahure!*

As if she'd said his name out loud, he beckoned to her. Tyema forced herself to walk to the crate and oversee the dismantling. "Wait to undo the final slats until Pharaoh arrives," she said to her staff members. "I'll walk the animal into the pond."

"Very good, my lady." Hotepre wiped his brow. "Hot here in Thebes."

"The crocodile will like it." She meant the remark as a small jest, but there was truth in the observation. After all, a group of crocodiles was named a 'bask' for good reason and Thebes was nothing, if not sunny.

The fan bearers had moved with her, taken up their station behind her shoulders and now endeavored to keep a languid breeze moving. It would be all too easy to get spoiled with such attentive service. With maternal relief she observed her niece had taken the baby into the shade, sitting on a soft bank of greenery. Renebti was tickling Seknehure's nose with a feather she'd found, much to the giggling baby's amusement. Turning her attention back to the partially opened crate, Tyema realized Sahure was watching her.

"Later," he said again.

There was another blare of trumpets, coming closer. Sahure took her elbow, positioning her to face in the direction of the palace. All around her, people were going to their knees, then fully prone as Pharaoh and his party approached. Tyema knelt in unison with Sahure but before they could kiss the earth Pharaoh held out his hand. "You may rise, we don't stand on full ceremony here in my private gardens."

As she got to her feet, Tyema tried to contain her awe at being in the presence of Pharaoh. Nat-re-Akhte was still handsome and virile, his features strong, although well into his fifth decade. His unusual green eyes, bequeathed to him by ancestors from the first civilization before Egypt, were kind as the monarch met her gaze. To her relief, she saw no flickers of black magic around him. Pharaoh was wearing a simple, perfectly pleated white linen robe, belted with a complicated woven red-gold-and-turquoise sash at the waist. A golden falcon was affixed to the center of the sash. The blue cloak pinned to the shoulders of Nat-re-Akhte's tunic with coral-and-malachite scarabs set in gold swept the ground. On his head sat the simple golden uraeus, a rearing Egyptian cobra symbolizing his royal rank, rather than a formal crown. His signet ring was the only jewelry, although an ornate dagger with a jeweled hilt rode at his belt. "I'm pleased to see you, Lady Tyema. I trust your journey was peaceful?"

Feeling overwhelmed by Net-re-Akhte's magnificence, Tyema's one conscious thought was to get this ordeal over with before she disgraced herself in front of Pharaoh. Or the baby, who she could hear beginning to fuss and whimper, set up a howl and made a scene. "Yes, yes, it was, Great One, thank you. Would you like to view the crocodile now?"

Beside her, she felt rather than heard Sahure tense. Apparently one didn't try to move Pharaoh along, but the ruler didn't seem upset by her suggestion, merely nodding. "The animal you've selected captures my interest. Sobek told me the keepers gave your beast the name 'Pharaoh'." He chuckled and there was a ripple of answering laughter from the courtiers in attendance. The guards maintained their stern mien and vigilant stance.

"We meant no disrespect, sir," Tyema said, feeling butterflies in her stomach. What seemed amusing in Ta'sobeksef might be deadly insult here. *So many ways to put a foot wrong in Thebes.*

Nat-re-Akhte paced toward the crate and she followed, conscious of the entire group trailing behind her. "No, I'm sure there was no disrespect intended, although there can be only one ruler at a time in Egypt," he said over his shoulder. "So long as your crocodile restricts his ambitions to the pond at the temple, the world can remain in harmony." There was a definite twinkle in his eyes.

Suddenly she felt at ease, even though her companion was Pharaoh himself. "I think we can safely assume the limited scope of my crocodile's ambitions, sir."

Her men scrambled to their feet from the prone position as Pharaoh nodded his permission. Tyema introduced them, thinking as she did so she'd never forget the awe on their faces. Nat-re-Akhte asked a few genial questions about the difficulties of keeping the crocodile healthy during the voyage, which Hotepre answered in loquacious detail while his assistants shuffled and blushed.

Curiosity apparently satisfied by the pond keeper's discourse, Pharaoh surveyed the assembled group of workers. "Where's my zookeeper?"

"Here, my lord." A burly man who had been waiting nearby took a step forward. "How may I serve you, Great One?"

"Open the fence so the crocodile can enter the water." Nat-re-Ahkte gave Tyema a sympathetic wink. "I'm sure he must be getting impatient and thirsty in his crate."

Once the gate was open, Tyema took her place next to the box and nodded to Hotepre to strike away the last bolt. As soon as the wooden panel fell to the ground, raising a small cloud of dust that sent one or two of the courtiers scurrying, she bent over, meeting the basilisk stare of the crocodile, his eyes practically glowing.

One hand resting on the emeralds of her golden pectoral, she pointed the other at the crocodile. "I command you in the name of the Great One Sobek, leave this box and move to your temporary pond."

The crocodile rose on its stubby legs and waddled past her, slipping through the makeshift gate in the fence and launching itself into the shallow pool in a smooth motion, drifting with just his eyes above the water, watching them.

"Had I not seen it myself, I never would have believed it," said the royal zookeeper.

"I *am* the high priestess of Sobek," Tyema reminded them.

Her son now burst into howls of outrage over his ignored needs. Tyema was embarrassed, torn between her desire not to offend Pharaoh and a mother's imperative to console her child. She took an instinctive step in Seknehure's direction before forcing herself to stop. "I'm sorry, Great One—"

"Please don't apologize." Pharaoh made a dismissive gesture, a broad smile on his face. "I remember when my son was of a similar age. Peace can't be restored until the child has its mother's milk. Take your babe from the girl. You and I will sit in privacy in the pavilion yonder and chat a bit, while you satisfy his demands." He spoke to the people surrounding them. "I'll not need you for the moment."

Tyema took a red-faced, wailing Seknehure from Renebti, bouncing him a bit and crooning a lullaby under her breath in hopes of calming him. Still humming the tune, she rejoined Pharaoh, courteously waiting for her while the others withdrew to a patch of shade beyond the pond, in the other direction. Sahure lingered beside the open crate but Nat-re-Akhte ignored him, indicating for Tyema alone to accompany him to the appointed seats. He led her to a pair of benches placed under a large shady tree and settled on the closer one, gesturing for her to take the other.

She sank onto the gilded wood, discreetly rearranging her dress and the baby's light blanket to allow Seknehure to nurse. Pharaoh leaned against the carved back of the opposite bench, watching gardeners in the distance work at caring for the banks of flowers and fruit trees. "There's a rare peace here in this area of the palace grounds. We used to bring my son to see the zoo, when he was little, as a special treat. He liked to catch the lazy fish in the pond." The memory appeared to please Nat-re-Akhte, judging by the softening of the lines in his face. "The queen and I seldom have time now for such activities."

"I can't imagine the cares and duties on your shoulders, Great One," Tyema said. "All of Egypt to deal with. The problems of a single temple complex exhaust me."

"Perhaps one day when I have grandchildren, the zoo will again become part of my day. I'd enjoy teaching a grandson to fish." Pharaoh took one more glance at his gardens before all his attention focused on her. "To business, Lady Tyema.

Sobek tells me there's someone in my Court using black magic, magic bearing the taint of the Usurper Pharaoh."

Sobek didn't tell me about the connection to the Usurper. I wonder if there's anything else he neglected to mention? "But surely the Usurper is long dead?"

Nat-re-Ahkte nodded. "Yes, she is. And Sobek himself carried her body away to be devoured by Ammit the Destroyer. But somehow, someone is invoking powers the Usurper called upon. The moment you know who this person is, I expect to be notified." His tone was steely, his gaze hard. A muscle in his clenched jaw twitched and his hand curled around the dagger's hilt as if he was ready to strike the enemy.

Tyema swallowed past the lump in her throat, remembering those telltale flickers of black magic coiling around Sahure earlier. *There's no proof he's using the magic. He might be a victim of it. I need to know more, to be absolutely sure before I accuse anyone of anything.* There was nothing to report yet, she assured herself. "Yes, Great One, I promise, at once."

"But in the meantime, my queen and I'll strive to make your visit to Thebes a pleasant one." He was relaxed again, a genial host. "We've set aside a suite of rooms in one of the quieter wings for you and your party. I've assigned Captain Sahure to be your personal liaison, since I believe he's the only individual you know here at Court?"

Dismay cascaded through her. *So I'll see him daily? How shall I bear the pain and longing, especially if he's married?* Realizing Pharaoh was watching her, she stammered out an appropriate response. "Th-thank you, sir. Most kind."

Nat-re-Ahkte glanced from her to the baby and then at Sahure, waiting at parade rest beside the crate. "Perhaps assigning him wasn't the blessing I intended it to be? Old matters to be settled between the two of you?"

"This is his son, sir," she answered, stroking the baby's downy cheek with pride. "But we've yet to speak of him or anything personal. I appreciate your concern for my well being. Just on the short trip from the harbor, I began to perceive how different life here must be from the way we dwell in my small village."

Pharaoh smothered a laugh, converting his mirth into a cough. "Sobek indicated this journey was a hardship for you and expressed his hope I'd do everything in my power to ease your way, while you're working to discover the traitor for me."

"Traitor?" The word struck a chill in her heart. *And so far the only person I've seen in Thebes with any sign of black magic attached is the father of my child. The man I love.*

"The source of the black magic traces to Qemtusheb, god of the Hyksos; therefore any who are involved are traitors to Egypt and to me." His tone made it clear there was no room for doubt. Pharaoh studied her for a moment. "A rare gift, to be able to see black magic in the air. Even I can't command the ability, more's the pity."

"The Great One Sobek gave me the power, for this trip." She wanted to change the subject, anxious about Sahure's involvement. If Pharaoh were to ask her any direct questions, she didn't think she could deceive him. "May I inquire what the plans are for dedicating the crocodile?"

"Tomorrow morning we'll have a planning session with the high priest of the temple here, probably conduct the ceremonies a day or so after. A procession, hymns, prayers, you perform your magic of making the beast go where you will him to be. A day of feasting for the populace of Thebes." Nat-re-Akhte shrugged. "Grateful as I am personally to Sobek over this matter of black magic, he isn't a major deity in this city. I myself am sworn to Horus, who lent me his strength in battle many a time. The patron deity of Thebes itself since time immemorial is Amun-Ra. But we'll give Sobek his due, never fear," Pharaoh said, almost as an afterthought. "Then you'll be at liberty to partake in entertainments the queen is arranging, over the next few weeks, and search for our sorcerer." He clenched his fists. "My vengeance will be swift and deadly, once you've named the culprit."

"I'll find the sorcerer for you, Great One." The baby had drowsed off, so she wrapped him in the light blanket, awkwardly fixing her dress.

Pharaoh rose and she hastily followed suit, Seknehure held close in her arms.

"There's a feast tonight," the ruler said as they strolled toward Sahure and the waiting courtiers.

Tyema couldn't stop herself from groaning at the idea of being on display to the entire Court so soon. She bit her lip in alarm at showing her reluctance, but Pharaoh laughed. "You don't have to attend, is what I was going to say. I can see the trip up the Nile has been tiring for a new mother. I'm sure my wife will understand your absence and be more than happy to set anyone straight who questions, although she's anticipating meeting you. Rest, get yourself ready for what's to come."

"Thank you, Great One." She understood he'd done her a large favor, granting her permission to skip the long evening of feasting and entertainment.

"Anything you need, you must request from my Chief Scribe, Edekh." Eyes narrowed, he gave her a meaningful glance. "There's no limit to my gratitude, Lady Tyema."

They'd reached the waiting courtiers and her companions. Pharaoh said, "Until tomorrow, then." He strode toward the palace, his guards and retainers hurrying to follow.

Tyema noticed Sahure staring at the baby as she handed the child to her niece, but she didn't try to reopen the conversation. Worn out from her private session with Pharaoh, she felt shy of Sahure, wary of the flickers of black magic she'd seen. Taking refuge in her status as a high priestess, she adopted a haughty tone. "I wish to be escorted to my rooms now."

"Certainly." Sahure addressed Hotepre and the two assistants. "You're to lodge with the household staff. The zookeeper can show you the way."

The men bowed and Sahure took Tyema's elbow, directing her to follow the path Pharaoh had taken a moment ago.

They walked in silence through the gardens toward the palace. Tyema felt reluctant to talk to Sahure, although there were so many things she needed to discuss with him. She also didn't want to reveal private matters in front of her companions or the fan bearers. *Already I can see there are far too many listening ears in the palace. And no way to tell who might be loyal to what faction.*

As she climbed up the many stairs leading to the palace entrance, Tyema realized someone was waiting for them in the shade. Coming forward as she took the final step, this newcomer bowed. "May I welcome you to the home of Pharaoh Nat-re-Akhte and his Royal Wife, Ashayet? I'm Edekh, Chief Scribe."

"I'm pleased to meet you," she said.

"Edekh runs this whole place," Sahure told her with a laugh. "Anything you need, he can get. In fact, he'll have figured out what you require before you know yourself. Good to see you again, old friend."

"We missed you while you were away in the desert." The two men clasped arms for a moment before Edekh returned his attention to Tyema. "Let me escort you to your chambers, my lady. I've ordered dinner for you and your niece."

As they walked into the cool halls of the palace, Sahure gave Tyema a quizzical glance, eye brows raised. "Yes," she said in answer to his unspoken question, "Pharaoh excused me from tonight's festivities."

"While I must attend," he answered.

"There would be a number of ladies of the court who'd be disappointed if you were absent tonight, after being in the southern deserts for a year. Certain ladies-in-waiting seem to be unable to talk of anything else but when you might be seen again in Thebes." Edekh poked Sahure in the ribs with his elbow and chuckled.

Tyema ground her teeth before she could stop herself, feeling a jealous pang of regret in her heart but steeled herself. *I found him so attractive, why wouldn't the women here?*

Brow furrowed in a scowl, Sahure glared at Edekh for a moment, before turning to her. "We should talk. Perhaps after dinner?"

"I—I'm going straight to bed. The voyage has tired me. Can we talk tomorrow?" She didn't feel up to the subjects they had to discuss. And the brief flare of black magic in the air around him had badly disconcerted her.

He shook his head. "I've an errand taking me out of the city tomorrow. Pharaoh gave me his permission. When is the ceremony to be?"

Unable to quell a feeling of alarm that he was leaving her on her own, in addition to annoyance at herself for needing his presence to support her, not to mention the audacity of his abandoning her so soon to cope with the terrors of Thebes alone, Tyema answered distractedly. "Pharaoh indicated the dedication might be in two or three days."

"I was given the same timeline," Edekh said. "You can take care of whatever business calls you away from Thebes and be here by the appointed hour to fulfill your duties, my friend." Pausing in the middle of the broad hallway they'd been traversing, the Chief Scribe indicated a gilded door, painted with a scene of water lilies and waterfowl, guarded by two sturdy warriors with spears crossed to bar entry. "We've arrived at your suite of rooms, Lady Tyema."

As the guards saluted, moving their deadly weapons aside to allow her to pass, Edekh ushered Tyema into a set of chambers so elegant and richly appointed that she was speechless. If she hadn't known better she'd have thought Pharaoh had given her his own rooms. The walls were painted with lovely scenes of the Nile, gardens and the like. Lotus-topped columns touched with gold supported ceilings decorated with a breathtaking vista of the starry skies ruled by the goddess Nuit. Tyema's bedroom, visible behind gauzy draperies billowing gently in the afternoon breeze, was huge, dominated by a large bed made of shiny ebony, the mattress supported at either side by carved, gilded, life-size lionesses. The headboard and footboard bore the eye of Ra symbol, painted in gold, accented with turquoise. More elegant draperies surrounded the bed. Nearby stood a wicker cradle for her son.

Her possessions were stacked neatly in their baskets and boxes by the door of the suite's main room.

Edekh paused in mid-step, seeming surprised by the tidy pile. "You travel lightly, Lady Tyema."

I brought my complete wardrobe. She bit her lip, remembering she was wearing her best dress this very moment, the one she was supposed to be keeping for the ceremony. "I've no occasion for a large wardrobe in Ta'sobeksef."

"I'll send the palace maids to unpack for you," he offered.

"No, I'm sure we can manage," she said, glancing at her niece for confirmation. Renebti was holding the baby close to her, staring wide-eyed from one fantastic piece of furniture to the next, but she managed a distracted nod.

"As you wish. Pharaoh has decreed members of his personal regiment will stand watch at your door, as you saw when we entered the room, so you need not fear intrusions." Edekh seemed to have an instinctive understanding that this might be high on her list of concerns, which Tyema appreciated. "Only those you wish to see will be granted entry."

"He does me great honor," Tyema said, her head spinning. All this pomp and ceremony and special treatment at Pharaoh's behest for a provincial priestess like her was overwhelming.

Again the Chief Scribe seemed to be reading her mind, disordered though her thoughts might be right now. "All things you deserve, being the personal representative of the Great One Sobek." Edekh smiled before going on to say, "A servant will be posted outside at all times so you can summon me, should you have a need."

The idea of bothering such an august person as Edekh with any trivial request of hers seemed impossible to Tyema. "You're too kind, everyone here has been so helpful. Where will my temple scribe be?"

Edekh glanced at Jemkhufu, who had trailed somewhat forlornly in their wake all the way from the gardens. "You'll be given quarters in the hall of scribes near the library, fellow. In a moment I'll direct your steps. Should the lady have need of your services during her stay, you'll be summoned."

There was one place Tyema wanted to see while she was in Thebes, not only because she hoped to research issues of black magic, but also because she loved to read. Feeling this was her best opportunity to request the favor, she said, "Are guests allowed to use Pharaoh's library?"

Apparently the idea pleased Edekh, who grinned. "It can be arranged. I'll have a word with the Chief Librarian in the morning and he can give you a tour whenever you like, locate anything you especially want to peruse."

"There are some accounts of journeys to the far lands, to Kush and Punt, you might enjoy," Sahure offered. "I prepared some addenda to those volumes after my own expeditions. Or perhaps the Tale of the Shipwrecked Sailor?"

The reference to the story they'd watched enacted by the strolling players on the night they'd first met unsettled her. *Why would he bring that up?* Before Tyema could say anything there was a knock and the gilded doors opened behind him, admitting a parade of servants, bearing portable tables and giant platters of fruit, roasted meats, pitchers of beer. The man in charge bowed to Edekh and supervised his staff as they set up the dinner.

"All this for just us?" her niece whispered, edging closer to Tyema, seeming overwhelmed.

The steward eyed the display as his staff left the room. He tweaked the arrangement of fruit on one platter, moving a leaf, adjusting a group of figs, before consulting Tyema. "Should there be any delicacy you crave besides what we've brought, you must let me know, my lady."

"I—I'm sure this will be fine." *We'll never manage to consume all of this, just Renebti and me.*

Apparently satisfied, the steward bowed and left.

"We'll leave you to your dinner then." Edekh drew Jemkhufu with him. The latter cast a glance over his shoulder as the door closed behind them. Tyema knew he'd been hoping she'd request him to remain and dine with her, but she was sure she'd have been committing a breach of etiquette, based on how Edekh had behaved toward her scribe. Truth be told, she longed to have privacy.

Sahure lingered. "I would see my child."

Without a word Tyema took Seknehure from her niece, who murmured something, grabbed a handful of grapes from the table, and walked off to explore her own adjoining bed chamber. The baby cooed and laughed, reaching to toy with his mother's earring.

"I know how to hold a baby," Sahure said as she hesitated. "I have nieces and nephews, friends with children. None of my own. Until now." He held out his arms and Tyema placed his son in them. Sahure held the baby carefully, securely. Father and son stared at each other, their solemn expressions almost comically identical. Tyema found herself blinking back tears, full of fierce pride in her sturdy baby. Sahure brushed one finger down his son's cheek and the boy grabbed it, gumming. Raising his eyebrows, Sahure glanced at her. "He's teething already?"

"So it seems. He's in a rush to grow up."

Pride written all over his face, Sahure grinned. "I'd expect nothing less from my son."

"He's a good baby," she said. Her heart ached, wanting Sahure to love the boy as she did. "Seknehure rarely cries but when he does, he has strong lungs."

"Yes, I heard for myself today in the garden," Sahure's cheerful expression faded as he glanced from the baby to her. "Why didn't you answer my letters? Did what we shared mean so little to you? Even though our son is the result? Were you still angry over the way we parted?"

Surprised, feeling attacked, Tyema put her hands on her hips and stared at him. "Letters? I had only the one, saying you'd been posted to the Southern Oasis, which arrived three months after you'd left. Why didn't you answer mine, when I told you I was with child?"

"I told you, I had no letters." His voice was sharp. "Do you think I'd ignore news of such importance? Even in the desert outpost of Kharga I'd have found a way to send you an acknowledgment, amulets to assure your safety in pregnancy and his at birth, *some* token of my concern and involvement. My affection."

Apparently upset by the tone of the adult voices, the baby's face crumpled into a frown and he wailed. Tyema reached for him, but Sahure put the infant to his shoulder, patting his back firmly. Seknehure subsided into hiccups, tugging on the black and gold *nemes* head cloth Sahure wore as part of his uniform. After a moment, he did hand the child back to Tyema.

"I don't know what to think," she said, remembering the flickers of black magic she'd seen earlier. She held the baby close. *I must tread cautiously. I don't know who in Thebes might be compromised by the black magic. It's been over a year since I saw Sahure.*

"Did you post your letters yourself? Does mail come to you unfiltered?" he said.

"Of course not, handling the temple's correspondence is one of Jemkhufu's duties—" She stopped, free hand going to cover her mouth. "You don't think, he wouldn't *dare*—"

"I've always thought your Jemkhufu had aspirations beyond his station. In Thebes a temple scribe wouldn't be so bold as to raise his eyes to a high priestess, much less forge his ambitions around a relationship with one."

Temper flaring, nerves stretched like a bowstring, head aching from all the events of the day and the heavy headdress, uncomfortable because the baby obviously wanted to nurse again and she craved privacy to sit with the child, Tyema was more brusque than usual. "I've heard quite enough about Thebes for one day. Don't you have to be on your way to Pharaoh's banquet?"

"Yes, I should be going." But Sahure made no move toward the door. "We'll have to talk about our son soon. He'll want for nothing, I assure you."

"I can take care of my child," she said.

Forehead wrinkling in a frown, Sahure seemed to exert effort not to respond angrily, maintaining an even tone of voice. "Our child, Tyema."

"So you keep reminding me." She moved toward the bed. "Do you mind? I've had a long day and the baby needs to nurse."

He bowed, "Of course. By the way, Edekh will watch over you tomorrow, while I'm out of Thebes. He'll ensure you're summoned to the meeting with Pharaoh and the local priests in good time."

Unbending a little, because Sahure was addressing one of her major concerns, which she appreciated, Tyema allowed her gratitude to show on her face and in her voice. "Thank you."

Without saying anything else, Sahure left the room, closing the door quietly behind him.

He acknowledged the guards' respectful salutes automatically and took a step toward the main cross-corridor, scarcely knowing where he was going, head whirling with all the day's events. He realized there was a servant in his path, attempting to get his attention.

The boy bowed. "Chief Scribe Edekh requests your presence in his quarters, sir, as soon as your duty to Pharaoh's guest is complete for the day."

"All right. I know the way, no need to escort me." Grateful to have a destination, knowing nothing would've escaped the keen eyes of his old friend, Sahure dismissed the page and hastened through the halls, relieved not to meet anyone he knew, until he arrived at Edekh's lavish chambers.

When Sahure knocked briskly and entered without waiting for permission, the Chief Scribe was alone, studying a malachite and ivory senet board, evidently playing against himself. A wine flask stood on the table nearby. As Sahure let himself into the room, Edekh glanced up, raised an eyebrow and poured a liberal amount into a mug. Handing the drink to Sahure as he sank into the empty chair, Edekh said, "Long day?"

Draining the wine in one rapid series of swallows, not even pausing to savor the quality of Pharaoh's finest libation, Sahure nodded and poured himself another.

"I gather the little Lady Tyema must be the mystery woman the queen had me send messages to, on your behalf?" The scribe moved a black pawn onto a malachite square outlined in gold leaf. "And perhaps the robust babe is your son?"

"Yes to both. Not that I doubt your word, old friend, but Ema says she never received more than the first message." Sahure sank down on the closest chair, setting his wine on a low table with cats' clawed feet that stood nearby. With a careless yank, he removed his nemes head cloth before burying his head in his hands for a moment. Straightening, rubbing his jaw, he said, "A letter which—as I recall to my embarrassment now—was written in haste and said little."

The scribe raised his mug. "I wish your son health and joy. And congratulate you on fatherhood."

Raising his head, stretching side to side to unkink his back muscles, Sahure nodded and drank in answer to the toast. "I confess my head is in a whirl."

"I thought you might need the safe ear of a friend before you appear at Pharaoh's dinner tonight." Edekh threw the counting sticks and moved a white pawn. "You've been under tight control today. I could tell."

Sahure nodded. "Aye, ever since I received Pharaoh's orders this morning to escort Ema while she's in Thebes." He shook his head. "She said she'd never leave Ibis Nome. She said it was impossible for her." A burning tide of anger rose in him as he remembered the way their night together had ended, with her outright, almost panicked rejection of his proposal. "Yet here she is. And it was plain to me this morning when I boarded her boat in the harbor, she'd no idea I was here as well. She certainly didn't come to Thebes in any hopes of seeing me." *And the knowledge burns.*

"To be fair, I understand the god Sobek ordered her to bring the crocodile to Thebes," Edekh answered, contemplating his senet board. "A woman might refuse a lover, but never a Great One." Head tilted, scratching his chin, he gazed at Sahure. "I quite like her. Refreshing lack of self importance. Certainly Pharaoh was favorably impressed. Apparently she held her own in their private conversation."

Sahure laughed. "She probably didn't know enough to be properly intimidated, my friend. You should have seen her on the boat this morning, dressed in a patched sheath, mended sandals, no jewels other than her amulet and a curious bracelet. Beautiful as always, but she's got no idea how any slightest detail carries significance at Court, the politics here, the intrigues—"

Leaning back in his chair, Edekh propped his bare feet on a small wooden stool in the shape of a kneeling gazelle. "Yet she's a high priestess. Even in a provincial temple such rank doesn't come to the naïve."

Rising, Sahure paced restlessly. "There's something more to the story of how she ascended to the position, which I could never get out of anyone in her small town. Her rank most certainly didn't come through a rise in established hierarchy. And I'd no time, nor was I in the right mood, to inquire of my uncle the nomarch when

I left Ibis at Pharaoh's command a year ago." He stopped, throwing his hands wide. "Edekh, I'm a *father*." He paused for a moment, savoring the words, basking in the proud notion, remembering how it felt to hold his sturdy son for the first time. "I was going to leave for Ibis within the week, to try and straighten out matters between us. My carefully measured speech was well rehearsed in my head." He laughed. "And then today not only is Ema here, but she brings a son I never even knew existed. I feel as if I've been tossed about in a sandstorm. My head aches."

Edekh held out the wine skin and poured more into Sahure's mug. "Do you still love her?"

"Yes." The answer was unhesitating, straight from his heart before his head considered the question. Surprised, Sahure paused for a moment to unravel the tightly wound braid of his feelings. Love warmed him when he thought of Tyema, but right now the deep emotion was tempered with anger and uncertainty. "While I was stationed in Kharga, I thought of her often, relived every moment of our two weeks together, tried to sound out the meaning of each word she said to me." He laughed with no mirth. "In the remembering, I could clearly see for every thousand words *I* spoke, she answered with fewer than ten."

Edekh paused in the middle of throwing the counting sticks. "Really? I've never known you to be a boastful or egotistical man."

"Ema has a way of drawing a person out, getting them to talk about their fondest dreams, their hopes and plans. She's not being false, she's genuinely interested," Sahure said, as if he expected his friend to venture some criticism.

The sticks clattered on the table as Edekh tossed them. "Such a quality is to be admired in a woman, no?"

"Yes, but I realize there's so much I don't know about her. I think she turns the conversation to the other person as a defense. Her version of a shield."

Moving another pawn, the scribe said, "You spent time alone with her today. Did you speak of all that lies between you?"

Sahure rubbed the back of his neck, thinking over the hours. "There were moments her behavior was odd, almost as if we were strangers, or enemies. As if she couldn't trust me. Then at other times, she was the Ema I fell in love with." He laughed. "She wanted to ride in my chariot through Thebes, can you imagine?"

"Highly improper." But the grin on Edekh's face softened the critical tone.

"Yes, well, I taught her to drive a team while I was there." The memory warmed him. "She's damn good at it too."

"She hardly brought any baggage at all," Edekh said, allowing his white pawn to capture a black one, sending it all the way back to the start of the board.

"Why do you bother to play against yourself?" Sahure gestured at the board. "You always win."

"Precisely. Sit then and we'll play a rapid game before we both must be off to the banquet."

"You're on." Sahure drew his chair over to the gaming table and sat. "But we haven't much time, so first to get one pawn through the board takes the win."

"Agreed." Edekh handed him the throw sticks. "What's your next move in the other game you're playing, the one with Lady Tyema?"

Rubbing the smoothly painted sticks between his hands for a moment, Sahure frowned. "I don't trust her scribe. I think he intercepted my letters and obviously never gave any courier the ones she wrote to me. There'd be no misunderstanding if I'd known she was with child, if she'd known I regretted my anger. Matters would stand differently between us today."

"The man does seem to think rather highly of himself." Edekh sipped his wine. "Apparently he's no idea of a mere temple scribe's proper station in life. I got the distinct impression he hoped to dine with Lady Tyema in her quarters this evening." Shaking his head, the scribe frowned. "I would've had to intervene. Totally improper. There would be too much gossip, reflecting poorly on your somewhat naïve priestess. And as she's Pharaoh's guest, even if I wasn't much taken by her already, I couldn't allow her to provide easy fodder for the nattering crows on the fringes of the Court."

"From my observations in Ta'sobeksef, the scribe has totally inappropriate ambitions for one of his station in life," Sahure agreed. "Yet Ema keeps him in check. Still, I think he and I are going to have a conversation but not just yet. I don't want her upset before the ceremonies have been completed."

"Somehow I doubt if this chat will be enjoyable for him." Chin resting on his hand, Edekh pondered his next move. "Perhaps we need to find Lady Tyema a new scribe or two for her temple and provide, um, other opportunities for this ambitious fellow."

"We do think alike. Sometimes." Sahure swept Edekh's pawn off the board, advancing his own several more spaces. "The sticks favor me tonight."

"And what of the lady herself?" Unperturbed, the scribe threw the gleaming black-and-white counters, earning enough points to get his pawn "reborn" onto the space marked with the golden ankh, where each game piece entered the board. He handed the sticks to Sahure.

Tapping one on the edge of the board while he thought, Sahure said, "I fear I must tread carefully there. I was too abrupt the first time, assumed too much, failed miserably—"

Contemplating the arrangement of their pawns on the board, Edekh nodded. "You don't like to lose."

Sahure drew back from the board, pawn suspended in his hand above the squares. "Do you think she's merely a challenge to me?"

"An observation only. You do have a pattern of laying siege to those ladies who affect indifference, until you've won. A point your self-proclaimed childhood sweetheart Lady Baufratet would have done well to consider in her endless pursuit of position as Mistress of your House."

"Ema is different from any other woman I ever met. I wanted to spend my life with her, have eternity with her." Sahure felt the rightness of the statement down to his bones. *Ema was no bored Court lady playing games we both understood, no mere bed partner. No ambitious social climber like Baufratet.* With distaste he remembered his original plans to marry the Theban lady in question or someone like her, to bolster his own efforts to rise in rank. *Gods, what a fate I escaped. Marriage without love would have been dry as the desert sands, no matter what rank I eventually achieved.* "I need to get her to let her guard down, talk to me, to explain. I need to find the real Ema hidden inside the exterior of the haughty priestess, find the woman who entranced me in Ibis province."

"She'll be in Thebes for a few weeks, or so Pharaoh has said."

Staring in surprise, Sahure said, "I wonder why? After the crocodile has been installed in his new home, what reason could she possibly have to linger? It's certainly not because she wants to see Thebes or experience the life at Court, trust me. Either would be totally out of character for her. And she knows no one here but me, I'm positive."

Edekh was silent, sipping his wine.

"Oh all right, keep your secrets, like the Sphinx. Whatever causes Ema to tarry here is a good omen for me, since her delay gives me time to wage my campaign for her heart. And become acquainted with my son." He threw the sticks so hard they rattled against the edge of the game board and one fell to the floor. Bending to retrieve it, Sahure laughed. "Ah, landed on the white side, by the gods, to give me my fourth point. This game goes my way, at least."

"I wish you success with the other as well," Edekh said. "Your pursuit of the reluctant lady will be interesting to observe."

CHAPTER FIVE

Breakfast was as bountiful as dinner had been, mounds of fruit and berries, freshly baked bread, honey. Tyema and her niece marveled at the variety as they picked morsels from the platters.

"You could feed the whole village with this," Renebti said. "And we never see fresh fruit out of season."

"I've heard there are special groves and gardens here at the palace, where the gardeners use secret incantations and appeals to Isis and Osiris to grow delicacies for Pharaoh's table year round." Tyema savored some pomegranate seeds.

The two women exchanged startled glances as there was a knock at the door. "Enter," Tyema called.

Stately as always, linen robes pleated to perfection, carrying the gold-and-cobalt staff of office, topped with a golden cobra's head, Edekh made his entrance. "I trust you slept well, my lady? And had an adequate breakfast?"

"All the details are done to perfection here," Tyema said truthfully.

Smiling, Edekh acknowledged the compliment before he said, "Her Majesty the Queen is on her way to your apartment."

"The Great Royal Wife visits me?" She wiped her hands, noticing a small juice stain on her skirt. Dismayed, Tyema closed her eyes for a second. *The queen of all Egypt and I'm dressed in my third best tunic and with no makeup or wig. What kind of impression will my disarray make?* "Do I have time to change? To be properly ready for such an exalted guest?"

Waving one hand, he attempted to reassure her. "It's not a formal audience, merely a friendly visit. Ashayet comes alone, without all the ladies-in-waiting and servants." He leaned closer. "I think she wants to see the baby."

And the next moment the queen herself was entering the chamber, followed by fan bearers and guards. Tyema and Renebti knelt in respect but Ashayet waved them to rise. Seating herself in a golden chair brought by an attendant, the sides of which were graceful gazelles, their backs serving as the arms and their legs supporting the woven leather seat, the queen said, "Please, go on with your breakfast. You'll need sustenance to deal with those crotchety old priests and city officials later this morning."

"May I offer you something to eat, Great One?" Tyema asked.

Ashayet waved an elegant hand. "No, I've breakfasted, thank you, but I'd love to see the child, if he's not asleep."

Tyema brought the baby to the queen, who took him in her arms with a smile. "I adore them at this age, so sweet."

A sense of sheer unreality swept over Tyema, seeing the queen of all Egypt cuddling her son. "He's a good baby, eats well, sleeps through the night." Honesty compelled her to add, "Mostly."

Cooing at Seknehure as he gurgled and gave her a toothless grin, Ashayet nodded, the golden beads in her elaborately braided black wig chiming. "Now then, what are you planning to wear today, for the meeting with my husband and the others?"

Startled, Tyema blinked. "Ma'am?"

"A little bird whispered to me yesterday you might not have brought quite enough of a wardrobe, being unfamiliar with our extravagant ways in Thebes." The queen turned her serene gaze on Edekh, who was unsuccessfully smothering his amusement.

Tyema gestured to Renebti, who hastily took a blue tinted linen dress, beautifully pleated, from the largest basket, shook the fabric out and held the garment up for Ashayet's perusal. Tyema walked over to take the dress from her niece, should the queen wish to examine it more closely. "I'm wearing this."

Ashayet clucked at the baby, playing with one of his chubby hands as he grabbed at her wig. "Beautiful seaming, but not quite up to the occasion, eh sweetling? Can't have your mother appear at a disadvantage in front of the pompous old priest from Sobek's Theban temple."

"Great One, forgive me, but I'm the same person here or in my village, wearing this dress or ceremonial finery." Tyema kept her voice even with an effort. "My authority stems from my selection by Sobek himself, not from whether I wear linen or spun cotton."

Still smiling, the queen met her eyes. "My husband has discussed with me some of the other reasons you visit with us. I say to you, here in Thebes one's appearance can be a tool, a weapon if you like. You need to move about in our Court freely, not attracting undue notice. You have to fit in, not look like—forgive me—a maid servant from a rural estate, wandering where she shouldn't be found." The queen's smile was impossible to resist. "No criticism is meant, dear, but what serves perfectly well for daily wear in the provinces, even beautifully stitched as I observe the dress is, doesn't stand scrutiny here."

"I see your point, ma'am." Tyema hadn't considered this added challenge of her assignment. "I wish I'd understood about the clothing before we came. But what am I to do now? My temple treasury has a surplus of deben, the Great One Sobek begrudges no expense where I'm concerned, but there's no time to send for the funds and have new, more elegant clothes made."

"No need for worry." Ashayet nodded at Edekh, who walked to the door. "I wouldn't raise the issue if I couldn't offer a solution."

When he opened the portal, a parade of servants marched in, arms full of dresses and cloaks. Another woman lugged in a basket of sandals. A fourth juggled several wig stands, with beautiful wigs in various lengths and styles. Bringing up the rear, carrying a large cosmetics box, was an elderly lady who was identified with much affection by Ashayet as her personal maid.

"I wasn't blessed with a daughter, so you must indulge me today and help me sort the most recent offerings from the suppliers to the queen," Ashayet said to Tyema. The Royal Wife waved a casual hand at Renebti, lingering shyly by the stack of baskets and papyrus fiber boxes they'd brought from Ta'sobeksef. "Both of you. I understand this is your niece?"

"I'm Renebti, ma'am. Tyema's niece." The girl bobbed an awkward curtsey, eyes wide at the honor of being addressed directly by the queen.

"Welcome to our city and my home," Ashayet answered.

Edekh ushered the guards and retainers out of the room, even the fan bearers, closing the door behind him so Tyema could try on dresses in privacy, the queen approving or rejecting as they went. There were a few in the pile that the queen directed Renebti to model, assisted by the haughty maids just as Tyema had been while she removed her clothing. Tyema strongly suspected the kindly Royal Wife had ordered her maids to find suitable items for a young girl, judging by the simpler, more modest cut of the dresses and the less flamboyant trimmings. Renebti was in awe, rendered speechless by the entire proceeding. When Ashayet declared they were done, Tyema had several fine linen garments laid aside and her niece had acquired two as well.

"I'm humbled by your generosity, your majesty," Tyema said to Ashayet as the queen's own maid helped Renebti arrange the intricate folds of the garment Tyema was now to wear to today's meeting. Pure white linen, crisply pleated, with a dyed blue hem, offset by lotus flowers worked in golden thread, the garment made Tyema feel as if she were a queen. Twirling, she relished the feel of the fabric swishing around her ankles. Even the lingering tightness of her new sandals couldn't detract from her satisfaction.

The queen laughed. "You notice I offer no jewelry from my husband's treasury. Sharing my gems would be generosity!"

Edekh reentered the room when Tyema had finished dressing, bringing the fan bearers with him. Tyema was grateful. The chambers were growing stuffy as the sun rose higher in the sky outside. Trying on new clothes was undeniably pleasant but made a person warm in the Theban heat.

The queen's maid set to work applying Tyema's makeup with skillful hands, the kohl and malachite tints drawn from a set of beautifully shaped, cobalt blue bottles, with stoppers of ivory carved in the shape of birds and flowers. Once that work was completed Renebti brought the ebony case, inlaid with ivory and turquoise, which bore the treasure of Sobek's temple— the six emerald Tears he'd given Tyema so long ago. As Renebti raised the lid, kneeling in front of her aunt, the queen stood and came to admire the gems, bouncing the baby on her hip. The tear-shaped raw emeralds were set into a golden collar, surrounded by highly detailed renditions of crocodiles embossed in the gleaming metal. Bigger than a man's thumb, the largest Tear sat in the center, with one only slightly smaller directly below it, offset on either side by the four remaining gems. As she lifted the collar from the box, the stones threw off green glints to sparkle on the wall and floor, the sun making the gems flash and gleam.

"Magnificent," Ashayet said, raising one hand to lightly touch the primary stone. "You're blessed by your god."

Picking up the necklace to allow Renebti and the maid to fasten it around her neck, Tyema nodded. "He has a special relationship with my temple and our town."

Ashayet's face grew somber. "I thank you for coming to Thebes, on your various missions," she said.

She must be so worried for her husband's life. Tyema longed to hug the queen, who had such a troubled expression on her face, but the distance between their respective ranks in society was too vast. "It's my honor, Great One."

"Well, I'll leave you now." Ashayet smoothed her wig with her free hand. "Good luck with the dyspeptic elderly First Priest. His nose is severely out of joint about all aspects of this ceremony, even as he exults in having the attention of the entire city and Pharaoh, for once. Edekh will conduct you to the meeting chamber and my husband will join you shortly."

Tyema bowed as the queen gave her son one more kiss on his chubby cheek, disentangling his determined fingers from her elaborate scarab-and-falcon earring. "He does have the features and the persistence of his father," Ashayet said, laughing.

Somewhat startled, Tyema took the baby from the queen, realizing a moment too late she should be more considerate of her new dress and allow Renebti to hold the baby rather than risk a mishap now. Hoping Seknehure wouldn't pick that moment to burp his breakfast, she said, "We've yet to discuss matters, Sahure and I."

"You may trust my discretion." The queen laid a finger on her painted lips for a second. "I'm intrigued to meet the mystery girl who captured his heart, where others vied for the honor and failed. Several of my ladies-in-waiting have their hopes pinned on becoming Mistress of his House. Sahure is known as a man on the rise in my husband's favor."

Taking a deep breath, Tyema asked her most pressing question. "Then he—he's not recently married?"

"Let me put your mind at rest, he remains unwed." The queen studied Tyema's face for a moment, brow furrowed. "I trust he took my advice and the letters we forwarded to you on his behalf were more beguiling in tone than his original proposal?"

Amazed how much the Royal Wife seemed to know about her relationship with Sahure, Tyema was at a loss for words. *How much had Sahure said about her to the queen? Or to anyone else in Thebes?*

Apparently deciding no answer was to be forthcoming, Ashayet leaned closer. "You'll find, my dear, most military men have no idea how to play games of true love, once their heart has been given. That his honeyed words and courtier's airs failed him when he made his rash proposal for you to abandon your own world and trail along in his wake to Thebes is actually a good indication his heart was truly involved. The captain is a favorite of mine. I would see him happy, so I hope you'll see fit to give him another chance while you're in Thebes. But be aware there are others intent on the position he wants to give you."

Not waiting to see what Tyema might reply, the queen left, the fan bearers and maids in her wake.

"Well." Drawing a deep breath, Tyema addressed the Chief Scribe who had reentered the chamber once the queen had departed. "After all the kindness and advice from her majesty, I feel I'm ready for this meeting."

"Indeed, I'm sure you are." He laughed as he opened the door to the corridor.

"Any other words of advice you'd offer me?" Tyema asked as they strolled into the main portion of the palace. "I'm not too proud to listen."

Edekh shook his head. "I think your power lies in the answer you gave my queen, a few minutes ago in your chambers. You have authority directly from Sobek and require nothing else. Ah, here we are."

Guards opened the doors and Edekh bowed, indicating for her to precede him.

The High Priest of Sobek was easy for Tyema to identify, dressed in layered raiment of white, gold and black, wearing a modified sun-disk headdress, all ten bony fingers adorned with golden rings set with chunky gemstones. He was flanked by five lower priests and a thin, nervous scribe sat close by to record orders. A much older man, the priest had a stern face, small eyes beneath bushy brows, flushed cheeks and thin lips. His wig was elaborately braided and he clutched a tall gilded staff topped with a representation of the god in his crocodile form. His pectoral was a depiction of Sobek as Crocodile, done in turquoise, coral and jet. It was eye catching, but nothing compared to the glory of her gold collar and emeralds.

"Lady Tyema, High Priestess of Sobek in the Ibis Nome," Edekh intoned, thumping his staff on the floor as if she were royalty.

The under priests bowed but the Theban high priest merely nodded, his eyes fastened on the Tears of Sobek around Tyema's neck. She suppressed a grin at his avaricious stare.

The door across the room, which only Pharaoh himself could use, opened and Nat-re-Akhte entered the chamber, saying as he crossed the gilded threshold, "No need to genuflect, this isn't a formal audience." Today he wore no crown but had the golden uraeus on his brow, held in place by a golden circlet. He carried the blue-and-gold crook and flail of his rank, ritually positioned across his chest.

She stood aside as Nat-re-Akhte walked past her to his chair, which was a golden marvel, depicting intricate scenes of himself with various gods that were far too detailed for Tyema to fully absorb in one glance. The chair rested on intricately carved lion paws, and was set on a slightly raised dais at the head of the gleaming wooden table. The ever present fan bearers took up station behind Pharaoh and Edekh walked to a place at his right hand.

"You may be seated," Pharaoh said, placing the crook and flail on the table in front of him. "Which day is going to be the most propitious for this ceremony?" He gave Tyema a conspiratorial smile. "My zookeeper tells me the beast has already devoured all the fish in his pond and they've had to restock."

"I've cast the omens, Great One, and the day after tomorrow is the ideal date for the new ruler of the bask to be presented to the people of Thebes and installed at our temple," said the High Priest, displaying no hesitation.

Pharaoh nodded and Edekh made a note. Tyema sat back in her chair as the men discussed the arrangements for the procession. The city officials were also silent for the most part, apparently in the meeting to receive instructions, not to make suggestions. She had no opinion about the parade, the local Sobek priests knew their own city and how to organize things here. Perhaps she would have put the second troupe of dancing girls before the sacred image of Sobek, not after as they were going to do, but Tyema had no feeling it mattered to the Crocodile God, so she only nodded when Pharaoh courteously asked her opinion.

The high priest continued his rundown of the sequence of events. "And when we arrive at the temple, I'll greet you with the hymn of the seventh hour—"

"After I've sung the hymn of the Abundant Nile," Tyema said. She felt a tightening in her gut, sure now they would be in opposition. *He'd rather I played no part in the day's ceremonies. He probably wishes I'd just sent the crocodile with only old Hotepre for escort. Well, for that matter, so do I, but the Great One wanted it otherwise.*

The older priest cleared his throat for a moment, blinking. Clearly he wasn't used to being interrupted. "No need for you to exert yourself, I'm sure. It's one of the *older*, less well known hymns after all. You can sing a brief blessing on the bask at the end of the ceremonies, if you wish. Now then, as I was saying—"

"The Great One Sobek particularly enjoys the 'Abundant Nile', since it praises his efforts to keep the life giving waters flowing freely," Tyema said, cutting across his words, her voice clear. "As he is sending his crocodile to you, personally selected by him, we need to thank him appropriately."

The men from the Theban temple gawked at her. Color becoming even hotter in his gaunt cheeks, the high priest blew out a breath. "My dear girl, we're duly conscious of the honor the Great One does us here at Thebes. I merely see no need to slow the tempo of the ceremony with additional music. The crowd will naturally wish to see the crocodile installed in the pond as soon as possible."

"As High Priestess, it's my responsibility to conduct the crocodile to your temple and to make the official transfer in proper order," she said, not at all abashed by his dismissive manner. When it came to anything regarding her duty to Sobek, Tyema felt as if some measure of his strength ran in her veins, and no condescending old man from Thebes could silence her. "I'll sing 'Abundant Nile,' after which you can sing whatever you feel is most appropriate to accept the gift of Sobek and *then* we'll proceed to the pond. Whether our audience is one person or ten thousand people, we must honor the Great One Sobek properly."

"Well," Pharaoh said, his voice solemn but his eyes twinkling, "The list of songs is decided then."

"Duly noted," Edekh assured him as the palace scribe by his side made rapid inscriptions on his tablet. The temple scribe shot a wary look at his superiors, but then scratched some notes as well.

There was an awkward moment of silence. Pharaoh raised his hand and gestured in a lazy circular motion at the priest. "Continue."

The man opened and closed his mouth several times before swallowing a sip of wine from the clay goblet his under priest handed him. "Um, yes, um, at the pond, we'll open the crate—"

"The child of Sobek doesn't travel through Thebes in a crate," Tyema interrupted.

"You're not seriously proposing to have a dangerous Nile crocodile carried loose in the procession, are you?" the old man spluttered.

"Sobek has given me the gift of controlling his children of the Nile when circumstances warrant. I'll ensure the animal remains calm during the parade through the city, docile until he's installed in the pond," Tyema said.

"I've seen this gift or power in action, exactly as the Lady Tyema indicates," Pharaoh agreed.

"It would be most exciting," said one of the younger priests, enthusiasm causing him to speak boldly, earning himself a glare from the High Priest. "Imagine the effect on the crowds, the crocodile on full display, yet posing no danger."

"Sobek has selected a magnificent animal to rule over your bask," Tyema said. "The beast has the rare purple underbelly. It can only benefit your temple to have the people of Thebes behold this marvelous creature, not have him hidden away in a crate."

"Consequences will be on your head if this goes awry, if the beast causes injury," the old priest said, his eyes flashing in anger. He bit his lip and glanced at Pharaoh, seeming to regret his outburst.

Tyema laid a hand on the collar, touching the emeralds. "Where's your faith in Sobek, the god we both serve?"

"Any other concerns?" Pharaoh asked the high priest, his tone mild.

"No, Great One. I'm satisfied with the arrangements," he said, sounding as if he was forcing the words out one by one.

"I'll need to inspect the pond," Tyema said, tapping her fingers on the table as she mentally reviewed her list of requirements. "I'm sure all your arrangements are in order, but I can't bring Sobek's gift to you with all the pomp and ceremony, only to find some problem in front of Pharaoh and the crowds."

Now she thought the old priest was going to have a full-on fit, especially as Pharaoh was nodding agreement with her. "Excellent forethought, Lady Tyema," the ruler said. "Captain Sahure can conduct you and your crocodile keeper to the temple tomorrow morning, leaving the afternoon for any repairs or alterations to be made. On the appointed day, the palace will provide the usual beer, bread and meat for the afternoon feasting after the procession in honor of Sobek. Edekh will see to the distribution." He rose, signaling the end of the meeting, and swept out of the chamber.

Edekh remained, moving closer to Tyema as the high priest came around the table at her. Shaking a finger in her face, the man talked so fast he was spitting. "There's nothing wrong with my temple's pond, girl, and I don't appreciate your trying to embarrass me in front of Pharaoh by suggesting there is."

The priest who'd agreed with Tyema before put a restraining hand on his elder's arm. "I don't think anyone took her words as carrying intent to insult, sir. The lady is being prudent, cautious with the Great One's living gift to us."

"Sobek gave me the responsibility for his crocodile and I don't take it lightly," Tyema said. "I can't."

"Some little nobody from the country, trying to make a place for herself here, no doubt," the High Priest blustered on.

"I've no desire to live here in Thebes. Running my own temple and managing my own concerns keeps me fully engaged," Tyema answered, her voice sharp. She leaned toward him. "I speak directly to the god, to learn his will and desire. Surely you do the same?"

The priest blinked, opened and closed his mouth like a floundering Nile perch, and sat down in the nearest chair, guided by his underling.

"Does he require some water? Or more wine perhaps?" Edekh asked, leaning on his gold-and-lapis staff.

"Either will be helpful, sir," the younger priest answered. He nodded at Tyema. "Since we didn't have time for introductions before Pharaoh arrived, allow me to tell you now I'm Lemertet, second in the hierarchy at the temple. I'll ensure we're ready for your visit in the morning."

"Perhaps it would be best if we withdraw and let them confer," Edekh said tactfully, taking Tyema by the elbow.

"Gentlemen." Tyema nodded at them all and swept out of the room on the Chief Scribe's arm, her head held high. A servant bringing wine passed them, heading toward the chamber.

"Your last arrow was a direct hit, I believe, Lady Tyema," Edekh said in a low voice as they proceeded back to her suite of rooms. "Well done."

"He seems so out of tune with what the Great One prefers," she said.

"Perhaps it's been some time since the god spoke directly to him," Edekh suggested tactfully.

"I hope my crocodile will be properly cared for here." Doubt made her slow her steps and she almost turned, as if to reenter the room they'd just left.

"I'm sure he will be. The temple is well run by all accounts, if not one of the most prominent in Thebes. Lemertet is a strong second in command. He's more than ready to step into the leadership position. Perhaps this series of events will precipitate such an outcome."

"Are you saying the temple here is run by the internal politics of men rather than by what Sobek commands?" Tyema stopped walking, placing her hand on Edekh's arm in her agitation.

The scribe was grave, no trace of amusement on his face. He patted her hand. "I think, Lady Tyema, few priests or priestesses are blessed to have as personal a relationship with their god as you do. In the absence of direct contact, men—and women—can only do what they think best."

"I never thought about it," she said. "I'm so used to the Great One telling me his will."

Edekh leaned even closer, practically speaking into her ear. "Rest assured Pharaoh communicates constantly with the Great Ones. I myself have seen a number of the gods when in Nat-re-Akhte's presence, including your Sobek on one memorable occasion. But the gods can't be everywhere, can't constantly be issuing orders to mankind. We must do our best."

She nodded, satisfied and comforted by his response. They resumed their leisurely stroll to her quarters.

"What will you do with your afternoon?" Edekh asked.

"I need to check on the crocodile but beyond that, I've no idea. Play with my son perhaps." Tyema shrugged. "It's rare for me to have so much time with no duties or responsibilities. Is there anything I should be doing, for Pharaoh or the queen?"

Edekh shook his head. "I was going to suggest you might take the baby to Pharaoh's zoo. Currently we have a good selection of animals. Captain Sahure sent us several shipments while he was in command at the Southern Oasis, once he took control of the place and drove the invaders out. The oasis fort is a crossroads for many caravans and an excellent location for acquiring rare goods. Having been on expeditions to the far lands himself, Sahure knows what animals are best suited to enhance Pharaoh's collection and thus his prestige."

Unable to stop herself, Tyema said, "Is Captain Sahure well thought of by Pharaoh?"

Although plainly curious, Edekh gave a neutral answer rather than ask any questions. "I believe he stands in high regard, yes. But if you'd rather have another escort—"

Tyema laughed. "Thank you, the arrangements are fine. Pharaoh offered me the same alteration yesterday. Sahure and I have things we need to discuss, but there shouldn't be any problems. What about this evening? Pharaoh excused me from attendance at the banquet yesterday, but should I be somewhere this evening? I dread giving offense, even inadvertently."

"There will be a small dinner for some of the courtiers." Edekh patted her hand. "I should warn you, small is a relative term here in Thebes."

She braced herself. "How many guests?"

"Perhaps a hundred. Captain Sahure is expected to escort you to the banquet chamber. Dinner will begin at sunset."

"I'll be ready then, but will he be back in time?" Tyema was comforted by the thought of the pretty dresses the queen had given her. She realized she didn't want to walk around the palace and attend dinners dressed like a person the Thebans would view as a country maid.

"Sahure meets his commitments, never fear."\

***

Many hours later, Tyema could see the sun setting through the archway to the small private garden attached to her quarters. Sahure, prompt as always, was standing by the door to the suite, waiting for her to finish refreshing her eye makeup and kiss the baby goodbye. After giving Renebti a quick hug and some last minute instructions about Seknehure's bath, Tyema found Sahure staring with longing at their son."Did you want to hold the baby for a little while before we go?"

"We can't be late. It's quite a breach of etiquette to enter after Pharaoh."

Tyema picked the baby up and handed him to Sahure, ignoring the faint discomfort from the lotus bracelet, signaling Sahure's exposure to black magic. "Just for a moment. He needs to get to know you."

"True. And we still have to discuss matters." He cast a glance at the niece, as he dandled the baby. Pressing a kiss on the child's forehead, he handed him to Renebti. "We must go."

Tyema allowed Sahure to escort her out of the room and through the confusing halls of the palace. An awkward silence fell between them. Tyema felt her small store of confidence seeping away, the closer they got to the banquet hall.

To distract herself, Tyema studied Sahure in quick, sidelong glances, noting new lines around his eyes. "You seem tired."

"I've had bad dreams since returning from Kharga," he admitted, rubbing a hand over his face.

She touched a curious amulet on his wrist. "I've never seen this before, so unusual. You weren't wearing the token yesterday, were you?"

There was an awkward pause, as if he was deciding how much he wanted to share with her. "Someone gave it to me, while I was in Kharga. She said I needed protection. I inferred at the time I only needed protection at the Southern Oasis, and indeed when I drove my chariot into Thebes, the amulet came untied of its own accord. I barely kept it from being lost in the road." Rubbing his forehead again, Sahure continued. "I put it on again this morning after a night of nightmares worse than any tale of the seven hells the scribes might write. I hope the amulet retains enough power to ward off whatever forces are building during the day to destroy my slumber."

A woman. "Was she beautiful? Did she drive your chariot as well?" Tyema knew her voice was full of sarcasm, but she couldn't seem to stop herself. "Like I did? Do you routinely offer that treat to women you wish to bed?"

Sahure stopped in the middle of the hall, hands on his hips. "What does it matter to you? Why do you care? You rejected my proposal if you'll recall. If I choose to take solace in the arms of a nomad beauty of the desert or the bed of a Theban lady, what business is it of yours?" His voice didn't carry the force of anger, more a tone of curiosity.

Fearful of revealing too much of her intense feelings for him, Tyema retreated a step. "I'm sorry, you're right, it's none of my business."

Footsteps sounded from ahead in the corridor. He took her elbow and urged her to start walking again as a servant bustled past them, carrying an armful of linens. "As it happens," Sahure said as soon as the young servant had gone by, "I received this from the goddess Sekhmet herself."

Shocked, Tyema stopped again. "What have you to do with Sekhmet?"

"Nothing, I would have said, other than the fact the people of Kharga claim to be descended from her. She appeared at the fort one evening, cloaked in disguise as the aged village headwoman till we were alone. She said her sister goddesses were engaged in combat on my behalf and she'd come to help me." Sahure glanced sideways. "I have a feeling now, calculating the age of our child, it must have been the night Seknehure was born, although I don't understand the reference to combat."

I do. Combat with the black magic someone had sent to find me. Did the sorcerer also seek to kill Sahure? Or to influence him? Chewing her lip, Tyema considered the ramifications of Sekhmet's involvement. Yet nothing in his story released her from Sobek's orders to keep her mission a secret. And there were still faint flickers of the magic around Sahure, amulet or no amulet.

"We're nearly there and as I said before, we can't arrive after Pharaoh." Raising one eyebrow, Sahure grinned. "I don't know what you're thinking over with so much intensity, but we need to continue our walk."

"Of course." Hastily Tyema scurried past him, her thoughts whirling. This mission Sobek had sent her on grew more complicated by the hour.

When she walked into the dining hall, the biggest chamber she'd ever seen, already packed with people, Tyema's heart sank.

Maids were stationed inside the door, to give each guest a flower garland. Sahure selected one for her, rejecting the offerings until he located one with red flowers, which he draped around her neck. Wondering what he was thinking, Tyema declined a perfume-scented wax cone for her wig, as did Sahure. The air in the room was close already and she could feel a headache coming on.

"Men and women don't sit together in Thebes, unless married," Sahure said in a low voice. "So I'll escort you to the table you've been placed at, introduce you, and move on to my own companions."

She nodded, trying to push away vertigo, reminding herself she was here for Sobek, to search for black magic, but the thoughts weren't helping under the stress of facing a crowd full of strangers, compounded by the physical assault of the perfume and smoke from the oil lamps. She had to battle a strong desire to spin on her heel and make her way out of the room as fast as she could walk.

Greeting people as they went, always with a joke or a light hearted comment, introducing her to scores of individuals whose names she'd never remember, Sahure escorted her to a table far up the room, flatteringly close to the dais where Pharaoh and the queen would sit when they arrived. Fan bearers stood at intervals along the walls, keeping the air moving, which helped her breathe a bit more easily.

So far, no serious flickers of black magic, not even around Sahure, thank the gods.

The table seemed like her worst nightmare, sixteen laughing and chattering young women who were obviously all old friends and greeted Sahure with cries of pleasure and flirtatious teasing.

"Ladies, you put the stars to shame tonight," he said, bowing. "Allow me to introduce Tyema, High Priestess of Sobek in the Ibis Nome. And these charming ones are numbered among the queen's ladies-in-waiting."

The women called out noisy greetings to her and, eyes locked on the centerpiece on the table to counter her vertigo, Tyema said, "I'm in Thebes to deliver a new crocodile to the temple here."

"Yes, we know, it's the talk of the city," said one girl, who got up and came to Sahure, getting artfully between Tyema and him, pushing her aside with a subtle hip thrust, taking his arm. "So did you give your lady mother that special amulet I found for her?" she asked Sahure.

Smoothly Sahure maneuvered the woman to face Tyema, saying as he did so, "Meet Lady Baufratet. This minx and I grew up together, on neighboring estates."

Tyema bowed her head and Baufratet did the same with a trill of laughter and then resumed her conversation with Sahure as if Tyema didn't exist, telling him how she'd found the amulet in question at the market by the temple of Amun-Re and a number of other irrelevant details, all of which she appeared to find fascinating. Tyema stood awkwardly next to them, completely shut out of the conversation, unsure what to do next, feeling as if all eyes must be on her.

The woman sitting closest to her touched her hand. "I'm Nidiamhet, come sit beside me, Lady Tyema." This girl slid over on the cushioned bench and patted the surface. "Once Baufratet has Sahure's attention, she's oblivious to anyone else. You'll have to forgive her manners, but he was gone from Thebes for a year and they were quite close before he departed for Kharga. We all missed him."

Grateful for any friendly gesture, Tyema did as she was told. Nidiamhet introduced her to the remaining ladies although Tyema knew she wasn't going to remember which name went with which woman. One or two asked her some perfunctory questions about her journey from the regions of the Upper Nile and then the heralds announced the arrival of Pharaoh and the queen. The crowd of courtiers fell silent, rising to show respect.

"We're not required to kneel or kiss the earth at dinner," Nidiamhet whispered to Tyema.

Baufratet came back to the table in a rush, crowding Tyema, forcing her to push Nidiamhet.

Sahure's old friend giggled as she said, "I almost got caught where I shouldn't be, talking to the unmarried men when Pharaoh arrived."

As soon as Nat-re-Akhte and his wife had taken their seats on the elevated dais, food was brought to them and servants carried heaping platters to the tables. Nidiamhet passed Tyema a plate of breads baked in different shapes, garnished with seeds and spice. She stared in amazement at the varieties. Picking one at random, Tyema gave the plate to Baufratet, who was busily chatting to the girl across the table. Next was a heaping platter of beef. Tyema was astounded. In her province cattle were almost never slaughtered for meat and even with her rank, the only times she'd eaten beef were on visits to the nomarch's capital.

"Well, either take some or pass the platter along, don't keep it all for yourself," Baufratet said, leaning on the table with her elbows. "The rest of us are hungry too." Her tone was teasing but Tyema became so nervous at her own display of naïve astonishment, she nearly dropped the heavy serving dish.

More delicacies kept coming, carried in by the steward's indefatigable staff. Though she had little appetite, Tyema made herself eat a few bites, balancing the dizziness of hunger against the fear of suffering public bodily ills from sheer nerves. The girls chattered on about court gossip and left her alone for the most part, although Baufratet had the disconcerting habit of asking her a rapid-fire question out of the blue at unexpected moments, barely listening to whatever answer Tyema stammered out. Musicians set up in an alcove were playing on harps, flutes, and drums, which was pleasant. Music always soothed Tyema when she was anxious. The hum of conversation kept her from fully appreciating the musicians' efforts.

A troupe of dancers performed, followed by a lively gaggle of acrobats. Tyema enjoyed the performances, especially since her companions focused on what was going on in the center of the floor, thus freeing Tyema from any risk of having to make conversation. She wondered when the dinner would end. She was going to need to feed Seknehure at some point. As far as her private mission for Sobek, there was no flicker of black magic anywhere in the vast room she could detect, which was something of a relief.

The girls were indulging freely in the beer and wine as the evening progressed. Their laughter was loud and shrieking and the jokes made no sense to Tyema, containing too many references to people and events of which she had no knowledge. She sat with her hands folded and watched the ever changing entertainment, trying to keep a pleasant expression plastered on her face, praying to Sobek for Pharaoh and the queen to signify the meal was over.

"I have an idea," Baufratet said suddenly, rising from her seat. "Let's toast to the health of Tyema's baby."

Startled, Tyema stared at her. *Where is this coming from?* Surprised by the hostility she felt underlying the girl's outwardly pleasant demeanor, Tyema picked up her clay goblet of beer. "Kind of you to wish my son well." She was dismayed to see the faint flickers of black magic dancing around Baufratet's head and shoulders, barely visible. *Is she the sorceress? Can my task be so easy? Or is she being influenced?*

Sloshing beer over the rim of her cup onto the table as she leaned in close, Baufratet asked, "What's his name again?"

"Seknehure." Shifting away from the spreading pool of beer, Tyema was conscious of an odd silence among the other women at the table. Glancing around she saw they were all watching her and Baufratet. Several of the faces displayed keen enjoyment of the awkward conversation, a few seemed to be pitying her and the others were embarrassed or bored.

The lady in waiting moved closer to Tyema, her breath like a brewery. "And who did you say the father was?"

"Baufratet—" One of the other girls rose to put a hand on her arm, trying to pull her to a sitting position. "People are staring."

"I didn't say," Tyema remarked, straightening her back and staring at the drunken woman. "We can toast my child without a discussion of his father."

Baufratet laughed, taking a gulp from her mug before raising it above her head. She addressed the occupants of the table. "But I think we should know before we make the toast. I heard it might be the Great One Sobek himself."

"Lady Baufratet, are you unwell?" Edekh stood at her elbow, his face set in serious lines. "Do you need to be escorted from the room? Pharaoh has given leave, if necessary."

"No." She drank her beer without toasting and sat down with a plop, leaning on the girl next to her. "I'm fine."

"I'm sure the Great Ones will be relieved to hear it." With a nod, Edekh moved on to speak to someone else.

More dancers flowed into the center of the room, whirling sistrums, and executed a complicated series of steps. Tyema was grateful for the loud music, underscored by the buzzing music of the hand instruments. *That whole exchange with Baufratet was odd. When will this interminable dinner be over?*

Mercifully, after the dance concluded Pharaoh and his wife left the chambers. Tyema gathered people were now free to leave if they wished, although most stayed. She didn't see Sahure in the crowd, which was mingling more, men and women chatting as they ate figs and honeyed dates, and continued drinking. Muttering some excuse no one paid attention to, Tyema left the table and made her way resolutely out of the banquet hall, walking along the perimeter, hoping to stay unnoticed. Peeling the wilting flower garland off her neck just before exiting the room, she dropped the blossoms on the last table in a puddle of wine.

She took a deep breath of the relatively fresh air in the corridor and then, conscious of the watching guards, she retraced her steps to her rooms. The halls were different at night, mostly empty, quiet, lit by torches and oil lamps shedding odd shadows.

"Tyema, wait!" Sahure hastened to catch up with her. "You shouldn't be wandering through the palace alone."

"Sobek protects me wherever I am." Touching her amulet with one hand, Tyema continued to walk.

"I'm sorry you feel you need his protection in the royal palace." He fell into pace with her. "Did you enjoy the dinner? The performers?"

"The food was excellent, as was the entertainment." She kept her answer short, hoping he'd get the hint she had no desire to make more conversation.

But Sahure was persistent. "Were the ladies good company? I know the queen hoped you might find subjects in common with some of her younger companions."

Tyema considered how best to reply. Honesty was her usual tack, but knowing the queen had selected the women especially in hopes of providing her with pleasing company kept her from giving him the full truth. "Lady Nidiamhet was cordial and did her best to include me in the general conversation at the table. We discussed the similarities between writing poetry and writing songs." She shrugged. "The others were fine, much caught up in their own affairs."

"And Baufratet? I'm sorry she was a bit thoughtless, even rude, when we first arrived, but she was so eager to tell me about the special amulet she'd had blessed for my mother. I've known Baufratet since we were children and she never learned to tailor her explanation of the most minute detail of her adventures for a less than enthralled audience."

Shaking her head, Tyema said, "Don't ask me about her behavior unless you want the truth. I know you two are longtime friends." The minute the words had left her lips, Tyema wished she hadn't said them. *But who could blame me for being annoyed when she went out of her way to be annoying, and the scene she created was ridiculous. No doubt she knows perfectly well Sahure and I've been lovers and she's jealous. Of all the ways to pick to embarrass me, that ploy has no teeth whatsoever.*

"Must we walk so fast? I was hoping we could stroll and converse as we used to do on the beach in your province, not race along the hallway like chariot horses." Chuckling, Sahure seemed to be having no difficulty keeping pace with her.

"This is Thebes, as you constantly remind me," she said, bad temper making her words bitter. "Everything is different here."

He reached out one hand and drew her to a stop, pulling her into an alcove between two pillars, where an alabaster statue of the goddess Isis was set on a marble shelf, flanked by small bronze oil lamps. "Even us? Must we be different here?" He pulled her into his arms, regarding her with such intensity, her heart stuttered. "I missed you. I longed to be able to talk to you, to reopen our last conversation in Ibis Nome and try again."

Tyema felt her pulse race and her head swam. Being held so close by Sahure was reawakening her senses, sharpening her desire for him in spite of her best resolves. *I'm not ready. Not to talk and certainly not to resume our love affair on a moment's notice. How can he expect me to be so willing tonight?* Although she hadn't resisted his initial embrace, had even melted into his arms which felt so good around her, now she struggled to get away. Instantly he released her. Stepping into the center of the hall, where torches threw a patch of bright illumination, she said, "It's late, I have a headache and I must nurse Seknehure. He's probably screaming down the walls by now."

Leaning against the column, a half smile on his lips, Sahure said, "Of course. I forget a mother's life is bounded by the demands of a baby."

"You don't need to accompany me. I know the way from here." Hastily, she set out.

Effortlessly he caught up. "Pharaoh commands I accompany you. The command isn't a hardship to obey." His voice was warm.

"We—we go to view the temple pond in the morning," she said, desperate to find a neutral topic. "Early in the morning."

"I know, Edekh told me the schedule. I'll be ready. I'm sure it'll be fascinating to compare this temple of Sobek to the charms of yours. I think the one here will suffer by comparison."

The rest of the walk to her suite was made in silence. Tyema wondered what Sahure was thinking but he offered no clue. Just before they were in earshot of the guards, voice barely above a whisper, he said, "We're going to have to talk, Ema, but I give you my word, not before the dedication ceremony is over, all right?"

Startled, she stared at him.

Ruefully, he put a hand to his forehead. "I probably had too much wine tonight. Being at the Southern Oasis for a year I'd forgotten military issue wine isn't as potent as the vintage, "three-times-good" label stuff Pharaoh serves here in the palace. I apologize if I was too forward just now, rushing you."

She cleared her throat, found her voice. "I think our entire relationship has been too rushed, right from the beginning."

He frowned, eyebrows drawing together in a vee. "Surely you aren't regretting the birth of our son?"

"No, of course not, Seknehure is wonderful and I'm so grateful I—*we*—have been blessed with a strong son."

"I poured my heart out to you, back there in Ibis," Sahure said. "You know me, Tyema. No one else knows me, understands me, the way you do. Rushed or not, you saw the heart of who I am."

She wanted to deny the assertion, but he was right, she did know him. *And I love him, but he still doesn't know me, doesn't know about my past, about my daily afflictions. And there's this question of the black magic.* Shaking her head, she stepped away. "Nothing permanent is possible between us, Sahure, nothing's changed just because Sobek ordered me to visit Thebes. And I can't handle an affair, not again."

At first she thought he wasn't going to say anything. His face was set in stern lines, accented by the ruddy torchlight. "I give you my word not to pressure you on the subject now, as long as you give me your oath we'll have an honest conversation about us. I want your promise you'll set forth in detail what you perceive to be the barriers to our being together, after the dedication, but before you leave Thebes." He raised his hand when she opened her mouth to reply. "You owe me an explanation."

"I promise."

"And we'll discuss our son's future," he added. "We owe him the establishment of an understanding between us."

"Agreed." She fled into her room, shutting the door with so much force that Renebti stared and the baby was startled into crying. Rushing to take her upset son from her yawning niece, Tyema blinked back tears. *Sahure wants a second chance for us, which should make me happy, but all the old obstacles still exist and there may be new ones. I wish Sobek had never sent me here.*

CHAPTER SIX

Hotepre reported to her chambers early next morning, dressed in his best brown cotton tunic, bald head gleaming. A single gold hoop was in his left ear.

"What's this?" Tyema asked, pointing at his earring.

He shuffled his feet a bit. "The zookeeper took me and the boys into Thebes last night. I thought I'd like a souvenir, to remind me of the trip, to have in my tomb for the Afterlife."

"Well, I like it." She drank her pomegranate juice. *This trip is changing all of us to some extent.*

One of the guards posted outside her door knocked, opening the portal at her command to allow Sahure to come striding into the room. He was wearing his dress uniform, the golden falcon badge of his unit gleaming on the broad leather straps across his bare chest, red cape swirling around his calves.

"You remember my crocodile keeper, Hotepre?" Tyema said.

"Of course." The two men shook hands.

"Are you ready, my lady?" Sahure asked, inspecting her as if she was one of his soldiers going on duty.

She felt confident in her new dress from the queen's trunks. "I just need to put on my pectoral with the Tears."

"Good idea." Sahure plucked the gleaming necklace from the tray where it sat waiting, emeralds glinting. He came to her and looped the collar around her neck, standing close behind her as he fastened the leather ties. "This adornment will impress them."

"Or infuriate them all over again." She laughed, stepping away to pick up a light cloak. "I got the distinct impression the high priest wanted to rip this off my neck yesterday and hide it in his temple's coffers."

Sahure took the cape and draped it over her shoulders. "How did your meeting with them go?"

"I thought it was fine. Pharaoh was apparently pleased. The high priest probably had stomach pains the rest of the day. I don't bend where the requirements of the god are being ignored or short changed."

"No, you certainly don't," Sahure said, his voice neutral.

"Must I ride in the litter again today? Is there any chance I can enjoy the freedom of the chariot?" Tyema knew she sounded a little wistful. "I never did obtain a chariot and team for the temple, because of my pregnancy."

He laughed. "Pharaoh has ordered the litter and the fan bearers and the guards to escort you. The whole impressive regalia, as if you were his relative. He continues to do you much honor, which would be a major insult to refuse. Hotepre and I'll be in my chariot." Standing by while she went to the mirror for a final adjustment of her pectoral, he made an offer. "This afternoon, if you like, I'll take you to the chariot manufacturer for Pharaoh's army. You can place an order. I'm sure Pharaoh will authorize it. And we can evaluate the available horses in the herd, see if we can put together a team or two. It's always best to have a backup team. Now that I'm aware you're the high priestess, with piles of deben at your command, there are no further obstacles beyond Pharaoh's permission. All chariots in Egypt are under his purview. You can send the considerable payment to Thebes later, via courier."

"Sobek expects me to take a certain monthly allowance," she said, annoyed at feeling so defensive over her expenditure.

"Aye, but you never do, Lady Tyema," Hotepre chimed in. "High time you indulged yourself a bit for all the hard work you do."

"The subject's settled then," Sahure said, as he escorted her and her crocodile keeper into the maze of palace corridors and eventually out a side door to where the litter and the chariot waited.

Tyema was braced for another unpleasant conversation with the old high priest, but when their small procession arrived at the entrance to the Theban temple of Sobek, Lemertet was waiting, backed by two under priests and a scribe. Bowing, he handed her out of the litter before Sahure could leave his chariot.

Tucking her hand into the crook of his elbow, Lemertet gave her a blinding smile. "I hope you won't mind touring the ponds with me, Lady Tyema. I'm afraid our high priest is indisposed."

"Oh, too bad," she said insincerely. "Stomach pains?"

Biting his lips, the priest only nodded. "But never fear, he'll be well enough to sing tomorrow and take full part in the ceremonies."

"I had no doubt." *He'd never miss his moment of glory, when even Pharaoh will be at his temple!* Tyema introduced Sahure and Hotepre and then they moved into the first temple courtyard, where six gigantic granite statues of Sobek in half human, half crocodile form lined the walkway made of alternating black and white bands of gleaming marble.

"Tomorrow of course we'll proceed around the perimeter of the temple grounds, since there will be crowds," Lemertet said as they walked. "But I thought you'd like to see the entire complex, since you're here."

"Oh yes, I'm most curious." Tyema gestured at the statue she was passing. "We've nothing so monumental at Ta'sobeksef."

"Your temple is scaled to its location, Lady Tyema," Sahure said unexpectedly. "It looks out over the Nile," he explained to Lemertet. "The Great One is said to be fond of walking the beach below the plateau, especially at sunset."

The Theban under priest raised his eyebrows and pursued the subject of Tyema's temple. "I understand your current structure was built on the ruins of an older one? From the days of the earliest pharaohs?"

Tyema nodded. "Correct. While we have no statues on the scale of yours, we do boast some beautiful murals. Similar to those over there, but smaller. So you expect crowds tomorrow then? I've been told repeatedly our deity isn't as highly regarded in Thebes as some."

"Oh yes." Lemertet was all but rubbing his hands together in anticipation. "There's a high level of interest in you, in the crocodile you've brought, in the fact Pharaoh himself plans to attend. Normally such attentions are reserved only for Horus and Amun-Re."

"No doubt your temple's coffers will be swollen with new offerings after this is over," Sahure said.

Lemertet gave him a sharp glance but didn't respond. Struck by a thought, Tyema asked, "How many scribes do you maintain for the temple? I've only the one—"

"One?" Both Lemertet and the scribe following them laughed. "Oh my dear lady, one man couldn't possibly keep up with our administrative needs unless he was the Great One Thoth, scribe to the gods. We have dozens on staff, which is fairly common here in Thebes. Why do you ask?"

"No particular reason." Tyema thought she might talk to Lemertet privately before she left Thebes and see if he would take Jemkhufu on as a transfer. Realizing the man might have dared to intercept the precious letters between herself and Sahure had left her deeply shaken.

After rounding the corner of the temple, Tyema stood still, marveling at the size and beauty of the pond in which the Theban crocodile bask dwelt. It was a veritable lake. Half of the sprawling pond was shaded by acacia trees and palms, while the other half lay open to the sun. A large statue of Sobek in his crocodile form stood on a granite pedestal in the center of the water. She saw a number of crocodiles basking in the warmth on the sandy shore, while others floated in the deep pond. The water was below the slight rise on which she now stood, and the pond was surrounded by a fairly high wall, keeping the denizens safely removed from the onlookers.

"So I'll be releasing the animal from my control here tomorrow?" Tyema asked.

Lemertet nodded. "There'll be a chute for him to slide down into the water, which as you can see is quite deep at this end."

"Seems like a good design," Hotepre said with approval. "Where are the hatching grounds? And the young ones?"

"We keep them in a separate area. Pilgrims often purchase the smaller ones, or the eggs that fail to hatch. If you'll follow me—" Lemertet led them farther into the extensive temple grounds, toward a series of less ornate buildings beyond the pond.

"I never thought about selling the young ones," Tyema said. "We do sell the unfertile eggs, however. I have a temple artist who paints Sobek's cartouche on them, beautifully detailed."

"What do you do with the juveniles you don't need for breeding or temple trade?" Lemertet took her elbow as they moved onto a path of more coarse gravel.

"Release them into the Nile," she said absently. It was fascinating to discuss temple business with another priest, especially one who oversaw such a bustling, prosperous temple. If this complex was one of the minor houses of worship in Thebes, what must the temple of Amun-Ra be like? "I'll want to chant a short farewell and blessing to Sobek's gift, before I leave the grounds tomorrow."

"Appropriate." Lemertet nodded his approval of the plan. "Then we'll all move into the temple for prayer and the ceremony will be concluded. The public can remain outside, by the pond."

"I'll be accompanying Lady Tyema," Sahure said from his position walking close behind them.

"Surely not into the temple? Aren't you sworn to Horus?" Lemertet was startled.

"As is Pharaoh, but he'll enter the outer sanctuary," Sahure reminded him. "I'm assigned to guard Lady Tyema while she's here in Thebes. Not that she'd come to any harm in a place dedicated to Sobek."

"I don't know, yesterday when the high priest was accusing you of trying to take over his job, my lady, I was happy he had no weapon to hand," Lemertet said with a chuckle. "The older he gets, the more violent his temper becomes."

In response to Sahure's instant, sharp glance, Tyema shook her head. "It was harmless enough. I've no desire to live here in Thebes. My place is in Ta'sobeksef."

"As you constantly remind us," he said.

He's never going to get over my rejection of his proposal, is he? Tyema allowed Sahure's remark to go unchallenged.

The rest of the tour was uneventful. Tyema and Hotepre were both more than satisfied with the accommodations for the crocodile they were chaperoning.

Lemertet served Tyema and Sahure a small luncheon on a private patio overlooking the crocodile pond, while Hotepre ate with the temple's animal keepers.

After a cordial parting from Lemertet when the simple meal was concluded, Tyema walked to the waiting chariot and litter. She allowed herself to be handed into the litter and her small procession headed to the palace. Leaning against the cushions, she fanned herself, even though the royal fan bearers walking on either side of the litter were doing their best against the rising heat. She closed her eyes for a long moment, thinking about tomorrow and the procession. She'd never been involved in anything as grandiose as this promised to be. Even the dedication of Sobek's new temple back in Ta'sobeksef hadn't been so huge. Yes, the nomarch and his court had attended and there'd been songs and ceremonies, but not with Pharaoh and half of Thebes in the audience.

And there I'll be, the priestess from the rural nome. She sighed. Well, this was all in Sobek's service and at his command, so she'd be fine. The crocodile would obey her, she never forgot her songs, the god would support her. Knowing all the things she had to do after the religious ceremonies was causing her chest to tighten and her head to spin. Tracking down the practitioner of black magic among hundreds of people at Court was going to be daunting. *And what if Sahure is involved?*

***

Her chambers were empty. "Do you know where my niece has taken my son?" Tyema asked the guards at the entrance to her suite.

"I believe they went to the gardens by the fountain, my lady."

"Let me escort you," Sahure said. "I wish to see my son again."

When Tyema walked out of the palace into the edge of the specified garden, she was surprised and displeased to find her baby being passed from hand to hand among a group of younger ladies of the court, while her niece and Jemkhufu sat deep in conversation with the Thebans. Her scribe was chatting with Lady Baufratet of all people. Tyema was amazed and suspicious the haughty young noblewoman would condescend to talk to a scribe. The lotus bracelet tightened around her wrist and Tyema saw the dark purple flickers of black magic's influence around Baufratet and Nidiamhet. *Victims? Or is one of them the magician? Hard to imagine.* She tried to eye Sahure without blatantly staring and was relieved to see no flickers. This time.

"Good afternoon, everyone," Sahure said as he and Tyema came closer to the group.

"How long has he been out here?" Tyema asked Renebti, as she went to take Seknehure from Nidiamhet.

"Oh don't be angry with your niece," Baufratet said with a laugh, breaking off her conversation with Jemkhufu. "The queen told us about your darling baby earlier today and we just had to come see for ourselves, right, girls?"

A chorus of voices agreed with her. Nidiamhet handed the boy to Tyema, saying, "I think he likes me." She patted Seknehure's rosy cheek. "He's so well behaved. Such gorgeous brown eyes."

"Thank you." Tyema was fuming, extremely annoyed her child had been taken from the safety of her guarded chambers and passed around like a doll to women she didn't know, two of whom were touched in some way by the black magic, although she couldn't explain her specific concern to anyone, not even her niece. Queen Ashayet was one thing, these women quite another. "He should be napping by now. He'll be cranky tonight."

Shifting from one foot to the other, her niece was ill at ease. "I'm sorry, Aunt Tyema. I didn't realize how much time had passed."

Coming to link her arm in Sahure's, Baufratet toyed with his golden falcon badge, allowing her hand to stray across his bare chest in a possessive caress. "If you're done escorting Lady Tyema for the day, I think you owe me a chariot ride, the one I won from you at senet last week?"

Tyema felt a flash of angry jealousy go through her like a wave of fire. *He takes her in his chariot? Just another of his seduction tactics? How foolish I was, thinking myself so special. Can I trust anything he tells me?*

Sahure shot her a glance, removing Baufratet's fingers from his person. "I told you as we played the game, a drive in my war chariot was an inappropriate thing to wager for, if you'll recall."

Another lady in waiting whose name Tyema couldn't recall chimed in on the topic. "Sahure never lets any woman ride in his chariot, you know that, Baufratet. None of the charioteers do. It's not allowed."

Placing her hand on Sahure's arm once more, his childhood friend pouted prettily, the red ocher on her plump lips calling attention to the perfection of her face. "I thought you'd make an exception for me. Well then, if you're going to be so stubborn and proper, I'll accept a stroll along the Nile, here in Pharaoh's garden."

"Don't linger on my account," Tyema said, although her heart was lightened by the information that only she had been invited into Sahure's chariot and equally pleasing was the knowledge he'd taught her to drive. "We'll be returning to my suite for the rest of the afternoon."

"We'll see you at dinner?" Nidiamhet asked.

The thought of another interminable meal with the courtiers was suddenly overwhelming to Tyema. "No," she said, reaching a sudden decision and feeling much better as she did so. "I must pray in solitude this evening, offer my thoughts to the god in preparation for his blessing on the procession and ceremonies tomorrow." *Hopefully Sobek can forgive one lie from me. I swear to dedicate all my time to finding the sorcerer after the day of the procession, no matter what it takes. And then I can go home.*

"Can you find your way back to your rooms?" Sahure asked, resisting Baufratet's tug at his arm.

"Of course I can, I'm not a child." Instantly Tyema regretted her undignified flash of temper.

Someone giggled. Nidiamhet raised her eyebrows but smoothed her expression when she saw Tyema glance at her. Sahure shrugged, lowering his head to listen to whatever Baufratet wished to say to him.

Tyema made herself walk slowly up the flight of broad stairs to the palace, holding her son close and nuzzling his hair, breathing in his sweet baby scent. Her niece and the scribe came behind her.

"There were some messages today, from the temple, sent by carrier pigeon," Jemkhufu said. He fumbled with his leather satchel. "I've got the most urgent ones right here."

"Not now," Tyema answered.

Renebti pulled at her arm. "I'm sorry if you're displeased, Aunt. The women came to our rooms after lunch, laughing and chattering and demanding to see the baby. Lady Baufratet said the queen had been talking about how sweet he was—"

"My son is *not* to be taken out of our rooms again, unless I've given my permission, do I make myself clear?"

"Of course, Aunt." Her niece bit her lip, unshed tears making her eyes shine. Wrapped in her anger, Tyema was beyond worrying about Renebti's feelings.

She was crisper than usual with her scribe. "The day after tomorrow, we can talk about these messages and any other temple business. I'll ask Edekh to set aside an office for us to use at midmorning."

"Will you need me tomorrow?" he asked.

She shook her head. Feeling a bit guilty, she said, "I hope they're taking good care of you, as far as lodgings?"

He nodded. "The surroundings are grand here, quite congenial. A man could get spoiled."

"I'm glad you like it in Thebes." *Since I may try to get you transferred to the temple here and not have you return to Ta'sobeksef with us.* Perhaps she was being unfair; she knew she needed to give Jemkhufu a chance to answer Sahure's charges regarding interference with their mail, but in her heart she knew Sahure was right. And trust, once broken, was impossible to restore.

Leaving the scribe to find his own way wherever he'd been assigned a room, Tyema and Renebti walked to their suite. As she sank down on the bed and opened her dress to allow the baby to nurse, Tyema closed her eyes and leaned back, suddenly exhausted. Her arms and legs felt as if they'd turned to marble and it was an effort to stay awake.

"I'm sorry to have upset you," her niece said, wringing her hands. "I didn't know how to refuse their request to take him outside. The Court ladies are so arrogant and self assured, and they serve the queen. I didn't want to cause trouble."

"It's all right, I hadn't thought to tell you I didn't want him in company." Tyema patted the side of the bed with her free hand. "Come, sit, tell me how the conversation went with your high born companions."

Bringing her a cup of water, Renebti had her brow furrowed in thought. "Most of them admired the baby, wanted to play with him, especially Lady Nidiamhet. Lady Baufratet asked a lot of questions about you, who the baby's father is, about Lord Sahure's time in our nome. I told her I didn't know anything about his visit. I certainly never met him."

"Good. We have gossips like her at home," Tyema said, striving for a light tone, although she wasn't at all pleased to know the woman tried to wheedle personal information out of her unsophisticated niece. "The less a nosy woman knows, the better."

"Well, she stopped pestering me and started batting her eyes at your scribe after that," Renebti said with palpable satisfaction.

And what did he tell her, I wonder? If she's the sorceress, she might have been able to loosen his tongue. But no, apparently she didn't try any spells on Renebti. Probably just batted those malachite-and-kohl rimmed eyes at my scribe and got him to reveal anything she asked. Wishing she had a better knowledge of how black magic was wielded, Tyema dropped a kiss on Seknehure's cheek. She blew kisses on his tummy, much to his chortling delight. Half her thoughts were of Jemkhufu, more than ever convinced he'd served his last day as scribe of her temple.

***

"Are you ready for this?" Sahure asked as he entered her chamber bright and early the next morning.

Tyema swallowed hard and nodded. "As ready as I can be, with nothing to compare the experience to. After the planning meeting day before yesterday with Pharaoh, I'm sure our little celebrations back in Ta'sobeksef don't begin to compare to what's going to happen."

He nodded but allowed the comment to pass. "How's your voice today? Ready to sing?"

She shrugged. "Yes, I practiced in the garden for a short time, at dawn, asking Sobek to bless the day and make the crocodile obey my will. The animals always do, but today would be an especially bad time for the gift to leave me."

He stepped aside so Renebti and one of the queen's own maids, on loan to Tyema for the morning, could adjust her wig and place the golden sun orb and plumes on her head. Tyema stood still under their ministrations. "I'm only sorry I had to wear the ceremonial dress through Thebes on the first day," she said. "I'm sure the other celebrants will be much more gloriously attired, and I feel I'm not going to do enough to honor Sobek."

"I've brought you something to address the issue." Sahure gestured for the servant who had followed him into the room to come forward.

The man placed a large black-and-red woven basket on the table close to Tyema and stepped back.

Puzzled but intrigued, she looked from Sahure to the basket, puzzled. "For me?"

He nodded.

She walked carefully to the table, so as not to disturb her headdress, and lifted the cover from the basket, gasping as she saw what was inside. "Wherever did you get such a marvel?" she asked, lifting a shimmering cloak from the container and allowing the folds to fall open. The cloak was a rich, dark blue in color, made of some sturdy fabric she didn't recognize. Iridescent feathers had been sewn in a collar at the neckline and in a deep border at the hem. The unadorned areas of fabric were worked with gold thread in a pattern repeating the natural shape of the green, aqua and dark purple feathers. Still clutching the cloak, she said, "It's amazing."

"I rescued some prisoners from the enemy when we retook the oasis. As it happened, they were kidnapped royalty from a tribe dwelling far south of the Nile's birthplace." Sahure took the cloak from her and draped it over her shoulders, where the fabric, gold thread, and feathers gleamed in the morning light, seeming to glow. He fastened the golden bracelets attached to the cloak at her wrists and upper arms, creating a dramatic silhouette. "Their king was so grateful to have his son and the others arrive home unharmed, he sent me this cloak as a gift. Couriers delivered the basket to me at the oasis just before I was summoned back to Thebes so I brought the cloak home, hoping I might have a chance to present it to you. I'd left it at my family's estate outside the city, with the rest of my gear and belongings. My errand yesterday was driving out to fetch this so you could have it today. You like it?"

"I've never seen anything so gorgeous." Tyema rubbed her chin on the downy soft feathers at the neckline and stroked along the grain of the rows of larger feathers ornamenting the opening of the cloak. "But should I have it? Should it perhaps have gone to the queen?"

Sahure leaned close, so only she could hear his words. "The gift was to me, personally, not to Egypt. And I'll give it to you or no one."

Blinking back tears, afraid to ruin her elegant eye makeup, she said, "Sobek isn't a god of the sky."

"But you sing like a bird on his behalf," Sahure answered.

"It's so beautiful, Aunt Ema," her niece said, touching the feathers delicately.

Tyema kissed Sahure lightly on the cheek and squeezed his hand. "Thank you."

He just nodded, stepping aside to let her precede him. "We'd better go. It won't do for you to arrive after Pharaoh."

"Oh no," she said with a gasp, speeding up her pace.

"I was teasing." He laughed, slowing her down again. "Edekh will ensure Pharaoh doesn't appear until the entire procession is in readiness, don't worry. He's the master of protocol and excels at the task, as he does with everything in his purview."

The procession was lined up alongside the palace, partly, Tyema supposed, because she had to bring the crocodile from the pond and get him to climb onto his litter. As Sahure escorted her along the line of marchers, she was impressed at how orderly and matter of fact the marchers were. The acrobats behind the heralds who led off the parade were doing flips and tumbles to warm up and she watched with delight as a truly spectacular series of tumbling runs played out.

"The temples must do processions often in Thebes," she said. "I sense little excitement among the celebrants and performers."

"Indeed, there are always parades for one thing or another," he agreed.

She bowed her head to acknowledge a polite greeting from Lemertet as she walked by the delegation from Sobek's Theban temple. Visibly grinding his teeth as he sat in his gilded chair beside Lemertet, the florid-faced High Priest stared at her.

"Jealous of your finery, no doubt," Sahure said as they paced farther, past the huge effigy of Sobek, ensconced in a cunningly fabricated "boat" of reeds, and then edged around more dancers, busy limbering up.

"Thanks to you. I'd have made a poor showing in the midst of all this glory on my own." Tyema took a deep breath, trying to calm the butterflies in her stomach. *Once the procession begins, I'll be fine. This day is all in honor of the god.*

Sahure stopped and swung her to face him. "You shine wherever you are, Ema. Never doubt that. My gift only frames your loveliness. And you're here for Sobek. "

For an aching moment she wanted him to kiss her, to let her take comfort in his strong arms, no matter if they were in public, but then a horse whinnied, breaking the spell. Tyema resumed her stately pace to the crocodile pond.

"Where do they get all these people? Surely the temple of Sobek can't have such a large staff, not even in Thebes?" she asked after walking by a third troupe of voluptuous dancing women, accompanied by musicians with drums, pipes and small harps.

"Indeed not." Sahure laughed. "Most are hired for the occasion. At other times they work in the taverns or at the marketplace. Besides the musicians and heralds who serve Pharaoh, almost everyone you see in the procession who isn't a priest is here for the deben the temple will dispense later."

"How odd."

"Not when you think about it. There are many temples here in the capital and a large number of festivals and occasions where pharaoh and other Great Ones must be honored. No one temple could afford to keep this many people on staff. Although some, like the temple of Amun-Re, do have their own company of dancers and keep a high priestess of the dance and a captain of musicians. But even the largest temple hires on additional women to perform for the major festivals."

Tyema took a deep breath of the morning air. "I can smell the meats being roasted."

"Pharaoh has authorized quite a feast for the people, later today. Gazelle, ibis, oryx, ducks, many kinds of bread, beer will flow like rivers," Sahure said. "Can you smell the myrrh in the air as well? The priests from the temple will have been adding it to the sacred incense burning on the temple's braziers since dawn."

"Indeed." Tyema enjoyed the scented air. "These smells are much better than some of the odors assaulting my nose the day we came through Thebes to arrive at the palace."

Sahure shrugged. "I can admit a big city has its drawbacks as well as its pleasures."

When they reached the pond, Hotepre and his men were waiting, accompanied by the palace zookeeper.

"They make a fuss over accepting their new crocodile, don't they, my lady?" Hotepre said with a grin.

Although she felt a pang of regret for not thinking of it herself, Tyema was glad to see someone— probably the tireless Edekh—had outfitted him in a new kilt and tunic, blue with red trim, and a *nemes* to match. He even had new sandals.

"Our crocodile is worthy of such attention," she said. "Shall we get him out of the pond and onto his litter?"

She was only vaguely conscious of all the bystanders as she, Hotepre and the zookeeper went to the pond, to open the gate. Unsurprisingly the crocodile was waiting close by, lounging in the morning sunlight.

"Are you ready?" she said to the creature.

He yawned, displaying a mouth full of jagged teeth, as if to say he wasn't overly impressed by all the fuss and might prefer to nap, but he did walk forward, past her. Gazing from side to side as he went, the crocodile clambered onto the litter, which had been set down in the middle of the road. He struck a pose.

"He's standing exactly like the statue of Sobek in crocodile form the priests will carry ahead of you in the parade," Sahure laughed. "Did you tell the beast to adopt the matching stance?"

She shook her head. "No, perhaps the god is giving him orders directly, as well as through me."

"And you're sure the animal will stay still during the parade?" the zookeeper asked her.

Tyema nodded. "He's obedient to my will because the Great One Sobek desires things to be done in such fashion today. The crocodile won't stir till I release him to his new pond."

She was to sit in a gilded chair at the back of the litter, visible to all, yet close to her animal. Sahure handed her into the chair, arranging the magnificent cloak in graceful swirls around her. The iridescent feathers shone in the sunlight.

"Pharaoh comes," he said.

While all the time maintaining her concentration on the mental leash she held on the crocodile, Tyema had to see.

Nat-re-Akhte wore the double crown of Egypt today, and carried the cobalt blue-and-gold crook and flail of power. His kilt was fine linen, pleated, tinted with gold, tied with the elaborate red sash. A leopard skin was draped across one side of the kilt. He wore the magnificent pectoral depicting Horus the Falcon on his chest, gold, coral and turquoise gleaming in the sun. Pharaoh's cloak was red, trimmed in gold and bearing his cartouche skillfully embroidered, guarded by a falcon on one side and the cobra on the other. The ceremonial braided beard adorned his chin today, although normally he was clean shaven, like most of his male subjects. It was almost painful to behold Pharaoh in all his glory. As he walked along the line of marchers, people knelt and genuflected.

Tyema's heart beat faster at the honor of participating in a procession with Pharaoh. *My astounding new cloak might be beautiful, but mere feathers can't outshine a living Great One.*

Paying the crocodile no heed, Nat-re-Akhte stopped for a moment beside her chair. "Are you ready for this, Lady Tyema?"

"Indeed, my lord. It's all so much grander than I'd imagined, but the procession pays proper tribute to Sobek. Thank you." She knew if Pharaoh hadn't taken a personal interest in this ceremony, things would have been done on a much lesser scale.

He nodded. "An outstanding cloak, my dear, quite unusual. The priests of the Theban temples will have yet another reason to feel cast into the shade. And so they should." He didn't wait for an answer but walked to his own chair, separated from hers by heralds and standard bearers with the insignia of the Nomes of Egypt, the one for Nat-re-Akhte's home province being foremost. The back of his chair was a glorious gilded rendition of the sun rising over the Nile. Uncut rubies set at the tip of each ray sparkled in the real sun as it rose higher. Six fan bearers took up position on either side of him as the burly litter bearers raised the chair high. In front of him soldiers stood ready to march, carrying his gold encrusted bow, shield and sword, accompanied by two handlers with Pharaoh's snarling hunting leopards on leashes. Behind him was another miniature boat, elaborately constructed and painted, bearing an effigy of the god Horus, Pharaoh's personal sponsor among the Great Ones. Depicted in falcon form, the statue was taller than a man, wings outspread, decorated in vibrant multicolored enamel and blue faience, with the head gold plated. Gleaming eyes, one a diamond and the other a yellow stone she couldn't name, gazed upon the scene. Tyema knew Horus and Sobek maintained a friendly rivalry, so she could find no fault with the parade concluding on a tribute to Horus.

Pharaoh must have made some sign she missed because suddenly her litter was raised into the air. Tyema clutched the arms of her chair as the eighteen men carrying her and the crocodile adjusted their hold on the ebony poles to achieve maximum stability. She glanced at Sahure for reassurance and he grinned, giving her a raised thumb of support. Far ahead, at the beginning of the procession, she heard the blare of trumpets. From her new position, supported on the shoulders of the massive litter bearers, three men at each corner and on both sides in the middle, she could see movement in the ranks of marchers. She took a deep breath, knowing she had to stay calm to play her part in this pageant, and more importantly, to ensure the crocodile played his. So far the animal stayed locked in his regal pose, watching his surroundings with the deceptively lazy demeanor of his kind. The litter bearers closest to him exuded almost palpable fear, and she wished she'd had time to reassure the men the crocodile was firmly under her control.

Music began, a somber march supported by the rhythmic pounding of drums and then a moment later, her litter was in motion. As she was carried through the gates of the palace road onto the wide street, the roar of the assembled crowd made her blink. The roadway was lined with excited, expectant people, at least ten deep, come to see the parade and marvel. Tyema stared straight ahead as she'd been instructed by Edekh, although it seemed wrong not to acknowledge the people who'd come to watch. The cheers for Pharaoh were deafening. Nat-re-Akhte was a popular ruler, much beloved. She glanced back once, and saw him sitting straight and unsmiling, the picture of a Great One come to life. She was glad she'd met him in private prior to today, knew what a kind and thoughtful person he was, despite wearing the Two Crowns and being a god walking the earth.

The procession wove through Thebes along the path they'd all agreed to, passing the large temples of other Great Ones and coming to a halt in front of the somewhat less impressive building that was Sobek's. As she arrived at the temple,

Tyema saw the marchers who'd gone before her had dispersed to prearranged places beside the building, along the towering pillars inscribed with hieroglyphics extolling the powers of Sobek or in the square in front of the main entrance. Sobek's cadre of priests had also regrouped, waiting to greet her.

Pharaoh was carried past her, directly to the stairs, which he alone ascended, so he stood above the crowd. His guards, heralds and attendants fanned out along the steps below him, creating a gorgeous pageantry, which drew the eye upward to the magnificence of Egypt's ruler.

Pharaoh raised his arms, nodding his head solemnly to the four corners of the compass, showing the crowd the crook and flail. The cheering cut off abruptly in response to his unspoken command and Tyema heard people whispering as they jockeyed to get a better view, waiting to see what would happen next.

"People of Thebes, it pleases us to welcome the gift of Sobek to this, his temple," Nat-re-Akhte said, projecting his voice to the crowd. He pointed the flail at Tyema, her cue to rise and sing.

Lost in the emotion of the moment, Tyema took a deep breath and launched into the song she'd insisted upon, an old and beautiful hymn to Sobek. She hoped her voice carried to the entire audience but all she could do was honor the god with the strength of her performance and other worries fell away. The applause when she finished was startling to her, but she supposed it must be the Theban custom.

The First Priest answered her song with one of his own, starting the verse in his own rather reedy voice and then being drowned out by the strong baritone chorus of his under priests, who stood ranked behind him. Lemertet sang the solo.

Pharaoh ascended the stairs and disappeared alone into the temple. Tyema knew he was going to join them at the pond. She sat down so her litter bearers could carry her and the still quiescent crocodile to their final destination of the morning. A much reduced set of marchers accompanied her around the side of the temple, through the gardens, to the pond, followed by an orderly crowd of Theban citizens. She'd been told a line of guards would cut off access once a certain number of lucky commoners had been admitted to the pool area.

Pharaoh was waiting, seated on his golden chair, held aloft by the seemingly tireless litter bearers.

As soon as the Theban priests took their places, Tyema's bearers set her platform down with barely a thump. She descended from her perch, aided by Sahure, and mentally commanded the crocodile to accompany her to the edge of the pond, where the gate had been opened. He walked briskly, long tail sinuously weaving as he went. Hotepre fell in behind her, marching proudly. When they reached the pond, the crocodile suddenly spun, rose to his full height on stubby legs, showing off his rare purple underside, and bellowed.

Tyema sensed the people behind her falling back in fright, but Sahure stayed close, hand on the hilt of his sword. Hotepre laid a restraining hand on his arm. Tyema stepped forward, spread her hands in a calming gesture and addressed the crocodile. "Be welcomed to your new home, child of Sobek, and dwell here in peace for many years as ruler of this bask." She sent the animal a firm thought of command, to enter the pond.

For the space of several heartbeats the crocodile stared at her, its yellow eyes gleaming. No one moved, the crowd was hushed. Tyema felt no fear, knowing herself secure in Sobek's grace and protected from attack. She just had to persuade this suddenly stubborn animal to go where she wanted him to be. Pointing at the pond with one hand and cupping the other over the largest emerald in her ceremonial pectoral, Tyema sent Sobek a mental plea for assistance. Thunder rumbled above in the clear sky and the waters of the pond trembled, waves racing across its previously undisturbed surface. A blaze of green sparks from the emerald under her hand cascaded down her other arm like liquid lightning and flew to outline the crocodile as another thunderclap split the air. Still ablaze with the illusion of green flames sent by Sobek, the crocodile moved in a rapid circle, demonstrating how fast he could be if he so desired, eliciting screams and gasps from the crowd. He slid and slithered down the embankment, diving into the pond with a small splash.

Temple workers hurriedly closed the gate.

Tyema felt drained. Her knees seemed to have turned to water. Sahure stepped forward and put his arm around her, guiding her back to the chair on the litter. Dimly she heard the Theban priests chanting a benediction, but she was too worn out from the excitement, the effort of controlling the beast and the singing, to pay attention. She sat in the chair, which had been moved into the shade, and did her best to look as if she was properly attentive to the conclusion of the ceremonies. Sahure made sure the fan bearers stayed with her to keep a constant breeze flowing. All thought of singing any more chants herself had fled. Thankfully Lemertet concluded the ceremony without making any requests of her, only giving a graceful speech directed at her, in appreciation for her conducting the crocodile to Thebes.

"Pharaoh has departed so now we can depart as well," Sahure said eventually. "Are you well enough to be taken to the palace in this litter? Do you need some wine to restore your strength first?"

"I should take my proper leave of the priests," she said, hearing how thready her voice was.

He put a hand on her shoulder. "Stay here. I'll bring Lemertet to you."

"I think serving as the channel for Sobek's power, to send the crocodile into the pond, wore me out." Tyema tried to breathe deeply. "No ceremony has ever affected me so deeply before."

"It was a spectacular effect," Sahure agreed. "Hotepre, stay close to your priestess while I fetch Lemertet."

He strode off, easily making his way through the thinning crowd of spectators and soon brought the jubilant under priest to speak with Tyema.

"This has been a once in a century day for our temple, thanks to you and your crocodile," he said to Tyema, clasping her hand and kissing her cheek. "The offerings and sacrifices today have been unprecedented."

"I'm glad we honored the god properly." Tyema was a bit taken aback at so much discussion of the financial gain for the temple's coffers.

"Of course, of course, and the song you insisted on was absolutely the right way to begin the ceremony here at the temple, quite a thrill for the crowd to hear one of the traditional paeans," Lemertet said smoothly. "Will you stay for the feast?"

"Lady Tyema is expected at the palace." Sahure's voice was firm. He gestured to the eight waiting litter bearers and they took their places, preparing to lift her chair. The rest of the "barge" on which she and the crocodile had ridden had been taken away earlier, leaving only the special chair and a reduced contingent of men to carry her.

"Will we see you again before you depart Thebes?" Lemertet asked.

"In a few days perhaps. I'd like to come and see how the crocodile does," she said.

"Any time." The priest waved as she was carried away.

"Must we travel through the streets of the city?" she asked Sahure, dreading the idea of being a spectacle again.

"No, we'll be taking side roads to the palace." He leaned closer, tucking the cloak around her more efficiently. "Retracing our steps in the open would tend to lessen the drama of the earlier procession. And the feasting will be going on, which can get rowdy, out here in the city."

CHAPTER SEVEN

Tyema had been left in peace the night of the procession, not expected to appear at any functions, going to bed early and sleeping soundly. In the morning she found herself well rested physically, but her mind was in a whirl. As she lay in bed, watching the pearlescent early sun creeping into her room, she pondered how to best begin the second half of her task, searching for the sorcerer. She hadn't the slightest notion where to begin and there's no one she could ask for guidance. *I refuse to believe Sahure is the one. Yet other than him, I've seen only a few people touched by the flares of the evil so far, and they're an odd assortment. Ladies of the court, a servant or two—how will I know who's at the center of the web? Maybe today is the right time for my first visit to the royal library.* Sighing, she rose to pluck Seknehure out of his cradle, since he was awake, making funny little noises, working himself up to announcing his hunger with his usual roar.

After a leisurely breakfast with Renebti, who assured her aunt she was enjoying the visit to Thebes, even if she was taking care of the baby most of the time, Tyema dressed in another of her new garments. She asked the servant outside the door to show her to the office Edekh was lending her for the meeting with Jemkhufu. Although not anticipating the encounter with any pleasure, she felt prepared, taking refuge in her high priestess role and drawing strength from acting on behalf of Sobek.

When she walked into the room she'd been given, Tyema was relieved to find herself alone. Awkward indeed if he'd arrived first and taken charge of the meeting. She took a seat behind the black lacquered table with gilded edges and falcon heads at the corners and toyed with the blank slate and sharpened reed pens which had been placed there in a small green basket. After a perfunctory knock at the half-open door, Jemkhufu sauntered in.

Tyema was astounded to see faint flares of the black magic in the air around her scribe. *I know he's not the sorcerer, but how in the name of Sobek has the evildoer managed to seek out my scribe? And why?*

"Good morning, my lady." Jemkhufu bowed and set his scribe's bag on the floor beside the table. With one hand he snagged the other chair in the room, arranging it so he could sit opposite Tyema. "I've brought the notes we've received from our temple."

"Unless your bag contains the letters I wrote to Lord Sahure and the ones he sent to me, don't bother unpacking the contents," she said.

Jemkhufu paused in the act of bending over and slowly straightened. All the color drained from his face as he opened his mouth to speak but she held up her hand.

"Don't waste my time with more lies. Pharaoh's Chief Scribe verified a total of three letters were forwarded to me from Sahure, after the initial one I received. You were in charge of all the temple's correspondence, so I have to assume you intercepted them. And never mailed mine. I want to know why you betrayed my trust?"

He swallowed hard. "My lady, I thought it for the best. You were so upset after the captain left Ibis Nome, and the first letter from him didn't seem to comfort you. It was obvious he was never going to set foot in Ibis again, never going to honor his responsibilities. I hated to see you hurt, hoping for something an arrogant noble from Thebes could never give." Jemkhufu rose from his chair and came around the table, reaching for her.

Alarmed, Tyema left her seat and backed away until she was at the wall. "Beware, scribe, Sobek protects me, even now, here in Thebes."

"I'd never harm you, how can such thoughts fly into your mind?" He frowned. "You mean more to me than anyone else in this world. Since I joined the temple I've sought to take care of you, and of the businesses you oversee. My only desire in this life is to continue in my role, running the temple's various enterprises, providing assistance and guidance to you on raising your son. I hope someday we can mean even more to each other, if you'll just—"

Disgust was a sour taste in the back of Tyema's throat as she realized she'd put up with him for much too long in her desire to avoid unpleasantries. She had one final question she very much wanted the answer to, before severing his ties with her temple. "Did you destroy our letters, mine and Sahure's?"

He nodded. "Unread, I swear to you."

"As if that makes the breach of trust any better," she said. "As of this moment you're no longer affiliated with the temple of Sobek in Ibis Nome, and I can't in good conscience recommend you to the temple here, or anywhere else, given what you've done."

Blinking, mouth falling open to reveal his crooked teeth, Jemkhufu retreated one step. "You—you can't do without me, what are you saying? You can't run the schools, conduct the cattle tally, you can't even step outside the temple compound walls without falling ill. Someone as weak and frail as you needs a man like me at her side. Don't let this warrior come between us, don't be overawed by his standing in Thebes. When we go home—"

"How dare you speak of me in such terms? I can see I've been lenient about your attitude for much too long, if your delusions run along these lines." White hot with fury over Jemkhufu alluding to her physical challenges, distressed she hadn't managed to conceal them from him, Tyema drew herself up and shook her finger at him. "You won't be journeying to Ibis Nome, not on my ship or any other way. I'll have the nomarch issue a writ of banishment from the province. Now get out and leave Sobek's property behind with me."

His face changed, lines of worry smoothing out, smile playing on his lips, a cunning glint creeping into his eyes. "You might not want to make threats against me, I know things about you other people might be interested in."

Appalled at the shift in his demeanor, Tyema felt her chest constrict. "And now you threaten me?"

"You need me more than I need employment at your rural, insignificant temple," he said. "I've made some connections, have better prospects already here in Thebes. Tread carefully with your high and mighty attitude, my lady."

"Issuing threats to a high priestess? A guest in Pharaoh's palace?" Sahure and Edekh stood in the doorway and it was the former who'd spoken, hand on the hilt of his dagger.

Tension easing, Tyema counted to ten and took a deep breath of relief. *If I'd had to appeal to Sobek to intervene to protect me from physical assault, who knows what might have happened? The Great One is never subtle in his approach to such things.* Remembering the scene years ago as he'd destroyed the Hyksos ships and killed the Hyksos commander in front of her when she was a child, Tyema grew dizzy.

Sahure was at her side, having shoved past the scribe. He put his arm around her waist. "Are you all right?"

Straightening her spine, but not pushing him away, she nodded. Wishing her mouth hadn't gone so dry from the stress of this meeting, she said, "Indeed. I've just relieved this untrustworthy scribe of all his duties and cut him from the temple staff."

"So he did intercept our letters?" Jaw clenched, Sahure glared at Jemkhufu.

Now Edekh spoke. "Tampering with mail sent under the seal of the Great Royal Wife is a crime punishable by death. Captain Sahure's letters were forwarded to Lady Tyema by Queen Ashayet's express command."

Angry as she was, Tyema didn't wish for Jemkhufu's execution. *I saw too much death as a child, during the Hyksos invasion.* "Please, I just want him out of my sight, exiled, not dead."

"You're too kind." Sahure's comment was virtually a growl. "He doesn't deserve mercy."

"He gave the temple many years of excellent service. I should have realized his expectations had grown unreasonable." *I knew I needed to take action and took the excuse of my pregnancy and new motherhood not to force a change. I have to do better in the future.* She sighed.

"Don't take any blame on your own shoulders for his criminal tendencies," Sahure said.

Edekh stood aside to allow two guards to enter the room. Pointing at Jemkhufu with his staff, he said, "Take this man into custody for offenses against Pharaoh."

Jemkhufu offered no resistance, standing with a sullen frown on his face as the soldiers twisted his arms behind his back and waited for Edekh to issue further instructions.

"My lady, he deserves a lashing at the least, for having abrogated his sacred duties as a scribe," Edekh said. "He's brought shame on the entire profession through his actions."

Tyema clenched her hands at her sides. "I don't want to broadcast this matter in Thebes. The crime is internal to my temple. No one else's business but mine and Sobek's."

"The only way to ensure his silence is to execute him." Edekh's enthusiasm indicated he'd relish giving the order immediately. "And I must correct you, but in strictest fact he committed the crime against the Great Royal Wife. Hard for me to overlook the offense, although I've no wish to share the news a scribe transgressed in such a manner."

Still in the grip of the soldiers, Jemkhufu fell to his knees, hands clasped. Fat tears rolled down his cheeks. "Mercy, Lady Tyema, have mercy! Remember all the years of faithful service I've rendered to you and your temple. I swear if you let me go, I'll never speak of this to anyone."

Sick to her stomach as the scribe groveled and begged, Tyema averted her eyes.

Striding forward, Sahure put his dagger to the scribe's throat, as the two soldiers held him immobile. "You committed a crime against me as well, jackal spawn. If the lady chooses to let you go free I'll honor her wish, but I swear on the eyes of Horus, I'll hunt you down and kill you myself if any word of what you've done, what you know or think you know, ever becomes public." He pressed the tip of the knife hard enough against Jemkhufu's neck to draw blood. "Swear yourself to silence."

"I swear, please don't kill me!" Tears poured down the scribe's cheeks and his voice was high pitched in terror.

Jaw clenched, Sahure nodded and stepped back, slamming the dagger into its sheath. "I'm satisfied."

"I'm not, not entirely, but I'll yield to the two of you, as being the most directly affected by his crime." Frowning, Edekh gave the appropriate orders despite his apparent misgivings about leniency. "Escort this man to his quarters to collect his possessions. Go through each item, ensure he's taken nothing else from the temple he served or this palace. Then escort him to the city gates and put him out of Thebes."

"You're banishing me from the city?" Jemkhufu's knees buckled.

"Pharaoh wouldn't want such as you inside the walls of his capital," Edekh said. "Best you make your way somewhere else before we change our minds. Leave Egypt." The Chief Scribe gestured to the guards. "Get him out of here."

As the guards dragged him from the room, Tyema groped for the chair and sat. Her mind was full of chaotic thoughts and worries. Sahure knelt beside her. "Are you all right?"

She nodded but words were beyond her. The sense of utter betrayal by a person she'd trusted with the business of Sobek's temple was like a knife in her own heart.

"I hate to prolong this scene," Edekh said, "But the odds are good the scoundrel was doing more than intercepting mail. A person who'd risk such a crime probably had no qualms about skimming from the offerings, filing incorrect tallies for assets—"

"When I was there I remember the two of you discussing some anomaly in the annual cattle tally," Sahure said. "How did you come to hire him when the temple was first reestablished? What were his references?"

"He came well recommended, from a temple in another nome." Tyema was horrified to think she might have unwittingly allowed Jemkhufu to steal from Sobek.

The two men exchanged glances. "Perhaps they were also ridding themselves of a troublemaker," Edekh said.

"What am I going to do now? Where will I find someone to replace him?" The thought of managing the temple's many enterprises for even a short time without a scribe to assist her was daunting. *And when can I get back to Ibis? I'm no closer to solving the black magic problem here.*

"If you'll allow me, I'd like to assign two men to your temple," Edekh said, sitting in the empty chair.

Hope lightened her heart for a moment, but then reality intruded. "The suggestion is kind of you, but scribes from Thebes aren't likely to want employment in a rural temple in Ibis Nome."

"On the contrary, it's an excellent thing for an up and coming scribe to be selected by me to sort out a complicated situation, no matter where in Egypt the problem lies." Edekh winked. "Having Pharaoh's Chief Scribe in his debt is a coup for any ambitious young man in our profession."

She chuckled. "I'm sure."

"My first order to the men I assign will be to review all records, every transaction conducted for your temple by that sniveling jackal and sort out any inconsistencies. Two men trained here under my eyes will be more than capable of doing an audit while running your scribe school, and all the other businesses Sahure has mentioned to me. Then they'll find local scribes to replace them, making recommendations to you as the final authority, of course."

"Of course," Tyema murmured, bemused by the way Edekh was solving her problem.

"I'll make the assignment for a year and the final requirement will be providing your new scribes with advanced training to keep the temple businesses running at top efficiency. The carrot of instruction from my men will attract high level candidates. A connection to Thebes is always to be valued."

Tyema reached out in gratitude to lay her hand on Edekh's. "You're being so generous to me, how can I ever repay you?"

"All things balance themselves in time," he said, resting his hand on hers for a moment and squeezing gently. "I'll have the two scribes selected before you leave Thebes. They can travel to Ibis with you?"

"Of course. There's plenty of room in the nomarch's ship."

"Well, this morning started badly but has now redeemed itself," Sahure said. "Have you plans for the afternoon?"

"None I'm aware of," Tyema said.

"I propose to take you to the chariot maker and help you commission your private vehicle, after which we'll go to the military stables and select four horses. We're going to spend your temple's deben like water today, I warn you." He grinned.

Tyema stared. "Are you serious?"

"Pharaoh has given permission," Sahure assured her. "He and I spoke of the matter yesterday. You're also going to need grooms."

"When the chariot is complete and ready to deliver, I can arrange for temporary stable workers," Edekh said. "Probably best if you find local men to care for the horses long term."

"Or perhaps your grooms can train some of my temple staff," Tyema said. "Hotepre has a few younger nephews who might prefer to work with horses rather than crocodiles or cattle. My brother-in-law, the commander of the town guard, has a chariot and a competent groom, so I'll get his opinion as well."

"Now the next steps are planned out, allow me to escort you, your niece, and our son for a walk in the gardens before the midday meal perhaps?" Sahure held out his hand. "Shake off memories of the recent unpleasantness?"

"I'd be delighted." She wanted nothing more than an escape from the small room and a chance to breathe fresh air.

Edekh cleared his throat. "I'm afraid the walk will have to wait for a few moments longer. I need to speak with Lady Tyema alone. I've a message from Pharaoh for her ears only."

Obviously displeased by this announcement excluding him, Sahure exchanged surprised glances with Tyema before bowing and leaving the room, closing the door behind him.

Heart beating faster, Tyema stared at Edekh. "How may I serve the Great One?"

"Pharaoh wished me to relay that he and the queen have established a full schedule of dinners, cruises and other events to fill your days, now the crocodile dedication is complete. He said this will allow you to meet and observe all members of his court closely and as rapidly as possible." Edekh paused, raising one eyebrow. "He seemed to feel you'd find this useful in some manner?"

I wonder how much Edekh knows of my true reason for being here? And clearly Pharaoh loses patience, for which I can't blame him. "Should I refuse to go to the chariot makers today, then?"

"No, I don't think cancelling the chariot buying trip is necessary. Pharaoh has approved the commission after all. There will be a large banquet tonight, tomorrow's plan is spending the day in leisure with the queen and her ladies-in-waiting, followed by an intimate dinner—"

"I need to visit the temple of Sobek tomorrow morning, to check on my crocodile," she said. "I gave my word to follow up within the week of his dedication, and then my duty to Sobek as far as the crocodile's welfare is concerned will be fully discharged. But otherwise the schedule of activities sounds wonderful."

Edekh stared at her, lips twitching as he allowed himself to grin. "Your words are fair, but why does your voice suggest we've consigned you to torture, or perhaps prison?"

She raised her chin. "While it's true I don't attend many gatherings in Ibis Nome, I'm in Thebes now, and of course I'll do as Pharaoh wishes." *And it's true with all these opportunities he's providing to observe the court, I should pinpoint the sorcerer more quickly. I just have to focus on my duty and try not to give in to my personal fears of unknown people and public events. And then I can take my child and go home.* Leaving Sahure yet again, for the last time.

"You didn't allow me to finish the list of enticements. The day after tomorrow the queen takes a party, including you, for a sail on the Nile in her barge, followed by another state dinner." He studied her face, a quizzical look in his eyes. Tyema tried to hide her frightened, rebellious thoughts deep inside and show only a bland expression. Tapping the table with his fingers, Edekh said, "I'll spare you the rest of the calendar for now. Perhaps it's best if I dole out the treats a day at a time."

"Yes, better not to overwhelm me with joy," she said, with a sigh. "Thank you, for all your help and support."

"If I know our friend Sahure, he's pacing a hole in the floor out there. Not patient, is our captain. Go then, enjoy the walk in the garden and later the process of ordering a chariot built to your specifications, which will be a ten-day sensation in Thebes, believe me. I don't think Pharaoh has ever granted permission to a woman to own a chariot before." Edekh rose and took her hand to assist her from her chair.

If I didn't want my own chariot so badly, I'd bow out of the meeting, to avoid being even more talked about and noticed than I already am. But no one in Ibis can construct a chariot or train horses properly to pull it. Tyema brought a smile from the depths of her unhappy soul and preceded Edekh into the corridor where, as predicted, a disgruntled Sahure was pacing.

***

Tyema was in restored spirits by the evening. Sahure had exerted himself to be amusing and charming while the two of them and Renebti walked in the gardens, taking turns carrying the baby. They revisited Pharaoh's zoo, where Sahure pointed out the animals he personally had supplied to the menagerie and told stories of life in the Southern Oasis.

The visit to the chariot maker and the military stables had been fascinating, and her order for a chariot bearing Sobek's cartouche had been placed. Much discussion had been required, and argument between the master chariot builder and Sahure. Eventually it had been decided she would receive a scaled down version of the standard war chariot. It was going to be at least a month before her chariot was built and then a few more weeks for it and the horses to be shipped to Ibis, but now her dream was becoming reality, she could be content.

Having bathed and changed into another dress from the queen, Tyema was trying to convince herself she was ready to brave the banquet chamber again.

When Sahure was admitted by the guards, she was relieved to see no flickers of the black magic in the air around him. Thinking back, she realized there's been none connected to him all day.

Nodding to Renebti, Sahure addressed Tyema. "Are you ready?"

"No, but I know I must be, so we might as well go." She picked up her ostrich feather fan, kissed the baby on the forehead and followed Sahure from the room.

As before, Tyema was placed at the table with the younger ladies-in-waiting, but at least now she felt she had some acquaintance with Niadiamhet in particular, although seeing the ever present flickers of black magic influence or presence around her and Baufratet was disconcerting. There were several newcomers at the table, including a young woman who was introduced as the daughter of a Minoan diplomatic attaché assigned to Pharaoh's court. Tyema was disturbed to see flickers of some other variation of black magic around her, a curious gray aura shot through with darker black tendrils. *Surely this person can't be the sorceress I'm seeking? Maybe the bracelet is detecting less than savory aspects of her worship of her gods?*

"And how long has Jadikiria been here in Thebes?" she asked, leaning over close to Nidiamhet when there was a lull in the general conversation.

"Oh, she's only recently arrived," Nidiamhet, who seemed overly friendly with the Minoan, answered. "Baufratet and I want her to become a lady in waiting with us—she's entertaining, knows such wonderful new stories—but so far the queen prefers to have only Egyptian attendants."

Eyeing the strange aura around the Minoan, Tyema thought the queen was being wise, even without the additional knowledge she herself possessed. *But Jadikiria hasn't been here long enough to have anything to do with the ripples of sorcery Sobek was worried about. Although I'll mention her when I make my final report.*

The troupe of dancers in the center of the room finished their graceful, swirling dance to enthusiastic applause and scampered off. Tyema noticed no other group of performers moved to take their place, and the room felt oddly quiet without the background of music. At the first banquet she'd attended, the stream of entertainment had been constant, no interruptions, each person eager to have their moment demonstrating their skills to Pharaoh and his court.

Edekh walked into the center of the floor, pounded his staff on the floor and announced, "Sobek's high priestess Lady Tyema has agreed to delight pharaoh's ears with traditional songs from the Lower Nile this evening."

There were oohs and ahs and a smattering of applause. Tyema thought she'd misheard, but as she stared, blushing and dizzy, the crowd was a sea of beaming, nodding courtiers. She could see Nat-re-Akhte and his queen smiling at the head table on the dais. Tyema pushed her chair back, feeling her chest growing tight. "No, I—there's some mistake. I can't sing tonight." Baufratet's expression was a mixture of triumph and secretiveness and Tyema had no doubt who had created this nightmare for her. *I wonder if Jemkhufu shared his secrets with her before he was banished?* The room was whirling around her now so fast she was afraid she was going to pass out or throw up or both. She regretted the few morsels she'd eaten.

Nidiamhet patted her arm. "Such an honor, to sing for Pharaoh. Lucky you!"

Tyema tried to respond to the compliment but couldn't focus on words.

Suddenly Sahure was at her side. "What's the matter? Are you ill? Pharaoh waits."

She clutched at his sleeve as if she were drowning. "I can't—"

"If it please you, Great One," Sahure said, pulling her to her feet, his grip impossible to resist. "A singer's voice is her instrument and Lady Tyema requires but a few moments to prepare herself for the concert. I believe she expected to sing a little later in the evening. A misunderstanding."

"She may take all the time she requires," Pharaoh answered graciously. "Edekh, show the lady to a suitable side chamber and bring her anything she needs."

"Some honeyed wine perhaps, to soothe her throat," Sahure said as Edekh walked to join them.

It seemed to Tyema her exit from the banquet hall took hours, with all eyes upon her, but in reality it was only a few moments before she'd been escorted to a private room and left alone with Sahure. He helped her sit in a gilt chair with feet in the shape of a gazelle's dainty legs, kneeling by her side as she lowered her head and tried to breathe.

"I—I can't sing in public," she said, wiping her brow.

He frowned. "You sang yesterday well enough, in front of thousands at the temple."

"I sang for Sobek, in his service, in my official role as his priestess," she answered, her voice escalating.

He put his finger to his lips, shushing her. "We don't want them hearing you in the banquet hall."

"This is me tonight, Tyema, the little girl from Ta'sobeksef, daughter of the village scribe, not the priestess wrapped in the power of Sobek." Tears poured down her cheeks. *I'm not making sense—I'm sure he thinks my wits have become disordered.* "With all those people staring at me, whispering about me, I can hardly stand without fainting, much less remember the words to any songs." She put her hand on her chest, feeling the telltale constriction worsening. "I can't breathe—how can I carry a tune?"

"Oh, sweetheart, I think I begin to understand. Why did you volunteer, then?" He held her close, smoothing her hair.

"I didn't. I'd never do such a thing. I wouldn't even be at the banquet tonight except—"

"Except?"

I can't tell him I braved the banquet to search out the source of black magic. Sobek forbade me to discuss it with anyone but Pharaoh. Tyema shook her head.

Edekh returned, followed by a servant bearing a tray with the requested wine. Pausing on the threshold, he glanced from Tyema to Sahure and back again. "Are you ill, my lady?"

Tyema hid her face in Sahure's shoulder, embarrassed to have the lofty Scribe see her in such distress. *This evening gets worse and worse.*

"She'll be fine," Sahure answered, rubbing her back. "Leave the wine and let me get her ready. Please tell Pharaoh we'll be there in a few moments."

Edekh bowed and retreated, closing the doors behind him.

"Don't worry about him, he's a good friend of mine and he likes you. He won't mention anything being amiss." Sahure handed her a mug of the wine. "Listen to me, you're going to have to go back in there and sing."

She pushed the drink away and shook her head. "I can't."

"Well, however this misunderstanding arose, Pharaoh has been promised a concert. Even a Great One as kindly and understanding as Nat-re-Akhte may be in private won't tolerate an insult in public." He wrapped her fingers around the mug and raised it to her lips. "You must sing."

She drank the wine and raised her tear stained face to him. "How will I get through it? I don't want to be a disgrace."

"Sing to me, sing only to me," Sahure said. "Pretend we're in the garden back at your temple. Or on the beach along the Nile. Sing what you sang for me on those occasions. I'll stay in your line of sight the whole time." He took the cloth sitting under the wine and gently wiped her face, trying to repair the damage to her makeup. "Sing two songs and in case he asks for an encore, have a third one ready. Then sit down and I'll get you out of the banquet hall as soon as I can."

Clinging to his sleeve, she took a deep breath. "You promise?"

"I swear, my oath as an officer." He kissed her forehead. "You'd better warm up your voice."

After taking another deep drink of the fortifying wine, Tyema stood. She smoothed her dress, closed her eyes and tried to picture her own garden. Experimentally she sang a few notes, which echoed pleasantly in the small room. Before she knew it, she'd sung half of the hymn of the inundation.

"Sounds fine." Sahure hugged her. "Are you ready?"

She sipped a little more wine, welcoming the warmth, and nodded. *Sobek, please lend me strength.*

He took her hand and escorted her back to the large chamber. After Edekh got the crowd's attention and announced she was ready to sing, a hush fell. Sahure escorted her into the center of the room. Detaching her hand from his, he bowed and walked to sit among the diners, but close to the head table, so she was able to keep him in her peripheral vision as promised. Tyema drew in a deep breath, crossed her arms over her chest and bowed to Pharaoh and the queen. She sang, trying to tell herself she was alone in her own garden, with only the royal couple and Sahure to hear. Her voice was wobbling during the opening verse. Clenching her hand in the fabric of her dress, tapping one toe on the marble floor, she made herself slow down to the appropriate tempo and lost herself in the music. She finished the first song and rushed into the second without stopping, afraid to lose the moment, and was surprised by the applause at the end of the last verse. Realizing she'd closed her eyes at some point, she opened them, focusing on Sahure, whose face bore an encouraging grin. He nodded.

"Lovely, Lady Tyema," Pharaoh said. "You've an exceptional voice."

"It's kind of you to say so, Great One," Tyema answered. Remembering Sahure's advice, she decided to offer the encore. *After all, my voice is fully warmed up now and the breath moves freely in my chest.* "If it pleases you, I have one more song prepared, a seafaring tune from the Tale of the Shipwrecked Sailor."

Smiling, Pharaoh gestured. "By all means, I'd enjoy hearing it."

She kept her eyes open this time and gave the rollicking song her all. The audience was clapping along by the time she reached the last verse and as she crossed her arms and bowed in respect again at the end, the applause was thunderous. True to his word, Sahure reappeared at her side and escorted her to her seat as a new troupe of dancers somersaulted and tumbled into the space she'd just occupied.

"Well done," he whispered as he handed her into her chair. "Do you want to stay after all?"

"Oh please, all I want is to retire to my room and lie down," she answered, trembling with reaction to the performance. *I'm just glad I survived and didn't disgrace myself or Sobek.* "Will you take me there?"

"You have to wait until Pharaoh and the queen have left the gathering," he said. "Hang on, have some more wine. But don't get tipsy." He waggled a cautionary finger at her."I'll escort you gladly once the evening is done."

He made his way back to his own companions. Tyema drank wine and accepted congratulations from the women around her and other members of the court who came to pay her compliments. In between accepting praise, she stared at the dancers without seeing them, desperate to escape the crowd and the noise. Her head was pounding. Baufratet sat in her chair scowling, drinking wine as if it were water. Tyema eyed the other woman with misgivings. *I hope she isn't going to make another scene, now that her plan for my downfall has gone awry.*

Unnoticed as he approached her, Edekh tapped her on the shoulder, causing Tyema to startle. "The queen has requested you sing for her in private."

"Now?" Tyema was confused.

The Chief Scribe pulled her chair away from the table, making it seem he was merely being courteous, subtly forcing her to rise. "Indeed."

"But I was told not to leave until Pharaoh had departed—"

"You may leave at the queen's command," he said with a laugh, taking her elbow. He steered her out a side door, into a long passageway. Queen Ashayet came down the hall, accompanied by her guards, fan bearers, and maids.

Tyema bowed her head as the queen walked up to her. "It will be my pleasure to sing whatever your majesty desires to hear."

Ashayet laughed and put a gentle finger under Tyema's chin, lifting her face. "Misery was written all over your expressive face, my dear. I told Pharaoh we needed to let you retire early, in gratitude for your amazing performance," she said, patting Tyema on the cheek as she might a young daughter. "Do you have a headache?"

Confused, Tyema looked from the scribe to the queen. "Indeed I do but—"

"Your songs were lovely and I hope to hear many more of them while you're in Thebes, but for tonight, I command you to seek your bed. Edekh, ensure Lady Tyema a safe arrival at her rooms."

Hand over his heart, he bowed low. "Yes, your majesty."

Ashayet leaned closer. "I warned Sahure you might find life here in Thebes quite a bit different than the pace you're used to in Ibis Nome. I think he begins to understand your qualms now. I pray to Isis the two of you can find some solution."

Straightening and stepping away from Tyema, the queen said in a louder voice, "Have the Royal Physician attend our guest with his best remedy for headache."

Edekh bowed again and Ashayet continued on her way, the members of her retinue trailing behind her, a few casting curious or pitying glances at Tyema. Holding her head high despite the pounding in her temples, she ignored them. As the last guard marched away, the Chief Scribe took Tyema's elbow. "The route to your suite of rooms lies in this direction, my lady."

"I'll escort her." Sahure came striding up.

"As you wish."

"As Pharaoh commands," Sahure contradicted.

Acknowledging the point with a slight tilt of his head, Edekh said, "I'll send for the Royal Physician to meet you at her chambers."

"No, please, I'll be fine," Tyema said. "I've a potion of my own to take, a recipe of my late grandmother's. Always effective."

Nodding, Edekh seemed happy to be relieved of any further duties in this case. "Until tomorrow, then." He left them, no doubt returning to the banquet.

"You won't get in trouble, will you? For leaving the dinner?" Tyema asked as Sahure walked with her in the direction of her chambers.

"Let me worry about any consequences," he said. "So tell me, how did it come about Pharaoh was told you'd sing tonight? Since you obviously didn't volunteer."

Hand pressing on her left eyebrow in an attempt to subdue the pain, Tyema stared at the floor. "I only have a suspicion. I can't very well name names with no evidence. Perhaps there genuinely was a misunderstanding."

"You pulled it off brilliantly. If someone was hoping to embarrass you, make you a laughingstock or worse, cause you to offend Pharaoh, they failed. He and the queen were highly entertained."

"Thanks to you."

"My pleasure," he said, taking her free hand.

***

Under the influence of her late grandmother's headache potion, Tyema slept well, dreamlessly. She was actually famished in the morning, sampling a variety of the dishes the steward's staff brought. Renebti wanted to hear all about the formal dinner of the night before, so Tyema indulged her with a cheerful version of the evening. "And then I had to sing for Pharaoh," she said.

Renebti's eyes grew wide. "You never sing for people outside the temple, do you? Only lullabies for the baby and of course songs for Sobek, when he visits."

"Well, I had no choice last night." Tyema laughed. She had to admit performing hadn't been such an ordeal, once she'd started.

A rapid knock at the door and Sahure came in, his face set in serious lines that smoothed away as he saw Tyema and Renebti sitting and laughing together. "I'm happy to find you so recovered," he said to Tyema.

She couldn't help smiling at him. The world was a wonderful place this morning. "Thank you for all the encouragement last night. I never would have managed to please Pharaoh and the company without you. The evening would have been a disaster."

"You were taken by surprise, nothing more." Sahure snagged a piece of fruit. "Are we still going to visit the crocodile today?"

"Indeed." Tyema felt buoyant, cheerful, and optimistic. She was looking forward to this trip.

As before, she traveled in the litter provided by Pharaoh, with attendants and guards, and Sahure trailed her little procession in his chariot, the horses high stepping as if in a parade, the ostrich feathers on their harness rippling in the breeze. Tyema thought they made a fine show and found the idea of being a two person parade through Thebes amusing today. *Am I becoming accustomed to life here? Maybe a bit.*

Lemertet met them on the steps of the temple.

"It's good to see you again," Tyema said as she was handed out of the litter.

"Welcome to our temple." He bowed. "I trust you'll find Sobek's crocodile has made himself at home already."

"Established dominance, has he?" Sahure climbed the stairs beside Tyema and the priest.

Lamertet beamed with satisfaction at the crocodile's behavior as if he could take credit for it. "A few small skirmishes with some of the older bulls, yes."

"But some fighting is to be expected," Tyema said. "It means he feels at home, in charge."

"Well, the females seem to find him fascinating." Lemertet grinned. "Maybe it's the purple belly. Our breeding program languished a bit under the old bull, but I'm expecting wondrous results this next time, with the addition of Sobek's gift to the bask."

As they walked across the grassy lawn to the pond, Tyema was surprised to see how many people were there on an ordinary day. "He apparently draws quite a crowd as well."

"The offerings have been bountiful, as I'd hoped." Lemertet all but rubbed his hands together in pleasure. "Right now we're mostly getting citizens of Thebes, but as word of the gift from Sobek spreads, including the details of the small miracle when he went into the pond wreathed in Sobek's magic flames, I'm sure we'll see pilgrims from afar as well. Our temple runs a bustling inn close to the harbor, among other businesses. If a pilgrim stays at our inn, he or she can receive an additional blessed amulet at the temple."

Tyema seized upon the opening to discuss business and soon was deep into the details of what other opportunities the priests in Thebes had explored, to bring more funds into the coffers of Sobek. Some, like the inn, were quite unique. At first Lemertet seemed only too happy to boast of what his temple had accomplished, but then Tyema felt he became a bit distant as her questions continued and grew more detailed. "I'm sorry," she said with a laugh, "But it's so rare for me to get an opportunity to talk business with someone who understands the workings of a temple. I'm afraid I'm boring you."

"Not at all," Lemertet answered, but his tone was cool. "I can fetch our chief scribe if you need to know more specifics of the sums and accounts."

"Well, I've been watching your crocodile while the two of you explored ways to increase temple revenue," Sahure said, breaking the tension of the moment. "He's doing nothing, as far as I can tell." He pointed to the small center island in the pond, which held the intricately carved statue of Sobek in full crocodile form.

Sure enough, the crocodile from Ibis Nome was sprawled across half the island's surface, basking in the sun, for all the world as if he was sound asleep. Tyema wasn't fooled. "He's doing what he's supposed to do, to lure unwary prey close enough to kill." She stared at him, a bit sad the animal made no acknowledgment of her presence, but he was being true to the cold nature of his kind. "He seems healthy."

"The purple color on his belly is the talk of Thebes, even as you predicted," Lemertet said.

"My crocodile keepers will be pleased to hear all is well. We got a bit attached to this one." Tyema realized some of the bystanders were pointing at her and whispering.

Sahure followed her line of sight and stepped closer, taking her elbow. "I'm afraid you're nearly as famous as your crocodile, my lady."

"A novelty in Thebes, both of you." Lemertet's comment wasn't entirely complimentary. "Shall we go inside? You did say you'd like to see some of the interior features when you visited us again."

"I'd love to. I remember you mentioned having some truly outstanding murals." Tyema was happy to leave the pond area, now she knew her duty was fully discharged. Being an object of public curiosity was always a difficult thing for her to bear. Sahure's presence was comforting. "I'd like to meet your priestesses today, if I could."

Lemertet stumbled. "Priestesses?"

"It's just, I'd enjoy comparing notes with some of the female celebrants," she said. "If any are available today of course."

"We uh, we have no female celebrants at this temple. Well, other than the mistress of dancers, and she concerns herself with nothing but the training of dancers and creating new steps for them to execute."

"She doesn't sing at ceremonies?" Tyema was hopeful.

"No." Lemertet's answer was just this side of rude. "In Thebes, other than the temples of Isis, Hathor and Mut, there are male priests only. It's the way things are done here, since time immemorial." He cast a desperate glance at Sahure as if seeking support from a fellow Theban. "Sobek is a male god, so therefore the celebrants and officials of the temples are men as well."

No wonder the high priest was so upset the day we had the meeting with Pharaoh. Not only was I an outsider, coming in to tell him how things were going to be done, but women have no place in this temple, other than as ornaments. Feeling she already knew the answer, she asked her next question anyway. "But surely if a woman felt the call to serve the Great One Sobek, she'd be welcome to become a priestess here?"

Lemertet cleared his throat. "I don't think what you suggest would happen, Lady Tyema. Theban women are called to serve the goddesses, principally the Great Ones Mut or Hathor."

She let the subject drop, aware of how uncomfortable she'd made him. They strolled through the outer chambers of the temple and she made suitably admiring comments about the murals, although privately she preferred the ones in her own temple. Smaller scale perhaps, but hers depicted the god as more approachable, she felt. Lemertet took them into the second courtyard and again she was unmoved by the stately artwork, other than on a superficial level. There was nothing to criticize, but the frescoes were formal, highly stylized.

"The colors are beautiful," she said truthfully.

One eyebrow raised, Sahure shot her a glance but said nothing.

Lemertet rambled on enthusiastically about how the pigments and crushed stones had been imported at great expense from other parts of Egypt and abroad. Tyema nodded as appropriate during his narrative but she grew more disgusted. *It's important to honor the god, but surely the funds spent on this were excessive. Think how many poor people could have been fed, or places at scribe school could have been provided to deserving but impoverished youths, with the deben required to import lapis lazuli from Ashvakas to create that exact shade of Nile blue.*

Aware Lemertet was winding down as her responses grew fewer and fewer, she broke into his final discussion of a mural featuring Sobek and the goddess Renenutet apparently enjoying a romantic encounter, as some traditions insisted they had done. *My sister Merys wouldn't appreciate this artwork.* Hiding a smile, she said, "I feel called to offer praises to the Great One today. I'd like to visit the inner sanctum. By myself."

Now her host frowned, eyebrows drawn together and jaw clenched. "I'm afraid what you request isn't possible. We've already done the morning devotions, clothed the god's image, offered the morning meal—"

She'd deliberately worn the golden collar of Tears, and now she ran her fingers across the gems, watching his gaze follow the motion of her hand. *The high priest isn't the only one who covets Sobek's Tears.* "Surely if the Great One Sobek is calling me to worship, there can be no objection? I won't disturb anything. I'm a high priestess, I know the protocol."

Lemertet put his hand out as if to physically bar Sahure from walking another step. "I'm sorry, but you can't venture any farther into the temple."

"Nor do I want to, with all due respect. I can wait for Lady Tyema right here." Sahure wasn't helping Lemertet raise obstacles to Tyema's request, which she appreciated. He seated himself on a conveniently located granite bench and waved one hand. "Please, don't concern yourself on my account. I'm sure she'll come to no harm in the temple of her Great One."

"I can find my own way, if you'd prefer, or if you're busy," she said, knowing the Theban would never allow her to roam his temple freely.

With little grace, Lemertet took her arm and escorted her through the next two courtyards, the rooms growing ever smaller as they approached the innermost sanctum, where the effigy of Sobek was housed. Finally they arrived at the last door, painted blue, with golden handles in the shape of crocodile heads, the eyes inlaid blue glass and the teeth gleaming ivory.

"I need to go alone," Tyema said. She splashed water on her hands and face from the silver basin waiting on a pedestal beside the portal. Putting her hand on the door before Lemertet could open it for her, she assured him, "I won't be long."

Not waiting for his answer because she knew he was unhappy at her insistence on having entry to the most sacred portion of his temple, Tyema opened the door just wide enough to slip inside and closed it firmly behind her. The inner sanctum was larger than the one at her temple, lit by numerous oil lamps on pedestals around the room. In the center, standing on a plinth carved with hieroglyphics extolling his many virtues, was the image of Sobek, half man, half crocodile. Carved with great skill from gray- and- pink granite, the statue was dressed in a golden kilt tied over the stone kilt, with a magnificent solar headdress and white ostrich plumes on his head touching the ceiling. His feet bore leather sandal uppers, inlaid with gold and gems, slid skillfully over the stone feet to give the effect of real shoes. Sobek's staff was also gold, with a stylized crocodile perched at the top, encrusted with gems. The statue wore a stunning pectoral on his bare chest, gold beads interspersed with faience, turquoise and coral, scarabs and lapis lazuli lotus flowers dangling along the edge.

Heaping platters of fruit and bread sat on tables next to the statue, along with pitchers of fine beer.

They've carried out all the morning rituals in proper manner. Tyema went to her knees directly in front of the effigy, arms crossed, head bowed and waited. Nothing changed, there was no slightest indication the god was present or intending to manifest himself to her. "Great One, I've come today to give final approval to the transfer of your crocodile," she said after a moment or two, staring at the statue towering above her. "All is in order, the beast is well cared for and content. I'd like to speak with you concerning my other mission in Thebes and…well, something else weighing on my heart."

No response. The great stone image of the god remained immobile in all its imposing, cold perfection.

Never had she felt more alone, more distant from the Great One she served. There wasn't the slightest hint of power in the room, no scent of the lotus, no humming of energy in her head. "Somehow I'm not surprised," she said out loud, standing up.

Should I search for the hidden effigy? The one made of silver covered in gold? The one the priests would bring out for the most sacred events? She stared at the walls surrounding her, searching for the telltale outline of the receptacle small enough to hold the most revered image of Sobek. *No. If the Great One was here, he'd make himself known to me as he does at home, with no need for any statue.*

One final test. She sang a few practice notes and then launched into the morning paean she knew Sobek enjoyed most. Singing brought her a warm happy feeling, as her music always did, but no sign of interest or appreciation from either the effigy or the elusive Great One himself.

As a high priestess, Tyema was well aware most temples had secret passages, ways for the priests to see into the inner sanctum and other rooms and to influence answers any oracle might provide, absent the direct intervention of the deity in question. Her temple had been designed without such enhancements at her direct order because Sobek was a reliably constant presence there. She suspected this temple was rife with mechanisms and clever devices, probably more than she could even think of. *I can't show my true feelings to these people. Let them think Sobek did communicate with me, or at least let them wonder.*

Bowing to the statue, she backed away until she reached the door. She took a moment to compose her feelings and then left the room. Lemertet was pacing the floor of the outer sanctum. He wheeled at the sound of the door and scrutinized her closely.

"Thank you for the courtesy of allowing me to worship here alone," she said. "If we can rejoin my military escort, I should be getting back to the palace."

"Will we be seeing you again, Lady Tyema?" asked Lemertet as they proceeded through the series of ever larger rooms to reach the spot where they'd left Sahure.

She shook her head. "No, I don't think so. I'm completely satisfied."

His mood seemed to improve at the news, although he made an attempt to look regretful that he'd never see her in his temple again. "Do you sail to Ibis Nome soon?"

Tyema was amused, hearing more than polite curiosity in his question. *I suppose he thinks I was inspecting the temple on Sobek's behalf. Maybe even probing to see if a proper amount was going into the god's treasury.* "I certainly hope to do so. There are matters there I need to attend to. But setting the date of departure is between Pharaoh and myself."

"Oh, of course." He walked faster.

Sahure rose from the bench where he'd been relaxing and came to meet her, searching her face for some sign about what had happened in the inner sanctum, she was sure. Keeping her emotions and thoughts from him was more of a challenge than fencing with Lamertet could ever be. "I'm ready to go back to the palace," she said to Sahure before he could open his mouth. "I'm expected in the queen's quarters promptly at the noon hour and mustn't be late."

"Of course, my lady. All is in readiness to convey you back to the palace." His bearing and tone were formal, to match hers.

"Good." She extended her hand to Lemertet. "It's been a pleasure to have a tour of the temple."

"Our honor to have you here, of course."

"Please tell the high priest how sorry I am we missed the opportunity to speak." *I don't even know that man's name, how ironic.* Despite her mood, Tyema did find a shred of amusement in the thought.

CHAPTER EIGHT

Next morning there was a quiet knock at her door shortly after dawn. Startled, glancing at Seknehure's cradle, wrapping her robe more tightly around her, Tyema went to open the door, knowing the guards wouldn't permit anyone to bother her without good reason.

Sahure waited on the other side, in an everyday uniform. "Ah good, I was hoping you'd be up already. I remember you always rose with the dawn at Ta'sobeksef. May I come in? I brought breakfast." He indicated a linen sack in his right hand.

She moved aside. "Keep your voice down, the baby's finally fallen asleep—he had a rough night."

"Poor little man." Sahure walked quietly past her, going to the cradle and peering at his now-snoring son. "Is he ill? Teething?"

"Teething, I think," she said, surprised yet again to learn this warrior knew so much of the ailments of babies. "The royal physician gave me soothing ointment to rub on his gums and eventually he drifted off to dream. The guards summoned the doctor for me, without asking. I think they wearied of hearing the crying."

Sahure laughed quietly. "Undoubtedly. Will he need to nurse soon?"

Blushing a bit at the intimate question, she shook her head and went to sit. "I just fed him, after the medicine dulled the pain enough. You've timed your visit well, but why are you here? You must know the palace steward brings Renebti and me a breakfast daily which is big enough to feed our entire village."

"Breakfast was just an excuse, although you're welcome to what I brought." He spilled some fruit and a roll onto the nearest table. "I want to show you something."

Tyema picked up the freshly baked roll and nibbled at the edge. "All right, but I've seen fruit before."

He chuckled at the small joke. "No, we'll have to leave the palace and drive a short distance. Unless you're too tired. We could do this another day, but I've waited so long to share this with you."

She considered. She was tired but knew she couldn't go back to sleep. And it might be a good thing to have some private time with Sahure, outside the palace, away from all the eyes and ears. "Are we going in the chariot?"

He nodded. "Absolutely."

"Won't seeing me in a chariot upset the populace?" She was only half teasing, but the temptation of a ride had her persuaded to venture out with him.

"It's early, no one who matters will see us. Please come."

Unable to resist the appeal on his face, she nodded. "Let me get dressed and warn Renebti to listen for the baby."

"Dress simply and bring a cloak," he said. "It'll be a bit chilly riding in the chariot at this early hour."

A few minutes later they stole out of her rooms, passing the saluting guards and hurrying down the hall together toward the closest exit.

"I feel like we're skulking, or escaping," Tyema said. "Where are we going?"

Sahure assumed an air of mystery, opening his eyes wide. "You'll know soon enough."

They came out onto one of the wide patios surrounding the palace and Tyema saw Sahure's chariot waiting at the bottom of the stairs, the impatient horses being held by his sergeant. She brushed her hair back and sighed in exasperation. "I never remember to bring them a treat to munch on."

Don't worry about my team— they eat far too much as it is." Sahure handed her into the chariot and took the reins from his man. "Let me get out of the palace complex and then you can drive for a few moments, before we reach the main street. If you want."

"Of course, I'd love to. I've missed driving." She bit her lip. *I've missed a lot of other, more important things since you left, but probably better not to speak of those.* Raising her face to the breeze, Tyema enjoyed the fresh air and the morning.

Her stint at the reins was short, but then Sahure skillfully drove them through light traffic to a sprawling temple complex on the far side of the city.

"What god is worshipped here?" she asked as she jumped down from the vehicle.

"A goddess, 'She Who Giveth Birth But Was Not Herself Born of Any,' " Sahure said. "Mut, the Vulture."

Tyema considered the information. "I've heard of the Vulture, of course. And Ashayet wore the most amazing golden vulture crown the other night at the dinner. I've never seen such intricate workmanship."

"Mut is the patron goddess of Thebes, wife of the mighty Amun-Ra," Sahure said. "Her worship rises in prominence as her husband becomes increasingly more favored and powerful among the gods. Or so it's said, mostly by his constantly growing, mortal priesthood." He held out his hand as she started to turn into the broad walkway, lined by sphinxes with rams' heads. "We're not going into the main temple, not today anyway. Walk with me."

Hand in hand they strolled along a path made of crushed white stones, bordered by larger rocks painted with red and turquoise hieroglyphics praising Mut. The path wound away from the imposing bulk of the central temple, which sat on a small hill behind them.

Sahure's clasp was firm, his fingers warmly possessive as they wrapped around hers. Tyema wished she could pretend they were back in Ibis and nothing had changed between them. Feeling the prick of tears as bittersweet longing swept through her, Tyema blinked hard and sought a topic of distracting conversation. "I wonder what Isis thinks about someone else being regarded as a queen among the Great Ones."

Sahure gave her a surprised glance. "I forget you're so close to Sobek. You must have unusual insight into the behavior of the gods."

Thinking of the various times Merys had spoken with fear of Isis, Tyema held her tongue. It wasn't her place to share any private information with someone else. Who knew when the gods might be listening? "Do you worship this Mut? Does Pharaoh? Or Queen Ashayet?"

"No, I don't. Most of Pharaoh's inner circle of courtiers and his warriors remain loyal to Horus. The queen, however, has become quite devoted to Mut over the years. I can see the day coming when Amun-Ra and Mut will be the most prominent deities in this city. Perhaps some future Pharaoh raised here in Thebes will swear allegiance to Amun-Ra, unlike Nat-re-Akhte, who grew up in a mountain province. I confess some fondness for Mut, for my own reasons." He paused on the path, grinning like a boy, barring her from going farther. "Close your eyes and let me lead you the last few steps, please?"

Unable to resist his laughing, pleading tone, Tyema ostentatiously closed her eyes, felt him take her elbow firmly and steer her forward, around a corner and down a gently curving path, until he said, "Now you can open your eyes and enjoy the surroundings."

Blinking, she found the view enchanting. "Oh how lovely!" She stood in a half circle courtyard, facing the Nile, surrounded by pillars inscribed with lavish hieroglyphics extolling the virtues, beauty and accomplishments of Mut, as well as the history of her marriage to Amun-Ra. Well trimmed trees framed the entire nook. Small statues of crowned vultures stood between the pillars and in the center was a greater-than-life-size statue of the goddess herself, shown as a woman but with the addition of great, outstretched white vulture wings, gleaming in the sun, each individual feather carved in relief and painted. Mut wore an elaborate vulture headdress, gilded to catch the sunlight, and held a large, ribbon-draped ankh in one hand. Her dress was painted rich lotus blue and she gazed serenely across the Nile. A small, crescent-shaped pond was directly in front of the statue, choked with water lilies. Several small turtles who'd been sunning themselves on the blue tiled edge of the pond plopped into the water, swimming away at Tyema's approach.

Staring at Mut, Tyema found herself strangely drawn to the deity's unusually peaceful face. *Her expression is so kindly, so welcoming. Much what I wish my mother had shown to me, not just to my older sisters.* Moved to tears by the sudden longing, Tyema brushed her hand over her eyes, glad she hadn't done her eye makeup yet, to be ruined by crying. *I've grown so weepy since coming to Thebes, which isn't like me at all.* Giving herself a mental shake, she concentrated on her surroundings. "I feel the attraction of this goddess. Mut seems unaccountably different from Isis." The entire effect of the area was to honor the goddess while still providing a peaceful spot for contemplation by mortals.

"I thought you'd like the place." Sahure drew her off to the side, to a bench, supported by twin sphinxes. "I designed it."

Tyema swiveled to stare at him as she sat. "You?"

He nodded, seeming pleased by her reaction. "Yes, as a boy. Well, to be fair, I did a rough sketch, handed off to more skillful hands for translation into architectural drawings. I wanted to show you this glade practically since I met you. When we were in Ibis Nome I talked often of my ambitions, my dreams. Probably too often." He grimaced and shook a finger at her. "You're entirely too skillful at getting a man to forget himself and ramble on about his own concerns."

She said nothing, feeling uncomfortable that however accidentally he'd realized it, what he described was indeed one of her favorite methods of deflecting attention from herself. "So how did you, as a boy, in training to be a warrior, come to design an aspect of a great temple?"

He answered her question with a question of his own. "Do you know who gets to build things in Egypt? Buildings and monuments standing for all time?"

"Pharaoh," she said, inserting a question into her tone.

He nodded. "Pretty much. Pharaoh and those he empowers or commissions to build on his behalf."

"Like the consideration he's giving to creating a new harbor and port city in my province?"

"If the river complex gets constructed, yes." Sahure sat beside her, leaving a small space between them. Tyema had to fight the urge to slide closer on the stone bench and put her arm around him as he went on speaking. "In my family there's only one career a man can follow—the military. We've been soldiers going back generations. Fortunately, my grandfather and father loathed the Usurper Pharaoh, hated the way she allowed the Hyksos to have authority in Egypt, which they used as an excuse to plunder and ravage. My relatives were happy to ally with Nat-re-Akhte when he decided enough was enough. They took their battalions of highly trained soldiers into the field on Nat-re-Akhte's behalf early in the rebellion, reversed the outcome of a hard fought, pivotal battle. He remembers that support with gratitude to this day. Members of our family have done well ever since, received honors and promotions, achieved positions of authority."

Tyema considered his explanation, never having stopped to wonder before how the current nomarch of Ibis Province had gained his position. "Like your uncle?"

Sahure nodded. "Yes, he was a successful general and Pharaoh appointed him to replace the old nomarch who'd given his loyalty to the Usurper. The elevation in rank was a reward for significant military victories. And as nomarch, my uncle's gotten to *build*, including monuments and temples to carry his name through the ages."

She thought she saw what he was driving at now. "Your uncle commissioned temples and government houses and a new granary—"

"Right. I want to do what he's done, but there's a great deal of competition at Pharaoh's court for the positions allowing a man to leave a mark on Egypt. And I want to have a hand in actually designing what I build." His voice was full of firm conviction. "Not merely oversee the execution of someone else's plans."

Tyema was fascinated by this new insight into the ambition driving Sahure. "You said your family was a military one, though?"

"Through and through." He nodded. "So of course I was destined for the sword and shield from birth."

Tyema heard an undertone in his voice, as if he hadn't been completely pleased to be born into the military strata of Egyptian society, honorable though it was.

"I know a man doesn't get invited into Pharaoh's Own Regiment unless he's one of Egypt's best warriors, proven himself." She touched the golden badge on his shoulder. "And Edekh mentioned the other night at dinner you received gold of valor for breaking the siege at Kharga. I was proud for you."

Smiling, he captured her hand. "Thank you. Fortune and fate favored me at Kharga."

"I was told you were there for a year? But surely it didn't require so long a campaign to defeat the Hyksos?"

Hardly," he laughed. "My commission from Pharaoh was to rebuild the place, create a stronger fortification, enhance the string of forts along the caravan route. I made a good beginning before my deployment ended and I was recalled to Thebes. Much remains to be done, but I'll not have the doing of it. Nor was the work on the scale of what I truly long to do."

"So, unless you were teasing me earlier, how did you come to design this peaceful little chapel to Mut? And how does this unusual fact concern us?"

"It concerns our son, primarily."

She tensed, withdrawing her hand to her lap. "Sahure—"

Eyebrows drawn together in a frown, muscle twitching in his jaw, Sahure insisted. "We have to talk about this, Ema, and if not now, when? I've no idea how long you're staying in Thebes, I have a feeling you misunderstand my intentions about the boy, and we get no privacy in the palace."

Swallowing hard, she nodded. *He's right, I'm worried about his plans for our son.* "The goddess Hathor attended Seknehure's birth and she said his future will be full of challenges befitting a warrior, but he'll prevail and bring honor to Egypt, and his parents." The words were engraved in her memory. *He deserves to know what Hathor prophesied for our son.*

Eyebrows raised, Sahure gave her an incredulous look. "You stand high indeed in regard of the Great Ones, if Hathor came herself to your childbearing."

"Tawaret was also there," she said, remembering that frightening time. *Best not to mention Merys. And I can't say anything about the black magic.*

There was a moment of silence, while Sahure apparently contemplated the idea of his son's birth having been assisted by two goddesses. "Thank you for sharing the prophecy with me. It makes what I want to say easier." He stared at her, eyes narrowed. "Although as always with you I have the feeling there's much you aren't sharing. What do you hide behind your beautiful façade, Ema? Why don't you trust me?"

Prickles of fear shot through her. She was hiding so much from him, more than she normally concealed from everyone. *I can't lose control of myself here, not now.* In an attempt to deflect her increasing shortness of breath, tight chest and vertigo, she rose from the bench and strolled to the crescent pond, saying over her shoulder, "Well?"

"When I was a boy, I spent much time with my mother's oldest brother, who was an architect. He designed the new portions of the greater temple complex." Sahure waved a hand in the direction of the sprawling buildings on the rise. "I was fascinated by his tools, by the models his draftsmen built, by the idea of creating something where nothing had been before. As it happens, I had an aptitude for architecture and I enjoy it. Since he was working on this large commission at the time, he indulged me with the assignment to design a nook for contemplation." His lips twisted in a wry grin. "I think he gave me the task to keep me out of his hair, but I surprised him."

"Here," she said, spinning in a leisurely circle to take in their peaceful surroundings.

He nodded. "My uncle did the final drawings, of course. No one but he and I knew the concept was mine. We couldn't tell my family."

"Because you were destined to be a warrior?"

"And I am, one of the best," he said as a simple statement of fact. "I was born with the necessary physical skills, and I had the right training from the moment I could walk. But my greater goal is to be in a position to create for posterity, to ensure what I design is built and acknowledged as *mine*. Done under Pharaoh's command of course, for the good of Egypt, but done by me, with my cartouche on the keystones."

She remembered some chatter at the dinner table the other night, regarding the possibility of Sahure being under consideration for the position of vizier, which would afford him the opportunities he sought, including the oversight of important construction. *And he'll need a wife who can help him navigate the politics and the intrigues. Not someone who spends entire dinners with important people unable to concentrate due to fear of vomiting or fainting from terror. I must set him free of caring for me, let him find a partner who can help him achieve his dreams, share his successes.* She squared her shoulders, positive of what she must do. "I need to get back to the palace. How does this all concern Seknehure?"

"I was going to swear to you the boy can pursue whatever career he wants, although now you tell me the gods decree he'll be a warrior, perhaps my concerns are groundless. I'd have been content had he chosen the priesthood or any other honorable pursuit, as long as he was happy."

"The boy is yet a babe who can't even walk," she reminded him.

"True, no rush right now." Sahure nodded. "But when he's old enough, we'll have to ensure he's accepted into the finest military school, here in Thebes."

She could hardly breathe, so painful was the idea of a future separation from her child. "I realize he can't get the proper training in Ibis Province, but must we speak of this today?"

"I want to recognize him as my heir, formally, before Pharaoh," Sahure said. "While you're here."

"I won't give him up," she said, panic making her voice shaky and harsh. "You and your wife can have other sons. Sobek will stand with me on this." Even as she uttered the threat, a little voice in her mind questioned whether the god would take her side. A career as a warrior for Egypt was a respected and honorable path for a man.

"Wife? I'm not married, nor likely to be any time soon at this rate," he said, eyes flashing in anger. "I just want to recognize my son, provide for him. All other things come in due time. My family has a large estate, Seknehure is entitled to his claim on it."

How can I argue? I can't deny my son what he's owed by birth. "Fine. Extremely honorable and generous of you." She occupied her shaking hands in smoothing the wrinkles in her gown.

He came toward her and instinctively she retreated a step. Eyes narrowing, he paused, letting the hand he'd extended fall to his side. "How did things come to this uneasy pass between us?"

"I don't know what you're talking about," she said, heart pounding as she prepared to lie, to renounce the one person she wanted in her life more than anyone other than her son. "We were lovers for one night, after a mere two weeks of acquaintance. The gods blessed us with a son and that's all, Sahure. A year has passed, life moved on and so should we. When my—my business in Thebes is concluded, Seknehure and I will return to Ibis Nome. Determining his future can wait until he's older."

He drew in a deep breath. "No slightest thought of staying in Thebes? With me?"

Shaking her head, she moved a few steps farther away. "I told you before, such a change in life is impossible for me." *And would be disastrous for you.*

"And of course you won't tell me why you of all the people in Egypt can't live in Pharaoh's capital city?" Following her toward the path out of the grove, his eyes were intent on her face. "You promised me an honest explanation, Ema. What is the barrier you think we can't surmount together?"

"I don't love you," she said, forcing the words out, even though her heart was breaking. Her sorrow made the words harsh.

His prompt answer surprised her. "And I'm not sure I believe you. My final night in Ibis, you swore you loved me, but there was some other impediment to our becoming man and wife, something keeping you in the province, unable to move to Thebes. I want the truth today, all of it."

"You fail to hear the truth when it's presented to you, then." Tyema made herself sound cold, hard as it was. "You were someone totally new in my world, a novelty, and I was the same to you. Having met the high born court ladies vying for the honor of Mistress of your House, I see this clearly. To have the future you desire, you need to marry one of them, follow your original plan. Don't let misguided infatuation and the fact you sired a son pull you from the high road you're destined for. Making me Mistress of your House will surely keep you from achieving your dreams of building for posterity." She gestured at the nook they stood in, although it seemed to her for a moment the statue of the goddess had taken on a disapproving air.

Sahure crossed the distance between them in a few strides, taking her in his arms. "Trying to save me from myself? What if I don't want saving?"

Averting her face, she made no other effort to break free, arms at her sides. "I wish to be driven back to the palace now. I'm done discussing this topic, and I must ask you not to raise the question again. Maybe I should request a new liaison from Pharaoh, someone who doesn't disturb my peace, doesn't ask for things I can't give. The Great One gave me permission to make a change, if I was uncomfortable spending time with you."

Sahure released her so suddenly she nearly fell. Startled, she stared as he paced away from. When he spun around, Tyema made herself look into his face.

Although clearly angry, he didn't seem as upset as she would have expected. Standing with his hands on his hips, jaw clenched, he said, "If the goddess Ma'at stood before us right now and challenged you to give me your answer again, with her red feather of truth in your hand, could you? Could you swear by Ma'at you don't love me and that's the reason you keep refusing to consider marrying me?"

Knowing the truth in her own heart, Tyema hesitated for a fatal second.

Apparently her momentary weakness was all Sahure needed. Pointing his finger at her, he said, "Aha. You couldn't swear, could you?"

"You didn't want to be one of my temple guards and I don't want to live in Thebes. I *can't* live in Thebes." Desperation and sorrow made her voice quiver. She took a deep breath, feeling her chest tightening under the stress of the conversation. "Our worlds are too far apart. Even if we did love each other, there's no bridge that can be built to make the situation work." Tears were close to spilling now. *If*

I start to cry, I won't be able to stop. Fear of weeping in front of him only added to her vertigo and nausea. "Please, I have to return to the palace."

He came toward her as cautiously as if she were a frightened baby gazelle, poised to flee. Halting in front of her, not touching her, Sahure said in a low voice, "I feel we're moving closer to the truth, although not there as yet, but I swear not to raise the subject again in Thebes. I give you my word of honor."

"Thank you." She wiped her eyes with a corner of her shawl and sat on the bench, feeling weak at the knees.

Sahure hunkered down in front of her, brushing her hair from her face so he could gaze into her eyes. "In exchange, I ask you not to request a new military escort. All right?"

Surprised, she supposed he feared her asking for him to be removed from her detail would impair his standing in the eyes of Pharaoh. "Agreed. I don't want to prevent you from seeing Seknehure freely while we're here, so it keeps matter simpler if you're still my escort."

"I'll take you back to the palace, then."

She glanced at the statue of Mut one last time, wishing she could have asked the goddess for help or consolation. Mut's serene face was so appealing. *But my life and loyalty are given to Sobek and I must walk the path he sets.* "May I have a moment alone here? To—to collect myself before we're seen in public on the way to the palace?"

"Of course. Take as long as you need. I'll be at the chariot." He strode away, seeming as relieved to be done with their conversation as she was.

Tyema remained on the bench for a moment before drawing in a long, shaky breath and rising. Overcome by desire to see the lovely face of the goddess one more time, she strolled to stand in front of the statue, gazing into Mut's serene visage. She rubbed one hand along the smooth top of the plinth where the statue stood, brushing a few windblown leaves to the ground. "I wish I could address you, Great One. I have the feeling you'd understand my dilemma more clearly than Sobek ever could, no disrespect to him." She glanced over her shoulder but

Sahure was out of sight. Turning back to the effigy, she said, "How do I make Sahure understand marrying me will ruin all his dreams? Without telling him how beset by terrors and ailments I am? I can't speak of those things to him, the sheer embarrassment of admitting all my failings would kill me. But maybe I should, since he'll accept no other answer?"

The goddess was silent, not that Tyema had expected anything else. It was comforting to speak freely, here in Mut's peaceful garden. *Almost like talking to Merys. Might as well unburden myself of all my worries.* "I love him, I trust him, I don't believe he's got anything to do with the black magic, but I can't explain the true situation there to him either."

A small breeze sprang up, winding through the trees and the statues, almost like a voice murmuring words too softly to be distinct. Tyema shivered, drawing her cloak more closely around herself.

Trust.

Did someone speak the word aloud? Startled, she took a step back, glancing around in fear.

As her gaze passed over the gracefully carved, outstretched wings of the goddess, she saw one gleaming feather work itself loose from the sculpture and drift ever so slowly to the ground, landing with the golden quill planted in the path, feather standing upright, vanes quivering in the slight breeze.

Tyema recoiled. "How can this be?" *The statue is carved from solid granite, I know it is.*

The breeze strengthened, giving her a push in the direction of the feather, or so it seemed. Tyema stumbled the few paces to where the uncanny plume stood. Bending over, half expecting to feel cold stone in her grasp, Tyema pulled the feather from the ground. Unable to resist, she stroked the downy softness along her cheek, closing her eyes in sheer awe. Facing Mut, she opened her eyes, drawing in a huge breath to steady her nerves. "I thank thee for this gift, Great One," she said, looking the statue full in the face. *Even if I have no clue as to the meaning or purpose of the gesture.*

There was no response, but Tyema hadn't expected one. She tucked the feather in her pocket before crossing her arms over her chest and bowing deep in respect, backing away from Mut until she knew she was at the edge of the chapel.

Sahure was waiting for her so she hastened down the path, wishing she didn't face the daunting day ahead. The queen's river cruise was bound to be tense, not pleasurable, even without watching all the passengers and crew for signs of black magic. An invitation impossible to avoid.

***

I should have skipped this river cruise, after the stressful discussion Sahure and I shared this morning, but Pharaoh made it clear he was losing patience. And I know the Royal Wife arranged the excursion for me, to more closely observe the most favored courtiers. Tyema brushed a few errant strands of hair from her face and sighed as she examined her surroundings for the tenth time since they'd left the royal dock. *And there are hours of sailing yet to endure.*

The queen's barge was huge, elegantly appointed, with a large shaded area in the center for Ashayet and her highest ranking guests to sit and talk. Honeyed wine and fruit were served and a trio of musicians—a harpist, a flutist, and a drummer— played softly at the bow. Not happy to be on a ship again, even a slow moving pleasure barge, Tyema went closer to the stern, leaning against the carved rail, a little hidden from view by the elaborate representation of lotus flowers decorating the ship's side. Nibbling a fig, she watched the courtiers laughing and talking. As always, her eyes were drawn to Sahure, in the middle of a group of officers and young women, the girls heavily made up, wearing the gauzy dresses that were all the rage in Thebes, colorful ribbons accenting the sheer fabric.

Tyema clenched her hand on the rail, averting her eyes to stare at the river rather than the people. It was none of her business what he did, who he talked to. *I refused any right to his attention, the night I rejected his marriage proposal and again this morning at Mut's temple.* Watching the Nile flow past as the rowers dipped their oars into the shining water, she sighed. Forcing herself to turn around again, she saw Sahure sharing a plate with Nidiamhet. Flickers of black and purple in the air around them riveted her attention. The magic was concentrated on the woman. Sekhmet's amulet was apparently affording Sahure some protection. *The sorcerer must be on this boat with us. Good. I want to be done with this hunt and free to go home.* Tyema scanned the crowd surrounding the queen but at first saw nothing out of the ordinary. Then a group of people shifted as new sweetmeats were brought from below by the servants and Tyema was staring directly at Baufratet.

The girl didn't see her, since she was glaring at Sahure and Nidiamhet. Rubbing one hand over the other as she observed the pair, Baufratet's face was set in petulant lines, elegantly arched brows drawn together in concentration. As Tyema watched, Sahure laughed at something his companion said and left her side to fetch more wine or food. As if stalking prey, keeping her gaze fixed on the woman she evidently perceived as a romantic rival, Baufratret crossed the deck toward Nidiamhet. A group of gossiping older ladies got between Tyema and her view of Nidiamhet and Baufratet, so she moved away from the safety of the alcove, walking closer to the edge of the deck.

All of a sudden a violent push struck in the center of her chest, as if someone was standing in front of her, trying to knock her off the boat. There was no rail behind her at this point on the barge. Instinctively, Tyema wrapped her hand around her emerald amulet and it was as if Sobek himself put his arms around her, holding her steady on the slippery planks of the deck.

Across the wide expanse, the two young ladies-in-waiting were wreathed in a cloud of black magic influence Tyema knew only she could see. While she watched in horror, both women were thrown off their feet by an invisible force, plunging into the Nile.

Did the black magic rebound on them when Sobek intervened to save me? Kicking off her sandals, Tyema sprinted across the deck. Shrieking, Baufratet was clinging to the edge of the barge, feet and lower legs dangling in the river. Two officers were already working to haul her back onboard. Hooking one arm around the nearest piece of ornamental fretwork, Tyema leaned over the river and searched in the ship's wake for Nidiamhet. The girl was nowhere in sight for a moment, then broke the surface, being carried away from the boat by the current. Clearly panicked, she was flailing her arms, eyes and mouth wide open in soundless terror.

Taking a deep breath, Tyema jumped into the water, clutching her amulet as she called orders to the Nile crocodiles sunning themselves on the far bank. "Find the woman who fell, help me!"

As she went under the cool surface of the water herself, Tyema heard someone else falling or diving next to her, but her focus was all for the helpless Nidiamhet. Holding her breath, opening her eyes under the water, Tyema saw the first crocodile arrowing toward her through the murky water. Reaching out, she gripped the spikes on its back. The creature immediately changed course and brought her to the surface. Craning her head, brushing clinging wet hair from her face, she saw Nidiamhet feebly attempting to swim. The girl was drifting with the current, moving perilously close to a group of curious hippos. As the crocodile carried Tyema nearer to the herd, she saw at least one baby in the cluster and knew even if Nidiamhet didn't drown, the hippos might attack her in the belief she was endangering their young.

In response to Tyema's earlier orders, another crocodile came up directly under Nidiamhet, raising her out of the water, draped across its back awkwardly. Shrieking, the girl fainted. Floating like the log it often pretended to be, the crocodile awaited further commands from Tyema. Meanwhile the hippos were becoming agitated, forming a circle around the calf, facing outward, mouths stretched open in challenge, exposing their powerful teeth.

"Ema!"

Checking behind her, she saw Sahure in the water, swimming strongly toward her. "What in the seven hells are you doing?" he yelled.

The crocodile supporting her rolled its gleaming eye at the new arrival but made no aggressive moves, obedient to Tyema's command. "I'm not sure how much I can get Sobek's creatures to do for someone else," she told Sahure, spitting out water as the Nile lapped at her. "Or how long I can control them. We've got to get Nidiamhet out of the river."

Treading water, he eyed the hippos. "Can you summon a few more crocodiles to put themselves between the herd and us?"

Getting a fresh grip on the spines of the animal beside her, she said, "I can try. I've never attempted to hold so many at once."

"Do that, and I'll fetch Nida."

Closing her eyes, she chanted a command, calling for guardians. She felt Sahure push off, swimming to meet the crocodile carrying Nidiamhet as the animal swam lazily nearer to them. A rush of water forced her to open her eyes, watching four crocodiles knife through the waves to take up positions between her and the hippos. Hippos could kill a crocodile, she knew, and she was anxious about endangering Sobek's children. She sent a prayer to Tawaret, visualizing the Hippo Goddess as she'd been on the night of Seknehure's birth. *Please hold your creatures in abeyance. We mean no harm to their young.*

"I've got her," Sahure yelled. He was swimming with powerful strokes to Tyema, pulling an unresisting, probably unconscious Nidiamhet along on her back. The crocodile which had been assisting the woman before Sahure arrived sank beneath the Nile's surface.

"I'm losing control, they don't want to be near the hippos," Tyema shouted. Tremors ran through the crocodile she was clinging to as it flexed its muscles, twitching impatiently. She stroked its head, just behind the eye. "I only need a few more moments, please." Blinking, the animal stilled, moving just enough to keep them afloat.

The queen's barge had come about and was bearing down on them. Although Tyema knew the crocodile wanted to be gone, it stayed, as did the four swimming in lazy circles between the hippos and her. "Quickly, get yourself and Nidiamhet out of the water," she said to Sahure. "The crocodiles will protect me, take me out of harm's way, but not the two of you." She was tired, cold, her arms were growing weak. As if sensing her condition, the crocodile adjusted, taking more of her weight.

A few moments later, Sahure was behind her, tugging her away from the crocodile, which rolled its eye at her and abruptly dove, swimming down and away with a flick of the powerful tail, leaving twin eddies in the surface of the Nile for a moment. Tyema was dimly aware of Sahure holding her tightly while sailors from the barge lifted the two of them in a net out of the Nile and safely on deck. Nidiamhet was nearby, coughing up water, being fussed over by her friends and her mother.

Baufratet was also being taken care of, weeping and lamenting her close call in dramatic fashion.

Queen Ashayet herself brought a robe to wrap Tyema, giving her a hug, heedless of her damp and muddy condition. "How fortunate you were right there when those foolish girls fell into the river."

Shivering now, Tyema couldn't speak. *One or both of those women is a sorcerer.* She reviewed the moments before the black magic rebounded from her protective amulet, trying to pin down which girl had been surrounded by the stronger aura, or might have made some gesture to hurl a spell. Her thoughts and memories were like the disjointed pieces of a puzzle which she was to tired to assemble, after the excitement and exertion of the time in the river.

Sahure was rubbing her arms, holding her tight. "As soon as we get to the palace landing, I'll have you to your rooms and into a hot bath," he said.

***

He carried her from the barge dock directly to her chambers, snapping orders at the waiting palace maids Edekh had dispatched to pour her a hot bath. Once the bathing pool had been refreshed with heated water, he banished the servants from the room. Even Renebti and the baby were sent to her chamber, so adamant was Sahure about privacy. After stripping Tyema's muddy, damp dress from her shivering body, he stepped into the pool with her curled in his arms and lovingly bathed her, washing her hair with sweetly scented oil before wrapping her in a large towel. Afterwards he carried her to the bed. Drying himself off, wrapping a towel around his loins, he joined her on the webbed mattress, but not before yanking the heavier curtains closed to provide additional privacy. Pulling her into his embrace, he held her close.

"I know you're protected by the Crocodile God himself," he said, "But I thought my heart would stop when I saw you jump into the Nile today."

"You're not protected and you came in after me," she said, covering her mouth as she yawned. The whole ordeal had taken a great deal out of her, particularly the tense minutes holding the crocodiles against their will to assist other people. She refused to think about the next steps she must take to sort out whether it was Nidiamhet or Baufratet wielding the black magic. She'd probably used her power over the crocodiles to save the sorceress, for the time being. All of that could wait until tomorrow.

"As if I'd stand by and watch the woman I love drown or be killed. In some ways you don't know me at all," he said, reaching out to pick up the sea shell-decorated comb on the side table. Using smooth, slow strokes he removed the snarls and tangles in her hair.

"Do you still love me?" Immediately wishing she could recall the forlorn question, she hated the plaintive tone in her own voice. *I sound like my younger self, the outcast, crippled child, begging for crumbs of my mother's affection. I swore I'd never do that again.*

Dropping the comb, he tightened his arms around her, holding her close to his heart. "I never stopped loving you, not even the night you first rejected me. I was angry, yes. Was I an idiot for leaving Ibis Nome in such a state? Absolutely. But have no doubt my love stayed true."

She retrieved the comb, stroking her finger along the edge of the teeth. "I'm sorry."

"No need to apologize." He kissed her cheek. "I think I understand more now, having seen you here in Thebes. What I proposed to you originally wouldn't have worked, would it?" Not waiting for her answer, he continued, "The queen warned me I'd failed to give proper consideration to what I was asking of you and she was right, as usual. You're like a special lotus, which can only grow in one place in the Black Lands, in the Ibis Nome, am I right? Take you away from your sheltered cove for too long and you won't thrive."

She took a deep breath. *Time for truth. Either I trust this man with the full story of my past and how it affects me to this day, or I let him go forever.* "No, I can't thrive, as you put it."

"So I must think of another solution, because I still intend us to be together as man and wife, with our son."

Surprised, her heart aching, Tyema twisted to gaze into his face. "There's no solution, my love. Your destiny calls for you to stay here, in Thebes, where you can do great things for Pharaoh and Egypt. Mine calls for me to stay in Ibis Nome."

"I refuse to accept your dreary interpretation of our fates. Just as I refused to become your temple guard." His tone was intimate and teasing. He kissed the soft spot where her neck joined her shoulders and she arched against him to invite more caresses. It was like a dream to be back in his arms, held close against his strong body. Unable to stop herself, Tyema ran a hand down his arm, tracing the curves of his muscles, well developed from all the military arts he excelled at.

Sahure whispered in her ear. "I want to understand the underlying problems because clearly there's something I don't know yet. Most of all, I want to apologize for being so high handed and arrogant on our final evening in your rooms. I was wrong to assume you'd give up all you'd achieved in your life for me and my precious career. I spent many a sleepless night in regrets."

She was too tired to keep her secrets from him anymore. He deserved to know what separated them. *Let me tell him with no softening of the ugly truth, put his surety we can overcome anything to the test. And if his love fails the test, better for us both to know.* "When I was born, my right leg was withered, misshapen." Pulling aside the sheets, she extended her right leg as if to be sure the limb hadn't reverted to its childhood state, pointing the toes and flexing them. "My mother said someone had put the evil eye on her, cursed her, that I was demon spawn, an animal, and should be killed," Tyema said. "Or so I was told, over and over."

His arms tightened. "Set's teeth, what mother would say such a thing of her baby? A child is a gift from the gods."

Somehow it was easier to talk because she couldn't see his face, yet his strength and love were wrapped around her. "My half-sister Merys saved me, treated me like her own child, saw I was given to a wet nurse. My father was the town's chief scribe at the time so there was plenty of deben, although Merys had to shame him into hiring the woman. Merys raised me. She taught me to walk as best I could, forced me to do exercises to strengthen my withered leg. She also taught me the traditional songs of the priestess since the gods had gifted me with a strong voice and sense of music." Tyema wiped away a tear. *Speaking of it is like reliving the horror.*

And yet somehow it wasn't. Telling Sahure was curiously simple, inflicted no pain. Maybe even felt good, like lancing a wound? Tyema decided to give him more details. "Other children in the village taunted me, threw stones at me sometimes when I tried to play with them. I'd no friends but Merys."

He rubbed her arms gently to warm them. "Children can be cruel to those who are different."

"In my tenth summer, the Hyksos raided the village. Merys was—was killed on the beach, below the old temple." She took in a breath, gulping as the tears threatened to overwhelm her. Even though she knew Merys was safe now, beyond the ability of anyone to harm her, the memories were overwhelming tonight. She'd never spoken of these matters to anyone and found she couldn't stop.

Turning her to face him, he put a gentle finger on her lips for a moment, before resting her head on his chest, holding her close, curled against him. "I know the unspeakable acts the Hyksos commit, no need to say more unless you wish to continue. May your sister's *ka* be at peace. And you?"

"When the Hyksos attacked the town, I was taken prisoner, along with most of the other women and children. The Hyksos commander said although I was flawed, I'd make an interesting sacrifice to their god. Something amusing for the demons to chew on, he said." Tyema knew if she closed her eyes she would still see the man, as if he'd stood taunting her now, not fifteen years ago. "We were carried away up the Nile in ships. I hadn't been on a ship since that day, in fact, until I had to sail to Thebes to bring Pharaoh the new crocodile for the temple. What an ordeal the journey was, but Sobek ordered me to come." She did close her eyes then, biting her lip. *Treading too close to the true reason why I'm here.*

"If sailing causes you distress, which I can understand it might, how did you manage the voyage to Thebes? Did your physician give you a potion or a spell?"

She shook her head slightly. "I thought of taking such an easy way out, drugging myself to make the journey, but my son—our son—was on board with me. He needed me."

"You could have left him in Ta'sobeksef, with a wet nurse."

Indignant, Tyema sat up. "I'm not a coward. I knew you might be in Thebes, the nomarch told me. I wanted you to know your son. I never intended to keep you from him."

Capturing her hand and bringing it to his lips for a kiss, he made reassuring noises. "No need to be so defensive, I believe you. So resuming your tale of years ago, how were you rescued from the Hyksos?"

"Sobek himself came to save us. He brought his crocodiles to destroy the enemy ships, just battered them to pieces. He led the attack as the White Crocodile, rescuing me, because he knew how much Merys loved me." She stared into Sahure's warm brown eyes, narrowed in concern for her and the painful past she was revealing. "Can I tell you something you must never repeat? I want no more secrets about the past between us, and I have Sobek's permission. The day he made you the map of the Nile he said I could share this truth with you, although I didn't understand why he was saying it at the time."

No hint of amusement in his demeanor, Sahure laid his free hand over his heart. "I swear upon my immortal *ka* not to ever speak of Sobek's secrets."

Satisfied, she nodded. "Not even the other members of my family know this, but Sobek and Merys were lovers. She was carrying his baby. When it came time for the judging of her heart, the goddess Isis granted Merys the special dispensation that she and the child could have eternity in the Afterlife with Sobek in the home of the gods."

Sahure was speechless for a moment. "No wonder the Great One insisted my uncle place your Merys in a lavish tomb, give her full honors as if she was a member of our family. He attends to its upkeep and protection to this day."

Tyema nodded. "I used to see Merys occasionally while I was growing up. Her *ka* was allowed to come from the Afterlife to the old temple every once in a while, and take on human form. She even brought Hathor and Tarawet to save my life and the baby's life the night he was born, but now Isis has forbidden her to travel to our world again. It's so strange, Merys is unchanged, and I'm older than she was when she passed into the Afterlife."

"Does Merys's spirit tie you to the village and prevent you from leaving?"

"No, I'll see Merys when I reach the Afterlife, if my heart be judged worthy. I'm not a child any more, Sahure. I don't need mothering from Merys to get through my tasks, my days. But to finish the tale of that awful day, many years ago, Sobek took us all back to the village, where he straightened my leg. He's not a healing god, but he said the task was simple to do. My entire life until then I'd been shunned, hated, an outcast, and he made my leg whole in the blink of an eye."

"But not your heart," Sahure said, raising his eyebrows.

She nodded. "He declared me to be his high priestess, gave me the six emerald tears. But I'd spent my entire life scuttling out of view, trying to stay away from people, not to disgrace my family or myself, avoiding torment and hurt—"

"And you can't bear to be in crowds of people unless you're carrying out tasks for Sobek. I understand now." He hugged her close to his heart, kissing the top of her head.

"I get physically ill, afraid I'm going to faint, or die, or lose control of some bodily function, which did happen to me on occasion as a child. Often I can't breathe." She tried to smile, knew she wasn't succeeding. "My heart races as if to pound its way from my chest. There are few people I can be comfortable with. Talking about anything besides temple business is hard for me. I never know what to say, my tongue ties itself into the shape of Isis's knot. You were the first person since Merys I felt completely at ease with, right from the first night. I fell in love with you. I'm sorry my love wasn't strong enough to overcome my malady."

"Shh, beloved, we'll find a way to work around the problem, now you've trusted me enough to tell me what the boundaries are." Stroking her back, he seemed thoughtful, brows drawn together in a frown. "You've done quite well here in Thebes though, all things considered. Not just at the temple ceremonies. You sang for Pharaoh in the midst of all his court."

Snuggling close to the warmth of his body, listening to the steady beat of his heart, she took a breath and pondered his words. "You're right, it hasn't been as bad in Thebes as I feared. Of course you were here. And Pharaoh and his queen are so kind. Another odd thing—ever since Seknehure was born, I can be fearless on his behalf, as I am for Sobek."

"My kitten is a lioness for her cub." Sahure hugged her.

"I want to be a lioness for you." She ran her hand over the smooth muscles of his abdomen, traced the raised white lines of an old battle scar on his flank. "You deserve someone who can help you achieve your dreams. They're good dreams, Sahure."

"I can take care of myself, sweetheart." His eyes crinkled as he laughed. "As long as I have you and Seknehure to come home to, I'm perfectly capable of building my own career, molding success. I understand now why you'll always serve Sobek from your own temple in Ta'sobeksef."

"Truly?"

With one hand he gently tilted her chin so their eyes met. "Truly," he said as he lowered his head to hers, kissing her lips with increasing pressure until she yielded, parting to allow his questing tongue entry. For several breathless moments she clung to him, returning his caress with all the pent-up ardor of the long months apart. When the kiss was done, he said, "I just wish you'd trusted me with this information earlier. We could both have been spared much unhappiness."

"You're so strong and capable, I didn't want to tell you how weak I was. I dreaded you'd despise me, regret having fallen in love with me. Or laugh at me." Even as she spoke, Tyema knew Sahure would never have done any of those things.

He might not have understood her problems before seeing how she fared in Thebes, but he never would have disrespected her. She'd done him and herself a serious disservice by not trusting him with her secret challenges.

"Sweetheart, you're one of the strongest women I know, in so many ways. I think you spoke the truth the other day when you said our relationship was too rushed in Ibis Nome. If you'd known me better, longer, I think you'd have realized my love was true. I'd give anything to protect you, in any situation." He grinned. "Even in the direst danger of a formal dinner in Pharaoh's palace."

They both chuckled and he recaptured her lips for another kiss so passionate she was left thrumming with arousal and desire.

Tyema was first to pull away this time, still curious. "But if we'd had months together in Ibis rather than weeks, if I'd eventually spoken of my concerns about how I could fit into your dreams for a shared future here in Thebes—"

"I have two dreams, which I thought were inextricably entwined, but now I know better. I wanted to rise in power and influence so I could be a builder of the future for Egypt, and I wanted a wife to be my partner. What I didn't know, being a fool, was if I had a wife who loved me for myself, I'd be truly blessed by the gods, wherever I ended up, whatever I did. We'll figure out the future, Ema, but we'll do it together." He pulled her closer, his tongue once again seeking hers, his arms holding her as if he'd never let go.

Tyema adjusted herself in his embrace as the caress continued, relaxing against his body, feeling the unmistakable evidence of his arousal as his hard cock thrust against her thigh. She couldn't quite surrender herself completely to the heady emotions, all too aware she hadn't told him about the black magic. He broke off the kiss, the expression on his face one of concern. "Am I rushing you again? I thought your desire matched mine tonight, but if not—"

Puzzled, she held him closer. "I've longed for you, for the intimacy we shared in Ibis, more than I can say. Why are you hesitating?" She stroked one hand across his chest, rubbing her palm ever so lightly on the flat nipple before bending to tease him with her tongue.

"You seem lost in thought. If you have any further doubts of me, I'd hear them now." His voice was firm.

But Sobek swore me to secrecy, and I'm still not sure how Sahure is involved or affected. She gave his nipple one final caress and sat. "No doubts." Her hand slid beneath the thin linen sheet, stroking his engorged cock as he took a deep breath in response to her bold possession of his manhood. She clasped her fingers around him, enjoying the feel of all that power, caged in her hand. Leaning forward, Tyema swirled her tongue across the head, savoring the salty taste of the moisture beaded there. Taking his cock into her mouth, she spent a few delicious moments with Sahure at her mercy as she licked and sucked, her other hand caressing his balls and the sensitive skin behind them.

With a groan he pulled her away and rolled her onto her back, kissing his way down her neck. "Many times I've dreamt of lying with you again." His hand parted the hair at the vee of her thighs, the long fingers skillfully penetrating her most private places, to rub and stimulate, coaxing her body into delicious spasms of feeling.

But she wanted more. Tugging at him, she urged him to move over her, plunging his shaft into her well prepared sheath. As she remembered, he filled her completely, even stretched as she'd been by childbirth. She matched her movements to Sahure's as he pumped in and out, holding him tightly, locking her legs around him to increase the sensation for them both. He captured her lips for a kiss that went on forever as their bodies moved in a well remembered unison, until the cresting pleasure sent her over the edge and she threw back her head, screaming his name. Sahure thrust deep into her, intensifying her pleasure as he reached his own release.

As they lay together afterward, his body warm against her back, she prayed to Sobek they might have made another child together this day. *Nothing would make me happier than to present him with another fine son or a beautiful daughter.*

CHAPTER NINE

The next day's schedule held plans for the ladies-in-waiting and other high born Theban women to play games and dine at Nidiamhet's home on the edge of Thebes. Tyema half hoped the event would be canceled after the dunking in the Nile, but word from her hostess came early in the morning by special courier how much Nidiamhet anticipated the gathering, and especially rejoiced in having Tyema as her special guest.

Queen Ashayet was not attending this event. Tyema wished the Great Royal Wife was to be there. She felt safer in the queen's presence, which of course was ridiculous. Ashayet had no power to thwart a sorceress. But after the incident on the royal barge the day before, Tyema felt she'd narrowed her search down to two candidates, both of whom would be in attendance. She hoped she might observe some sign which would allow her to eliminate either her hostess or Baufratet from suspicion. *And then I report to Sobek and to Pharaoh and let them take action while I flee home.*

After bidding a lingering farewell to Sahure at midmorning in the privacy of her chambers, giving Seknehure a kiss, she walked through the now familiar halls of the palace to the area where a number of litters waited to carry the invited guests through Thebes to Nidiamhet's family compound.

The first few hours went well, Tyema gradually relaxing as she saw no vestiges of the black magic. While disappointed to realize her mission wasn't going to be resolved today after all, she was happy the gathering was so informal and cordial. Since Ashayet hadn't attended, the guests weren't required to observe royal protocol and decorum. Tyema was now somewhat acquainted with many of the women in attendance, and as the activity centered around tables of senet and other games, it was easy to relax and let the conversation flow over her while she threw the counters and moved her pawns along with her companions.

There was an ebb and flow of the black magic around Nidiamhet today, very little in evidence near Baufratet. But matters had been that way before so Tyema still wasn't sure who was the instigator. She debated leaving the gathering early and giving Pharaoh a report of what she did know. Only the concern that the impatient ruler would order the death of both women in order to have the problem resolved, kept her at the house party, in hopes of seeing something definitive.

About an hour after the delicious luncheon had been served, Tyema felt nauseous and dizzy. Puzzled, because she'd been having a good time with the ladies of the Court, feeling more relaxed than normal in a social gathering, she put her hands over her stomach. Pain was growing on her left side. Whatever this was, the illness was definitely not her usual malady.

"Are you all right?" asked the woman she was playing jackals and hounds with, eyes open wide in concern. "You've gone pale."

"Perhaps something I ate at lunch disagreed with me," Tyema said, setting the black and white counters on the table. "I'm not used to all the spices used here in Thebes." Cringing, biting her lips, she choked back a moan as a new flare of nausea combined with hot pain clawed at her.

"Have some wine? Or some water?" The woman, whose name she'd forgotten, searched the room for a servant to summon.

"Water perhaps." Tyema put a hand to her forehead.

Nidiamhet came hurrying over. "What ails you, my friend?"

"My—my stomach," Tyema said, barely able to speak for the nausea. She clutched at Nidiamhet's arm, despite the swirls of black magic in the air. Tyema's pain was such that she could only think about getting some relief. "Please, I need to lie down."

"Of course." Nidiamhet drew Tyema to her feet with surprising strength, putting one arm around her waist. "Lean on me and I'll take you to one of our spare bedrooms."

Tyema closed her eyes for a moment, allowing the other woman to lead her through the room. "I'm sorry to cause a fuss, but I think I need a basin. I'm going to be sick."

"Probably a passing thing," her hostess said in soothing tone. "Maybe the food was too rich for one unaccustomed to our northern cooking. You'll be fine by sunset."

"May I help?" The Minoan attaché's daughter joined them, taking Tyema by the other arm.

Alarmed despite the onslaught of nausea, Tyema raised her head, searching for some other assistance, only to realize in her pain and confusion she'd allowed herself to be led from the chamber where all the women were gathered. Nidiamhet and Jadikiria were guiding her rapidly down a corridor. She pulled back against them. "Please, you're both very kind but I'd rather go to the palace. Just call my litter. The court physician can treat this."

"Nonsense," Nidiamhet said, gripping her arm more tightly. "You're under my roof and my responsibility for now. I know what's best. You're far too ill to travel."

Tyema tried to dig in her heels but strength was rapidly leaving her body. The two women half dragged her the length of a corridor and then into a smaller side hall, ending the journey in a windowless room dominated by a small bed. They dropped her onto the mattress and she turned her head to be sick on the floor. Wiping her mouth a few moments later, trembling, she said, "I insist you call for my litter and let me seek help at the palace."

"You can insist all you want, but you're wasting your breath," Nidiamhet said, reaching to get a grip on Tyema's crocodile amulet. "You'll be going somewhere else all right, but you'll find no one to help you. Quite the contrary." With a yank that jerked the weakened Tyema half off the bed and sent hot pain through her neck and back, Nidiamhet broke the fine gold chain holding the amulet, slipping the stone into her pocket. "Your precious Sobek won't hear you now." Her hostess grabbed some linens from a nearby table and mopped the floor where Tyema had been sick, swearing under her breath.

Head spinning, Tyema tried to stand, but the Minoan woman waiting nearby easily shoved her flat on the bed. Head pounding, barely conscious from the nausea, Tyema said, "You poisoned me?"

"Nothing fatal."

Those were the last words Tyema heard for a few moments until Nidiamhet started shaking her roughly by the shoulder, jarring the bed. "Open your eyes, I want you to see this."

Blinking, surprised and frightened she'd passed out without even realizing it, Tyema took a deep breath and opened her eyes as ordered, the lamplight in the room making her nausea worse. The intensity of black magic in the air and the aura around Jadikiria only heightened her fear. Between agonizing abdominal cramps, curling into a ball, Tyema whispered, "What could you possibly want to show me?"

Nidiamhet reached down and yanked a few hairs from Tyema's head. "I think I got the resemblance remarkably right, don't you?" She held a wax figure close to Tyema's face. The tiny figurine was female, wearing only a loose kilt. Tyema's name was inscribed in hieratic on the doll's bare chest. Seating herself on the end of the bed while Jadikiria hovered nearby, Nidiamhet busied herself wrapping the strands of stolen hair around the neck and head of the effigy. "I learned to make these spell dolls from a most excellent book of black magic I discovered, locked in a cabinet in Pharaoh's library. The librarian was almost no challenge at all. A few simple spells and he was only too happy to reveal the deepest secrets, the most forbidden tablets, to me." One eyebrow raised, she glanced at the Minoan. "He admires my poetry, you see, which gave me a starting place for my magic to work on him. Hand me a quill from the basket on the table, will you?"

Hand on her head, which stung where the hair had been yanked out, Tyema made another futile effort to rise. Again Nidiamhet shoved her flat, scratching Tyema's shoulder with her long fingernails in the process. Unable to control her urge to be ill, Tyema retched, holding her aching stomach. Scarcely above a whisper, she asked, "Why are you doing this?"

"Because you stand in my way. Until he met you, Sahure was eager to marry me, use my connections to further his career." Nidiamhet stood taller, smoothing her wig with one hand. "I only had to influence that stupid girl Baufratet. Cause her to disgust Sahure by being too openly eager for his attention, and then there was no other rival. Our marriage was just a matter of time. Now you've had his child and all he can think about is you and your problems." Nidiamhet snorted as she leaned closer. "I'll be a good mother to the brat, I promise. All Thebes will sing my praises as a doting stepmother."

Thoughts of her baby in peril gave Tyema renewed strength. Kicking out, she knocked Nidiamhet off balance. Rolling off the bed in the next moment, Tyema staggered to her feet, heading for the door, screaming for help. The Minoan launched herself at Tyema, carrying them both to the floor, where she continued to struggle as best she could, slapping at the other woman's hands and face. Suddenly she lost all feeling in her arms and legs, falling on her back as if paralyzed, head striking the floor with a jarring thud. The Minoan extricated herself from Tyema's limp embrace and stood, aiming a swift kick at her ribs, saying as she did so, "No one heard you, we're in the farthest wing of the house."

Nidiamhet bent over, showing Tyema the doll, whose hands were now tied behind its back with Tyema's hair, wax ankles similarly hobbled. "Your god was a fool to send you to Thebes. Neither you nor he has the slightest idea how to fight the kind of magic I can wield, even if he did somehow protect you from me while you were in Ibis Nome last year. Of course I wasn't as powerful then, and I didn't know much about you."

"You've been an excellent student since I was sent to tutor you this year." Working to replace the ivory pins in her complicated hairdo as she complimented her accomplice, Jadikiria said, "Granted you started from a strong place, owning the magic ring your mother looted from the Usurper Pharaoh's bedchamber during the chaos when Nat-re-Akhte took Thebes. Our god still hungers for domination over Egypt and our group of exiles would be only too happy to regain the Black Lands for him, with you as our secret agent inside the Court."

"Help me put her back on the bed." Placing the wax doll on the table, Nidiamhet took Tyema by the shoulders and Jadikiria scurried to pick up her feet. Unceremoniously the women dumped her onto the bed, flopping helplessly as if she'd become the doll.

"I'm not sure you're ready for this level of spell casting, though," Jadikiria said as Tyema's head banged against the head rest, unable to control her own movements or even cry out with pain. "I wish you'd consulted me first. This course of action is risky, invoking Qemtusheb's demon servants without the proper preliminary sacrifices, lacking a consecrated altar, no priests to support you—"

Sobek, help me! Tyema couldn't move a single finger now. She felt tears trickle down her cheeks as she thought of her son. There was no answer from the Great One. Anger at her god and her own naiveté fought with the nausea and pain in her gut. *I never should have come to Thebes, and he should have known I'd be no match for a true sorcerer. It was exceedingly reckless to come here today. Why didn't I just report Baufratet and Nidiamhet to Pharaoh and let him sort the matter out?* Tyema prayed Sahure would resist Nidiamhet's black magic, would shield their child from her evil intentions.

"I know what I'm doing. The book of spells was clear enough. I send the *ka* of a living being as a sacrifice to Qemtusheb, for his pleasure, and he grants me tremendous power as a result." Nidiamhet shrugged. "Her being a priestess, and a mother, just makes her more valuable as a sacrifice."

Jadikiria stared at Tyema, who tried to project her hate and loathing in a glare, her powers of speech having fled under the influence of the spell doll. Jadikiria glanced away, rubbing her arms as if cold or uneasy, frowning. "Still, my high priest is due to arrive in Egypt within the next week or so. I wish you'd wait till he was here, to consult and assist. All your guests saw how unwell the priestess was, you could administer a fatal dose of the poison now and no one could possibly question her death. Your rival would be removed and you could pick another target to be your sacrifice later. Rituals are important to approaching Qemtusheb. This is rushed and not according to form, which worries me."

"Watch then, and let your fears be assuaged." Nidiamhet came back into Tyema's field of vision, holding the doll. Speaking to Tyema, she said, "Pay attention, she-viper, for now I'm sending your *ka* to the realm of Qemtusheb's demons." With the quill, she wrote something on the doll's left leg. She yanked Tyema's dress up and peered closely at her leg.

Tyema screamed soundlessly as raised red weals appeared on her skin, symbols spelling out a word or name she didn't know as if she was being branded.

Nidiamhet leaned over to check the results. Apparently satisfied, she started writing on the effigy's other leg. "In case you're curious," she said to Tyema in a conversational tone that was horrifyingly matter of fact, "These are the names of the demons I'm calling to accept you as my sacrifice, names which can't be uttered aloud. It may take some time, but they'll collect your *ka* all right."

The pain was fading in her left leg even as it increased in her right. The weals disappeared as the next name was written, the symbols seeming to sink into Tyema's body through her skin. As Nidiamhet began scrawling the final two names on the doll's arms, Tyema—unable to bear the pain any longer—lost consciousness. Her last prayer was for her child to be safe in Sahure's arms.

***

Sahure's day had been excellent, doing practice drills with some of his comrades on the training ground, followed by a round of archery and an impromptu chariot race. It was good to be back in Thebes among his fellow warriors. Anticipating escorting Tyema to Pharaoh's banquet later in the evening, followed by another leisurely session of lovemaking in the privacy of her rooms, he'd bathed and shaved and was donning his dress uniform when there was a peremptory knock on the door.

"Enter!" Fastening his cloak, he turned to greet the newcomer.

It was the scribe who'd been appointed to sit outside Tyema's door in case she had need of Edekh. He leaned on the door jamb, breathing hard as if he'd been in a race. "You must come quickly, sir."

"What's amiss? Did Lady Tyema send you?" He grabbed his dagger and pushed past the scribe into the hall, striding rapidly in the direction of Tyema's rooms.

Hurrying to keep up, the scribe said, "No, my lord, it was Lady Renebti. She insisted you be summoned. Lady Nidiamhet wished to deal with the situation herself but—"

Alarmed, Sahure stopped, grabbing the other man by the arm. "Speak plainly. Where's Tyema?"

The scribe gulped. "She fell ill, sir, and has been brought to her quarters unconscious. The ladies argue over how to care for her, as I understood matters."

At a dead run, Sahure left the scribe behind and reached Tyema's suite moments later, passing the saluting guards in an instant and coming to a halt in the first chamber.

"Thank the gods," Renebti cried. White-faced, wig askew, makeup ruined by tears, she was clutching a screaming Seknehure. Backed into a corner, she was facing Nidiamhet, who'd apparently been trying to wrest the baby from her arms. Renebti seized the distraction afforded by Sahure's entrance to dart around the lady-in-waiting and scoot across the room to the door of Tyema's bedroom.

"What is the meaning of this? What's going on?" Sahure stood in the center of the room, hands on his hips, dread like a knife in his heart.

Niadiamhet sauntered to him, her eyes soft with unshed tears, although he noted in passing her elaborate eye makeup was untouched. Placing one hand on his arm, she leaned closer. "Your lady was taken ill today at my home. I've brought her back to the palace as she requested, but I'm afraid now she's unconscious."

Removing her fingers from his forearm, Sahure strode to the entrance to Tyema's room, shoving aside the draperies, Renebti meeting him at her aunt's bed. Tyema lay in the center, a small, still figure. Makeup smudged and running, her eyes were closed and sweat beaded her brow.

Sahure bent over her, hand on her shoulder, calling her name, but she didn't open her eyes. "She was healthy this morning," he said in disbelief.

Leaning over, Nidiamhet smoothed the hair away from Tyema's face in a maternal gesture. "And she was fine at my family's home, until shortly after luncheon concluded. Then she began to complain of stomach pains. I took her to lie down in peace in a spare room and when it was time for the party to break up I found her as you see her now, feverish and unresponsive. Perhaps I should have left a maid to sit with her in the afternoon. I feel badly not to have checked on her sooner, but Tyema insisted on being alone to nap."

Sahure had no time or patience for any excuses. "Has the royal physician been sent for?"

Holding the furiously crying child as best she could, Renebti nodded. "As soon as they carried my aunt into the room, I asked the scribe outside to fetch the doctor, then to get you."

"Then where is the man?" Sahure reached for his son. "What ails Seknehure? Is he also falling ill?"

"He's hungry, my lord." Renebti handed him the baby, who was momentarily distracted by Sahure's golden falcon badge. "I gave him water and juice, but he needs milk."

Edekh hurried into the room, followed by the royal physician, who went immediately to the bedside, setting down his box of instruments and potions. He made a shooing gesture as he did a quick visual examination of Tyema's limp form. "Give me space, if you please, my lord, ladies. Let me have a chance to assess my patient."

Sahure carried his son to the outer room, Edekh at his side. Nidiamhet lingered in the bedroom, as did Renebti. Sahure heard them talking over each other as they sought to explain Tyema's symptoms to the doctor.

"Edekh, will you do me a favor?" Sahure asked.

"As long as it isn't anything to do with the screaming baby," he answered, eyeing the red-faced, howling Seknehure with misgiving.

"Send a courier and a chariot to my family's estate, tell my mother to dispatch our best wet nurse from the village immediately." Sahure cast a glance at the bedroom. "I fear Tyema won't be able to care for my son anytime soon. I can't allow him to go hungry and sicken as well."

Edekh bowed. "A wise precaution. I'll see to it." He spoke to the waiting scribe, who rushed off. Turning his back to the bedroom, Edekh said, "This is all unnervingly odd. Lady Tyema seemed fine this morning when I saw her."

Sahure kissed his son's forehead and patted his back. "I don't like it either."

Leaning closer, Edekh lowered his voice. "I understand Nidiamhet was bidding her guests farewell when the gaming party ended, as if nothing had happened. One of the more senior ladies of the court— General Kaminhotep's wife, I believe— insisted upon saying farewell to Lady Tyema, knowing she'd been unwell, wishing to see how she was faring. When she saw your priestess in this state, she ensured Tyema was brought to the palace. It wasn't Nidiamhet's doing, although she came along and now takes credit."

His thoughts racing, Sahure glanced at the bedroom. "What are you insinuating?"

"Nothing, merely reporting all the facts, in order for you to properly assess the situation."

"Perhaps this fever is an effect of her immersion in the river yesterday," Nidiamhet said, walking over to them, either not having heard or uncaring of what Edekh had said. She held her arms out. "I can hold the child."

"My aunt didn't want anyone touching Seknehure without her permission." Renebti, who'd also left the bedroom, rushed to put herself between Sahure and the lady-in-waiting. "Other than his father, of course. Please, my lord, I'll take him if need be."

"Thank you." Sahure had misgivings about the entire situation, without being able to identify the source of his unease. "It's kind of you to offer, Nidiamhet, but the child knows his cousin and will be less upset in familiar arms." He transferred Seknehure to Renebti, who hugged him close as she edged a few steps away.

Nidiamhet laid her hand on his arm. "Of course. I understand." Waving a graceful hand at the bedroom, she said, "I'll be glad to sit with Lady Tyema, make sure she's well tended during the night, help in any way I can."

"You might be sickening yourself, Lady Nidiamhet," Edekh said before Sahure could say anything. "You were in the Nile yesterday too."

Laughing she shook her head, slipping her arm around Sahure's waist and leaning close. "No, I'm fine, I assure you. Lord Sahure rescued me with no thought for himself."

His skin crawling at the casual way she was touching him in this inappropriate moment, Sahure kept his temper with an effort. *As if now Tyema has fallen ill, I'd be happy to move on to another woman.* Removing her arm from his waist, Sahure took Nidiamhet by the elbow and escorted her to the door. "I'm grateful to you for bringing Tyema safely back to the palace. We can't ask more of you."

She had sense enough not to argue with him. "You'll keep me informed how she does?"

He nodded. Nidiamhet went on tiptoe and kissed his cheek. "I'm so sorry, Sahure, I know she means a great deal to you. May the gods bless her." She slipped out the door before he could say anything else.

Rubbing his cheek as if to erase the unwanted kiss, he stalked to the bedroom, where the doctor was just completing his examination. "Well? What's your diagnosis?"

The doctor pinched the bridge of his nose. "Fever of unknown origin."

"Lacking any shred of medical training, I could have written that papyrus," Sahure said, frustrated. "What can be done for her?"

Apparently used to dealing with irate family members, the doctor merely shrugged. "I've given her something to relieve the symptoms and left you a packet of herbs to mix into another dose in the middle of the night. Frankly, she'll have to be watched closely. Prayers must be offered to the appropriate deities. Try to get her to drink water at any opportunity."

Sahure gazed at the pale, unconscious figure of his beloved and searched his heart in vain for hope.

"Don't hesitate to summon me if there's any change," the doctor said, packing up his scrolls and potions. "I'll return in the morning to check on her."

Carrying the baby on her hip, Renebti came to peer around Sahure as the doctor bowed and left. "What are we going to do, my lord?"

"Pharaoh and the queen have offered any assistance you desire," Edekh said. "Her majesty regrets she can't come in person, but Pharaoh has forbidden her to risk exposure to this virulent fever."

Sahure sat on the edge of the bed, taking one of Tyema's limp hands in his, alarmed at how hot her skin felt to his touch. Propping her up with one arm, he poured a mug of water from the pitcher and held it to her lips. Encouraged by the fact she drank a few sips even though her eyes didn't open, he had a thought. "Can we have two of the palace maids assigned to help us care for her?" He smoothed her tousled hair away from her face.

"Of course. And the wet nurse will be brought to you the moment she arrives, even if it be in the middle of the night." Edekh frowned. "I wish there was more to be done."

"When I was sick with fever and spots last year, my mother put cooling rags on my forehead," Renebti offered.

"We'll try the suggestion. We'll try any remedy, no matter how farfetched," Sahure said, fists clenched. "When the maids get here, we can give her a refreshing bath."

"I'll send two of the most senior serving girls right away. Let me know if there's anything else." Edekh bowed and left them alone.

Renebti leaned close, her voice lowered. "I didn't want to speak of this while anyone else was here, but there's something seriously amiss, my lord."

"What? What do you mean?"

"Her amulet from the Great One Sobek, where is it?" Renebti's eyes were wide and her voice shook ever so slightly. "Aunt Tyema never takes it off."

Startled, chagrined he hadn't noticed, Sahure took another look. "I'll talk to Nidiamhet tomorrow, but perhaps the chain was broken somehow, or the amulet fell when they placed her in the litter. I'm sure the Great One will give her another." Gazing at Renebti's face, so youthful under the ruined makeup, he saw again how frightened she was. What she needed to hear right now was reassurance she'd done the right thing and encouragement that Tyema would recover. "I didn't get a chance to thank you for sending for me so promptly. I'm grateful."

Renebti blushed, lowering her eyes for a moment, shifting Seknehure on her hip. "I knew my aunt would want you in charge of her care, and of your son. I couldn't win an argument with Lady Nidiamhet, her being a grand court lady, couldn't do more than delay her intentions at best, but I knew you'd agree with me."

The odd choice of words caught his attention. "Argument?"

Hugging his son close, Tyema's niece frowned. "She wanted to take the baby away, sir, to keep him safe, she said. I know Aunt Tyema would never agree, no matter how sick she was. You're an entirely different matter, being his father."

What in the name of Set's teeth would make Nidiamhet believe my son should be removed from his closest female relative other than his own mother, and given into her care? She has no experience with babies and no right to take custody of my son. Disturbed, he was glad he'd followed his instincts to keep the woman from participating further in nursing Tyema. Nidiamhet undoubtedly meant well, with a healthy portion of wanting to make herself appear helpful and gracious in his eyes, but he'd no time for games.

***

Why am I lying on cold rock? Tyema rolled over, arms and legs numb, as if she hadn't moved in quite awhile. She opened her eyes and immediately blinked them shut again against the odd, brassy yellow glare all around her. She heard the quiet hiss and sizzle of fire. Gathering her determination, she sat up and opened her eyes again. She was sitting on a cold stone ledge, surrounded by an odd cage made from ropes of fire burning without consuming itself. The lattices were too narrow for her to safely climb through, but she could see a vast cavern stretching into the distance.

Where did Nidiamhet send me and what's going to happen to me next? Instinctively she reached for the comfort of her amulet, before remembering how the sorceress had pulled it from her neck. Tyema sent a prayer to Sobek, in the slim hope he might hear her, but there was no sign the Great One was listening. Massaging her stiff calf muscles for a moment first, she rose, examining her surroundings. The ledge beneath her bare feet was flat, not even a pebble she might use as a weapon. The fire cage was about eight feet in diameter and reached above her head, coming to a point. Tyema saw no door, no gap where she might squeeze through.

"How long was I unconscious?" she said, wanting to hear her own voice. There was an unpleasant echo, bouncing from the rocky walls of the cavern. Tyema bit her lip, deciding against further speech. Checking her arms and legs, she saw the names Nidiamhet had somehow branded her with no longer disfigured her skin. She was wearing the sleeveless white linen dress she'd had on at the luncheon, although missing the shawl and the embroidered overskirt.

No amulet, no way to call upon Sobek. Refusing to surrender to despair, Tyema searched the cell more closely in the light of the fire, but there was nothing on the ledge. Rubbing her arms, she realized she wasn't hungry or thirsty—her body made no demands of her at all. *So am I even here in body? Or is this my eternal ka imprisoned in this place?* Fear swept through her, causing her to tremble and grow dizzy.

Thoughts of Seknehure growing up without her poured through her mind, bringing anger and defiance in their wake. *No.* Defiantly she straightened her spine. "I won't be afraid. No matter what happens here, I refuse to make it easy for whoever comes to kill me. My fear is their weapon. I'll find a way to get back to my child. And Sahure." *I still have my songs and they have power, even if Sobek isn't listening. Maybe someone else is. Might there be a guardian of the innocent here I could appeal to?* She sang, one of the oldest songs she knew, a hymn to Mother Nile herself, praising the power of the floods. The tune gave her strength and hope, vibrating in her bones, echoing off the eerie walls around her as if she was but one member of a sacred choir. When she opened her eyes as the song came to an end, she thought the fires making up the cage might be flickering somewhat. Searching her repertoire for another hymn of equal antiquity and power, she stuck her hand in her pocket, only to feel her fingers brushing something.

Amazed, she brought out the white feather from Mut's chapel. The vane gleamed with a pure white glow. Tyema contemplated the gift. *Might this carry some magic I can use? I know I left this in my keepsakes box at the palace before going to that cursed woman's home, so how it got in my pocket*—She ran her finger over the quill, astounded at the sharpness of the point, which she hadn't noticed before. *A weapon, then.* Feeling a bit encouraged, she slid the lovely soft feather through her fingers before hiding it in her pocket. *For all I know I'm being watched. No need to reveal my slight advantage.*

Settling on a new song, equally old and powerful as her first selection, Tyema launched into a full voiced rendition. This time she kept her eyes open as she sang the praises of the oldest gods, Sobek among them, who had created the world in the before-times. The flame bars of her prison flickered and dimmed each time she named another of the most primeval deities. Stepping closer to the odd enclosure, she directed her song to one area of the latticework and was gratified to see the colors growing dark, as if the fire was being smothered by her voice.

I might be able to crawl out, if I can make even a small hole. She refused to consider what might happen after escaping from the cage. Time enough for those worries later. Midway through the third song, Tyema saw the section of the cage she was concentrating on go dark, the flames winking out. They sputtered for a moment and then black ashes rained down on the ledge. Still singing, if a bit distractedly, Tyema got on her knees and crawled through the hole. Safely on the other side, she stopped the song in mid-note. Walking away from her prison, she craned her neck to examine the possibilities in all directions. The ledge was one in a long series, she discovered, so close together she could easily hop from one to the next.

But do I want to travel in that direction? Although no flaming cages sat on any of the ledges as far as she could see, the feeling of being in a prison remained. Tyema leaned over to see what lay below the ledge. Full of shadows, the cavern was dimly lit by a glow emanating from pale veins in some of the rocks, which was enough for her to realize the drop to the cavern floor wasn't far. Huge stalagmites and stalactites made an obstacle course in all directions, although Tyema couldn't identify any obvious destination. There was a glow in the distance to the west so she decided to go there, for lack of anything better to try. *Maybe it's daylight and I can escape this place.*

But even as the comforting thought flitted through her head, she knew in her bones Nidiamhet hadn't physically placed her in a cave.

The ledge shook beneath her feet, vibrating. The remaining flames of the cage danced and settled, before wavering again as another impact hit. *Not an earthquake. As if something large is coming in this direction.* Tyema went to the edge of the stone shelf and awkwardly climbed over, hanging by her fingertips for a moment, gathering her courage, when the next tremor knocked her loose. As she fell, she heard a voice roaring in anger. Stunned for a moment by the impact of her fall, she rolled onto her back and found herself looking into a face from a nightmare—vaguely human, drool dripping from fanged yellow teeth, bulging red eyes glaring at her. Screaming, she backed away, rising to her feet and dodging behind the nearest stalagmite.

Were those tentacles it was waving? Shuddering, trying to catch her breath, Tyema peeked around the stone pillar, ducking back before the demon could see her. *Even more hideous than I thought.* Trying to stay in the shadows, she flitted toward the next stone formation, tripping on the loose gravel underneath her feet and falling. The ground shook as the demon jumped from the ledge to follow her, bellowing, "I'll sniff you out, human. It's been a long time since sacrifices were sent from above, and I haven't traveled all this way only to be cheated of your sweet liver."

Needing no extra encouragement, Tyema ran to the next stalagmite, but she could tell from the creature's pounding footsteps, it was gaining on her. *Maybe it sees better in the dark than I do.* She leaned her head on the rock for a moment.

"I think you want to come out," the demon said. The echoes in the cave made it seem the creature was right in front of the jagged rocks sheltering Tyema. "Fighting me isn't the wisest idea right now. My master has been promised your *ka*."

She bit her lip and tried to quiet her breathing.

Lowering its voice and injecting a note of cunning, the creature said, "You're not the only one sent here by the would-be sorceress."

Tyema's thoughts flew to her beloved. *Sahure? But why would Nidiamhet curse him? She wants to marry him, be Mistress of his House. Maybe he found out about her treachery—*

A baby's cry sent chills through her entire body. *Could the wretched bitch have gotten her hands on Seknehure as well? Sent his ka here?*

"No, not my child!" She ran from her hiding place in the direction of the sound, all her thoughts on protecting Seknehure.

A tentacle as big as the largest desert cobra wrapped itself around her waist, squeezing the breath from her lungs and she was carried into the air. Kicking and tearing at the scaled appendage as she was lifted from her feet, Tyema came face to face with the demon that'd captured her.

"Where's my child? Don't you dare hurt my child," she said furiously.

The demon peered at her with its rheumy red eyes. "I can speak with many voices, foolish human. The one who sent you here told us you were a mother, for mothers have additional energies my master enjoys feasting upon." Throwing its head back, the demon wailed in an uncanny imitation of a baby's cry, rapidly changing into a hiccupping laugh as the demon's shoulders shook with mirth. "I needed no other snare. A mother will always sacrifice herself for the babe. But there's no child here, more's the pity."

Furious with herself for having been lured out of hiding, terrified at what might happen next, Tyema closed her eyes, breathing a silent prayer to Sobek, the appeal somehow becoming a plea to Mut. Then, opening her eyes again, she spoke to the demon, which was carrying her tightly wound in its tentacles, a few feet off the ground, as it headed toward the glowing light she'd hoped might offer escape from the nightmare. "Please, let me go. The Great One Sobek would reward you richly for your mercy, I promise."

Blinking its eyes, the demon laughed. "Save your breath, human. I'm a creature of the god Qemtusheb and answer only to him. I've no use for rewards from any other being of power."

"Where are we going?" Tyema grasped at straws, for any information about her fate. Thoughts of the stiletto-tipped feather in her pocket were a slight comfort. *I'd rather kill myself than die at a demon's command.*

Her captor glanced at the cavern surrounding them. "We don't use this area, not for centuries now. Too close to where the newer gods hold sway. I'm taking you to the current arrival point for sacrifices. Someone is meeting us there. I hope he's in the mood to share." The last was said almost as an afterthought. "I'm doing all the hard work, taking the risks, coming here to collect you." He shook her slightly, as if his current toil was all her fault. "We wouldn't have responded to this clumsy summons, except you're a priestess and close to Pharaoh."

She closed her eyes, sickened at the idea of waiting in the cage of fire forever, sentenced to prison for eternity at Nidiamhet's whim. The idea the schemer would have failed to gain the power she sought in return for Tyema's *ka* was small consolation. *The first chance the demon gives me, I'm using the feather to gain my freedom from this nightmare.* Better to be a shade condemned to roam the Afterlife aimlessly forever than a pawn in the grasp of the enemy god.

CHAPTER TEN

It had been a long night, followed by a depressing day, during which Tyema never once awoke, never stirred from the position they'd arranged her in, not even when the baby was brought and Renebti attempted to place him in her arms. Sahure and the maids bathed her fever-wracked body in cool, refreshing water twice, again to no effect. He found the most frightening aspect of her illness was how still and quiet she lay in the bed. *Almost as if she isn't really there, this is a doll or a statue, not a person.*

He tried to shake off the bleak thoughts as the sundial in the garden outside Tyema's bedroom measured the passage of hours. Meals were brought and removed. Pharaoh and the queen sent their good wishes. The court physician paid another visit, with no results. Nidiamhet visited twice, although Sahure wouldn't allow her into Tyema's presence. Later, she sent a bouquet of flowers Sahure couldn't bring himself to put in his beloved's room, sweet as their perfume was. He gave the blossoms to one of the maids, with instructions to destroy it.

He knew he was probably doing Nidiamhet an injustice, but more and more the fact Tyema had been stricken with this strange illness at her home weighed on him and the sight of the woman's beautiful face, perfectly adorned with cosmetics, only produced unreasoning anger in his heart. When asked, Nidiamhet claimed no knowledge of the missing amulet, and later said her home had been searched roof to subfloor with no result. He didn't believe her report, either.

Finally, as the second night fell with no improvement in Tyema's condition, Edekh prevailed upon him to seek his own chambers for a few hours of rest. "You can't do her any good if you fall ill yourself."

Sahure shrugged. He straightened a wrinkle in the coverlet laid across Tyema's body. "I'm a soldier, used to keeping watch without true sleep. I want to be here if she awakens, if she needs anything."

"I must speak plainly, old friend. The chance Lady Tyema is going to awaken grows more slim with each passing hour. The doctor is afraid to speak bluntly to you, but he's given me a complete report. Whatever ailment she has isn't going to release its grip on her. You need your strength to cope with the loss, to take care of your son." Edekh's face was shadowed in the candlelight. "I pray the outcome will be more positive, but if the gods decree otherwise, you must be prepared."

Snatching up the half empty mug of wine on the table next to him, Sahure drank. "I feel as if I leave her alone, even for a few moments, she'll die," he said in a low voice, barely above a whisper. "I'd admit my fears only to you. Yet nothing indicates she even knows I'm here."

Edekh patted his shoulder. "I'm sure Tyema herself would be the first person to wish for you to stay healthy. Go, get some rest and return in the morning. Her niece watches for her, the maids are here, I'm sure Sobek must be paying attention. I have a scribe on duty with no other task than to summon you should anything change."

"All right." Rising, Sahure kissed Tyema on the forehead and followed Edekh from the room into the outer chamber. "No one is to be admitted while I'm gone, understand?"

"The strictest order will be given."

And so Sahure sought his own quarters, hoping for a few hours of sleep.

***

He woke suddenly, feeling as hot as if he was lying on desert sands in the middle of the day. Sitting up in bed, he startled at the sight of the goddess Sekhmet, standing in the center of his room, dressed in a kilt and tunic of her customary red, leaning on a spear, a shield strapped to her back as if she was an infantry soldier.

Behind her, in the western wall where he knew perfectly well there was no door, a closed portal glowed fiery orange, as if heated by unimaginable fires beyond. Sekhmet's cartouche was inscribed in the center in black, outlined by radiant red. With a shiver he realized the goddess had installed a *ka* door in his bedchamber, such as would be found in his tomb, a portal between life and death, a place where his spirit could receive offerings from those who survived him. Inside a rectangular frame, the door had a long, narrow recessed panel, above which was a half rounded molding representing the reed mat used to close most doors in Egyptian homes, other than Pharaoh's palace. His heart thumped. *Am I to die tonight? Is Tyema?*

"You humans can be unforgivably obtuse at times," Sekhmet said, pointing one clawed hand at him, her green cat eyes gleaming in the reflected light from the uncanny portal. "It's fortunate for you I count my debt from Kharga as yet unfulfilled."

Hot desert winds blew around him. Hastily Sahure threw off the linen sheet and put his feet on the floor to rise. "Forgive me, Great One, I don't understand."

She unslung the shield and pitched it at him with a peculiar curved motion of her paw and wrist. Instinctively Sahure caught it, realizing as his fingers grazed the surface that while the shield might resemble black and white spotted cowhide, it was actually made from stone, yet lightweight. Examining the sturdy leather straps on the reverse side, he said, "You—you need a shield mate, my lady? Of course I'm proud to stand with you—"

"It is I who will stand with you in battle tonight, if you so desire."

As she eyed him up and down, purring a bit under her breath, tail curling around her ankles, he belatedly remembered he'd gone to bed unclothed. He groped for his kilt at the foot of the bed. "In what combat? Is Pharaoh in danger?"

She came closer, slinking a bit, tail lashing the air as it swished from side to side. "Do you love this woman? Is she your mate or not?"

"Tyema?" He wiped his brow, as he realized the room was becoming even hotter. "Great One, I love her with all my heart but she has misgivings, even now."

Sekhmet hissed at him, fangs bared. He recoiled, barely preventing himself from raising the shield in self protection. If a goddess wished him dead, even a magic shield wasn't going to save him. "You're a lion, born for great things, as is your son," she said. Pointing one claw at him, she tilted her head, the pupils in her eyes expanding as if he was prey. Sniffing the air, she said, "Not to rule, for you haven't the bloodline to be Pharaoh, but to accomplish much, nonetheless. The girl understands your drive to create and build. What she doesn't understand is that mates must balance each other, fit each other, not necessarily match strength for strength. She fears she can't help you achieve your dreams, thinks she isn't lioness enough because she has weaknesses she hides from you."

"Ema is the world to me," he said. "Every human, including me, has weaknesses. There's no shame in that, as I've told her. She lies sick in her chambers tonight, out of her mind with a fever for two days now—can you help her? I'd thought to petition Sobek in the morning if she's no better, go to his temple, force them to let me into the inner sanctum and beg the god on my knees for help, even though I'm not pledged to him."

Sekhmet made a huffing sound, almost a growl. "She's not sick. Useless for you to talk to the Crocodile—Sobek has no power over black magic unless it threatens Pharaoh himself."

Sahure rocked on his heels as if she'd struck him. "Black magic? Ema's been affected by black magic? How—"

Sekhmet shook her head. "Not my place to explain. But I'll help, to clear my debt to you. I loathe being in debt." Baring her fangs for a moment, ears flattening against her skull, the goddess laughed. "And because I relish a good fight." She pointed over her shoulder at the ominously glowing door. "Your woman battles for her life and the survival of her *ka* in the realm beyond. And all the answers you seek are there with her."

"Why are we wasting time talking, then?" Sahure laid the shield carefully on the bed and bent to grab his sandals. "I need my sword."

Sekhmet purred his name, a sound sending shivers up his spine. *Unpredictable, ferocious, bloodthirsty—and apparently my ally in a battle I didn't even know I was fighting.* When he checked on her, the goddess held a sword, the pommel a golden lion's head, set with rubies blazing in the odd light seeping from the closed portal. She presented the weapon to him with formality. "Here, forged by me, in the holy fires I control, to be wielded only by a consummate warrior such as yourself."

The blade was some metal unknown to him, silver-colored, covered in golden hieroglyphics. His swift perusal of the characters in the red light revealed a prayer, or perhaps a spell. The markings swirled and changed even as he read them, as if written in sand. *Magic.* The weight of the blade in his hand was perfect, and he knew he could cut a swath through enemy ranks with ease, if the foe was human. Glancing past the goddess to the sacred door, he doubted he'd be facing anything recognizable.

"Stay close to me, follow my lead," Sekhmet ordered as she walked past him. With one paw, she rotated the door handle, which appeared to be solid gold in the shape of the hieroglyph for the word *ka.* The portal opened into a scene straight from the nightmare he'd been having before her arrival.

The hallway beyond the door sloped downward, the coal black walls and ceiling covered in detailed paintings glowing red. One glance was enough to imprint his mind with scenes of demons torturing humans, death and destruction lovingly depicted. Warmth poured out, surrounding him, taking his breath away for a moment, but he hefted the odd shield and marched after the goddess. The hall was narrow, no room for them to walk shoulder to shoulder. Heat radiated from the ground, penetrating the stout leather of his sandals. A distant drumbeat punded like an uncanny heart. He had to draw a deep breath of the acid smelling air to keep his own heart from beating in time with the ominous sound. After a few moments the climate became more bearable and as his breathing eased, Sahure realized they'd come to the end of this tunnel.

Whiskers twitching, Sekhmet turned, paw to her lips in a warning. More lioness than human, she crept out of the passageway to a narrow plateau which ended in a sheer drop. Following her, Sahure found himself on a ledge, barely wide enough to stand. Gazing beyond the goddess, he saw a dizzying set of stairs carved into the stone, going straight down at an angle that was going to be hard to navigate without tumbling headlong to whatever waited below.

Whiskers flared, she pointed with her chin. "Your lady."

He stared at the scene in the midst of the cavern ahead.

Huge yellow and green stalactites dripped from the ceiling, shedding red drops of water like blood onto a floor spiked with black stalagmites big enough to impale a giant, were he to fall. Open fissures in the ground breathed steam and burning vapors. In the middle of this underground room, the floor rose to become a flat plateau, oddly shaped into a series of ledges.

Sekhmet growled, pointing in the direction of the plateau. "An *utukkai*, a demon in the service of Qemtusheb."

Sahure squinted, wishing he could see better in the gloomy cavern, envying the goddess her cat-eyes. A faint vibration rumbled through the stone under him and he caught a glimpse of the otherworldly denizon.

Easily twice Sahure's height, he estimated, with horns, the demon stood on hoofed legs, spiked tail lashing the ground, tentacles like those of an octopus waving in the air where arms should have been. An imposing sight and a daunting opponent. Sekhmet, however, seemed oddly pleased as she began to move. "They send only one low level uttukkai, which tells me their god is wary of angering us or provoking us too far. This is good news."

Sahure hefted the sword as Sekhmet sidled toward the precipitous stairway. He had to give his attention to the treacherous footing, but kept glancing at Tyema and the demon, who had now lifted her above his head, wrapped in one thick tentacle like the body of a huge black serpent. He was taking her in the opposite direction, apparently heading toward the fiery glow in the distance to the west.

When Sahure hit the cavern floor after jumping from the fifth step, he didn't wait for the goddess but began running after Tyema and the demon, using the nooks and crevices of the cavern as cover. Sekhmet was at his shoulder in a moment, easily keeping pace.

As he got closer to the source of the fierce light, he realized it was a lake of fire. Stretching farther than the eye could see, gigantic roiling flames of red, yellow and orange flame crashed against the land mass with a thunderous impact that echoed in the cavern. *The* Lake of Fire? "Are we in the Afterlife?" he whispered to Sekhmet as they paused for a moment, taking shelter behind a stalagmite while the goddess reconnoitered. Sahure was impatient to rescue Tyema, but the Great One was his commander on this field of battle and must be obeyed.

"The Afterlife you know is but one of many destinations in this realm," she said. "The Lake of Fire spans all boundaries."

The demon paused at the edge of the lake, attempting to improve his hold on Tyema, who screamed defiance, kicking his face and punching as best she could at the muscular coils wrapped around her midsection.

Unable to sit and watch this scene unfold, terrified for Tyema, Sahure broke into a run. "If you value your miserable life, put her down and move away," he yelled, sword raised to impale the demon.

Quick as a desert whirlwind, the monster spun around, clutching Tyema closer until she squeaked like a mouse in the grip of a snake. Eyeing Sahure from a set of bulging eyes, the demon appeared to be amused. "What's this? A second human where none should be? Are you a willing sacrifice, then?" The tail seemed a living thing, weaving a sinuous pattern of defense between Sahure and the creature's body. Studded with spikes dripping green ichor, the appendage ended in a dangerous black stinger, extended like a dagger, ready to strike.

"I'm no sacrifice and neither is she." Sahure couldn't get a clean stroke with the sword, although he hacked off the tip of the tail with a mighty blow as the stinger slashed toward him, which sent the demon screaming and sidling away. Tentacles waving in apparent anguish, the demon swore in Hyksos, but retained its hold on Tyema, closing the tentacle more tightly.

"Go back, save yourself, you can't help me," Tyema shouted in between panting efforts to breathe or to tear the tentacle loose. Tears cascaded down her face. "We can't both die here. You have to protect our son, warn Pharaoh."

"Listen to her words," the demon advised, curling the damaged tentacle close to its body and cradling it with a smaller arm. "Escape to your world however you came here, for if you linger, I'll have you. I was summoned to take this one," he said, waving Tyema in the air like a trophy. "But two *kas* to harvest is even better. Interfere with me again and I'll add you to my tally."

"I won't let you take her," Sahure said, trying to get close enough to do more damage, wondering where in the Seven Hells Sekhmet was. *Some shield mate!* "And you'll never defeat me, demon."

"You delay me, mortal." The demon glanced out across the lake and seemed to come to a decision. It reached one sinuous tentacle into a pouch slung on a belt around its portly middle and threw a handful of glowing stones on the ground between them. "You humans like games, play senet with these." Extending the tentacle holding Tyema straight above his head and holding her there, the creature waded into the lake of fire, immersed in flame to his waist, which didn't seem to affect him, covered as he was in an almost stonelike green leather skin. Laughing with a shrieking sound like wind clawing at crevices in a canyon, he strode away through the fiery waves.

The small coals grew into man-sized, featureless, many-armed blobs, much like the octopus Sahure had once seen, captured at sea and brought to Pharaoh's court as a curiosity. If these beings had mouths or eyes, they were well hidden. Whipping their barbed tentacles through the air, the group blocked his access to the lake. One managed to graze Sahure's arm before he shifted the shield to protect himself and the contact left a pattern of small red welts, as if he'd been burned by poisonous thorns. Arm throbbing, he backed away, frustrated, shield raised. *Now what?*

Green light flared behind him, a shower of green sparks falling beside him, accompanied by the roar of an enraged lioness. Sekhmet in lion form bounded past. Launching herself at the new enemy, claws tearing huge holes in their unarmored bodies, she was seemingly unaffected by the poison in the tentacles. Whenever one of the creatures sought to wrap itself around her body, the tentacles blackened and shriveled away. Yelling a battle cry, Sahure waded into the fray behind her, now acting as her shield mate, slicing off tentacles as he went, doing as much damage as he could to the ones she injured as she whirled and pounced.

One attached itself to her back as she rolled and yowled defiance. He slashed at it and then pursued it across the black sands as the thing crawled away, pinning it with the edge of the shield and slicing through what seemed to be a neck. He ran back to the battle in time to watch the goddess bite the head from one of the demon assailants, spitting it aside with disgust and crushing another between her front paws, long talons punching holes in the bodies. He hurled the sword at the center of a larger demon about to launch itself at Sekhmet's haunches and the enemy fell. Retrieving his weapon a moment later, he realized they'd vanquished the army of uncanny warriors Tyema's captor had unleashed on them.

But we've wasted much time. Seeing no one left to battle them or bar his access to the lake, Sahure ran forward to follow the demon and Tyema. The furnace-like heat drove him from the shore's edge. Clearly whatever power the demon possessed to walk unscathed through the flames didn't apply to humans. Swearing, he spun around in the gray sand to face his companion. "By Set's teeth, goddess, do something to get me across this lake! I have to follow them, I have to either save her or grant her a clean death myself, to ensure her safe passage to the Afterlife."

Sekhmet sat daintily cleaning her claws with her sinuous pink tongue, but at his words she morphed into her human state as green light flashed and sparks flew.

"I'm the goddess of fire," Sekhmet reminded him calmly. Walking past him, to the edge of the lake, she raised both arms, paws facing the fire, lethal claws unsheathed. Her tail lashed the ground, raising clouds of gray dust as she intoned, "I am she who rules your fierce heart and I command the living flames to give way."

As Sahure watched, breathing hard after the battle, impatient to be on his way, the flames parted, drawing away from each other, until there was a six foot wide path down the center of the lake in the direction the demon had gone. Almost out of sight, apparently on the far shore, the demon wheeled in place for a moment, bellowing defiance, and then sprinted to the east. Sahure stepped onto the hot lakebed, full of glowing coals and glittering black sand. Sekhmet snagged his arm, nearly yanking him off his feet.

"I can only go this far, mortal, now we've killed the interlopers and driven off the higher order demon to the other side of the lake. My king Osiris forbids direct confrontation with the enemy in their own land, but they're fair game if they trespass on our side."

He shook off her grasp. "Thank you for bringing me here, for arming me."

"The waves will remain parted for a time, if you can rescue her and return. The portal I opened will remain as well. You only have until dawn in your own world." Sekhmet tapped her claw three times on the amulet she'd given him. Heat and fire pulsed through his arm from the enameled disk. "You've proven yourself to be an excellent battle comrade this night, so I grant you one additional boon, resistance to the effects of being in this place where humans shouldn't be. Touch your lady and she too will be protected for a time. Our debt is discharged, agreed?"

"Agreed." He didn't care whether Sekhmet felt she'd done enough or not. It was plain the goddess would offer no more help, and he had to be on his way to have any hope of rescuing Tyema. "Thank you, Great One."

Purring, she released her grip on his arm and he sprinted forward, into the lake, running down the center of the path she'd cleared for him. Uncanny, glowing creatures flopped on the black sands, gasping for the world of fire they normally swam in. The stench from the lakebed was overwhelming. He tried to avoid the grotesque fish and other animals as he went, nearly falling when something squished under his sandal. Catching his balance, he ventured too close to the wall of fire and a long, suckered tentacle snaked out to encircle him. He parried the blow with the shield, bringing the sword down on the thick ropy limb a second later, severing it. Accompanied by a deafening scream from below the fire's surface, the stump withdrew into the lake. The piece curled around his waist fell away. Kicking it aside, breathing hard, Sahure broke into a run again, realizing he had to keep his distance from the boundaries.

Glancing over his shoulder to see how far he'd come, he could barely see the shore any longer. Sekhmet was still watching, a tiny figure in the distance, raising one paw to acknowledge him. *I don't understand any of this, even whether I'm awake or dreaming, but the stakes couldn't be higher. Thank the gods I was properly respectful to her people when I was at Kharga.* Shifting his attention to what lay ahead, he settled into the ground eating trot of a trained warrior, a pace he could maintain for hours. It wouldn't do Tyema any good if he arrived at the far shore unable to fight. He refused to think about what action he'd take if the demon had already moved on, away from the lake. *I'll track the bastard through all Seven Hells if need be, to save her.*

Ahead he saw the shore and soon was making his way up a slight incline onto the dry ground. He half expected the fiery waves to crash together behind him, but the path remained open. *I wish I knew how much time Sekhmet gave me.* But then he shrugged as he searched the ground for traces of the demon and Tyema. *This rescue attempt will take as long as it takes.* Glancing around, he noticed an odd statue. Taking a moment, he went closer. It was a larger than life-sized baboon, carved from pink-flecked gray granite, seated on a platform resting on a tripod of carved flame bearing traces of red and yellow pigment. *Had I entertained any doubts, this makes it clear I'm in the Afterlife, standing beside the Lake of Fire, just as the Book of the Dead describes.* The line of baboon statues stretched off to his left, as far as he could see, but no trace of his quarry.

Searching to the right, he spied a trail of fat droplets, glowing dull orange against the dark sands. Wishing he had a water skin with him to ease his parched throat, Sahure swallowed hard and proceeded in the direction the wounded demon had gone.

Strange trees with trunks of black stone and withered gray leaves grew here and there in this uncanny land, but otherwise nothing relieved the grim landscape. No sounds other than the crunching of his sandals across the gravel broke the silence. The droplets were showing up more and more, which gave Sahure hope he'd caused the demon some real problems by hacking off the stinger at the end of its tail.

As he passed through a thicket of the trees, still following the drops, he heard the demon's raspy voice, muttering to itself, somewhere close by. Creeping to the edge of the grove, using the spike tree trunks for cover, Sahure found his quarry.

Tyema was bound by yellow fire ropes to two posts set in the ground, each inscribed with deeply carved runes, filled in with red like dried blood. She stood, seemingly unharmed to this point, pale but resolute. Her eyes widened as she saw him but she said nothing, not even a gasp. He put one finger to his lips just in case. She nodded ever so slightly.

The demon crouched on the ground in front of her, back to Sahure, using two tentacles to awkwardly bind a strip torn from Tyema's dress over the stump of a tail, muttering to itself in a language Sahure had never heard before. Getting a firm grip on the sword's hilt, Sahure raised the shield and burst from the tree line, slashing at the beast's thick neck even as the creature belatedly realized the danger. Although his sword left a deep wound in the demon's neck, its tentacles came whipping around, striking at him from two different directions. He fended one off for the moment with the shield and sliced the other away. Circling the demon, which was struggling to rise, Sahure feinted and then hacked at its left ankle.

Roaring defiance, lashing out with the other razor-sharp hoof, the demon rolled away from him, orange blood spurting like a fountain from the neck and tentacle stump. Sahure pressed his advantage, launching an attack of furious blows, making deep cuts in the creature's hide. Surprised the demon wasn't putting up a more efficient resistance, Sahure hoped the effectiveness of his attack was due to the magic sword. Certainly his blows were having more effect on the enemy than he would have expected. He slashed the blade across the back of the creature's neck as it curled and felt the spine sever. The gruesome head rolled away from the body and Sahure danced out of the way as a gush of orange, viscous blood heralded the deflating of the corpse, until it was virtually flat on the ground.

He wasted no time pondering the strangeness of a demon's death but ran to free Tyema.

"Madness for you to follow me here," she said. "But I'm so grateful. I've never seen anything like the way you fought the demon. You were magnificent."

He kissed her on the lips hastily, needing a moment of human touch, skin to skin, in this alien, hostile place. "Once Sekhmet told me the true danger you were in, how could I do anything else?" Setting the shield aside, he examined the odd ropes of fire binding her to the cross-tree. Although they appeared to be made of pure flame, there was no heat and her skin was unblemished. "More magic," he grunted. "Thank the gods Sekhmet gave me a magic sword." Carefully he inserted the tip of the blade under the edge of the nearest restraint. The symbols along the blade shifted and altered in a dizzying display. Tyema gasped as the metal touched her skin and he stopped. "Are you all right?"

She nodded. "A tiny bit of pain, nothing to stop over. Keep working on it," she said. "I feel the ropes loosening."

A tiny increment at a time, he moved the sword, so the edge of the blade sliced through the bonds and left her untouched. In a moment he had one of her arms free and moved to the other side. "You're going to owe me some explanations," he said. "We're caught up in black magic on a scale unheard of outside a scribe's most terrifying tale. I deserve to know how we came to this."

"I'll tell you the whole once we're safe, I promise." She fell into his arms as the last strand of fire yielded to the blade's touch. Winding her arms around his neck, she hugged him tight and he could feel the violent trembling of her entire body. He spared a moment to embrace her before stepping away to retrieve the shield, sliding his arm through the leather straps.

"We have to be going," he said. "Sekhmet wouldn't say how long my safe passage through the lake of fire would last."

"I'm afraid your departure from my realm won't be possible," said a deep, gritty voice from behind them.

Pushing Tyema behind him so hard she nearly fell, Sahure wheeled to face this new menace.

If the other demon had been misshapen and ugly to human eyes, this creature was terrifyingly beautiful. From the waist up he had the appearance of a handsome man, save for the two small horns protruding from his forehead and iridescent black wings jutting straight out from his shoulders. Those resembled the wings of a summer dragonfly, and Sahure found their utter blackness disturbing. His eyes were red, bulging as the other demon's had, but otherwise there was scant similarity. As the newcomer regarded them in apparent good humor, black-stained, pointed teeth were revealed. A sparkling gemstone had been set into one front tooth, and rays of smoky red light flickered from the gem. The demon's head was covered with flowing locks of red, and a twisted black metal circlet set with a larger red stone kept the curls of hair off his face. From the waist down, the demon was scaled, with muscular legs ending in clawed feet, as if he was some giant lizard. Sahure saw no tail on this *utukkai*, nor tentacles. The enemy rode a black and white goat large as a horse, and the animal lowered its head and snorted, as if threatening to charge. Sparks flew from the metallic gravel as the goat pawed the ground.

Two smaller demons resembling the one Sahure'd just killed flanked the animal.

Not wonderful odds. And this new arrival seems to be higher in the scale of things, judging by jeweled tooth and crown. Probably more powerful. Sahure backed away a step, moving Tyema with him.

The demon glanced beyond Sahure, eyeing the spot where its fellow demon lay deflated and already smelling of noxious gasses. "Interesting," he said, stroking his chin, running his fingers through the curling beard. "Few mortals have ever managed to slay an *utukkai*, much less in our own realm."

"He kidnapped my lady. I was justified in taking his life," Sahure said.

The demon raised a finger. "Not precisely true, mortal. We kidnapped no one." He pointed an elegantly clawed finger at Tyema, who stepped out from behind Sahure despite his muttered order to her to remain where he could defend her. "She was sent to us, you see. My poor servant was merely carrying out his assigned duties, collecting a sacrifice offered by one who wishes to become strong in the service of Qemtusheb, our ruler. But you know these facts, don't you?"

Realizing the demon was questioning Tyema, Sahure stared at her. Tyema swallowed hard and nodded.

"Who? Who sent you here?" Sahure demanded.

Tyema shook her head, staring at the demon. "I think it's better not to speak the name."

"A little late to be wary and wise, but you're right. Names are power, in this realm and, to a lesser degree, in the world where you dwell." The demon's eyes widened and his lips curved in seeming good humor. Hands on his muscled abdomen, he laughed, the sound echoing in the caverns like a roaring wind. "Your Crocodile god was strong at the beginning of time, girl, when brute force was all the universe required. I suppose we owe him a debt for helping to create the world my gods and yours brawl over." Still chuckling, the demon went back to combing his beard. "But the Crocodile is elemental, not smart enough for the world as it exists today, in this flicker of time. He sent you to find the sorcerer with just a flimsy lotus bracelet offering no protection, and an amulet easily removed." The demon chuckled again, shaking his head, the strange wings undulating with his mirth, creating a faint buzzing noise.

"I don't see any cause for humor," Sahure said. Out of the corner of his eye he noticed Tyema rubbing the odd bracelet she'd been wearing since she arrived in Thebes.

The demon laughed harder. "The tale is full of jokes, warrior. You're her champion, yet she suspected even you of black magic."

"You lie." Sahure pushed away the anger building inside him, strongly suspecting there was an element of truth in the demon's charges. *Tyema and I will get to the bottom of this subject later. She owes me an explanation, but I can't allow him to pit us against each other here.*

She turned to him, her face in worried lines. "I swear, I didn't. There were flickers but—"

"Not now," he said, putting a hard tone in his voice he'd never ordinarily take with Tyema, but the demon was trying to create discord between them. *Can't she see his ploy?* "We don't belong here, she didn't ask to be sent here, and now we're leaving." He raised the sword, pointing the tip at the demon. "Anyone who tries to stop us will suffer the same fate as your ugly servant there." He backed up another step, Tyema keeping pace with him. "Get behind me," he hissed at her.

The demon appeared to be thinking things over. "You could leave, warrior, having earned your passage by killing the *utukkai*. Having done nothing to earn her freedom from sacrifice, she must stay. The price for your woman's capture has been paid, and we own her."

"Price? What price?" Tyema asked.

"A fine spell, deadlier than a cobra, useful for killing instantly, leaving no telltale traces. It was an acknowledgment of your adversary's accomplishment in delivering you, clumsy though she was. My master was content to consider her petition, subject to sampling your usefulness." The demon bowed his head to Tyema but when he raised his eyes, they were glowing and he snapped a command at his attendants. "Seize them!"

The two smaller creatures bounded forward, but Sahure met them with slashing blows of the sword, beheading one and severely injuring the other. *Too easy, this is too easy.* He grabbed Tyema by the wrist but they'd hardly run more than a few steps before coming to a horrified standstill. The two small demons had fallen to the ground, true enough, bleeding more of the orange blood, but this time wherever the blood ran, more demons sprang from the ground, tiny at first, like dolls, but growing rapidly to the size of the original pair. And all intent on overwhelming the two humans in their midst.

"Run!" Sahure yelled.

Tyema took off like a gazelle, sprinting toward the Lake of Fire with him right on her heels. He could hear the demons coming after them and the staccato beat of the giant goat's hooves on the rocky soil. One pursuer caught up with them and Sahure cut it off at the knees with a sideways slash. But soon five of them piled onto him from behind and he saw an equal number overpowering Tyema. As the enemy bore him to the ground, Sahure continued to fight, Sekhmet's sword killing demons with a mere touch of the enchanted blade. He could hardly breathe from the weight of his opponents swarming over him. Hearing Tyema scream, Sahure redoubled his efforts but the demons got him spread-eagled, even though he still had the sword in his grasp and the shield on his arm.

"Best stop killing my troops now, soldier," said the demon in charge, nudging his goat a few steps closer. "I have your woman and your resistance accomplishes nothing. Other than making me more servants, of course. Release him!"

The creatures pinning him to the ground stood up and moved away. Sahure rose to his feet, adjusting his grip on the sword and shield. Tears streaming down her face, Tyema struggled against the tentacles of two demons restraining her. "I'm so sorry you were brought into this battle, my love."

"You may go, warrior," the demon said. "Although you'll have to thank me all your days for my generosity." He patted his mount's neck. "Sacrifice a few goats in my honor, eh? Call me— Idimuuzul for the purpose of your thanks, which isn't of course my name, but it'll do. I need no quarrel today with the goddess who gave you entry to this level."

"Please, you must go," Tyema pleaded. "One of us has to be there for our son as he grows up. I'm clearly too deep in this coil of black magic to get away. It's me they want."

Affecting a calm he didn't feel, Sahure leaned down and cleaned his sword on the hair of a slowly regenerating demon. He slung the odd shield across his back, adjusting it comfortably as if he hadn't a care in the world and had accepted defeat. He looked at Idimuuzul. "I know when I'm beaten. What will you do with her?"

"Well you see, the person who sent her here hoped the act would win Qemtusheb's favor, draw more power unto herself and achieve some goals, one of which concerned you, I believe." Idimuuzul's voice was amused. "Although the fledgling sorceress started well enough, sadly for her, things have gone awry. But Qemtusheb will be pleased to take the sacrifice, or what's left of her, after I eat the sweetmeats—the liver and such." The demon lifted a hand to caress Tyema's cheek as his servants dragged her closer. "Her *ka* will be destroyed of course—no

Afterlife for you, my lovely. Then we'll pour the essence of one of our female demons into your shell, send you back to see what mischief she can do in your form. Seduce Pharaoh? Kill him? Maybe even wreak a little havoc on old Sobek before the Egyptian gods catch on to our ruse."

Acid in the back of his throat as his gorge rose at the things the demon was describing, blood running cold, Sahure met Tyema's eyes. "I'll kill her myself rather than let her suffer such a fate." Showing no fear, she nodded.

"Oh it's too late for that," Idimuuzul assured him. "If she dies here in our realm, whether by my hand or yours, her *ka* is destroyed. Not to worry, soldier, you won't remember any of this when you wake tomorrow in your bed. No terrible memories to trouble your sleep in the future. I might even let the sorceress have her desires where you're concerned. An amusing concept, with you all unknowing of the role she played in your lover's destruction here."

"Even if I won't remember, I ask for one last embrace," Sahure said, rolling his shoulders. "I've earned the right."

Idimuuzul considered. "Bound to be amusing. You humans are so sentimental."

Sheathing the sword, Sahure stepped to Tyema. The demons clutching her checked with their master and then retracted their tentacles, retreating a few feet. Taking her firmly in his arms, he lowered his lips to hers and behind her back at the same time tapped the fingers of his left hand on the blue enameled amulet of Sekhmet, breathing a silent prayer to the goddess for the promised last surge of energy. Blue flame sprang out around them, bolts of fire crisping the nearest demons where they stood, no chance for regeneration. Screaming in an unknown tongue, Idimuuzul yanked his mount into furious retreat. Realizing they were bathed in sizzling blue light, buzzing with Sekhmet's power, Sahure grabbed Tyema's wrist and dragged her stumbling into a sprint toward the Lake.

"What did you do?" she said, in between panting breaths.

"Sekhmet, not me. Run, don't talk!" He knew they were pursued and he'd no idea how long the borrowed magic of the goddess would last. He only hoped the fiery "waters" of the lake were still parted. A moment later they approached the shoreline and he saw thunderous waves of fire crashing against the beach in sets of three. Not slackening the pace, he pulled Tyema to the right, running along the line of baboon statues. "This way. I think we'll be in our own area of the Afterlife, maybe the demons can't follow us there."

The azure light of the amulet was fading, growing less by the moment. He heard yelling behind him and risked a glance over his shoulder. Shaking his fist, Idimuuzul was gaining on them, urging his mount to renewed effort.

Tyema stumbled, the force of her fall sending her sprawling headlong and knocking Sahure to his knees. Idimuuzul vaulted from his saddle to capture Tyema by the arm as she struggled to her feet. "I have you now, bitch, and you'll not escape again."

With a scream of pure rage, Tyema brought her free hand up, holding what appeared to be a white knife with a gold hilt. She plunged the weapon into the demon lord's eye, burying the blade to the hilt in his skull. Cursing with power enough to set the ground quaking beneath their feet, Idimuuzul staggered away, holding his face. Grabbing Tyema, Sahure yanked her in the direction of the lake.

Hunched over, falling to his knees, the demon roared, "You may have escaped me this day, mortals, but you'll never get out of the underworld now. Wander long enough, grow careless, and we might meet again. You won't survive a second encounter with me."

Still running, Sahure said, "You had a weapon all this time? What was that?"

"A gift from Mut—I'll explain later. What are we going to do?" Tyema was breathing hard, barely moving now, and he had to reduce his pace to match hers.

Impatiently he swept her into his arms and kept going. "I don't know, but we need to get as far away from the demons as possible. Will your god aid us?"

"I can't call upon Sobek for help," she said. "Not without my amulet."

Ignoring the pain in his tired legs, he forced himself to run at a steady pace. Idimuuzul might change his mind and give pursuit after all. "You're sure the god won't hear you without it?"

"Not here. Beside the Nile maybe, if he was listening. I tried, when I first woke here, in the fire cage."

He asked the question uppermost in his mind. "Are they pursuing us?"

She checked the cavern behind him. "No. I see nothing but the lake and the statues. How do we get back to the place we belong? Are we doomed to roam the Afterlife as exiles? Will Sekhmet help us?"

Sahure slowed and stopped, letting her slide down his body to stand on her own feet, steadying her as she got her balance. "The fire of the amulet was my final gift from Sekhmet. She made the limits of her assistance clear. I hope the portal she created still exists, if we can only get to it."

Tyema gestured at the body of liquid flame beside them. "This— this is the Lake of Fire, the one the Book of the Dead tells of?"

He barely glanced at the barrier. "Apparently."

Brow wrinkled in thought, she asked, "Was it still night when you came into this realm?"

He tried to remember. "Yes, why?"

"Ra's Boat of the Million Years might still be on this side of the lake, then."

Astonishment kept him silent for a moment before responding to her remark. "Are you proposing we try to stowaway on the Great One Ra's sacred boat?"

She shrugged. "Why not? The *Mandjet* would take us to the other side, where the god starts the day. It's as mad an idea as anything else we've endured in this realm."

"I've never heard Ra carries anyone other than gods as passengers on his daily course with the sun."

"We can be the first mortal passengers, then," she said with a little smile that faded despite her best effort. "I don't know what else to try, do you? I guess if our bodies die in the real world, Pharaoh might give us each a proper funeral. Then our hearts could receive Judgment and our souls might be released from wandering in these fringes of the Afterlife forever, allowed to pass into the blessings of the *duat*. But I want to live. I want to see our son grow up." She glanced at him. "You were so brave, coming into this hellish place to save me. I'm sorry the rescue may have doomed you to share my fate."

"Let's just do our best to get out of here," he said. "Do my eyes deceive me or is there something up ahead?"

Peering into the hazy distance, then rubbing her eyes and staring some more, she nodded. "Maybe it's the ship."

He took her hand and they broke into a slow run again. A few moments later he could clearly see the ship of the sun god, pulled up on shore and sitting empty, waiting for its moment to sail to the other side of the lake, in preparation for the next day's journey across the sky. As they came closer, he realized the boat was pulled up onto the black sands.

Built of gleaming cedar, whose sharp clean smell cut through the fetid air on the lakeshore, the craft was more of a barge, flat bottomed, without mast or sail. Sahure eyed the trim lines of the boat with appreciation. No sails were needed. *Fitting. Where Ra travels there is no wind.* The prow was taller than two men, rising straight up, ending in a carved bouquet of giant lotus blossoms, painted in bright blue and red with gold ribbons tied around the graceful stem. At the stern was a similar carving, curving protectively over the small cabin. The ship was more than sixteen cubits in length, with six pairs of long, sweeping oars. A helmsman would normally be stationed at the stern, manning the rudder. The workmanship was astoundingly good, the planks in the hull joined together smoothly.

The gangplank had been left in place when the god Ra and his party departed, to transfer to the *Mesektet* or evening boat, which would even now be carrying the Great One on his perilous rounds of the underworld, heading for the glorious rebirth of morning over the Nile.

"If we don't try this, we may never see our son again," Tyema said as they walked along the boat toward the gang plank.

He glanced at her. "Are you trying to convince yourself or me?"

She laughed. "Both. I hate to travel by boat, as you know."

Dutifully he chuckled at her small joke, glad she could still find anything humorous. "If we allow ourselves to be exiled here, whoever sent you to be a sacrifice triumphs. I'm not going to allow the sorcerer to win, gods willing," he said, hand on the hilt of the sword as if taking a vow.

Tyema laid her hand over his and squeezed gently. "Saving ourselves may not be so simple."

"Best we don't discuss the matter here," he said. Drawing a deep breath for the sheer audacity of what they were trying to do, Sahure stepped onto the gangplank. He waited a heartbeat, making sure he wasn't going to be blasted for the trespass, then offered his hand to Tyema. "We can't delay. No telling how soon the boat will depart."

She walked beside him, up the shiny black ramp, stepping onto the deck of the *Mandjet* together. He drew Tyema toward the cabin at the stern. "We mustn't be seen. I doubt if whoever comes to sail the barge back across the Lake bothers to check the cabin."

"Who would stowaway on the god's boat?" Tyema laughed.

They were halfway down the deck when the sound of the gangplank being drawn inboard caused Sahure to halt, wheeling as he drew the sword. He saw no one, yet the ramp was now resting on the deck. The ship lurched a bit, Tyema clutching at his arm.

"Quickly, to the cabin," he said as the barge floated away from the shore and began turning, the rudder moving as if a skilled helmsman was standing there. Slamming the blade back into the scabbard, he led her down the long deck towards the uncanny rudder. Sahure felt the ship gathering speed as the vessel set out across the lake. He and Tyema reached the cabin and he wrenched the door open, pushing her inside, closing the panel behind him. He saw black spots in his vision and his head swam as vertigo assaulted him.

"I feel so ill," Tyema moaned, sinking to the deck, putting her head between her knees. "How can I be sea sick already?"

"Not the effect of the waves, I think. There may be something we don't know about the way this boat travels, some magic we can't handle, being human." He got his arm under her elbow and half carried her to the long bench built into the back wall of the simple cabin. Wedging himself into the corner, holding Tyema as tightly as he could, Sahure prayed to Horus, then Sekhmet and finally Sobek, begging the deities to grant them a safe passage. It was difficult to breathe as the air in the cabin became hot and stifling. *We must be in the middle of the lake by now, surrounded by flames.* He knew Tyema had passed out and his last conscious act was to adjust her more securely in his arms.

***

He surged to his feet, grabbing at the sword as someone lifted Tyema away from him. Gentle hands pressed him against the smooth wood of the bench, soft voices murmuring reassurances. Blinking, he tried to focus on the beings around him, as someone handed him a water skin, which he shoved away. "No, can't—"

"You may drink of the water in the Afterlife, for the Nile flows freely here as in your world," said a melodious voice, pressing the water skin to his lips. "It's food you must avoid in our realm if you ever hope to leave."

The cool liquid felt wonderful on his throat. Wiping his mouth, he needed two tries to get his voice to work. "Where's Tyema?" Absence of motion told him the boat had stopped moving.

The beautiful woman bending over him, lines of concern on her face, had long black hair tied in braids with red ribbons, matching the stripes on her dress. She tried to wipe his brow with a square of linen. "The woman is safe for now, out on deck. My sisters carried her there to revive."

"If you can stand," said another woman, twin to the first save that her simple dress was green striped rather than red, "We should get you on deck as well. It isn't proper for you to be in the god's cabin."

"It isn't proper for you to be here at all, human," said another voice crisply.

Sahure paused in the middle of rising with the help of the two women. A flash of annoyance burning through him because he only remained steady with their help, he found himself facing an officer in someone's military, judging by the man's crisp black kilt and gold-accented *nemes* head cloth. An officer's flail was tucked into the waistband of his kilt and on his chest he wore a glittering black pectoral in the shape of Isis's knot. The newcomer seemed Egyptian to all intents and purposes, yet was not, some subtle difference in the features of his face putting Sahure on the alert.

Straightening, shaking off the gentle hold of the two girls, Sahure met this officer's hostile gaze. "I'm Captain Sahure, in the service of Pharaoh Nat-re-Akhte."

"And I am Captain Intefiqer-Duaen, in the service of the queen of the gods, Isis herself."

"We sent for him after finding you and the lady," the girl in red explained to Sahure, her voice still soothing and low pitched. "To find a human stowaway on the Great One Ra's boat is something never before recorded in all of time. My sisters and I saw you wear the amulet of Sekhmet, who is daughter to Ra." She stretched out a graceful hand to touch the eye in the center. "I sense the residue of the goddess's gift of power."

"And your lady wears the lotus bracelet of Sobek," the girl in green said. "Which alerted us that you may be more than simple lost souls."

Captain Intefiqer-Duaen stood aside to allow Sahure to pass onto the deck where he found Tyema leaning on the gunwale, another of the slender serving girls at her side.

Hastening to join his beloved, he was alarmed at how pale and gaunt she seemed. "Are you all right?" Sahure asked, putting one arm around her shoulder.

"Yes." She nodded as if the single word had exhausted her.

"You won't be if you're still here when the Great One Ra arrives," said Captain Duaen. He leaned casually on the rail, tapping the fingers of one hand on the shiny wood. "Don't waste my time if you want my help to avoid the god's wrath. Tell me what's going on."

"You're Ushabti?" Sahure realized the truth, gazing from one girl to the next and back to the captain.

"Servants to the gods, yes." The other man nodded. He indicated the women with a wave of the hand. "It's their job to prepare the *Mandjet* and the *Mesektet* for the Great One Ra and his guests each day, before the god sets sail with the sun. As she told you in the cabin, the women sent for me to deal with you. One of my many duties is to keep the unJudged shades who wander the fringes of the Afterlife out of areas they've no right to enter."

The girl in the red striped dress put her hand on Duaen's arm. "Ra comes soon."

"Get your woman off the ship now," he said to Sahure.

Concerned by Tyema's obvious fragility, Sahure got her to her feet and supported her down the long, polished deck to the gangplank, Isis's captain following. They had to stand aside while a parade of Ushabti servants came aboard the vessel, bearing platters of the most luscious food Sahure had ever seen, and carrying refinements for the cabin—draperies, pillows and rugs in beautifully colored fabrics, accented in gold thread. A quartet of Ushabti musicians followed, giving Sahure a curious glance as they hurried by.

The moment the way was clear, Sahure descended to the shore, escorting Tyema. Duaen touched his arm lightly. "Over here."

The Ushabti captain gestured and a small group of acacia trees sprang full grown from the arid black ground in a shower of green sparks. A white stone bench materialized in similar fashion, under the trees. "She can sit for a moment longer while we talk."

"Thank you." Gratefully Sahure took Tyema to the bench, where she sank down with a whispered word of gratitude.

"You're not dead in the Upper World," Duaen said, following them. "Not yet. If you were, we'd have an entirely different set of problems." Hands on his hips, the officer surveyed them from head to toe. "I can see you're both touched by black magic, even though you wear symbols of two powerful Great Ones. How this can be, I don't understand. Neither Sekhmet nor Sobek traffic in sorcery, although both can combat it in their own way."

"A human sorceress sent me out of my body," Tyema said. "She meant me to be a sacrifice to Qemtusheb, in exchange for more power. With the help of Sekhmet, Sahure came after me, fought with the demons to save me." She reached up and squeezed his hand.

He nodded. "I had nothing to do with the sorcerer."

"You're mistaken, mortal," Duaen said. "I can see the signs plainly—the evil one has attempted to influence you, wants something from you."

"I haven't even heard the person's name," Sahure protested. "Although I have my suspicions."

"Captain Duaen's right," Tyema said. "She's been trying to affect you. I saw the signs back in the real world. Sobek sent me to Thebes to observe, to find the sorcerer and report to him."

With difficulty, Sahure tamped down the anger rising in him. *What else has she been keeping from me? How could Sobek send her into such peril so unprepared?* "We can discuss the many other aspects of your assignment later." Addressing Duaen, he said, "All we want is to get back to the Upper World. I'm hoping the portal Sekhmet created to bring me here will still be open for us as she promised."

Brows drawn together in a frown, Duaen shook his head. "The Great One Sekhmet meddles in ways my lady Isis won't be happy to hear when I make my report. Truly, you two mortals are living out a scribe's tale. Well, since your bodies yet breathe, you're not my concern. I need take no action other than issuing a most stringent caution not to attempt travel in these realms again until it's your time to be Judged."

Sahure was relieved, although he found it hard to accept such a simple resolution. "Will the Great One Ra—"

"Sekhmet can answer to him," the Ushabti captain said with confidence, holding up a hand to interrupt Sahure's question. "She's his daughter, after all." Closing his eyes, he pressed one hand to the pectoral on his chest for a moment, the black knot of Isis glowing with a curious violet light. "Your portal remains open." Duaen blinked and addressed his remarks to Sahure. "I sense the disruption, the eddies of Sekhmet's power holding it for you." He pointed one hand to the east. "In that direction. The Great One must have felt she owed you a great debt, mortal, to do so much."

"We should be on our way, then." Sahure felt his impatience rising along with his concern for Tyema. She'd been in this realm longer than he, maybe the magic here was sapping her life-force. *Or maybe her body lies near death in the world above.* "My lady weakens the longer we stay here."

"A final question, then I'll delay you no longer. On the other side of the lake, did you see the guardians of the boundary?"

He had to think for a moment to understand what Duaen was asking. "The baboon statues? Yes. Finding them told me we must be on the fringes of the Afterlife."

Duaen shook his head. "Much more than mere statues. They should have torn you limb from limb, for trespassing where you didn't belong." He pointed with his flail before tucking it back into his belt. "You see, the guardians line the lake in the direction you must travel."

"If they didn't bother us before, why would they take action now?" Tyema asked.

"I think you were protected by the energy Sekhmet poured into your man's amulet," Duaen answered. "The magic also helped you survive the voyage on the *Mandjet*. But now the power is much depleted, fading."

"We'll keep our eyes open and travel fast," Sahure said.

"If the baboons come to life, they'll swarm you in a pack and you'll be dead. A *ka* is a delicacy to them, and the pack cares not whether the mortal still lives in the upper world. They can run faster than any human. Even I'd be hard put to outrun them in full cry." Duaen plucked the flail from his belt and held it out to Sahure, golden handle first. "Take this. They'll recognize the symbol of my authority derived from Isis and let you pass."

Sahure reached to take the flail, its weight familiar in his hand as if it was his own blue and gold symbol of an officer's authority from his commander, although the handle of his wasn't decorated with a golden Knot of Isis. The Knot glowed with magic power. "Thank you."

Duaen shrugged. "From one warrior to another, in recognition of your courage. Any man who would voluntarily descend to the Afterlife and battle Qemtusheb's demons to rescue his woman has my admiration." He made a slight bow to Tyema. "An equal honor to meet a woman who inspires such gallantry." His tone turning businesslike again, Duaen continued giving information. "Once you pass the end of our boundaries and enter the no man's land, the baboons should lose all interest in you. There are other dangers, but as you made it through the area before, I imagine you can make your way again. Now, the final problem you face is time, which moves differently here than it passes in your world above."

"What can I do about time?" Sahure felt ready for anything at this point in the mad adventure. He took Tyema's arm and brought her to her feet, in preparation to depart the boat landing area before Ra got there and took umbrage at the presence of humans.

"Hope Sekhmet remembered the issue and established her portal in such a way as to place you back in the correct moment." Duaen shrugged. "There's no other remedy I can offer. Such things require a Great One's power and I'm only Ushabti. But I thought you should be aware of the possibility. Sekhmet can be a bit careless in her arrangements."

Sahure held out his hand. "Thank you."

Duaen's clasp was strong as he said, "I wish you well. Perhaps we'll meet again one day, when your *ka* has traveled to the Afterlife properly." With a half wave, he walked in the direction of the activity surrounding the boat. In Duaen's absence the trees and the bench behind Sahure vanished as if they'd never been, a slight breeze springing up as the items disappeared.

Sahure linked hands with Tyema and set off at a fast walk, skirting the lake. He kept glancing at the amulet on his wrist, noting how the enamel was fading, losing its vibrant blue color. Only the eye at the center retained its original brilliance.

"I think one of the statues twitched as we went by it just now," Tyema said, her voice low.

He showed her his wrist. "Sekhmet's magic is nearly gone." Pulling the flail from his belt and drawing his sword, Sahure fell behind Tyema by a step or two, turning to check behind them.

The eyelids of the baboon sculpture they were passing snapped open, revealing glowing red orbs which the guardian immediately focused on his face. Sahure raised the flail as the creature shifted from stone to flesh and fur, the transformation moving rapidly from face to haunches. The guardian bared its impressive teeth at him in a deceptive yawn. "Can you see the last of the statues yet?" he asked Tyema over his shoulder.

"I think so. Maybe ten more." Her voice was so weak he had to strain to hear her.

They were hurrying past the next baboon, already awake on its pedestal of frozen flame. Snarling, the animal reached toward Sahure with one paw, snatching it back when he showed it the flail, golden Knot flaring a bit brighter. Still glaring at him, the creature subsided. "We've got to go faster," he said to Tyema.

They broke into a run. The next baboon was in the act of climbing down from the pedestal. Sahure heard snarls and the pattering of many footsteps behind them. Grabbing Tyema, he said, "Stop. Stand still. Be ready to run if I tell you to, but right now I think we're acting too much like prey, rather than beings who have a right to be here." Moving with great deliberation, he turned, sword at the ready, flail clutched in his fist. What he was facing set him to swearing under his breath. "Set's teeth!"

A pack of baboons confronted him, their ranks swelling by the moment as more of the statues came to life and swarmed to join the group. The alpha male at the head of the pack was impressive, nearly five feet tall, long canines exposed in its doglike face as the creature growled at him. Sahure focused on this baboon, showing it the flail. The alpha's eerie eyes flicked their gaze to the symbol of authority for a moment and back to Sahure's face. *I can almost see it thinking I'm not the proper owner of this.* Sahure straightened. "We pass through these lands by the authority of Sekhmet and the permission of Isis," he said to the baboon, putting as much authority into his voice as he could muster. *Well, we're here by permission of Isis's captain.* He felt no embarrassment to be addressing an animal as an equal. The alpha baboon held his life and Tyema's in its grasp. "Walk forward," he hissed to Tyema, giving her a nudge in the ribs with his elbow.

They traveled on, Sahure guarding Tyema's back, the baboons following them, keeping just out of reach of his sword, silent for the most part, red eyes glowing. Occasionally one or two of the younger ones would make a threatening noise or gesture but the alpha maintained his icy silence, never glancing away from Sahure. As he and Tyema passed the last of the pedestals, the baboons stopped, forming a line.

Making it clear we'd better not try to retrace our steps. Gods willing nothing ever pitches me or Tyema into this cursed realm again. Taking a deep breath, he turned his back on the throng of deadly baboons, although the move required every iota of his willpower, and took Tyema's hand. "We're close to the portal," he said, recognizing some of the particularly spectacular rock formations. "There's a steep staircase. Can you manage?"

"I'll have to." She stumbled badly and he caught her.

He examined her in his arms, did a double take as for a moment she seemed almost transparent to him, like a will of the wisp or a mirage in the desert. He blinked and she regained form in his eyes. They dodged around stalagmites. Sahure knew he was dangerously focused on Tyema, but her fragility alarmed him. From time to time he heard slithering noises, saw eyes gleaming yellow in the crevices of the cavern, but thankfully they weren't attacked by any of the other terrors the Book of the Dead listed as dwelling in this region. *Maybe the flail conveys more protection than even Captain Duaen realized. I'll have to make sacrifice to Isis in gratitude for his help.*

They reached the base of the staircase. "I can't carry you, not even on my back," he said, sheathing the sword. "The angle is too steep. But I'll be right behind you, should you slip."

"How far is the portal, once we get up there?" Tyema bent over, hands on her knees, breathing hard for a moment.

"Not far," he said, trying to remember exactly. "I can carry you through the tunnel. And then we're through the spirit door and safe in the palace where we belong."

Straightening, she came to him, putting her arms around his neck and pulling his head down so she could kiss him. For a long moment there was only the warmth of her embrace and the feel of her body against his. Sahure savored the closeness in this awful place. Pulling back, she framed his face with her hands, rubbing his nose with hers for a moment. "I love you. I'm sorry I couldn't tell you what I was doing in Thebes, my true mission from Sobek."

A throng of questions crowded his mind but the priority was to get to safety in the Upper World. He hugged her. "I won't deny I'm angry to have been under suspicion of black magic. I'm also furious with your god for sending you on such an errand, so unprotected. But do we have to discuss this here?"

"I'm fading, Sahure. I might not make it back to the real world." Allowing her hands to fall to her sides, she leaned on the rock wall next to the stairs and closed her eyes.

Not liking the defeat in her voice, he gave her a gentle shake. "I refuse to listen to such words. We need to be going if your weakness is so overwhelming."

As if waking from a nap, Tyema blinked. "I couldn't even smell the food, back at Ra's ship. I'm not hungry or thirsty. I just feel…empty. I've been here too long perhaps. Maybe I can't leave."

Seriously alarmed, he hoisted her in the air to put her bare feet on the third step. "Climb. No more talking, save your breath."

She went up about five risers and stopped, breathing hard. "I need to tell you what I know, in case I don't make it, in case this realm won't release its hold on me. I think I can risk giving voice to the name now. Pharaoh needs to know who the sorceress is. You won't like the answer," she said, moving slowly up a few more stairs as she continued to speak. "But you must believe me."

"Keep climbing." He put his hand in the middle of her back, to urge her onward and to give her a boost. His own balance was better than most and he'd no fear of falling.

"Nidiamhet," she said as she toiled up a few more of the stone steps. "With some help from Jadikiria, the daughter of the Minoan attaché."

"Two more unlikely candidates to be all powerful sorceresses I can't imagine," he answered. "I'm not doubting you, but the Nidiamhet I knew was a sweet, gentle girl who thought only of her music and poems. How would she be able to wield black magic associated with the Hyksos god? Enough magic to send you to this hellish place as a sacrifice?"

"I can't explain it to you." Tyema kept moving upward. "I know what I saw. She's the traitor."

"No more talking right now," he said, grappling with the idea Nidiamhet was the cause of their current danger. Her involvement fit with the circumstances under which Tyema fell ill, and he'd certainly had misgivings about the woman's behavior toward him in the past few days. *I need to hear Tyema's evidence, I need to know what caused Sobek to send her to accomplish this task, but she's barely moving on these stairs.* He took a glance at his amulet in the gloom and found reassurance in the fact the eye remained colorful, even as the rest of the bracelet had faded to dull silver.

"I see the top of the stairs." Tyema's voice was a mere whisper.

A few moments later she was proven correct as first she and then Sahure reached the last step and moved into the tunnel. Picking her up, he took off in a dead run, worry gnawing at him that Tyema's time was nearly done. Noxious fumes had them both gasping and the heat emanating from the walls of the tunnel was worse than he remembered, but fear for his lady gave him extra strength. Soon he saw the portal glowing red in the distance.

"Thank the gods, the door still waits for us," he said, shifting Tyema in his hold. She mumbled something but seemed almost unconscious, limp in his arms, her head lolling against his chest.

Sahure burst through the portal with so much force he fell, managing to cushion the impact for Tyema at the last moment. Sprawled on the floor of his bedroom, Tyema lying on top of him, he slowly rolled her off his body, onto the floor as the first rays of the dawn sun reached through the door to his private patio. The mysterious portal to the Afterlife vanished before his eyes. The original detailed frieze of hunters covered the wall, unbroken, as if nothing else had ever been there.

"Where are we?" Tyema asked, putting a hand to her forehead.

"My room in the palace." Rising, he drew her to her feet with him, gasping in shock as he saw the bed. His gut ached as if he'd been punched by an enemy or kicked by a mule.

His body lay stretched on the mattress, arms flung carelessly, legs akimbo. Touching a hand to his chest to reassure himself, Sahure watched in horror as the man on the bed, which was also him, snored and rolled onto his side. "More black magic," he whispered.

"No, I don't think so. Didn't you say my body was still in my bed?" Tyema asked.

He nodded.

"I think our souls journeyed to the Afterlife while our physical bodies stayed safely here. Like a scribe's tale."

I could have sworn I rose from the bed in bodily form at Sekhmet's command. Swallowing hard against the nausea at the idea his *ka* had been sundered from his physical being, he took another quick glance at the sleeping man. "How do we get back into our bodies, then?"

What Tyema would have said he was never to know. Some undeniable force jerked her from his grasp, like a crocodile taking prey. Eyes opened wide, screaming soundlessly, Tyema became a wisp of blue smoke even as he reached desperately for her. The Tyema-shaped cloud rearranged itself into an arrow shape, passing through the wood of his door as he stared. *I pray her ka goes to reunite with her body. Now I've got to figure out how to do the same for myself.*

He doubled over in pain as violent cramps assaulted him, as if someone was trying to pull his body's entrails out. Falling to the floor, he crawled to the bed, using all the strength left in his sinews to fight the agony. Clawing at the webbed mattress, Sahure managed to get to his feet, staring at his own oblivious, sleeping form on the bed. He tried to speak, to curse or to pray, but no words emerged. A glow from the amulet on his wrist drew his eye and then he found he couldn't look away from what was left of Sekhmet's gift. The colors seemed to expand, filling his entire field of vision, while the bodily aches and pains grew more intense. Collapsing on the bed, he saw nothing but the vivid blue of Sekhmet's symbol, not able to feel the surface below him. All he knew was the agony. He realized black was creeping in at the edges of his vision and then he knew no more.

CHAPTER ELEVEN

"Gods, what a nightmare." Rubbing his forehead to soothe an incipient headache, Sahure groaned and sat up. He ached from head to toe and he coughed, feeling as if he'd been breathing fumes from a particularly badly tended campfire. *But what if it wasn't just a dream? Tyema!* Worry for her got him moving, swinging his legs over the side of the bed, standing up while steadying himself by clutching one of the carved posts. His foot brushed against something on the floor and, bending over, he saw an unfamiliar black and gold officer's flail. *Duaen's. So, not a dream.* The sword of Sekhmet lay beside the far wall, where the *ka* door had been. Of the shield there was no sign. Grabbing the wine flask on the bedside table he drank directly from it to slake his raging thirst before grabbing his uniform and struggling to dress as fast as he could. Despite his terror for Tyema, and what he might find in her room, he couldn't roam the halls of the palace naked.

Going to the sword, he found it covered in a light film of ash. Shaking the dust off, he buckled it on in place of his normal weapon. A gift from the goddess, the blade had more than proven itself in the underworld. In passing he noted the golden hieroglyphics no longer moved on the surface of the blade, but had settled into a pattern praising the power and beauty of Sekhmet, which brought a faint smile to his lips, even in this dire moment. He hesitated over the flail. *It doesn't belong to me, and it won't be recognized here as a symbol of my rank.* He decided for now to carry it, in case there was any lingering magic attached, which he might need before the situation with the sorcerer was resolved. The Knot of Isis on the handle was plain, beaten gold now, no unearthly glow of magic remaining. *Later perhaps Tyema and I can present it to the temple of Isis as an offering.*

Hurrying into the halls, he found only a few sleepy servants and yawning guards. He made the trip to Tyema's rooms in record time, answering the crisp salutes of the soldiers on duty before pushing the door open and going inside. Heart pounding, he ran to the bed, pushing aside the draperies.

She lay there, seemingly sound asleep, hands at her sides, head pillowed comfortably on the curved headrest. He thought there was more healthy color in her cheeks this morning.

"Gods, Tyema, you don't know how relieved I am to see you," he said, sinking onto the bed next to her, kissing her cheek, relieved to find no fever burning. Gently he shook her shoulder. A sinking feeling crept into his gut as she failed to respond.

"Her fever broke just before dawn," whispered Renebti, coming into the room barefoot, wrapping herself in a thin robe over a plain cotton gown. "She cried out, a single gasp, and I came running but she was still asleep. She rests more comfortably, at least."

"She's got to wake up." Sahure scanned the room, hoping some solution would present itself. *Does the niece know anything about this black magic situation? Or how to summon Sobek?* He assessed Renebti as she bent over the cradle, checking on his son, tucking the covers more closely around him as he slept. No, she was just what she seemed, a good hearted rural maiden, not even a fledgling priestess. "I have an idea," he said. "Where are Sobek's Tears?"

"In their case." Renebti pointed to one of the small tables, where the beautifully decorated jewelry box sat.

Rising, he went to get the gilded box, hesitating a moment. But the container was just painted wood, no matter how miraculous the contents might be. Carrying it easily, he returned to the bed, sparing a glance for the baby as he passed the cradle. *I thought I might never see you again in this life, my son.* Too worried about

Tyema to hesitate now, he opened the box and lifted out the golden collar set with the crocodile-shaped emeralds. Putting the box aside, he laid the diadem on her chest, arranging the links to lie flat. With some difficulty he fastened the necklace securely behind her neck and then sat back, taking one of her hands and rubbing his thumb across the soft skin. "Great One Sobek, if you're listening, your priestess needs your power and protection now," he said, repressing his anger at the god for the danger Tyema had been placed in. *Please let this work.*

It seemed to him the largest emerald glowed more vividly than the others for a moment. He bit back a curse as a thin gray mist congealed in the air above Tyema on the bed, as if pushed from the pores of her body by the gem's flickering green light. Renebti screamed and he put out a hand to shush her. Sparks flew from the emerald, and the cloud eddied, recoiling from any contact with the green fire. There was a faint odor in the room now, reminiscent of the stench in the demons' part of the Underworld. Horrified, he watched as the miasma flowed off the bed and across the floor. The doors to the balcony flew open of their own accord and he saw a puff of mist drift into the dawn skies before he was distracted as Tyema drew in a long, shaky breath and her eyes fluttered open. "Thank the gods," he said, bending to kiss her.

She returned his kiss a bit distractedly, struggling to sit up. Immediately Sahure braced her with his arm as Renebti, weeping tears of joy, rushed to give her aunt a hug.

Patting the girl's shoulder at an awkward angle due to her position, Tyema met Sahure's gaze. "I'm fine, truly. Just tired. And hungry, I believe."

"The best sign of all." Sahure laughed, sheer relief flooding over him like a cool wave. "What do you remember?"

"All of it, even things I'd rather forget." Her answer was flat, but she smiled as the baby whimpered and then broke into full cry. "Someone else is hungry as well, it seems."

"I'll bring him to you." Renebti rushed to the cradle. "Let me change his body linen first."

"I had a wet nurse come in from my family's estate while you lay fevered," Sahure told Tyema as the girl took a wailing Seknehure to change him. "We couldn't rouse you even for his hunger. Of course now I know it was black magic holding you in its grip, not a true fever."

Tyema took his hand, squeezing it tenderly. "How can I ever thank you for coming to the underworld after me?"

Sahure leaned close. "I love you." *What other answer could there be, foolish one?* "In all fairness, I confess I needed the goddess Sekhmet to alert me to the true state of affairs." He brushed her hair back behind her ears. "I think it's past time you tell me everything."

Tyema hesitated, biting her lip. "Are you angry?"

He considered, holding his tongue while Renebti handed Tyema the baby and adjusted pillows to make mother and child comfortable. Tyema murmured her thanks and then sent her niece to her own room. Sahure settled at the end of the bed, enjoying the simple sight of his son and the woman he loved together. *Thank the gods we survived to reach this peaceful moment, but the battle isn't over yet.*

"Well?" Tyema glanced up from cooing at the baby.

"I have so many thoughts mixed up at this moment I don't think I dare name any emotion," he said. "Other than my love for you and my determination to keep you safe, keep my son safe, find a way for us to be together." He held up a hand as she started to speak. "Since I came into this fantastical scribe's tale of black magic in the middle, I'd like to know the whole."

"Fair enough." Tyema gave him a rapid rundown of what Sobek had told her about the mysterious traces of black magic at Pharaoh's court, and how she used the bracelet. "I saw flickers of the black magic in the air around you the first day I came to Thebes."

He sat up, mouth gone dry, dread like a stone in the pit of his stomach. "Have I been reported to Pharaoh for such?"

"No, for I—I couldn't believe it of you." Tyema swallowed hard. "I thought I needed to know more before speaking of it, about you or anyone here."

He squared his shoulders and nodded. "I'm grateful you had that much good opinion of me left at least."

"Sahure—"

"We've been over this before." Clasping his hands around one knee, he leaned back and chose his words with care. "I think we both know the true heart of the other now."

Tyema nodded. "As if Lady Ma-at had weighed us in her golden balance."

"Then if you didn't truly suspect me, why not share this burden with me on the day we had the plunge into the Nile? When we made love?" He was rueful, frowning. "I thought all walls between us had broken down that day, but it seems I was wrong."

"Sobek ordered me to strict secrecy. I was to discuss the matter with Pharaoh only." Tyema narrowed her eyes and frowned as some new complication apparently occurred to her. "I think the queen knows, though."

"Probably. Nat-re-Akhte keeps no secrets from her." Sahure raised a hand to forestall her answer. "I meant nothing extra by my remark, beloved lady. I believe the Chief Scribe knows as well. He was oddly reticent to discuss why you were remaining here as a guest after the dedication ceremony."

"Well, I soon discovered the flickers of black magic affected a number of people here, but such an odd mix—servants, scribes, members of the Court—there seemed no pattern. But two people stood out to me."

Determined to have all the facts now, Sahure followed up on her last remark. "Lady Nidiamhet and who else?"

"Baufratet." Casting her eyes down, as if she feared the name would bring him pain, Tyema identified the woman. "But now I realize she was an unknowing pawn for Nidiamhet."

He nodded. "Baufratet told Pharaoh you'd sing at the dinner, in hopes of embarrassing you. She and I had harsh words later, once Edekh told me what he knew of how the impromptu concert came about."

Tyema put the baby to her shoulder and burped him, before settling the child to nurse at the other side. "I'm grateful I still have sufficient milk for him, after three days of fever. Where was I? Oh yes, Baufratet. I'll admit I didn't care for the way she acted. Nidiamhet was friendly, right up till the moment she poisoned me and sent my *ka* to the Afterlife. I believe she tried to influence others, like yourself, or has bent them unknowingly to do her will, which is why I saw the fainter flickers around various people, a residual effect, I guess." She laughed without humor. "I probably have flickers myself now, since I've been a direct victim."

"Your pendant was missing when Nidiamhet brought you to your rooms," Sahure told her.

"Easy enough to steal from me, unfortunately, once I was sickened from whatever drug was in my food or wine. Sobek wouldn't think to guard me from poison. He worries about physical force or outright use of black magic."

"It's beyond me to answer the riddle how she could possess powers of black magic deriving from the god of the Hyksos, but I think you need to set this in Pharaoh's hands now," Sahure said, prepared to argue the point vehemently if necessary. "Let him get at the truth with no further risk to you. Sobek can't expect more from you, not after what we just went through."

Tyema seemed to be in full agreement. "Yes, I need to speak with Pharaoh, put him on alert, let him decide how to proceed. We should ask to see him immediately, although I'm not sure how we can prove she's the sorceress, other than through our testimony about what happened."

"I forget you've been unconscious for three days. He's gone on a hunting expedition. I was given leave to remain here, since you were so ill. He should be back in Thebes in two days." Sahure drummed his fingers on the bed. "We have another problem. Nidiamhet will surely know she's failed. Whatever result she was expecting to reap from sacrificing your *ka* to Qemtusheb obviously didn't happen, although she does have the curse the demon told us was her reward for sending your *ka* to the underworld."

Tyema shivered. "What will she try now?"

Sahure considered their options. "Can you summon Sobek?"

"He made it clear he can only intervene if Pharaoh is directly, physically threatened. If I called him, if he came, he'd most likely tell me to speak with pharaoh. Back to square one of the senet board."

"Loyal as I am to Nat-re-Akhte, my concern is for you, my heart," Sahure said. "Without your amulet, you're unprotected. What if you went to the temple?"

"I—I don't know. I did go there, remember?"

"To check on your precious crocodile, I know." He chuckled, remembering how discomfited the second priest had been when Tyema insisted on praying in the sanctuary alone.

Tyema was shaking her head. "No, the crocodile was just an excuse. I actually went to speak with Lemertet."

Her statement was news to Sahure. "Oh? For what reason?"

"To see what the situation at the temple might be, if I asked Sobek to allow me to move here."

Sahure was speechless. "That was the purpose of all those questions you threw at him like darts? And?" he said, swallowing hard.

She shook her head, toying with the baby's curly hair. "You heard Lemertet—there's only one female of any importance at this temple, and she's mistress of the dance. She performs none of the daily rituals of worship, does no singing. Remember how cordially Lemertet started out explaining the running of the temple and its business affairs? His demeanor changed as he began to suspect there was deep purpose behind the questions. I think he feared I was evaluating his temple and its affairs for Sobek. Rather than make him an enemy with too many questions, I asked to be allowed into the inner sanctum to pray."

She fell silent, holding the baby more closely.

After a minute Sahure said, "What happened when you went to the sanctum?"

"I couldn't feel the presence of the god at all." She raised a grief stricken face to Sahure. "Even when he's absent from our temple for days or weeks, I can always sense a connection between us when I stand on his beach or in the ancient sanctuary. How can I serve in a place where I can't reach Sobek? Can't sing for him? I owe him so much."

Sahure was connecting a chain of events now. "And the next day I showed you the little temple I'd designed and asked you again to marry me. You told me you never loved me," he said.

"Yes." Blushing, she focused on the baby. "I thought I should set you free of—of trying to figure out a future together, since I couldn't even be a priestess in Thebes."

"Thank the gods you went into the Nile later the same day then!" He held up a hand to stop her protest. "At least we had an honest conversation as a result. We've much to settle between us, my heart, but I think first we have to finish your hunt for the sorceress, see her captured and defanged. You're in danger while she goes free. Sekhmet made it clear she'd discharged any debt she owed me, and I doubt if Duaen's flail will get me back into the underworld should you be taken again. Do those emeralds detach from the collar?"

She put her hand protectively over the pectoral, rubbing her thumb across the largest emerald. "They do. Why?"

"I want you to wear the largest one as your amulet then, from this moment onward. I want you protected." He knew he was using his officer's voice, giving commands, but the idea of Tyema being flung back into the underworld tormented him.

Thankfully, Tyema apparently shared his concerns and took no objection to the way he was dictating to her. "All right, you'll get no argument from me. I've no desire to walk around Thebes without Sobek's protection."

Having reached a decision, Sahure stood up. "I'm going to take my chariot out to the hunting grounds, talk to Pharaoh, tell him you sent me with urgent news, implore him to make an early return to Thebes. I hate to leave you alone here, but I can't protect you against black magic. No human can." Idly, he flicked the leather thongs of Duaen's flail against the bed.

"I have my makeshift amulet and I'll not eat or drink unless I've seen the dish prepared." She smiled. "I'll tell the Chief Steward my illness has given me strange food cravings."

He grinned. "I'm sure they'll be happy to oblige you, no matter what outlandish favor you request. We can drop a word in Edekh's ears as well. In fact, I think we'll tell Edekh you don't remember anything after plunging into the Nile. Ask him to spread the word."

"As if the high fever destroyed my memory? Excellent idea." Beaming, Tyema said, "I particularly like your plan for going to Pharaoh. He'll know what to do next, being a Great One himself."

The baby was done nursing, so Sahure extended his arms to take the child and do the final burping, grabbing a cloth from the nearby table to protect his uniform. "I want you to stay in your rooms today. No one will be offended, as you're recovering from a fever as far as the court is concerned."

Tyema got out of bed, running her fingers through her disheveled hair. "On the contrary, I think I should go to Pharaoh's library today. I can research methods for defeating sorcery." She took the baby back. "I'm not likely to run into anyone there. It's a feast day for the Great One Thoth, so all the scribes and librarians will be celebrating. The place will be locked and empty. I'll be safe. Edekh gave me a key and the Chief Librarian gave me a tour the other day. I paid extra attention to the location of the section on magic."

"Better if you stay in your rooms." Sahure came for a kiss, hugging her and the baby in the circle of his strong arms. "I'll have a word with Edekh before I set off to find Pharaoh, give him some instructions regarding your meals and increasing the guards on your rooms. " He patted the baby's chubby cheek. "Keep your mother safe until I come back."

***

Sitting in her rooms playing with Seknehure and chatting with Renebti grew tedious. Tyema wasn't the least bit tired, not after three days asleep, and even with the largest Tear as her amulet, she felt uneasy. *After all, I was wearing my amulet in Ibis Nome and safe in my temple and Nidiamhet's power sought me out there.* Though she'd barely dipped into the appropriate texts on her first visit to the library, she felt there might be valuable information on how to protect oneself against black magic. Nidiamhet wasn't going to give up easily when confronted by Pharaoh. Deciding it was her duty to gather as much knowledge as she could, and sure the library would be empty today, Tyema finally decided to venture to that end of the palace. Straight there, borrow the best books and hasten to her chambers to read them.

Having reached a decision, she dressed in one of her own garments and slipped out into the corridors. With Pharaoh away and most of the scribes at the festival honoring their god, the palace was quieter than usual and she met few people as she headed to the library wing. She blended in with the servants and no one took any notice of her, apparently just another maid on an errand.

"I was going to go mad, sitting and waiting all day for Sahure and Pharaoh, with nothing to do but twiddle my thumbs and amuse the baby. They might not even be back until tomorrow," she said to herself as she turned the complicated key in the library door. Locking it behind her again, she hurried to the area where the tablets and scrolls on aspects of magic had been set aside for her, some piled on tables and others neatly standing on end, arranged in baskets on the floor.

Having forgotten there were so many, Tyema sat down to sort through the collection, pulling out the oldest first and skimming. She lost track of time, engrossed in deciphering some old hieratic on a promising scroll from hundreds of years past, when suddenly she heard the lock on the door opening.

She was annoyed, not wanting to be disturbed as she pored through the ancient, crumbling papyri, but simple irritation became terror when one of the newcomers spoke and she realized it was Nidiamhet.

"Are you sure we won't be disturbed here?" asked another woman.

Blood running cold, Tyema recognized the lilting tone and unusual accent of Jadikiria.

"Positive. The librarians are all at the Feast of Thoth today and I've stolen the only other key. I'll have it back on Edekh's wall before tomorrow." Nidiamhet sounded confident. "I have the complete run of the palace."

Tyema glanced down at the key hanging from her belt, the spare one Edekh had ordered made for her. *Schemers always overlook something. But then, so did I. Nidiamhet said she'd done much research here.* She slid off her chair with great care, slid her sandals from her feet and tiptoed deeper into the stacks of tablets and scrolls. From the sounds, the two women had seated themselves at the large table right by the door. Crouching behind a set of tall wooden shelves crammed with papyri, Tyema prayed she could remain undiscovered, while eavesdropping. *I wish I'd checked to see if the library had another exit.*

"You have to abandon this obsession with Sahure," Jadikiria said, her voice a mix of exasperation and chiding. "Your trick the other day on the queen's barge was much too obvious. You only succeeded in making the little mouse of a priestess into a heroine, while you became the fool. And now your plan for sending her *ka* to the underworld as a sacrifice has failed, it's time to move on, start a fresh path."

Nidiamhet's response was a whine. "Sahure was supposed to be mine. Of all the eligible unmarried men at Court, he met my requirements in full. Between his accomplishments, my blood connections, and my magic, we could have risen to the highest levels in Egypt. I was so close to ensnaring him. It was ridiculously easy to exert a little influence here and a touch of magic there." Nidiamhet laughed and the sound was chilling from one who'd pretended to be Sahure's friend. A moment later, Tyema jumped as Nidiamhet evidently shoved a pile of tablets to the floor in anger. "But now, who is this—this *nobody* from Ibis Nome, to steal Sahure from me? To have his child?"

"I know the situation burns, is unfair, but perhaps you should set your aim higher." Jadikiria's voice was now honey sweet, wheedling. "Even if Sahure could be separated from the provincial priestess, he can only rise so far, being limited by his birth. *You* might be destined for higher things."

She's like a seller of poisoned perfume or unguents. Tyema's fear remained strong as she listened to the smooth Minoan trying to manipulate Nidiamhet, who was protesting Jadikiria's last suggestion. "What do you mean? The crown prince is barely into manhood, much too young for me."

"But Pharaoh himself is not too old for a young wife." The Minoan's answer was prompt.

Tyema wished she could see the other women's faces as they conducted this treasonous discussion.

"Nat-re-Akhte is an untraditional pharaoh in that regard, he'll take no other woman to wife but Ashayet. He won't even take concubines." Nidiamhet paused. Tyema heard her gasp. "Are you suggesting I use the curse Qemtusheb's demons gave me to kill the queen?"

"I'm suggesting since you wield the sorcerer's ring your mother took from the Usurper Lynefaraht's jewel box when she was overthrown, use the power to fullest advantage. The Usurper rose to the throne by marrying an older Pharaoh, after which he conveniently died, leaving her as regent for their child. You might be able to use the magic in a similar fashion." There was a meaningful pause. "If the queen was removed first."

"I could be the regent after I bore Pharaoh a son and then killed him, maybe even marry Nat-re-Akhte's older son eventually to cement my hold on the throne. Or kill him as well if he failed to succumb to my spells." The enthusiasm in Nidiamhet's voice showed how much she was enjoying this macabre picture of a possible future.

How can any sane woman think this plot has a chance of success? Tyema wondered if Nidiamhet had always been unbalanced, seeking power, or had the Usurper's ring affected her sense? Either way, she was doomed now, as soon as Pharaoh and Sobek knew she was the sorceress.

"Not so fast," Jadikiria was issuing warnings. "Although you have the ring and are gifted with inherent powers, you're self taught, with significant gaps in your knowledge, which leads to mistakes such as the one on the queen's barge, or much more significantly, the failure to sacrifice Tyema's *ka*. You were lucky the *utukkai* gave you a death spell in exchange for her and didn't demand repayment and more from you when she somehow escaped."

"The *utukkai* said she'd been promised to them as a child. They were pleased when I offered her. It's not my fault she escaped." Nidiamhet was back to whining.

"Foolish one, even approaching the *utukkai* of Qemtusheb without safeguards and proper rituals of appeasement can be fatal. You had almost no chance of actually winning Qemtusheb's favor with the sacrifice of the priestess, and you expended a huge amount of energy needlessly when you summoned his lower level servants to strike the deal." There was a pause as Jadikiria evidently took a few breaths to calm herself. "The ring is powerful, but no one talisman is enough to bring victory. The gods themselves fought when Nat-re-Akhte defeated the Usurper. But you can learn other powers, become a disciple of Qemtusheb directly, not have to work through his servants."

Nidiamhet apparently felt a bit suspicious of Jadikiria, as her next question held a tinge of cynicism. "With your help?"

"Of course. I'm a loyal servant of Qemtusheb. My parents fled to the land of Minos when the Usurper fell. We've quite a colony of believers there nowadays. King Minos is tolerant as long as we take no steps against his throne or his gods. Qemtusheb has no appetite for Crete, he craves Egypt, which was so nearly his."

"I might ally with Qemtusheb, but I wouldn't hand my country over to the Hyksos," Nidiamhet said, her tone lofty.

Yes, you would, stupid girl. You'd be nothing but their puppet. Tyema was impatient for the women to conclude whatever else they wanted to discuss and leave, so she could make her escape. She craned her head to see if there might be another exit, just in case.

"Clearly the ring was meant to pass from Lynefaraht to you, as one queen to another." Jadikiria was so fawning now Tyema became even more suspicious of the Minoan's true motives. Did this group of Hyksos she represented really want to enact a convoluted plan in hopes of seating spoiled, arrogant Nidiamhet on the throne someday? Or were the enemy perhaps after the ring and the death spell?

"So what are my next steps?" It seemed Nidiamhet was capitulating.

"You'll need an advanced tutor," Jadikiria said. "To acquire such a level of skill is beyond what I can teach you."

"Where am I to find such a person in Thebes? Pharaoh forbids the use of black magic on pain of death. Not that he'd ever suspect *me*. I'm a great favorite with the queen."

The very woman you now want to kill and replace. Tyema's disgust roiled her gut.

"I told you, a small party of my people, including priests skilled in the use of devices like the ring, was traveling to Egypt in secret. This morning I've received word they're camped in the Forbidden Valley, waiting to meet you."

Tyema wondered where this valley might be.

Nidiamhet's question gave her a partial answer. "Where the Usurper built her tomb?"

"She was also building a small temple to Qemtusheb there, which is where they wait to meet you." Unsuspecting they were being overheard, Jadikiria enlightened both her pupil and Tyema. "We should go there today, in case the priestess regains her memory and accuses you. You need to be able to deal with her without wasting the death spell."

"I can leave now," Nidiamhet said. "Let me just secure the scroll we came for and we can take your donkey cart and be off."

Panic struck Tyema as she realized the women were leaving the table and coming in her direction. Barefoot, she ran down the aisle, trapped between the shelves, seeking a hiding place, knowing she only had a moment before her enemies would come around the corner and discover her. Nidiamhet wouldn't hesitate to use Qemtusheb's death spell if she had to. Tyema wasn't any too sure her amulet was enough protection, and was afraid to rely on Sobek appearing in time to save her.

She reached the back wall of the library and spun, trapped. Frantically she tried sending a mental plea to Sobek but felt no sign he was listening. Closing her eyes in despair, she resolved to fight as hard as humanly possible, once the enemy discovered her. *At least Sahure is on his guard, at least he'll warn Pharaoh.*

A white glow penetrated her closed eyelids and Tyema cautiously reopened them. The Great One Mut stood in front of her, face to face, expansive white wings curving to embrace her. Thinking she was dreaming, Tyema opened her mouth to speak but Mut shook her head, finger to her lips.

"Close your eyes," the goddess whispered.

Obediently, Tyema shut her eyes and the soft feathers closed around her like a blanket. Next moment there was a rush of air and she felt herself being lifted. Tyema knew wind gusted past, for she could feel the feathers fluttering against her bare skin, but how they left the library or where they were going she had no idea. It seemed but a moment before she felt hot sand under her feet and Mut unfolded her wings.

"You can look now. You're quite safe." The goddess sounded somewhat amused.

Tyema found herself standing in the middle of a road, out in the deserted countryside. "Where are we?"

"On the trail between Pharaoh's private hunting grounds and Thebes. He and your man will be along soon." Mut's wings arched and she flung them wide open, obviously preparing to ascend.

Tyema reached out and touched her arm. "Thank you, Great One, for rescuing me today and for your gift of a feather the other day. I put it to good use as a weapon against one of the *utukkai*."

"Then you did well with my present and I give you another."

Tyema saw Mut was holding her hand out, a small, carved ivory feather on a golden chain resting in her soft palm. As she took the necklace, Tyema said, "I'm grateful but—"

"But why am I helping you?" Mut smiled and Tyema felt warm and comforted just gazing at the goddess's beautiful face.

Nodding, she said, "Well, yes. I'm sworn to Sobek."

"I heard your prayer the day you visited my temple. And I have a soft place in my heart for a young mother who's been given a nearly impossible task by one of the old gods. You've done amazingly well, my dear, but what Sobek sent you to Thebes to do was beyond human scope. So I helped a little." Mut glanced at the sky, where a flock of white vultures circled, calling to her in their hoarse voices.

"And while this pharaoh doesn't swear fealty to me or my husband Amun-Ra, his son will, if their bloodline retains the throne. It has been foretold, this family is the key to the rise of my husband's power among gods. So I have an interest in Nat-re-Akhte's health."

"Oh." Tyema was at a loss for words, dismayed by discussion of changes among the gods and unable to agree to any criticism of Sobek. She busied herself putting the new amulet around her neck.

Mut leaned closer and the delicious perfume of the Nile lotus wafted around Tyema. "But the main reason I involved myself is that the perfect little meditation grove your Sahure designed for me is my favorite place in all of the Black Lands. You may tell him I said so." She laughed and the sound was like lilting music.

Tyema wished she could capture the beauty of Mut's laughter in a song. "I would have gladly served you, my lady, if I weren't already a priestess for another."

Mut hugged her close. "I know, daughter, and I would have been the fortunate one."

Tyema allowed herself to relax into the motherly embrace of the goddess for a moment, heartened, encouraged and consoled to the depths of her *ka*, all at once, in a way the touch of no other being—not even Sahure or Merys—had ever accomplished. It was as if an old wound had been healed and ceased to hurt, scars vanishing.

All too soon Mut kissed her on the forehead and stepped away, great wings flaring to catch the wind. As she rose into the sky, the goddess pointed to the west. "They come. You won't have to wait in the sun more than a moment or two. And Tyema, although Ibis Nome is far removed from my domain, I *will* hear you, if ever you sing for me."

Shielding her eyes with one hand, Tyema watched as the Great One continued her rapid ascent, vanishing into the sun, until only a flock of white vultures could be seen, winging their way to the Nile. With a sigh, Tyema turned to face the oncoming chariots.

In a great, choking cloud of dust, the drivers of the five speeding chariots reined their horses to a halt a few feet short of where Tyema stood. The next moment Sahure jumped from his vehicle, running to embrace her. "What in the seven hells are you doing out here? How did you get here? What's happened?"

"Yes, Lady Tyema, I too will be most curious to hear your answers." Pharaoh came striding through the settling dust, cobalt-and-gold flail in his hand, body-guards at his heels.

Kissing Sahure quickly on the cheek, keeping her hold on his hand, Tyema turned to Nat-re-Akhte. Making a small head bob to show proper deference, she said, "The goddess Mut brought me to meet you on the road, Great One. She rescued me when I was trapped in the library." She coughed as she inhaled some of the clogged air.

Pharaoh gave an order to the nearest soldier. "Bring water for the lady." He gestured to Sahure. "Escort her to my chariot, where she may sit and tell us of the new developments."

"You promised me you'd stay in your rooms," Sahure said in a low, angry voice as he followed orders and conducted her to the large, gold-encrusted chariot in the center of the group.

"Just as well I didn't, since I now know vital new information." Tyema sank down on the end of Pharaoh's chariot and gratefully accepted the water skin from a soldier.

Nat-re-Akhte ordered his guards to stand watch in a loose perimeter before he was ready to confer with Tyema. "Sahure has told me of your terrifying journey in the underworld, gave me the name of the traitor, whose life is now forfeit, let me assure you. As soon as I lay hands on her, Nidiamhet is a dead woman and her bones will be scattered in the desert."

His cold anger was terrifying to behold, but Tyema was compelled to give him the new information she'd gleaned. "Matters grow even worse, sir. I overheard her plotting in the library earlier today with Jadikiria, her accomplice. There's no delicate way to say this, so forgive me, Great One, but now they plan to kill your wife with the spell the *utukkai* gave Nidiamhet in exchange for sending me to them."

Pharaoh swore a violent oath. Hands on his hips, he stared at Tyema. "Imagining they can then beguile me to look to Nidiamhet herself to console my broken *ka*? When there has *never* been any other woman for my heart but my Ashayet? Fools." He spat.

Tyema nodded. "The threat isn't imminent, not to be carried out at once. Nidiamhet needs more training in the black arts to accomplish the entire plot, or so Jadikiria says. A party of Hyksos and priests of Qemtusheb has traveled into the Black Lands to tutor Nidiamhet and assist her. They're camping out somewhere in the Forbidden Valley. At a temple the Usurper Pharaoh was building there, next to her tomb?"

Pharaoh pondered the information. "Are these infiltrators there now?"

Tyema nodded. "Nidiamhet and Jadikiria were going to drive to the temple today to meet with the priests."

Nat-re-Akhte and Sahure exchanged glances. "We're closer to the Forbidden Valley than to Thebes, sir," Sahure said. He asked Tyema, "How many were in this party of Hyksos, did Jadikiria say?"

She shook her head. "No, just described them as a small group."

"We know where the enemy is today," Pharaoh said. "By tomorrow they may have scattered or moved to a new location. Mount up, we're going to the Forbidden Valley. No time to summon reinforcements."

Sahure took Tyema's hand and drew her away from Pharaoh's chariot. "You ride with me."

"Are we actually going into battle?" she asked.

"Probably." Sahure helped her into the chariot. "It's not a thing I'd normally ever do, taking the woman I love into mortal danger but—"

"But we've been there together before." She squeezed his hand as he unhooked the reins and prepared to give the horses the signal to move. "I'll be fine. I think it's meant for me to be with you and Pharaoh for the final chapter of this adventure."

His jaw was clenched, one muscle twitching. "Our child can't lose both of us." As the horses accelerated from a walk to full gallop, Sahure shouted over the rumbling of the wheels, "When the fighting begins, take my shield to protect yourself and stay in the chariot. We'll keep the enemy too occupied to even notice you."

"And what of Nidiamhet?"

"She's my first target," he said. "I plan to kill her before she can use the death spell."

I only hope preventing disaster is going to be that easy. Tyema clung to the top rail of the chariot for dear life as they barreled along in formation behind and to the right of Pharaoh's vehicle.

***

Some indeterminate time later, Pharaoh signaled for them to halt. Tyema unclenched her stiff fingers from the rail and hopped from the chariot behind Sahure, anxious to know what the plans were.

"The Forbidden Valley lies over the next ridge," Nat-re-Akhte was saying to Sahure as she walked up to join them. "I've sent a man ahead on foot to reconnoiter and report back. Never charge blindly into a situation, Lady Tyema." He grinned. The prospect of combat seemed to have energized Pharaoh, making him appear younger and more care-free than she'd ever seen him.

"I'll remember your advice, sir."

Sahure glanced at the sky. "We have a few hours of daylight left, thank the gods. I wouldn't want to be fighting over this terrain in the dark."

"True. And the enemy might slip away under cover of night. I intend to make an example of them, execute at least a few publicly if we can capture rather than kill them outright. I need to send King Minos a strong message to keep better control of the exiles he gives sanctuary within his borders. He should also choose his own diplomatic personnel with more care. But the traitor within my own Court won't survive the day." Eyebrows raised, Nat-re-Akhte gave Sahure a sharp glance.

"No, sir."

There wasn't much further conversation while they waited for the scout to report back. Sahure took Tyema to his chariot and gave her his belt dagger. Sitting on the tail of the chariot, he watched her tuck the knife into her belt. Catching her hand, he said, "Tell me why you broke our agreement and went to the library?"

"Does it matter now? I wouldn't have known about the enemies in the valley if I hadn't gone." Tyema was surprised to find how calm she felt. Apparently an incipient battle didn't set off her physical ills the way any social gathering would. "I hope Sobek will be listening. We'll need his help."

"Should you pray to him now, perhaps? Before we get into the heat of the battle?" Sahure pulled her into a hug. "Gods, listen to me—I can't believe I'm taking the woman I love into combat."

"No choice," she said. "I'm not going to wait here while you and Pharaoh finish this."

"And I hear no trace of fear in your voice." His tone was admiring.

"Apparently I've moved beyond fear." The next moment they were summoned to Pharaoh's side to hear what the scout had to report.

"A detachment of five men guards the entrance to the half finished temple. There are three small carts and two chariots waiting."

"One of the carts belongs to Nidiamhet and Jadikiria," Tyema volunteered.

"So probably only another five or six people inside, at most." Nat-re-Akhte glanced at his own party consisting of Sahure, four chariot drivers, and six heavily armed members of his select regiment. "Some of those at the temple are noncombatants, which further reduces the odds. Better and better."

"But there will be a threat of magic," Tyema warned, not shy at all about speaking up in this gathering when it came to aspects of the coming battle which concerned her.

"I expect you and Sobek to combat the sorcery, priestess." The seriousness in Pharaoh's voice implied he wasn't making the declaration lightly.

Hand on her amulet, comforted by the feeling of Mut's feather alongside the emerald, Tyema straightened her shoulders and sent a swift prayer for assistance into the sky. *If only Sobek isn't otherwise occupied with some problem concerning the Nile today and thus oblivious to my appeal. Even Merys herself couldn't reach him when she faced the Hyksos by herself on the fateful day long ago.*

"Is there a back door to the temple?" asked one of the soldiers.

"No, we have them nicely trapped, like vipers in a basket, which makes now the ideal time to strike, as I'd hoped," Pharaoh answered. "Mount up."

Tyema walked back to Sahure's chariot, still fingering her amulet, thinking to Sobek. *I need your help, Great One! Pharaoh requires protection.*

Sahure grabbed her elbow, hustling her into the chariot, breaking her train of thought. "Come on, Pharaoh is moving out already. We're to bring up the rear, but we mustn't lag."

She barely had a chance to grab at the rail before the horses were galloping to catch up with the rest of their war party. The chariots swept up the road leading to the valley and crested the rise with a dizzying burst of speed. Tyema almost lost her footing as the vehicle rose in the air when it hit a rut and landed again on the sturdy wooden wheels, charging forward in Pharaoh's wake. She saw the archers taking aim as the Egyptian chariots barreled down the slope toward the enemy. Just when it seemed the chariot horses would surely slam into the stone walls of the cliff housing the temple, the drivers wheeled their teams and the arrows flew, taking down the Hyksos soldiers guarding the entrance.

Sword and shield raised, Pharaoh jumped from his still moving chariot and ran toward the temple entrance, his bodyguards close behind. Sahure pulled his team to a halt, grabbed his sword and sprinted to join the battle as more soldiers boiled from the temple.

Crouched low in the chariot, shield angled to protect herself as ordered, Tyema peered through the opening, doubly terrified for Sahure now she realized the Hyksos party had been twice the size originally believed to have been present. She saw one of Pharaoh's bodyguards fall, but the Great One and his men, including Sahure, were fighting fiercely and gaining the upper hand as far as she could tell.

Movement in another direction caught her eye. As the fighting shifted away from the temple entrance and toward the more open ground beyond, several figures swathed in cloaks emerged from the half-built temple, scurrying toward the Hyksos chariots and carts.

Sure Nidiamhet was among this group, Tyema cast aside the shield, rose and unfastened the reins. Skillfully she brought the horses around as she'd been trained to do by Sahure and galloped them through the field of battle, scattering the clusters of combatants, halting the chariot in position to block the enemy vehicles from leaving.

Nidiamhet threw off her cloak and stood forth. "Now you'll die, priestess!"

Tyema grabbed the belt knife and threw it as best she could, but the oncoming enemy easily dodged her throw. Two men in the rusty robes of Hyksos priests attempted to pull her from the chariot as the high strung horses reared and lashed out. Tyema screamed for Sahure as the priests dragged her to the ground.

"Take the chariot," yelled a third priest, an older man who'd been watching this struggle. "I care nothing about this Egyptian woman."

The men released Tyema abruptly, leaving her lying on the ground, bruised and winded but for the most part unhurt. One Hyksos went to the horses' heads, while the other jumped into the chariot to take up the loose reins.

Tyema scrambled to her feet as the high priest pushed past her, Nidiamhet and Jadikiria in his wake. The Minoan woman quickened her pace and yanked on the man's robe with enough force to stop him in his tracks and make him face her. "What about us? We can't all fit into the chariot?"

He attempted to tug his garment from her grasp. "You're on your own now. You've botched this entire assignment and deserve whatever fate the Egyptians mete out. I'm not rescuing you!" As Jadikiria continued to argue and implore him to reconsider, delaying his escape, the man drew a knife and slashed at her hands. Letting go of his garment, she retreated with a high pitched scream, blood dripping from her fingers. Face set in lines of rage, eyes flared wide, he followed her, stabbing the knife into her chest several times before releasing the hilt as she fell. "And as for you," he said to Nidiamhet with a twisted smile and a beckoning motion, "Come here."

She seemed reluctant, glancing at the combat still raging a little farther down in the valley. "Where will you take me? What am I to do now, go into exile?"

"You're out of choices, it seems." He held out one hand and step by step Nidiamhet walked forward to clasp his fingers. The priest drew her closer as if embracing her, putting his face close to hers as he said, "I take you nowhere, fool. Throw yourself on the mercy of your pharaoh. But to save this expedition from being a total loss and myself from Qemtusheb's wrath, I'm taking the ring and the curse. At least I know how to use them properly." He fought to take the ring from her, holding her with one hand and working frantically to strip the ring from her finger.

Unsure what she should do next, Tyema prayed to Sobek as she watched the life and death struggle play out. Reluctant as she was to allow the ring and curse to be taken by the Hyksos, was the fate of those objects her affair? Wasn't she only charged with removing Nidiamhet as a threat to Pharaoh? It seemed the enemy was going to resolve the issue for her. Sidling in tiny increments at a time, Tyema worked her way to the dagger she'd thrown so ineffectually a few moments before and scooped it up. The feel of the weapon in her hand was reassuring.

"Take me with you," Nidiamhet was begging the priest, even as she fought him with surprising strength. "I have power, you said so yourself. I can wield the death spell, your god respects me, I'm an asset you need."

"You have nothing we need, stupid Egyptian bitch." The priest struck her across the face, stunning her for a moment and knocking her off her feet.

Anxious for reinforcements to help her with whatever was going to happen next, Tyema glanced at the skirmish winding up. To her relief, Sahure and Pharaoh had broken free of the fighting and were heading in her direction at a dead run.

Just as the two Egyptians reached the area in front of the temple, the priest in Sahure's chariot panicked and set the horses to gallop. Pharaoh threw his belt dagger with deadly effect and the enemy fell over, dead or dying. The other priest had been knocked aside as the horses bolted and seemed dazed, a bloody slash on his temple where the left-side animal had kicked him as he fell.

"Surrender, Hyksos," Pharaoh advised, shield raised and bloody sword at the ready. "Your day in Egypt is long over. Only death awaits you now."

Nidiamhet slithered out of the priest's slackening grip and put herself with her back to the wall. She raised her hands, the large oval black stone in her ring catching the setting sun and throwing violet shadows everywhere. Tyema saw the foglike aura of black magic growing ominously dark and thick around her.

"She's going to cast a spell," Tyema screamed, having had a heartbeat of warning as the lotus bracelet around her wrist tightened, before Nidiamhet launched a sinuous coil of the vile black magic directly at her. Instinctively, Tyema raised her arm like a shield to ward off the threat. Although feeling buffeted, as if by high winds, she was unscathed, the tendrils of evil parting like water around her arm, dissipating in the air with a hiss, as if acid had rained.

"Not so fast, Egyptians." Nidiamhet's attack on Tyema had distracted the group's attention long enough for the lone remaining Hyksos priest to draw a knife. He stabbed Nidiamhet in the side and slid the ring off her finger, yanking the leather cylinder from around her neck for good measure. The thong parted with a whiplike crack. "She'd no idea what power she was playing with, no clue how to use the ring or the *utukkai* spell, but I—"

Interrupting the boastful harangue, Sahure threw his sword with deadly aim. At the last second the priest waved the ring and the blade swerved in midair, striking the rock at his side instead of lodging in his heart. The weapon fell to the dirt. Laughing, the man kicked the blade away with one sandaled foot. He pointed the ring's gemstone toward the Egyptians facing him. "Fool, even a bespelled weapon can't touch an adept like me, not when I possess the ring of Qemteshub. My spell will lock you all in place, like a collection of statues. You can watch as I kill your so-called Great One, the exalted pharaoh of all Egypt, nothing but a bird ensnared in my net and waiting to die."

Caught in the backlash of whatever spell the priest was working to freeze Nat-re-Akhte, Sahure and the others in one spot, Tyema's vision blurred and it seemed as if her every breath was labored. Appalled at how dangerous the priest was, far more of a threat to Pharaoh and Egypt than the untrained Nidiamhet could ever have been, she struggled to take some action. *Pharaoh trusted me to protect him and I'm failing miserably.* With great difficulty she turned her head to find her companions in the grip of a paralysis even more immutable than the lethargy affecting her, as if the dusty floor of the Forbidden Valley had become quicksand, trapping them where they stood. Pharaoh alone was trying to move, apparently afforded some shielding by his semi-divine nature, fighting the black magic to place himself between his people and the priest. Wreathed in a cloud of gray and black, the latter was shouting words of power in Hyksos.

"Qemtusheb will reward me well, for killing Pharaoh in his own land. Egypt will be thrown into chaos, easy to invade." The priest gloated in Egyptian as he fumbled with the cap on the container holding the death spell.

Where's Sobek? Can't he recognize the danger to Pharaoh? Tyema felt some strength flowing to her from the lotus bracelet and the large emerald, but not enough. She'd no idea how to channel the energy and cast it into a spell. Such things were beyond the knowledge and experience of a rural priestess. Fighting the magic compulsion, she took one step, then another toward the enemy priest, but she knew she wouldn't reach him soon enough to distract him, not that she had any plan other than a physical assault with her fists. The priest raised the ring, chanting something in his own language as he peered at the tiny papyrus Nidiamhet had been given by the demons. Black lightning arced out, sweeping toward Pharaoh.

"No!" Tyema screamed.

Half crocodile, half man, Sobek materialized in front of Pharaoh, the great golden sun in the god's crown blazing, illuminating the valley, engulfing and counteracting the black magic. Standing taller than any mortal, Sobek pointed at the now cowering priest. "Your evil recoils on you, Hyksos, and will trouble my brother the Pharaoh no more." His voice echoed around the rock walls of the valley like thunder and Tyema covered her ears.

The black light retracted upon itself and seemed to flow from the ring to coat the priest in ooze. He fell, screaming and convulsing, as the dark oily illumination spread over his entire body. The ring went rolling away in the dirt, clinking against pebbles as the Hyksos died.

Sobek walked to where the two bodies lay, the priest's now nothing but a blackened husk, Nidiamhet's untouched for the most part, her face set in a final expression of surprised horror. Baring his imposing, jagged fangs, he made a motion with his hand. Green light flared and the priest's corpse fell in upon itself, reduced to ash. The Crocodile God pointed one taloned finger at the ring, which rose from the dirt to hover at eye level like an evil hummingbird, glinting and gleaming with deadly allure. Turning his head to stare at Pharaoh from blazing citrine eyes, Sobek said, "This ring must be destroyed, which can only be done in the court of my king Osiris, by means known to him."

"Do what you think best," Pharaoh answered. "I certainly don't want that cursed object to remain in Egypt. Thank you for coming to our aid, Great One."

The god inclined his head. "It's my duty. And my honor." He contemplated Nidiamhet's body. "Ammit the Destroyer has already eaten her heart in the Underworld, for she was sadly tainted. There will be no Afterlife for this woman. Her *ka* has been extinguished."

"This valley can be her tomb, for all I care," Pharaoh said. "Scatter the bones. There's to be no mourning for this woman, no mention of her name ever again. Her family shall be banished from Egypt, I so decree."

"We need to make sure whatever other jewelry she has is destroyed," Tyema said. "Who knows what else her mother stole from the Usurper? And if she possessed books of black magic, those must be given to the Librarian for safekeeping."

"Wise precaution." Pharaoh nodded his approval of Tyema's point.

"What of the spell she was given in the Underworld?" Sahure asked. "Surely the papyrus the words are inscribed on must be destroyed as well."

Sobek nodded, quirking one finger at the tiny papyrus now protruding from the heap of ash representing the remains of the priest who'd sought to kill Pharaoh. The sheet drifted into the air, whatever was written upon its surface glowing bright red in the gathering twilight.

As if the spell was written in fire. Maybe it was. Tyema shuddered, remembering her *ka* had been the price of this evil object.

Sobek reached out, placing his hand under the spell as it floated in the early evening breeze. He uttered three syllables in a language Tyema had never heard before. The pronouncement echoed through the Valley and drew thunder and lightning to batter at the valley rim above them in an awe inspiring spectacle, although no rain fell. A single bolt of lightning raced down, terminating at the spell. Sobek stood rock steady under the assault and when Tyema's vision cleared, she saw him blow a tiny pyramid of ash from his hand.

She felt a twinge in her chest, as if someone had plucked her heart like a harp string, and then a wave of warmth spread through her. The smell of the blue lotus was in the air, comforting as always.

"You've done well, my priestess," Sobek said, walking over to her. "The curse is dispelled and its link to your immortal *ka* is no more." He made a fist for a moment, blew on it and then extended his fingers to reveal sizzling green sparks dancing on his flesh. A moment later a new emerald crocodile-shaped amulet dangled from a gold chain. "A replacement for the one stolen by the would be sorceress. Your duties in Thebes are now concluded."

"And I'm grateful," Pharaoh said, coming to join them, sheathing his sword. "Whatever reward is in my power is yours to command, Lady Tyema."

Hesitating, Tyema stared at the amulet, raising one hand before allowing it to fall to her side. She moved closer to Sahure for a moment, gazing into his eyes while addressing Sobek. "May it please you, Lord Sobek, Pharaoh, I wish only to be the wife of Sahure, living wherever he is, with our child."

Sahure took up a position behind her, putting his arms around her, holding her tight. "Ema."

"I'll do my best to be the kind of wife you need," she said. "To conquer my fears."

"I don't want you to change anything about yourself for me," he said. "I love you as you are."

"Renouncing your duties as my high priestess, little sister, to wed a mortal?" the god asked, his voice curiously gentle. "You've served my temple and me faithfully."

"Allow me to add to this discussion," Pharaoh said. "As part of the conversation between myself and Sahure this day, Lady Tyema, I offered him a choice of two long term assignments. One to serve as Lord of all Thebes, my vizier for the capital city." Pharaoh clapped Sahure on the shoulder with a grin. "He's more than proven his talents for such a job."

An amazing position of power and authority. The culmination of any man's ambition, lacking the blood to be royal. Surely Sahure accepted. The pit of her stomach burned as she contemplated spending the rest of her life in Thebes, running the vizier's palace, holding court in support of Sahure's duties. The wife of a vizier wielded her own power and influence, or could, if she so chose. Tyema stood tall, raising her chin. *If running a vizier's house is my fate, in order to be his wife, so be it. I'll manage in my own fashion.* Belatedly, she realized Sobek and the men were still watching her. "And the other choice?" she asked, holding her breath.

"To take his uncle's place as Nomarch of the Ibis province." Nat-re-Akhte grinned. "I'll not keep you in suspense, Lady Tyema. The latter was his decision."

"To be with you," Sahure said. "And our son. You could still be High Priestess."

"But the nome's capital lies a day's travel from the temple." Exasperated with herself for always seeing the difficulties, Tyema stopped speaking.

"You've devoted yourself to my service as no other priestess for all these years," Sobek said. "I'll allow you to become the senior high priestess, still in charge, but with someone else running the day to day duties of the temple." He leaned closer, golden eyes gleaming. "I'd miss your voice at the major ceremonies, little sister. Participate in those special occasions, keep an eye on the overall affairs of the place, and I'll be satisfied."

"But, Sahure, to renounce *Thebes*, for me—"

"I do it gladly, no second thoughts," he said, kissing her hand. "My heart is in the Ibis Nome. I told you that truth when we first met beside the Nile, and nothing has changed. If anything, I feel more strongly my destiny lies there. Besides, I want to oversee the building of Pharaoh's new port city." He winked.

Pulling away from Sahure, Tyema reached for the amulet the god was still holding. "I accept the new position, Great One, with humble thanks."

Sobek let her take the necklace and then he changed to his fully human form for a brief moment, reaching to hug her close, heedless of the men surrounding them. "Many years of happiness lie before you, little sister," he whispered. Addressing Pharaoh, he said, "The structures in this valley must be destroyed, lest the place continue to be a magnet for those seeking to create footholds in the Black Lands for Qemtusheb."

"I don't disagree," Nat-re-Akhte said. "Yet there are those entombed in the Usurper's building who lie there in all innocence, victims of her evil."

"And the *ka* of each of her victims has been properly accepted into the Afterlife, long ago." Although Sobek smiled, his expression was daunting in the fierce set of his jaw and the glare in his eyes. "Never fear, I myself will do the destruction, as soon as you've left this place."

"It'll be night soon," Pharaoh said. "We'd best be on the road to Thebes without further delay." He extended his hand to Sobek, who shook it firmly.

Sahure ushered Tyema to his chariot, the well trained horses having stopped in place after the man trying to steal them was killed. Taking a moment to heave the body from his vehicle, Sahure helped her step inside. "Good thing I taught you to drive."

"Indeed." She was distracted, watching Sobek as he stood there while the Egyptian chariots made a circle on the flat plain in front of the elaborate tomb and temple the Usurper had never lived to complete. The god raised one hand in farewell as she looked back, the chariot moving up the road to leave the valley.

Then, with a shower of green and white fire, accompanied by the sound of thunder, Sobek shifted into his full Crocodile form. Tyema gasped as she took in the enormous size of the white crocodile he became. *This is what he was the day he rescued me and the others from the Hyksos ships.* Her last view of Sobek was as he began rending the temple apart, tearing at it with his powerful forelegs and sweeping the enormous tail across the valley, knocking the giant granite columns down as if they were children's toys. The earth shook under his ferocious, methodical assault on the Usurper's buildings.

And then she was carried over the ridge and she lost sight of Sobek.

"Are you all right?" Sahure glanced at her sideways.

"I'm fine. I'll see the Great One again in Ibis Nome, I've no doubt." She felt carefree now, a huge weight lifted from her shoulders. Pharaoh was safe, the practitioner of black magic was no more, the Hyksos had been repelled— and most importantly to her, she and Sahure were free to be together as man and wife, to build the happy future she'd despaired of ever claiming.

"We can leave Thebes within the week," Sahure said. "I was between assignments, on leave, so I've no commitments to keep me here. Pharaoh said something about a gold of valor ceremony, and he'll have to invest me with the title of nomarch, of course, but then we can sail to Ibis. You should meet my mother before we go," he said as an afterthought. "You'll like her. And she'll dote on Seknehure."

"So maybe what, another one or two banquets to suffer through?" Tyema said, amused at the idea."I can handle a few dinners. Now Pharaoh has recognized us as man and wife I can sit with you and not be marooned at the table of simpering ladies-in-waiting."

He put one arm around her shoulder and planted a kiss on her cheek. "I don't think there's anyone in the Black Lands happier than I am this evening."

"There's just one tiny cloud on my horizon," she said.

He did a double take and the chariot swerved under his lack of attention. "Name the thing and I'll resolve it."

She leaned close. "I want to drive."

***

Thanks so much for reading *Magic of the Nile!* If you enjoyed the book, please consider leaving a review at the retail site of your choice or on Goodreads, to help other readers discover the Gods of Egypt series.

Much more to come so make sure you join my mailing list at *http://veronicascott. wordpress.com/* to be updated when new books are available.

Be sure not to miss Priestess of the Nile, Warrior of the Nile and Dancer of the Nile!

www.ingramcontent.com/pod-product-compliance
Lightning Source LLC
Chambersburg PA
CBHW071059250626
47159CB00002B/527